JO NESBØ

The Bat

Jo Nesbø's books have sold more than eighteen million copies worldwide, and have been translated into forty-seven languages. His other Harry Hole novels include *The Redbreast*, *Nemesis*, *The Devil's Star*, *The Snowman*, *The Leopard*, *Phantom*, and *The Redeemer*, and he is the author of *Headhunters* and several children's books. He has received the Glass Key Award for best Nordic crime novel. He is also a musician, songwriter, and economist and lives in Oslo.

www.jonesbo.com

BOOKS BY JO NESBØ

Headhunters

The Harry Hole series

Phantom

The Leopard

The Snowman

The Redeemer

The Devil's Star

Nemesis

The Redbreast

The Bat

The Bat

The Bat

JO NESBØ

Translated from the Norwegian by Don Bartlett

VINTAGE CRIME/BLACK LIZARD
Vintage Books
A Division of Random House, Inc.
New York

FIRST VINTAGE CRIME/BLACK LIZARD EDITION, JULY 2013

The Cataloging-in-Publication Data is on file at the Library of Congress.

Vintage ISBN: 978-0-345-80709-0

www.weeklylizard.com

Printed in the United States of America
10 9 8 7 6 5 4 3 2 1

WALLA

I

Sydney

Something was wrong.

At first the female passport official had beamed: "How are ya, mate?"

"I'm fine," Harry Hole had lied. It was more than thirty hours since he had taken off from Oslo via London, and after the change of planes in Bahrain he had sat in the same bloody seat by the emergency exit. For security reasons it could only be tipped back a little, and his lumbar region had almost crumbled by the time they reached Singapore.

And now the woman behind the counter was no longer smiling.

She had scrutinized his passport with conspicuous interest. Whether it was the photograph or his name that had initially put her in such a cheery mood was hard to say.

"Business?"

Harry Hole had a suspicion that passport officials in most places in the world would have added a "sir," but he had read that this type of formal pleasantry wasn't especially widespread in Australia. It didn't really matter; Harry wasn't particularly accustomed to foreign travel or snobbish—all he wanted was a hotel room and a bed as quickly as possible.

"Yes," he had replied, drumming his fingers on the counter.

And that was when her lips had pursed, turned ugly and articulated, with a pointed tone: "Why isn't there a visa in your passport, sir?"

His heart sank, as it invariably did when there was a hint of a catastrophe in the offing. Perhaps "sir" was used only when situations became critical?

"Sorry, I forgot," Harry mumbled, searching feverishly through his inside pockets. Why had they not been able to pin a special visa in his passport as they do with standard visas? Behind him in the queue he heard the faint drone of a Walkman and realized it was his traveling companion from the plane. He had been playing the same cassette the whole flight. Why the hell could he never remember which pocket he put things in? It was hot as well, even though it was getting on for ten o'clock at night. Harry could feel his scalp beginning to itch.

At last he found the document and placed it on the counter, to his great relief.

"Police officer, are you?"

The passport official looked up from the special visa and studied him, but the pursed mouth was gone.

"I hope no Norwegian blondes have been murdered?"

She chuckled and smacked the stamp down hard on the special visa.

"Well, just the one," Harry Hole answered.

The arrivals hall was crowded with travel reps and limousine drivers, holding up signs with names on, but not a Hole in sight. He was on the point of grabbing a taxi when a black man wearing light blue jeans and a Hawaiian shirt, and with an unusually broad nose and dark, curly hair plowed a furrow between the signs and came striding toward him.

"Mr. Holy, I presume!" he declared triumphantly.

Harry Hole considered his options. He had decided to spend the first days in Australia correcting the pronunciation of his surname so that he wouldn't be confused with apertures or orifices. Mr. Holy however, was infinitely preferable.

"Andrew Kensington. How are ya?" the man grinned and stuck out an enormous fist.

It was nothing less than a juice extractor.

"Welcome to Sydney. Hope you enjoyed the flight," the stranger said with evident sincerity, like an echo of the air hostess's announcement twenty minutes earlier. He took Harry's battered suitcase and began to walk toward the exit without a backward glance. Harry kept close to him.

"Do you work for Sydney police?" he initiated.

"Sure do, mate. Watch out!"

The swing door hit Harry in the face, right on the hooter, and made his eyes water. A bad slapstick sketch could not have started worse. He rubbed his nose and swore in Norwegian. Kensington sent him a sympathetic look.

"Bloody doors, eh?" he said.

Harry didn't answer. He didn't know how to answer that sort of comment down under.

In the car park Kensington unlocked the boot of a small, well-used Toyota and shoved in the suitcase. "Do you wanna drive, mate?" he asked in surprise.

Harry realized he was sitting in the driver's seat. Of course, they drove on the bloody left in Australia. However, the passenger seat was so full of papers, cassettes and general rubbish that Harry squeezed into the back.

"You must be an Aboriginal," he said as they turned onto the motorway.

"Guess there's no fooling you, Officer," Kensington answered, glancing in the mirror.

"In Norway we call you Australian Negroes."

Kensington kept his eyes trained on the mirror. "Really?"

Harry began to feel ill at ease. "Er, by that I just mean that your forefathers obviously didn't belong to the convicts sent here from England two hundred years ago." He wanted to show he had at least a modicum of knowledge about the country's history.

"That's right, Holy. My forefathers were here a bit before them. Forty thousand years, to be precise."

Kensington grinned into the mirror. Harry vowed to keep his mouth shut for a while.

"I see. Call me Harry."

"OK, Harry. I'm Andrew."

Andrew ran the conversation for the rest of the ride. He drove Harry to King's Cross, holding forth the whole way: this area was Sydney's red-light district and the center for the drugs trade and to a large extent all the other shady dealings in town. Every second scandal seemed to have a connection with some hotel or strip joint inside this square kilometer.

"Here we are," Andrew said suddenly. He pulled in to the curb, jumped out and took Harry's suitcase from the boot.

"See you tomorrow," Andrew said, and with that he and the car were gone. With a stiff back and jet lag beginning to announce its presence, Harry and his suitcase were now alone on a pavement in a town boasting a population roughly equivalent to the whole of Norway, outside the splendid Crescent Hotel. The name was printed on the door next to three stars. Oslo's Chief Constable was not known for largesse with regards to accommodation for her employees. But perhaps this one was not going to be too bad after all. There must have been a civil service discount and it was probably the hotel's smallest room, Harry reflected.

And it was.

2

Gap Park

Harry knocked warily on the door of the Head of Crime Squad for Surry Hills.

"Come in," boomed a voice from inside.

A tall, broad man with a stomach designed to impress was standing by the window, behind an oak desk. Beneath a thinning mane protruded gray bushy eyebrows, but the wrinkles around his eyes smiled.

"Harry Holy from Oslo, Norway, sir."

"Take a pew, Holy. You look bloody fit for this time of the morning. I hope you haven't been to see any of the boys in Narc, have you?" Neil McCormack let out a huge laugh.

"Jet lag. I've been awake since four this morning, sir," Harry explained.

"Of course. Just an in-joke. We had a pretty high-profile corruption case here a couple of years back, you see. Ten officers were convicted, among other things for selling drugs—to one another. Suspicion was raised because a couple of them were so alert—round the clock. No joke really." He chuckled contentedly, put on his glasses and flicked through the papers in front of him.

"So you've been sent here to assist us with our investigation into the murder of Inger Holter, a Norwegian citizen with a permit to work in Australia. Blonde, good-looking girl, according to the photos. Twenty-three years old, wasn't she?"

Harry nodded. McCormack was serious now.

"Found by fishermen on the ocean side of Watson's Bay—to be more precise, Gap Park. Semi-naked. Bruising suggested she had been raped first and then strangled, but no semen was found. Later transported at the dead of night to the park where the body was dumped off the cliff."

He pulled a face.

"Had the weather been a little worse the waves would definitely have carried her out, but instead she lay among the rocks until she was found. As I said, there was no semen present, and the reason for that is that the vagina was sliced up like a filleted fish and the seawater did a thorough job of washing this girl clean. Therefore we have no fingerprints either, though we do have a rough estimate of time of death . . ." McCormack removed his glasses and rubbed his face. "But we don't have a murderer. And what the hell are you gonna do about that, Mr. Holy?"

Harry was about to answer but was interrupted.

"What you're gonna do is watch carefully while we haul the bastard in, tell the Norwegian press along the way what a wonderful job we're doing together—making sure we don't offend anyone at the Norwegian Embassy, or relatives—and otherwise enjoy a break and send a card or two to your dear Chief Constable. How is she by the way?"

"Fine, as far as I know."

"Great woman, she is. I s'pose she explained to you what's expected of you?"

"To some extent. I'm taking part in an invest—"

"Great. Forget all that. Here are the new rules. Number one: from now on you listen to me, me and me alone. Number two: you don't take part in anything you haven't been instructed to do by me. And number three: one toe out of line and you'll be on the first plane home."

This was delivered with a smile, but the message was

clear: paws off, he was here as an observer. He might just as well have brought his swimming things and a camera along.

"I gather that Inger Holter was some kind of TV celeb in Norway?"

"A minor celeb, sir. She hosted a children's program broadcast a couple of years ago. I suppose before this happened she was on her way into oblivion."

"Yeah, I've been told that your papers are making a big thing of this murder. Couple of them have sent people here already. We've given 'em what we've got, and that's not a great deal, so they'll soon be bored and bugger off home. They don't know you're here. We've got our own nannies, so you won't have to take care of them."

"Thank you for that, sir," Harry said, and he meant it. The thought of panting Norwegian journalists looking over his shoulder was not a welcome one.

"OK, Holy, I'll be honest with you and tell you how the land lies. I've been told in no uncertain terms by my governor that councillors in Sydney would like to see this case cleared up as soon as possible. As usual, it's all about politics and dosh."

"Dosh?"

"Well, we reckon unemployment in Sydney will rise to over ten percent this year, and the town needs every cent we can get from the tourists. We've got the Olympic Games just round the corner, in 2000, and tourism from Scandinavia's on the up. Murder, especially one which hasn't been cleared up, isn't a good advert for the town, so we're doing what we can. We have a team of four detectives on the case plus high-priority access to the force's resources—all the computers, forensic staff, lab people. And so on."

McCormack pulled out a sheet of paper which he studied with a frown.

"In fact, you should be working with Watkins, but since you specifically asked for Kensington, I see no reason to refuse your request."

"Sir, to my knowledge I haven't—"

"Kensington's a good man. There are not many Indigenous officers who have come up through the ranks like him."

"No?"

McCormack shrugged. "That's just the way it is. Well, Holy, if there's anything else, you know where I hang out. Any questions?"

"Er, just a formality, sir. I was wondering whether *sir* was the right mode of address to a superior officer in this country, or whether it was a little too . . ."

"Formal? Stiff? Yes, I guess it probably is. But I like it. It reminds me that I am in fact the boss of this outfit." McCormack burst out laughing and concluded the meeting with a bone-crunching handshake.

"January's the tourist season in Australia," Andrew explained as they lurched forward in the traffic around Circular Quay.

"Everyone comes to see the Sydney Opera House and go on boat trips round the harbor and admire the women on Bondi Beach. Shame you've got to work."

Harry shook his head. "Doesn't matter. I break out in a cold sweat around tourist traps."

They emerged onto New South Head Road, where the Toyota sped eastward to Watson's Bay.

"The East Side of Sydney's not exactly like the East End of London," Andrew explained as they passed one fashionable house after another. "This district's called Double Bay. We call it Double Pay."

"Where did Inger Holter live?"

"She lived with her boyfriend in Newtown for a while before they split up and she moved to a little one-room flat in Glebe."

"Boyfriend?"

Andrew shrugged. "He's Australian, a computer engineer and met her when she came here on holiday two years ago. He's got an alibi for the night of the murder and is not exactly the prototype of a murderer. But you never know, do you?"

They parked below Gap Park, one of Sydney's many green lungs. Steep stone steps led up to the windblown park that lay high above Watson's Bay to the north and the Pacific Ocean to the east. The heat hit them when they opened the car doors. Andrew put on a big pair of shades, which made Harry think of a laid-back porn king. For some reason his Australian colleague was wearing a tight suit today, and Harry thought the broad-shouldered black man looked a bit comical as he rolled and pitched up the path in front of him to the viewpoint.

Harry looked around. To the west he saw the city center with the Harbor Bridge, to the north the beach and yachts in Watson's Bay and, further in the distance, verdant Manly, the suburb on the northern side of the bay. To the east the horizon curved in a spectrum of various shades of blue. The cliffs plunged down in front of them, and way below the ocean breakers ended their long voyage in a thunderous crescendo among the rocks.

Harry felt a bead of sweat running down between his shoulder blades. This heat was giving him goose pimples.

"You can see the Pacific Ocean from here, Harry. Next stop New Zealand, after about twelve hundred wet miles," Andrew said, spitting a thick gobbet off the edge of the cliff. They followed it down for a while until the wind dispersed it.

"Good job she wasn't alive when she fell," he said. "She must have hit the cliffs on the way down; there were large chunks of flesh torn from her body when they found her."

"How long had she been dead before she was found?"

Andrew pulled a grimace. "The police doctor said forty-eight hours. But he . . ."

He put a backward-facing thumb in front of his mouth. Harry nodded. So the doctor was a thirsty soul.

"And you become skeptical when the figures are too rounded?"

"She was found on a Friday morning, so let's say she died some time during Wednesday night."

"Any clues here?"

"As you can see, cars can park down below and the area is unlit at night and relatively deserted. We haven't got any reports from witnesses, and to be frank, we don't reckon we'll get any."

"So what do we do now?"

"Now we do what the boss told me, we go to a restaurant and spend a bit of the force's entertainment budget. After all, you're Norway's highest police rep in a radius of more than twelve hundred miles. At least."

Andrew and Harry sat at a table with a white cloth. Doyle's, a seafood restaurant, was situated at the furthest end of Watson's Bay with only a strip of sand between itself and the sea.

"Ridiculously beautiful, isn't it?" Andrew said.

"Picture postcard." A small boy and a girl were building sandcastles on the beach in front of them, against a background of a deep blue sea and luxuriant green hills with Sydney's proud skyline in the distance.

Harry chose scallops and Tasmanian trout, Andrew an Australian flatfish which Harry, quite reasonably, had never heard of. Andrew ordered a bottle of Chardonnay Rosemount, "quite wrong for this meal, but it's white, it's good and it's smack on budget," and looked mildly surprised when Harry said he didn't drink.

"Quaker?"

"No, nothing like that," Harry said.

Doyle's was an old family-run restaurant and considered one of Sydney's best, Andrew informed Harry. It was peak season and packed to the rafters and Harry presumed that was why it was so difficult to gain eye contact with the waiters.

"The waiters here are like the planet Pluto," Andrew said. "They orbit on the periphery, only making an appearance every twentieth year, and even then are impossible to glimpse with the naked eye."

Harry couldn't work up any indignation and leaned back in his chair with a contented sigh. "But they have excellent food," he said. "So that explains the suit."

"Yes and no. As you can see, it's not exactly formal here. But it's better for me *not* to wear jeans and a T-shirt in places like this. Because of my appearance I have to make an effort."

"What do you mean?"

Andrew stared at Harry. "Aboriginal people don't have very high status in this country, as you may perhaps appreciate. Years ago the English wrote home that the natives had a weakness for alcohol and property crime."

Harry listened with interest.

"They thought it was in our genes. 'All they were good for was making a hell of a racket blowing through long pieces of hollow wood, which they call didgeridoos,' one of them wrote. Well, this country boasts that it's managed to integrate several cultures into one cohesive society. But cohesive for who? The problem, or the advantage, according to your perspective, is that the natives aren't seen anymore.

"Aboriginal folks are as good as totally absent from social life in Australia, apart from political debates that affect Indigenous interests and culture. Australians pay lip-service by having Aboriginal art hanging on the walls of their houses. However, we Blackfellas are well represented in the dole queues, suicide statistics and prisons. If you're

Aboriginal the chances of ending up in prison are twenty-six times greater than for any other Australian. Chew on that, Harry Holy."

Andrew drank the rest of his wine while Harry chewed on that. And the fact that he'd probably just eaten the best fish dish in his thirty-two years.

"And yet Australia's no more racist than any other country. After all, we're a multicultural nation with people from all over the world living here. It just means that dressing in a suit whenever you go to a restaurant is worth the trouble."

Harry nodded again. There was no more to say on that subject.

"Inger Holter worked in a bar, didn't she?"

"Yes, she did. The Albury in Oxford Street, Paddington. I thought we could wander up there this evening."

"Why not now?" Harry was beginning to be impatient with all this leisure.

"Because first we have to say hello to her landlord."

Pluto appeared unbidden in the firmament.

3

A Tasmanian Devil

Glebe Point Road turned out to be a cozy, not too frenetic street where small, plain and, for the most part, ethnic restaurants from various parts of the world stood cheek by jowl.

"This used to be Sydney's bohemian quarter," Andrew explained. "I lived here as a student in the seventies. You can still find typical veggie restaurants for people with conservation on the brain and alternative lifestyles, bookshops for lesbians and so on. But the old hippies and acidheads have gone. As Glebe became an 'in' place rent went up—I doubt if I'd be able to live here now, even on my police salary."

They turned right, up Hereford Street and went through the gate to number 54. A small furry black animal came toward them, barking, and revealing a row of tiny, sharp teeth. The mini-monster looked seriously angry and bore a striking similarity to the picture in the tourist brochure of the Tasmanian Devil. Aggressive and generally unpleasant to have hanging from your throat, it said. The species had been almost completely exterminated, which Harry sincerely hoped was true. As this specimen launched itself at him with jaws wide open, Andrew raised his foot and kicked the animal in mid-flight and volleyed it yelping into the bushes alongside the fence.

A man with a large gut who looked as though he had just got up was standing in the doorway with a sour expression on his face as they came up the steps.

"What happened to the dog?"

"It's admiring the rose bushes," Andrew informed him with a smile. "We're from the police. Crime Squad. Mr. Robertson?"

"Yeah, yeah. What do you lot want again? I told you I've told you everything I know."

"And now you've told us you've told us you've told us . . ." A long silence developed as Andrew continued to smile and Harry shifted his weight from one foot to the other.

"Apologies, Mr. Robertson, we won't try to kill you with our charm, but this is Inger Holter's brother and he would like to see her room if that's not too much trouble."

Robertson's attitude changed dramatically.

"Sorry, I didn't know . . . Come in!" He opened the door and went ahead of them up the stairs.

"Yeah, in fact I didn't even know Inger had a brother. But now you say it of course I can see the family likeness."

Behind him, Harry half turned to Andrew and rolled his eyes.

"Inger was a lovely girl and a fantastic tenant—indeed, a source of pride for the whole house and neighborhood too, probably." He smelled of beer and his diction was already a bit slurred.

No attempt had been made to tidy Inger's room. There were clothes, magazines, full ashtrays and empty wine bottles everywhere.

"Er, the police told me not to touch anything for the moment."

"We understand."

"She just didn't come back one night. Vanished into thin air."

"Thank you, Mr. Robertson, we've read your statement."

"I told her not to take the route round Bridge Road and the fish market when she came home at night. It's dark there and there are loads of blacks and Chinks . . ." He looked at Andrew Kensington in horror. "Sorry, I didn't mean to . . ."

"That's fine. You can go now, Mr. Robertson."

Robertson padded down the stairs and they heard bottles clinking in the kitchen.

The room contained a bed, a few bookshelves and a desk. Harry looked around and tried to construct an impression of Inger Holter. Victimology: putting yourself in the victim's shoes. He could just about recall the impish girl off the TV screen with her well-meaning, youthful commitment and innocent blue eyes.

She was definitely not a home bird. There were no pictures on the walls, just a poster of *Braveheart* with Mel Gibson—which Harry remembered only because for some incomprehensible reason it won an Oscar for Best Film. Bad taste, as far as films go, he thought. And men. Harry was one of those who felt personally let down when *Mad Max* made a Hollywood star out of him.

A photograph showed Inger sitting on a bench in front of some colorful Western-style houses with a gang of long-haired, bearded youths. She was wearing a loose, purple dress. Her blonde hair hung down flat against her pale, serious face. The young man whose hand she was holding had a baby in his lap.

On the shelf there was a pouch of tobacco. A few books about astrology and a roughly hewn wooden mask with a long, bent nose like a beak. Harry turned the mask over. *Made in Papua New Guinea*, it said on the price tag.

The clothes that weren't lying on the bed and floor hung in a small wardrobe. There wasn't much. A few cotton blouses, a worn coat and a large straw hat on the shelf.

Andrew picked up a packet of cigarette papers from the drawer in the desk.

"King Size Smoking Slim. She rolled herself some big cigarettes."

"Did you find any drugs here?" Harry asked.

Andrew shook his head and pointed to the cigarette paper.

"But if we'd hoovered the ashtrays I wouldn't mind betting we'd have found traces of cannabis."

"Why wasn't it done? Didn't the SOC people come here?"

"First of all, there's no reason to believe that this was the scene of the crime. Second of all, smoking marijuana is nothing to shout about. Here in New South Wales we have a more pragmatic attitude to marijuana than in certain other Australian states. I wouldn't rule out the possibility that the murder could be drugs-related, but the odd reefer or two is hardly relevant in this context. We can't know for sure if she used other drugs. There's a fair bit of coke and designer drugs on the go in the Albury, but no one we've spoken to has mentioned anything, and there wasn't a trace of anything in the blood tests. At any rate, she wasn't on the serious stuff. There were no needle marks, and we have a reasonable overview of the hard-core users."

Harry looked at him. Andrew cleared his throat.

"That's the official version, anyway. There is one thing they thought you could help us with though."

There was a letter in Norwegian. "Dear Elisabeth," it started and obviously wasn't finished. Harry skimmed through it.

> Well, I'm just fine, and even more important, I'm in love! Of course, he's as handsome as a Greek God with long, curly brown hair, a pert bum and eyes that tell you what he's already whispered to you: he wants you now—this minute—behind the closest wall, in the loo, on the table, on the floor, anywhere. His

name's Evans, he's 32, he's been married (surprise, surprise) and has a lovely little boy of 18 months called Tom-Tom. Right now he doesn't have a proper job, but drifts around doing things.

And, yes, I know you can smell trouble, and I promise not to let myself be dragged down. Not for the time being, anyway.

Enough about Evans. I'm still working at the Albury. "Mr. Bean" stopped inviting me out after Evans was in the bar one night, and that at least is progress. But he still follows me with those slimy eyes of his. Yuk! Actually I'm beginning to get sick of this job, but I'll just have to hang on until I can have my residence permit extended. I've had a word with NRK—they're planning a follow-up to the TV series for next autumn and I can carry on if I want. Decisions, decisions!

The letter stopped there.

4

A Clown

"Where are we going now?" Harry asked.

"To the circus! I promised a friend I would pop by one day. And today is one day, isn't it."

At the Powerhouse a small circus troupe had already started the free afternoon performance for a sparse but young and enthusiastic audience. The building had been a power station and a tram hall when Sydney had trams, Andrew elucidated. Now it was functioning as a kind of contemporary museum. A couple of well-built girls had just completed a not very spectacular trapeze number, but had reaped a great round of friendly applause.

An enormous guillotine was rolled in as a clown entered the stage. He was wearing a brightly colored uniform and a striped hat, obviously inspired by the French Revolution. He tripped and got up to all sorts of pranks to the huge amusement of the children. Then another clown came onto the stage wearing a long white wig, and it gradually dawned on Harry that he was meant to be Louis XVI.

"By unanimous vote, sentenced to death," announced the clown with the striped hat.

Soon the condemned man was led to the scaffold where he—still to the amusement of the children—laid his head, after much screaming and yelling, on the block below the blade. There was a brief roll of the drums, the blade fell and to everyone's amazement, Harry's included, it cut off the monarch's head with a sound reminiscent of an ax blow in the forest on a bright winter's morning. The head, still bearing the wig, fell and rolled into a basket. The lights went out, and when they were switched back on, the headless king stood in the spotlight with his head under his arm. Now the children's cheering knew no bounds. Then the lights went out again, and when they came back on for the second time, the whole troupe was assembled and bowing, and the performance was over.

As people poured toward the exit, Andrew and Harry went backstage. In the makeshift dressing room the performers were already removing their costumes and makeup.

"Otto, say hi to a friend from Norway," Andrew shouted.

A face turned. Louis XVI looked less majestic with makeup smeared over his face and without his wig. "Well, hello, it's Tuka the Indian!"

"Harry, this is Otto Rechtnagel."

Otto proffered his hand elegantly with a kink in the wrist and looked indignant when Harry, slightly perplexed, made do with a light press.

"No kiss, handsome?"

"Otto thinks he's a woman. A woman of noble descent," Andrew said, to illuminate.

"Stuff and nonsense, Tuka. Otto knows very well she's a man. You look confused, handsome. Perhaps you'd like to check for yourself?" Otto emitted a high-pitched chuckle.

Harry felt his earlobes go warm. Two false eyelashes fluttered accusingly at Andrew.

"Your friend, does he talk?"

"Sorry. My name's Harry . . . er . . . Holy. Clever number out there. Nice costumes. Very . . . lifelike. And unusual."

"The Louise Seize number? Unusual? On the contrary. It's an old classic. The first time it was done was by the Jandaschewsky clown family just two weeks after the real execution in January 1793. People loved it. People have always loved public executions. Do you know how many reruns there are of the Kennedy assassination on American TV stations every year?"

Harry shook his head.

Otto looked up at the ceiling pensively. "Quite a lot."

"Otto sees himself as the heir of the great Jandy Jandaschewsky," Andrew added.

"Is that so?" Famous clown families were not Harry's area of expertise.

"I don't think your friend here is quite with us, Tuka. The Jandaschewsky family, you see, was a traveling troupe of musical clowns who came to Australia at the beginning of the twentieth century and settled here. They ran the circus until Jandy died in 1971. I saw Jandy for the first time when I was six. From that moment I knew what I wanted to be. And now that's what I am."

Otto smiled a sad clown smile through the makeup.

"How do you two know each other?" Harry asked. Andrew and Otto exchanged glances. Harry saw their mouths twitch and knew he had committed a gaffe.

"I mean . . . a policeman and a clown . . . that's not exactly . . ."

"It's a long story," Andrew said. "I suppose you could say we grew up together. Otto would have sold his mother for a piece of my arse of course, but even at a young age I felt a strange attraction to girls and all those awful hetero things. It must have been something to do with genes and environment. What do you think, Otto?"

Andrew chuckled as he ducked away from Otto's slap.

"You have no style, you have no money and your arse is overrated," Otto squealed. Harry gazed round at the others in the troupe; they seemed quite unfazed by the performance. One of the well-built trapeze artists sent him an encouraging wink.

"Harry and I are going up to the Albury tonight. Would you like to join us?"

"You know very well I don't go there anymore, Tuka."

"You should be over that by now, Otto. Life goes on, you know."

"Everyone else's life goes on, you mean. Mine stops here, right here. When love dies, I die."

"As you wish."

"Besides, I have to go home and feed Waldorf. You go, and I may come a bit later."

"See you soon," Harry said, putting his lips dutifully to Otto's outstretched hand.

"Looking forward to that, Handsome Harry."

5

A Swede

The sun had gone down as they drove along Oxford Street in Paddington and pulled up by a small open space. "Green Park" the sign said, but the grass was scorched brown, and the only green was a pavilion in the middle of the park. A man with Aboriginal blood in his veins lay on the grass between the trees. His clothes were in tatters and he was so dirty that he was more gray than black. On seeing Andrew, he raised his hand in a kind of greeting, but Andrew ignored him.

The Albury was so full they had to squeeze their way inside the glass doors. Harry stood still for a few seconds taking in the scene before him. The clientele was a motley collection, mostly young men: rockers in faded denim, suit-clad yuppies with slicked hair, arty types with goatees and champagne, blond and good-looking surfers with bleached smiles, and bikers—or *bikies* as Andrew called them—in black leathers. At the center of the room, in the very bar itself, the show was in full swing with long-legged, semi-naked women wearing purple, plunging tops. They were cavorting about and miming with wide, red-painted mouths to Gloria Gaynor's "I Will Survive." The girls took turns so that those who were not performing served the customers with winks and outrageous flirting.

Harry elbowed his way to the bar and ordered.

"Coming up right away, blondie," said the barmaid in the Roman helmet with a deep voice and a mischievous smile.

"Tell me, are you and I the only straight guys in this town?" Harry asked, returning with a beer and a glass of juice.

"After San Francisco, Sydney has the biggest gay population in the world," Andrew said. "The Australian outback is not exactly known for its tolerance of sexual diversity, so it's not surprising that all the queer farmer boys in Australia want to come to Sydney. Not just from Australia, by the way, there are gay people from all over the world pouring into town every day."

They went to another bar at the back of the room where Andrew called a girl behind the counter. She was standing with her back to them and had the reddest hair Harry had ever seen. It hung down to the rear pocket of her tight blue jeans, but was unable to conceal the willowy back and pleasingly rounded hips. She turned and a row of pearly-white teeth smiled from a slim, radiant face with two azure eyes and innumerable freckles. What a waste, if this isn't a woman, Harry thought.

"Remember me?" Andrew shouted above the noise of seventies disco music. "I was here asking about Inger. Can we have a word?"

The redhead became serious. She nodded, passed on a message to one of the other girls and led the way to a little smoking room behind the kitchen.

"Any news?" she asked, and Harry needed no more to be able to determine with some certainty that she spoke better Swedish than English.

"I met an old man once," Harry said in Norwegian. She

glanced at him in surprise. "He was the captain of a boat on the Amazon River. Three words from him in Portuguese and I knew he was Swedish. He had lived there for thirty years. And I can't speak a word of Portuguese."

At first the redhead looked perplexed, but then she laughed. A trill of cheery laughter that reminded Harry of some rare forest bird.

"Is it really so obvious?" she said in Swedish. She had a deep, calm voice and softly rolled *rrr*s.

"Intonation," Harry said. "You never completely get rid of intonation."

"Do you know each other?" Andrew scrutinized them skeptically.

Harry looked at the redhead.

"Nope," she answered.

And isn't that a pity, Harry thought to himself.

The redhead's name was Birgitta Enquist. She had been in Australia for four years and working at the Albury for one.

"Of course we talked when we were working, but I didn't really have any close contact with Inger. She kept herself to herself mostly. There's a gang of us who go out together and she occasionally tagged along, but I didn't know her that well. She had just left some guy in Newtown when she started here. The most personal detail I know about her is that the relationship became too intense for her in the long run. I suppose she needed a fresh start."

"Do you know who she hung out with?" Andrew asked.

"Not really. As I said, we talked, but she never gave me a full rundown of her life. Not that I asked her to. In October she went up north to Queensland and apparently fell in with a crowd from Sydney there who she stayed in contact with afterward. I think she met a guy up there—he came by here one night. I've told you all this before though, haven't I?" she said with an inquiring glance.

"I know, my dear Miss Enquist, I just wanted my Norwegian colleague here to have a firsthand report and see where Inger worked. Harry Holy is regarded as Norway's best investigator after all and he may be able to put his finger on things we Sydney police have overlooked."

Harry was overcome by a sudden fit of coughing.

"Who's Mr. Bean?" he asked in a strange, constricted voice.

"Mr. Bean?" Birgitta eyed them in bewilderment.

"Someone who looked like the English comedian . . . er, Rowan Atkinson, isn't that his name?"

"Oh, him!" Birgitta said with the same forest-bird laughter.

I like it, Harry thought. More.

"That's Alex, the bar manager. He won't be here till later."

"We have reason to believe he was interested in Inger."

"Alex had his eye on Inger, yes, he did. And not just Inger, most girls in this bar have at one time or another been subjected to his desperate efforts. Or Fiddler Ray, as we call him. It was Inger who came up with Mr. Bean. He doesn't have an easy time of it, poor thing. Over thirty, lives at home with his mum and doesn't seem to be going anywhere. But he's perfectly OK as a boss. And quite harmless, if that's what you're thinking."

"How do you know?"

Birgitta patted the side of her nose. "He hasn't got it in him."

Harry pretended to jot notes down on his pad.

"Do you know if she knew or met someone who . . . er, had it in him?"

"Well, there are so many types of guy that drop in here. Not all of them are gay, and there were quite a few who noticed Inger—she's so attractive. Was. But off the top of my head I can't think of anyone. There was . . ."

"Yes?"

"No, nothing."

"I read in the report that Inger was working here the night we assume she was killed. Do you know if she had a date after work or did she go straight home?"

"She took a few scraps from the kitchen, said they were for the mutt. I knew she didn't have a dog, so I asked her where she was going. She said home. That's all I know."

"The Tasmanian Devil," Harry muttered. She sent him a curious look. "Her landlord has a dog," he said. "I suppose it had to be bribed so she could enter the house in one piece."

Harry thanked her for talking to them. As they were about to leave, Birgitta said, "We're really upset at the Albury about what happened. How are her parents taking it?"

"Not too well, I'm afraid," Harry said. "They're in shock, of course. And blame themselves for letting her come here. The coffin's being sent to Norway tomorrow. I can get hold of the address if you want to send flowers for the funeral."

"Thank you. That would be very kind of you."

Harry was on the verge of asking something else, but couldn't bring himself to do it with all the talk about death and funerals. On the way out her farewell smile was burning on his retina. He knew it was going to be there for a while.

"Shit," he mumbled to himself. "Should I, shouldn't I?"

In the club all the transvestites plus a fair number of the other customers were standing on the counter miming to Katrina & the Waves. "Walking on Sunshine" boomed out of the speakers.

"There's not much time for grief and reflection at a place like the Albury," Andrew commented.

"Suppose that's the way it should be," Harry said. "Life goes on." He asked Andrew to hang on for a minute, went back to the bar and waved to Birgitta.

"Sorry, just one last question."

"Yes?"

Harry took a deep breath. He was already regretting his decision, but it was too late. "Do you know a good Thai restaurant in town?"

Birgitta had a think. "Mmm, there's one in Bent Street, in the city center. Do you know where that is? It's supposed to be pretty good, I'm told."

"So good you would go with me?"

That didn't come out right, Harry thought. Besides, it was unprofessional. Very unprofessional, in fact. Birgitta gave a groan of despair, but the despair was not so convincing that Harry couldn't see an opening. Anyway, the smile was still in residence.

"That one of your more frequent lines, Officer?"

"Fairly frequent."

"Does it work?"

"Statistically speaking? Not really."

She laughed, inclined her head and studied Harry with curiosity. Then she shrugged.

"Why not? I'm free tomorrow. Nine o'clock. And you're paying."

6

A Bishop

Harry jammed the blue light on top of the car and got behind the wheel. The wind rushed through the car as he took the curves. Stiansen's voice. Then silence. A bent fence post. A hospital room, flowers. A photograph in the corridor, fading.

Harry sat bolt upright. The same dream again. It was still only four o'clock in the morning. He tried to go back to sleep, but his mind turned to Inger Holter's unknown murderer.

At six he reckoned he could get up. After an invigorating shower, he walked out to a pale blue sky with an ineffectual morning sun to find somewhere to go for breakfast. There was a buzz coming from the city center, but the morning rush hour had not yet reached the red lamps and black mascara eyes here. King's Cross had a certain slapdash charm, a lived-in beauty that made him hum as he walked. Apart from a few late, slightly worse-for-wear night birds, a couple sleeping under a rug on some steps and a wan, thinly clad prostitute on the early shift, the streets were empty for the moment.

Outside a terrace cafe the owner stood hosing down the pavement and Harry smiled his way to an impromptu breakfast. As he was eating his toast and bacon, a teasing breeze tried to whisk away his serviette.

"You're up at sparrow's fart, Holy," McCormack said. "It's good. The brain works best between half past six and eleven. After that it's mush, if you ask me. It's also quiet here in the morning. I can hardly add two and two with the racket after nine. Can you? My boy claims he has to have the stereo on to do his homework. He gets so distracted if it's bloody quiet. Can you understand that?"

"Er—"

"Anyway, yesterday I'd had enough and marched in and switched off the sodding machine. 'I need it to think!' screamed the boy. I said he would have to read like normal folk. 'People are different, Dad,' he said, pissed off. Yup, he's at that age, you know."

McCormack paused and looked at a photograph on the desk.

"You got kids, Holy? No? Sometimes I wonder what the hell I've done. What rathole did they book you into, by the way?"

"Crescent Hotel in King's Cross, sir."

"King's Cross, OK. You're not the first Norwegian to have stayed there. A couple of years ago we had an official visit from the Bishop of Norway, or someone like that, can't remember his name. Anyway, his staff in Oslo had booked a room for him at King's Cross Hotel. Perhaps the name had some biblical connotation or other. When the bishop arrived with his retinue one of the seasoned prostitutes caught sight of the clerical collar and harangued him with a few juicy suggestions. Think the bishop checked out before they'd even carried his bags up the stairs . . ."

McCormack laughed so much there were tears in his eyes.

"Yeah, well, Holy, what can we do for you today?"

"I was wondering if I could see Inger Holter's body before it's sent to Norway, sir."

"Kensington can take you to the morgue when he comes in. But you've got a copy of the autopsy report, haven't you?"

"Yes, sir, I just . . ."

"You just?"

"Think better with the body in front of me, sir."

McCormack turned to the window and mumbled something that Harry construed as "fine."

The temperature in the cellar of South Sydney Morgue was 46 degrees, as opposed to 82 degrees on the street outside.

"Any the wiser?" Andrew asked. He shivered and pulled his jacket tighter around him.

"Wiser, no," Harry said, looking at the earthly remains of Inger Holter. Her face had survived the fall relatively well. On one side the nostril had been torn open and the cheekbone knocked into a deep hollow, but there was no doubt that the waxen face belonged to the same girl with the radiant smile on the photo in the police report. There were black marks around the neck. The rest of the body was covered with bruises, wounds and some deep, deep cuts. In one of them you could see the white bone.

"The parents wanted to see the photos. The Norwegian ambassador explained that it was inadvisable, but the solicitor insisted. A mother shouldn't have to see her daughter like that." Andrew shook his head.

Harry studied the bruising on the neck with a magnifying glass.

"Whoever strangled her used his bare hands. It's difficult to kill someone with that method. The murderer must be either very strong or very motivated."

"Or have done it several times before."

Harry looked at Andrew.

"What do you mean by that?"

"She has no fragments of skin under her nails, she has none of the murderer's hair on her clothes and she has no grazing on her knuckles. She was killed so quickly and efficiently that she never had a chance to put up much of a fight."

"Does this remind you of anything you've seen before?"

Andrew shrugged. "When you've worked here long enough all murders remind you of something you've seen before."

No, Harry thought. It's the other way round. Work long enough and you see the tiny nuances each murder has, the details that distinguish one from another and make each one unique.

Andrew glanced at his watch. "The morning meeting starts in half an hour. We'd better get a move on."

The leader of the investigative unit was Larry Watkins, a detective with a legal background, on a swift upward curve through the ranks. He had narrow lips, thinning hair and spoke fast and efficiently without intonation or unnecessary adjectives.

"Or social antennae," Andrew said, not mincing his words. "A very able investigator, but he's not the person you ask to ring the parents when their daughter has been found dead. And then he starts swearing whenever he's stressed," he added.

Watkins's right-hand man was Sergey Lebie, a well-dressed, bald Yugoslav with a black goatee that made him look like Mephisto in a suit. Andrew said he was usually skeptical of men who were so fussy about their appearance.

"But Lebie isn't really a peacock, just very *meticulous.* Among other things he has a habit of studying his nails when anyone talks to him, but he doesn't mean it to seem arrogant. And then he cleans his shoes after the lunch break. Don't expect him to say much, not about himself or anything else."

The youngest member of the team was Yong Sue, a small, skinny, pleasant guy who always wore a smile above his bird-like neck. Yong Sue's family had come to Australia from China thirty years ago. Ten years ago, when Yong Sue was nineteen, his parents went back to China on a visit. They were never seen again. The grandfather reckoned the son had been involved in "something political," but he wouldn't venture any deeper. Yong Sue never found out what had happened. Now he provided for his grandparents and his two younger sisters, worked twelve-hour days and smiled for at least ten of them. "If you've got a bad joke, tell it to Yong Sue. He laughs at absolutely everything," Andrew had told him. Now they were all assembled in a tiny, narrow room in which a noisy fan in the corner was supposed to provide some air movement. Watkins stood by the board in front of them and introduced Harry to the others.

"Our Norwegian colleague has translated the letter we found in Inger's room. Anything interesting you can tell us about that, Hole?"

"Hoo-Leh."

"Sorry, Holy."

"Well, she had obviously just started a relationship with someone called Evans. From what the letter says, there is good reason to assume that it's his hand she's holding in the photo above the desk."

"We've checked," Lebie said. "We think he's one Evans White."

"Uh-huh?" Watkins raised a thin eyebrow.

"We don't have much on him. His parents came here from the US at the end of the sixties and were given a residence permit. It wasn't a problem at that time," Lebie added by way of enlightenment. "Anyway, they traveled round the country in a VW camper, probably on the diet of veggie food, marijuana and LSD that was the norm in those days. They had a child, got divorced, and when Evans was eighteen the father went back to the US. The mother's into healing, Scientology and all sorts of spiritual mysticism. She runs a place called the Crystal Castle on a ranch near Byron Bay. There she sells stones of karma and imported junk from Thailand to tourists and soul-seekers. When Evans was eighteen he decided to do what an increasing number of young Australians do," he said, turning to Harry: "Nothing."

Andrew leaned over and muttered in a low voice: "Australia is perfect for those who want to travel around, do a bit of surfing and enjoy life at the taxpayer's expense. Ace social network and ace climate. We live in a wonderful country." He leaned back.

"At the moment he has no fixed abode," Lebie continued, "but we think that until recently he was living in a shack on the outskirts of town with Sydney's white trash. Those we spoke to out there said they hadn't seen him for a while. He has never been arrested. So I'm afraid the only photograph we have of him is as a thirteen-year-old when he got his passport."

"I'm impressed," Harry said without any dissimulation. "How did you manage to find a guy without a record from one photo and a Christian name in a population of eighteen million in such a short time?"

Lebie nodded to Andrew.

"Andrew recognized the town in the photo. We faxed a copy to the local police station and they came up with this name. They say he has a role in the local milieu. Translated, that means he's one of the spliff kings."

"It must be a very small town," Harry said.

"Nimbin, just over a thousand inhabitants," Andrew

interposed. "By and large they lived off dairy products until Australia's National Union of Students took it into their heads to arrange what they called the Aquarius Festival there in 1973."

Chuckles rippled around the table.

"The festival was actually about idealism, alternative lifestyles, back to nature and that sort of stuff. The newspapers concentrated on the young people taking drugs and having rampant sex. The festival lasted for over ten days, and for some it never stopped. Growing conditions around Nimbin are good. For everything under the sun. Let me put it this way: I doubt that dairy products are the most important business up there any longer. In the main street, fifty meters from the local police station, you will find Australia's most open marijuana market. And LSD market, I'm sorry to say."

"At all events," Lebie said, "he's been seen in Nimbin recently, according to the police."

"In fact, the Premier of New South Wales is about to launch a campaign there," Watkins interjected. "The Federal government has apparently been pressing him to do something about the burgeoning trade in narcotics."

"That's true," Lebie said. "The cops are using spotter planes and helicopters to take photos of the fields where they're growing hemp."

"OK," Watkins said. "We'll have to catch this guy. Kensington, you obviously know your way around there, and you, Holy, I don't suppose you would object to seeing a bit more of Australia. I'll get McCormack to give Nimbin a bell so they know you're coming."

7

Lithgow

They mingled with tourists and took the single-track railway to Darling Harbour, got off at Harbourside and found an outside table with a view of the quays.

A pair of long legs stalked past on stilettos. Andrew rolled his eyes and whistled in a very un-PC way. A couple of heads in the restaurant turned and sent them an irritated glare. Harry shook his head.

"How's your friend Otto?"

"Well, he's devastated. He's been abandoned for a woman. If their lovers are bi they always end up with a woman, he says. But he'll survive this time as well."

To his surprise, Harry felt some raindrops, and sure enough: heavy cloud cover had drifted in from the northwest almost without his noticing.

"How did you recognize this Nimbin place with no more than a photo of a house front?"

"Nimbin? Did I forget to tell you that I'm an old hippie?" Andrew grinned. "It's claimed that anyone who can remember the Aquarius Festival wasn't there. Well, I remember the houses in the main street at least. It looked like an outlaw town in a middling Western, painted in psychedelic yellow and purple. Well, to tell the truth, I thought the yellow and purple had been the result of taking certain substances. Until I saw the photo in Inger's room."

On their return from lunch Watkins called another meeting in the Ops Room. Yong Sue had unearthed some interesting cases on his computer.

"I've been through all the unsolved murder cases in New South Wales over the last ten years and I've found four cases that have similarities with this one. The bodies are found in out-of-the-way places, two in landfill sites, one on a road by the edge of a forest and one floating in the Darling River. The women have probably been killed and sexually abused elsewhere and then dumped. And crucially—all of them have been strangled and show bruising to the neck from fingers." Yong Sue beamed.

Watkins cleared his throat. "Let's hold on to our hats here. After all, strangulation's not such an unusual type of killing after rape. What's the geographical distribution, Yong Sue? The Darling's in the bloody outback, more than a thousand kilometers from Sydney."

"No luck, sir. I couldn't find any geographical pattern." Yong Sue looked genuinely sorry.

"Well, four strangled women scattered across the whole state over a period of ten years is not a lot to—"

"One more thing, sir. All the women were blonde. I mean, not blonde hair, but fair hair, almost white."

Lebie released a silent whistle. The table went quiet.

Watkins was still looking skeptical. "Can you do your sums on this, Yong? Have a squiz at statistical significance and all that, find out if the odds are within reasonable limits before we cry wolf. For safety's sake perhaps you should check all of Australia first. And include the unsolved rapes. We might dig up something there."

"That'll take a bit of time. But I'll try, sir." Yong smiled again.

"OK. Kensington and Holy, why aren't you on your way to Nimbin?"

"We're going early tomorrow morning, sir," Andrew said. "There's a recent rape case in Lithgow I'd like to investigate first. I have a feeling there may be a connection. We were just heading there now."

Watkins frowned. "Lithgow? We're trying to work as a team here, Kensington. That means we discuss and coordinate and we don't wander off on our own. To my knowledge, we've never spoken about any rape cases in Lithgow."

"Just a hunch, sir."

Watkins sighed. "Well, McCormack seems to believe you have a kind of sixth sense."

"We Blackfellas have closer contact with the spiritual world than you whities, you know, sir."

"In my department we don't base our police work on that sort of thing, Kensington."

"A joke, sir. I've got a bit more than that on this matter."

Watkins shook his head. "Just be on the plane early tomorrow morning, OK?"

They took the freeway from Sydney. Lithgow is an industrial town of ten to twelve thousand inhabitants, but it seemed more like a medium-sized village to Harry. Outside the police station there was a flashing blue light nailed on top of a post.

The chief there received them warmly. He was an overweight, jovial type with a stack of double chins and went by the name of Larsen. Distant relatives in Norway.

"Do you know any of the Norwegian Larsens, mate?" he asked.

"Well, there are quite a few of them," Harry replied.

"Yes, I heard Gran say we've got a lot of family there."

"You sure do."

Larsen remembered the rape case, no problem.

"Fortunately, that doesn't happen so often here in Lithgow. It was at the beginning of November. She was bundled over in a backstreet while walking home from the night shift at the factory where she worked, dragged into a car and driven off. He threatened her with a big knife, took a turning onto an isolated forest road at the foot of the Blue Mountains, where she was raped on the backseat. The rapist had his hands round her throat and was squeezing when a car hooted behind them. The driver was on his way to his log cabin and thought he had surprised a couple making love on the deserted forest road, and for that reason did not get out. When the rapist got into the front seat to move the car, the woman managed to scramble out of the rear door and ran over to the other car. The rapist knew the game was up, jumped on the accelerator and made a break for it."

"Did either of them get the registration number?"

"Nope, it was dark and everything happened too fast."

"Did the woman get a decent look at the man? Did you get a description?"

"Sure. Well, sort of. As I said, it was dark."

"We've got a photo. Have you got an address for the woman?"

Larsen went to the filing cabinet and began to flick through. He was breathing heavily.

"By the way," Harry started, "do you know if she's blonde?"

"Blonde?"

"Yeah, fair-haired, white."

Larsen's double chins began to wobble as he breathed even harder. Harry realized he was laughing.

"Don't think so, mate. She's a Koori."

Harry searched Andrew's face.

Andrew looked up at the ceiling. "She's black," he said.

"As coal," Larsen said.

* * *

"So Koori's a tribe, is it?" Harry asked as they were driving away from the police station.

"Well, not quite," Andrew said.

"Not quite?"

"It's a long story but when the whites came to Australia there were 750,000 Indigenous Australians spread between many tribes. They spoke over 250 languages, several of them as different as English and Chinese. Many tribes are now extinct. As the traditional tribal structure collapsed, Indigenous people started to use more general terms. The Aboriginal groups who live here in the southeast are called Kooris."

"But why on earth didn't you check if she was blonde first."

"A slip. I must have misread. Don't computers flicker in Norway?"

"Shit, Andrew, we don't have time to waste on such long shots."

"Yes, we do. And we have time for something which will put you in a better mood as well," Andrew said, suddenly taking a right.

"Where are we going?"

"To an Australian agricultural show, the real thing."

"An agricultural show? I've got a dinner date, Andrew."

"Oh? With Miss Sweden, I assume? Relax, this is done in two shakes. By the way, I take it you, as a representative of the legal authorities, are aware of the consequences of having a private relationship with a potential witness?"

"This dinner forms part of the investigation. That goes without saying. Important questions will be asked."

"Of course."

8

A Boxer

The marketplace was in a wide-open expanse with a few scattered factory buildings and garages as the only neighbors. The final heat in the tractor race had just finished and the exhaust fumes still lay thick over the field as they pulled up in front of a large tent. The market buzzed with activity, the stalls rang with calls and shouts and everyone seemed to have a glass of beer in their hand and a smile on their face.

"Party and commerce in splendid union," Andrew said. "Don't suppose you have anything like this in Norway."

"Well, we have markets. They're called *markeder.*"

"Maaar . . ." Andrew essayed.

"Never mind."

By the marquee there were some huge posters proclaiming "The Jim Chivers Boxing Team" in big red letters. Below were pictures of the ten boxers who obviously comprised the team. Name, age, birthplace and weight of each were also given. At the bottom was: "The Challenge. Are you up to it?"

Inside, young men were queuing by a table to sign a piece of paper.

"What's going on?" Harry asked.

"These are young men from the area who are going to try and beat some of Jimmy's boxers. If they can there are great rewards, and even more important, local honor and fame. Now they're signing a declaration that they're fit and healthy and have accepted that the arranger will not take any responsibility for any sudden deterioration in their physical condition," Andrew explained.

"Sheesh, is that legal?"

"Well . . ." Andrew hesitated. "There was a kind of ban in 1971, so they had to change the procedure a bit. The original Jim Chivers led a boxing team that traveled round the whole country to rallies and fairs after the Second World War. Many of those who went on to become boxing champions were from Jimmy's team. There was always a variety of nationalities—Chinese, Italians, Greeks. And Aboriginals. In those days volunteers could choose who they wanted to box. So, for example, if you were an anti-Semite, you could pick out a Jew. Even though the chances of being beaten up by a Jew were pretty high."

Harry chuckled. "Doesn't that just stoke up racism?"

"Maybe. Maybe not. Australians are used to living with different cultures and races, but there's always some friction. And then it's better to have a scrap in the ring than in the streets. An Aboriginal guy in Jimmy's team who did well would have been a hero to his own wherever he came from. He created a tiny sense of solidarity and honor in all the humiliation. I don't think it widened the gulf between the races, either. If the white boys were given a hiding by a black boy it created more respect than hatred. Australians are pretty sporting on that front."

"You sound like a fully signed-up redneck."

Andrew laughed. "Almost, I'm an ocker. An uncivilized bloke from the outback."

"You are not."

Andrew laughed even louder.

The first bout started. A short, compact red-haired guy with his own gloves and his own gang of supporters against a much smaller man from the Chivers team.

"Mick against Mick," Andrew said with a knowledgeable expression.

"Your sixth sense?" Harry asked.

"My two eyes. Red hair, so Irish. Tough buggers. This is going to be a hard fight."

"Go, Johnny, go-go-go!" the gang chanted.

They managed two more choruses before the fight was over. By then Johnny had been punched on the nose three times and didn't want to go on.

"The Irish aren't what they were," Andrew sighed.

The speakers crackled, and the MC introduced Robin "The Murri" Toowoomba from the Chivers camp and Bobby "The Lobby" Pain, a local giant who entered the ring with a leap over the ropes and a roar. He pulled off his T-shirt and revealed a powerful hairy chest and bulging biceps. A woman dressed in white was jumping up and down close by the ring, and Bobby blew her a kiss before two assistants tied his boxing gloves. The marquee began to buzz as Toowoomba slunk in between the ropes. He was an erect, unusually black and good-looking man.

"Murri?" Harry asked.

"Aboriginal from Queensland."

Johnny's gang came to life as they realized they could use "Bobby" in their choruses now. The gong was struck and the two boxers approached each other. The white man was bigger, almost a head taller than his black adversary, but even to the untrained eye it was easy to see that he didn't move with the Murri's light-footed elegance.

Bobby rushed forward and launched a missile of a punch at Toowoomba, who swayed backward to avoid it. The audience groaned and the woman in white screamed encouragement. Bobby punched holes in the air a couple of times before Toowoomba glided in and planted a careful, probing right in the Lobby's face. Bobby staggered back two paces and it looked as if it was goodnight nurse for him.

"I should have put *two* hundred on him," Andrew commented.

Toowoomba circled Bobby, threw a couple of jabs and swayed back with the same ease when Bobby swung his log-like arms. Bobby was panting and yelling with frustration while Toowoomba never seemed to be where he had been a moment before. The audience started to whistle. Toowoomba raised a hand as if in greeting, then buried it in Bobby's stomach. He folded and stood doubled up in the corner of the ring. Toowoomba drew back a couple of paces and looked concerned.

"Finish him off, you black bastard!" Andrew screamed. Toowoomba turned in surprise, smiled and waved a hand above his head.

"Don't stand there grinning, do your job, you dingbat! I've got money on you."

Toowoomba turned to get the whole thing over and done with, but as he was about to give Bobby the *coup de grâce*, the gong went. The two boxers approached their corners as the MC took the microphone. The woman in white was already in Bobby's corner and giving him an earful while one of his assistants passed him a bottle of beer.

Andrew was annoyed. "Robin doesn't want to hurt the whitie, fair dinkum. But he ought to respect the fact that I've put money on him, the useless bugger."

"Do you know him?"

"Yes, I know Robin Toowoomba," Andrew said.

The gong went again and this time Bobby stood waiting in the corner for Toowoomba, who approached with a determined gait. Bobby was holding his arms high to protect his head and Toowoomba fired a body punch. Bobby collapsed backward against the rope. Toowoomba turned and looked imploringly at the MC—who was also working as a kind of referee—to make him stop the fight.

Andrew screamed again, but too late.

Bobby's punch sent Toowoomba flying and he hit the canvas with a thud. As he staggered to his feet, dazed, Bobby was on him like a hurricane. The blows came straight and true, and Toowoomba's head was batted to and fro like a ping-pong ball. A thin stripe of blood issued forth from one nostril.

"Shit! A hustler!" Andrew shouted. "Bloody hell, Robin, you fell for that one."

Toowoomba had his hands in front of his face and was retreating as Bobby went after him. Bobby's left arm was pumping in and out, followed by powerful haymakers and right uppercuts. The crowd was in ecstasy. The woman in white was on her feet again, screaming the first syllable of his name and holding the vowel in a long, shrill tone: "Boooo . . ."

The MC shook his head as the gang of cheerers quickly launched its new chorus: "Go, Bobby, go-go-go, Bobby-be-good!"

"That's it. It's over," Andrew said, dispirited.

"Toowoomba's going to lose?"

"Are you crazy? Toowoomba's going to kill the bastard. I'd been hoping it wouldn't be too gruesome today."

Harry concentrated, to try and see what Andrew could see. Toowoomba had fallen back on the ropes; he appeared almost relaxed as Bobby pummeled away at his abdomen. For a moment Harry thought Toowoomba was going to sleep. The woman in white pulled the ropes behind the Murri. Bobby changed tactics and went for the head, but Toowoomba avoided the punches by moving his body forward and backward in a slow, lazy glide. Almost like a hooded snake, Harry thought, like a . . .

Cobra!

Bobby stiffened in mid-punch. His head was half turned to the left, with an expression suggesting he had just remembered something, then his eyes rolled back, the mouth guard slipped out and blood spurted in a thin, even jet from a tiny hole on the bridge of his nose where the bone was broken. Toowoomba waited until Bobby fell forward before hitting him again. The marquee went quiet, and Harry heard the awful crunch as the blow hit Bobby's nose for a second time, and the woman's voice as she screamed what remained of his name:

". . . bbyyy!"

Red spray composed of sweat and blood flew off Bobby's head and showered the corner of the ring.

The MC charged over and signaled, somewhat superfluously, that the fight had finished. The marquee remained silent, just the clatter of the woman in white's shoes as she ran up the central aisle and out of the tent. Her dress was spattered at the front, and she wore the same surprised expression as Bobby.

Toowoomba tried to get Bobby to his feet, but the two assistants shoved him away. There were scattered claps, but they faded. The whistles increased when the MC went over and raised Toowoomba's hand in the air. Andrew shook his head.

"Must have been a few blokes who put their money on the local champion today," he said. "Idiots! Come on, let's collect the cash and have a few serious words with this Murri drongo!"

"Robin, you bastard. You should be locked up—and I mean it!"

Robin "The Murri" Toowoomba's face lit up in a big smile. He was holding an ice-filled rolled towel over one eye.

"Tuka! I could hear you out there. Have you started gambling again?" Toowoomba spoke in a low voice. A man who is used to being listened to, Harry thought instantly.

The sound was pleasant and gentle, not like someone who had just broken the nose of a man almost twice his size.

Andrew snorted. "Gambling? In my days betting money on a Chivers boy could never be called gambling. But now I suppose nothing is certain anymore. Fancy allowing yourself to be taken in by a bloody white yahoo. Where's it all going to end?"

Harry cleared his throat.

"Oh, yeah, Robin, say hello to a friend of mine. This is Harry Holy. Harry, this is Queensland's worst hoodlum and sadist, Robin Toowoomba." They shook hands and Harry felt as if his hand had been trapped in a door. He groaned a "How are you?" and received an "Absolutely magnificent, mate—how are you yourself?" and a gleaming smile by way of an answer.

"Never better," Harry said, massaging his hand.

These Australian handshakes were crippling him. According to Andrew, it was important to say how unimaginably well things were going; a bland "fine, thanks" could be interpreted as very cold.

Toowoomba pointed his thumb at Andrew. "Talking of hoodlums, has Tuka told you that he once used to box for Jim Chivers?"

"I suppose there are still quite a few things I don't know about . . . er, Tuka? He's a secretive guy."

"Secretive?" Toowoomba laughed. "He speaks in tongues. Tuka will tell you everything you need to know so long as you know what you have to ask. Of course, he hasn't told you he had to resign from the Chivers team because he was considered too dangerous, has he. How many cheekbones, noses and jaws have you got on your conscience, Tuka? Everyone reckoned he was the best young boxing talent in New South Wales. But there was one problem. He didn't have any self-control—no discipline. In the end he knocked down a ref because he thought he had stopped the fight too soon. In Tuka's favor! That's what I call bloodthirsty. Tuka was suspended for two years."

"Three and a half, thank you very much!" Andrew grinned. "He was a real drongo, I'm telling you. I only nudged the bastard of a ref, but you wouldn't believe it, he fell and broke his collarbone."

Toowoomba and Andrew clapped their hands and collapsed in laughter.

"Robin was hardly born when I was boxing. He just quotes what I've told him," Andrew said. "Robin was one of a group of disadvantaged kids I worked with whenever I had time. We did some boxing sessions, and to teach the boys the importance of self-control I told them a couple of half-true stories about myself. As a deterrent. Obviously Robin here didn't understand, he followed me instead."

Toowoomba became serious. "We're usually good boys, Harry. We let them have a few heaves before we chuck in the odd punch so they can see who's boss, know what I mean? After that it's not long before they give up. But this bloke could box, he could have hurt someone. Blokes like him get what they ask for."

The door opened. "Fuck you, Toowoomba—as if we didn't have enough problems already. You only broke the nose of the local police chief's son-in-law." The MC looked furious and underlined this fact by spitting on the floor with a resounding splat.

"Pure reflex action," Toowoomba said, examining the snuff-brown liquid. "It won't happen again." He sent Andrew a surreptitious wink.

They got up. Toowoomba and Andrew hugged each other and uttered a few concluding remarks in a language which left Harry mystified. He gave Toowoomba a pat on the shoulder to render any more handshaking redundant.

* * *

"What was the language you were speaking there?" Harry asked after they had gotten into the car.

"Oh, that. It's a kind of Creole, a mixture of English and words of Aboriginal origin. It's spoken by lots of Aboriginals across the country. What did you think of the boxing?"

Harry took his time to answer. "It was interesting to see you earn a few dollars, but we could have been in Nimbin by now."

"If we hadn't come here today you wouldn't have been able to go to Sydney this evening," Andrew said. "You don't have dates with women like her and just run off. We might be talking about your future wife and mother of two tiny Holies, Harry."

They both smirked as they passed trees and low houses as the sun went down on the eastern hemisphere.

Darkness had fallen before they reached Sydney, but the TV mast stood like a massive lightbulb in the center of the town and showed them the way. Andrew drew in at Circular Quay, not far from the Opera House. A bat whirled in and out of the car headlights at great speed. Andrew lit a cigar and motioned for Harry to remain in the car.

"The bat is the Aboriginal symbol of death. Did you know that?"

Harry did not.

"Imagine a place where people have been isolated for forty thousand years. In other words, they haven't experienced Judaism, never mind Christianity and Islam, because a whole ocean has separated them from the closest continent. Nevertheless they come up with their own history of creation, the Dreaming. The first man was Ber-rook-boorn. He was made by Baiame, the uncreated, who was the beginning of everything, and who loved and took care of all living things. In other words, a good man, this Baiame. Friends called him the Great Fatherly Spirit. After Baiame established Ber-rook-boorn and his wife in a good place, he left his mark on a sacred tree—yarran—nearby, which was the home of a swarm of bees.

"'You can take food from anywhere you want, in the whole of this country that I have given you, but this is my tree,' he warned the two people. 'If you try to take food from there, much evil will befall you and those who come after you.' Something like that. At any rate, one day Ber-rook-boorn's wife was collecting wood and she came to the yarran tree. At first she was frightened at the sight of the holy tree towering above her, but there was so much wood lying around that she did not follow her first impulse—which was to run away as fast as her legs could carry her. Besides, Baiame had not said anything about wood. While she was gathering the wood around the tree she heard a low buzzing sound above her head, and she gazed up at the swarm of bees. She also saw the honey running down the trunk. She had only tasted honey once before, but here there was enough for several meals. The sun glistened on the sweet, shiny drops, and in the end Ber-rook-boorn's wife could not resist the temptation and she climbed up the tree.

"At that moment a cold wind came from above and a sinister figure with enormous black wings enveloped her. It was Narahdarn the bat, whom Baiame had entrusted with guarding the holy tree. The woman fell to the ground and ran back to her cave where she hid. But it was too late, she had released death into the world, symbolized by the bat Narahdarn, and all of the Ber-rook-boorn descendants would be exposed to its curse. The yarran tree cried bitter tears over the tragedy that had taken place. The tears ran down the trunk and thickened, and that is why you can find red rubber on the bark of the tree nowadays."

Andrew puffed happily on his cigar.

"Gives Adam and Eve a run for their money, doesn't it."

Harry nodded and conceded there were a number of parallels. “Perhaps it’s just that people, wherever they live on the globe, somehow share the same visions or fantasies. It’s in our nature, wired into the hard drive, so to speak. Despite all the differences, sooner or later, we still come up with the same answers.”

“Let’s hope so,” Andrew said. He squinted through the smoke. “Let’s hope so.”

9

A Sea Nettle Jellyfish

Harry was well down his second Coke when Birgitta arrived at ten minutes past nine. She was wearing a plain white cotton dress, and her red hair was collected in an impressive ponytail.

"I was beginning to worry you wouldn't come," Harry said. It was said as a joke, but he meant it. He had started worrying the moment they agreed to meet.

"Really?" she said in Swedish. She sent Harry a mischievous look. He had a feeling this was going to be a great evening.

They ordered Thai green curry with pork, chicken with cashew nuts cooked in a wok, an Australian Chardonnay and Perrier water.

"I must say I'm pretty surprised to meet a Swede so far from home."

"You shouldn't be. There are about ninety thousand Swedes in Australia."

"What?"

"Most emigrated here before the Second World War, but quite a lot of young people left in the eighties with unemployment on the rise in Sweden."

"And there was me thinking Swedes would be missing

their meatballs and the midsummer dancing before they'd reached Helsingør."

"That must be Norwegians you were thinking about. You're crazy, you lot! The Norwegians I've met here started yearning for home after a few days, and after two months they were back in Norway. Back home to woolly cardigans!"

"But not Inger?"

Birgitta fell quiet. "No, not Inger."

"Do you know why she stayed here?"

"Probably the same reason as for most of us. You go on holiday, fall in love with the country, the climate, the easy lifestyle or a man. You apply to have your permit extended. Scandinavian girls don't exactly have a problem getting jobs in bars, and suddenly it's such a long way home and it's so simple to stay."

"Is that how it was for you, too?"

"More or less."

They ate in silence for a while. The curry was thick, strong and good.

"What do you know about Inger's last boyfriend?"

"As I said, he popped by the bar one night. She'd met him in Queensland. On Fraser Island, I think it was. He looked like the version of hippie I thought had died out long ago, but is alive and well here in Australia. Long braided hair, colorful, baggy clothes, sandals. Like he'd walked in off Woodstock beach."

"Woodstock's inland. New York."

"But wasn't there a lake they swam in? I seem to remember that."

Harry ran a closer eye over her. She was sitting hunched over her food, concentrating. The freckles were bunched in a cluster over her nose. She was pretty, that was Harry's opinion.

"You shouldn't know that kind of thing. You're too young."

She laughed. "And what are you—past it?"

"Me? Well, some days I might be. It comes with the job—somewhere inside you age all too quickly. But I hope I'm not so disillusioned and jaded that I can't feel alive now and then."

"Oh, poor you . . ."

Harry had to smile. "You can think what you like, but I'm not saying that to appeal to your maternal instinct, even though that might not have been a bad idea. It's just the way it is."

The waiter passed the table and Harry took the opportunity to order another bottle of water.

"You're a tiny bit damaged every time you unravel another murder case. Unfortunately, as a rule there are more human wrecks and sadder stories, and fewer ingenious motives, than you would imagine from reading Agatha Christie. At first I saw myself as a kind of knight dispensing justice, but at times I feel more like a refuse collector. Murderers are generally pitiful sorts, and it's seldom difficult to point to at least ten good reasons why they turned out as they did. So, usually, what you feel most is frustration. Frustration that they can't be happy destroying their own lives instead of dragging others down with them. This probably still sounds a touch sentimental . . ."

"I'm sorry—I didn't mean to appear cynical. I understand what you mean," she said.

A gentle breeze from the street caused the flame of the candle on the table to flicker.

Birgitta told Harry about how she and her boyfriend had packed their rucksacks in Sweden four years ago and set off, how they had traveled by bus and hitched from Sydney to Cairns, slept under canvas and in backpacker hotels, worked there as receptionists and cooks, dived by the Great Barrier Reef and swum side by side with turtles and hammerhead sharks. They had meditated on Uluru, saved their money to catch the train from Adelaide to Alice Springs, been to a Crowded House concert in Melbourne and hit the wall in a motel in Sydney.

"It's strange how something that works so well can be so . . . wrong."

"Wrong?"

Birgitta hesitated. Perhaps she was thinking she'd said too much to this rather direct Norwegian.

"I don't really know how to explain it. We lost something on the way that had been there and we'd taken for granted. We stopped looking at each other and soon we stopped touching each other. We came to be no more than traveling companions, someone it was good to have around because double rooms were cheaper and tents safer with two. He met a rich man's daughter, German, in Noosa and I kept on traveling so that he could continue the affair in peace. I didn't give a shit. When he arrived in Sydney I told him I'd fallen in love with an American surf freak I'd just met. I don't know if he believed me, perhaps he understood that I was giving both of us a pretext for finishing things. We tried to argue in the motel room in Sydney, but we couldn't even do that anymore. So I told him to go back to Sweden first and I would follow."

"He would have quite a head start on you now."

"We were together for six years. Would you believe me if I said I can hardly remember what he looked like?"

"I would."

Birgitta sighed. "I didn't think it would be like that. I was sure we would get married and have children and live in a little suburb of Malmö with a garden and *Sydsvenska Dagbladet* on the doorstep, and now—now I can hardly remember the sound of his voice, or what it was like to make love with him, or . . ." She looked up at Harry. "Or how he was too polite to tell me to shut up while I was babbling on after a couple of glasses of wine."

Harry grinned. She hadn't commented on the fact that he hadn't drunk any of the wine.

"I'm not polite, I'm interested," he said.

"In that case, you'll have to tell me something personal about you, other than that you're a policeman."

Birgitta leaned across the table. Harry told himself not to look down her dress. He sensed her aroma and greedily breathed in the fragrance. He must not let himself be duped. Those cunning bastards at Karl Lagerfeld and Christian Dior knew exactly what was required to trap a poor man.

She smelled wonderful.

"Well," Harry began, "I have a sister, my mother died, I live in a flat I can't get rid of in Tøyen, Oslo. I have no lengthy relationships behind me, and only one has left any marks."

"Really? And there's no one in your life now?"

"Not really. I have a few uncomplicated, meaningless relationships with women I occasionally ring if they don't ring me."

Birgitta frowned.

"Something wrong?"

"I'm not sure if I approve of that kind of man. Or woman. I'm a bit old-fashioned like that."

"Of course, I've put all that stuff behind me," Harry said, raising the glass of Perrier.

"And I'm not sure I like these glib answers of yours, either," Birgitta said, raising her glass.

"So what do you look for in a man?"

She rested her chin on her hand and gazed into the air considering the question. "I don't know. I think I know more about what I don't like in a man than what I do."

"What don't you like? Apart from glib answers."

"Men who try to check me out."

"Do you suffer a lot?"

She smiled. "Let me give you a tip, Casanova. If you want

to charm a woman, you have to make her feel unique, make her feel she's being given special treatment, something no one else gets. Men who try to pick up girls in bars don't understand that. But I suppose that means nothing to a libertine like you."

Harry laughed. "By a few I mean two. I said a few because that sounds a bit wilder, it sounds like . . . three. One, by the way, is on her way back to her ex according to what she told me the last time I saw her. She thanked me because I had been so uncomplicated and the relationship had been so . . . well, meaningless, I assume. The other is a woman I started a relationship with and who now insists that since it was me who left, it is my duty to ensure that she has a modicum of a sex life until either of us finds someone else. Hang on—why have I gone all defensive here? I'm a normal man who wouldn't harm a flea. Are you implying that I'm trying to charm someone?"

"Oh yes, you're trying to charm me. Don't deny it!"

Harry didn't deny it. "All right. How am I doing?"

She took a long swig from her wineglass and gave the matter some thought.

"B, I reckon. Moderate anyway. No, I think it will have to be a B . . . you're doing quite well."

"Sounds like B minus."

"There or thereabouts."

It was dark down by the harbor, almost deserted, and a fresh wind had sprung up. On the steps to the illuminated Opera House an unusually overweight bride and groom posed for the photographer. He directed them hither and thither, and the newlyweds seemed to be very annoyed at having to move their large bodies. In the end, though, they came to an agreement, and the nocturnal photo session in front of the Opera House ended in smiles, laughter and perhaps a little tear.

"That's what they must mean by bursting with happiness," Harry said. "Or perhaps you don't say that in Swedish?"

"Yes, we do, you could be so happy you burst in Swedish, too." Birgitta took off her hairband and stood in the wind by the harbor railing, facing the Opera House.

"Yes, you could," she repeated, as if to herself. She turned her freckled nose to the sea, and the wind blew her red hair back.

She looked like a sea nettle jellyfish. He didn't know a jellyfish could be so beautiful.

10

A Town Called Nimbin

Harry's watch showed eleven as the plane landed in Brisbane but the stewardess on the speaker insisted it was only ten.

"They don't have summer time in Queensland," Andrew informed him. "It was a big political issue up here, culminating in a referendum and the farmers voted against it."

"Wow, sounds like we've come to redneck country."

"I reckon so, mate. Up until a few years ago long-haired men were refused entry to the state. It was banned outright."

"You're joking."

"Queensland's a bit different. Soon they'll probably ban skinheads."

Harry stroked his close-cropped skull. "Anything else I ought to know about Queensland?"

"Well, if you've got any marijuana in your pockets you'd better leave it on the plane. In Queensland the drugs laws are stricter than in other states. It was no coincidence that the Aquarius Festival was held in Nimbin. The town's just over the border, in New South Wales."

They found the Avis office where they had been told a car would be ready and waiting for them.

"On the other hand, Queensland has places like Fraser Island, where Inger Holter met Evans White. The island's actually no more than a huge sandbank, but on it you can find a rainforest and lakes with the world's clearest water and sand that is so white the beaches look as if they've been made out of marble. Silicon sand it's called, because the silicon content's so much higher than in normal sand. You can probably pour it straight into a computer."

"The land of plenty, eh?" said the guy behind the counter, passing them a key.

"Ford Escort?" Andrew wrinkled his nose, but signed. "Is it still going?"

"Special rate, sir."

"Don't doubt it."

The sun was frying the Pacific Highway, and Brisbane's skyline of glass and stone glittered like crystals on a chandelier as they approached.

From the freeway eastward they drove through rolling green countryside alternating between forest and cultivated field.

"Welcome to the Australian outback," Andrew said.

They passed cows grazing with lethargic stares.

Harry chuckled.

"What's up?" Andrew asked.

"Have you seen the comic strip by Larson where the cows are standing on two legs chatting in the meadow, and one of them warns: 'Car!'"

Silence.

"Who's Larson?"

"Never mind."

They passed low wooden houses with verandas at the front, mosquito nets in the doorways and pickup trucks outside. They drove past broad-backed workhorses watching them with melancholy eyes, beehives and penned pigs blissfully rolling in the mud. The roads became narrower. Around lunchtime they stopped for petrol in a little settlement a sign informed them was called Uki, which had been chosen as Australia's cleanest town for two years running. It didn't say who had won last year.

"Holy macaroni," Harry said as they trundled into Nimbin.

The town center was about a hundred meters in length, painted all colors of the rainbow, with a crop of characters that could have come from one of the Cheech & Chong films in Harry's video collection.

"We're back in 1970!" he exclaimed. "I mean, look over there. Peter Fonda in a clinch with Janis Joplin."

They slowly cruised down the street as somnambulist eyes followed them.

"This is great. I didn't think places like this existed anymore. You could just die laughing."

"Why?" Andrew asked.

"Don't you think it's funny?"

"Funny? I can see it's easy to laugh at these dreamers nowadays. I can see that the new generation thinks the flower-power lot were a bunch of potheads with nothing else to do except play guitars, read their poems and screw one another as the whim took them. I can see that the organizers of Woodstock turn up for interviews wearing ties and talk with amusement about the ideas of those times, which obviously seem very naive to them now. But I can also see that the world would have been a very different place without the ideals that generation stood for. Slogans like peace and love may be clichés now, but back then we meant it. With all our hearts."

"Aren't you a bit old to have been a hippie, Andrew?"

"Yes. I was old. I was a veteran hippie, a slyboots," Andrew grinned. "Many a young girl received her first introduction into the intricate mysteries of lovemaking with Uncle Andrew."

Harry patted him on the shoulder. "I thought you were just talking about idealism, you old goat."

"Of course. This was idealism," Andrew said with indignation. "I couldn't leave these fragile flower buds to some awkward, pimply teenager and risk the girl being traumatized for the rest of the seventies."

Andrew glanced out of the car window and chuckled. A man with long hair, a beard and a tunic was sitting on a bench and making the peace sign with two raised fingers. A placard with a drawing of an old, yellow VW camper announced "The Marijuana Museum." Beneath, in smaller letters: "Admission: one dollar. If you can't pay, come in anyway."

"This is Nimbin's dope museum," Andrew explained. "It's mostly crap, but I seem to remember they have some interesting photos of the Mexico trips with Ken Kesey, Jack Kerouac and the other pioneers when they were experimenting with consciousness-expanding drugs."

"When LSD wasn't dangerous?"

"And sex was just healthy. Wonderful times, Harry Holy. You shoulda been there, man."

They parked further up the main street and walked back. Harry took off his Ray-Bans and tried to look like a civilian. It was clearly a quiet day in Nimbin, and Harry and Andrew ran the gauntlet between the vendors. "Good grass! . . . Best grass in Australia, man . . . Grass from Papua New Guinea, mind-blowin.' "

"Papua New Guinea," Andrew snorted. "Even here in the grass capital people walk around thinking grass is better if it comes from somewhere far enough away. Buy Australian, I say."

A pregnant yet thin girl was sitting on a chair in front of the "museum" and waved to them. She could have been anything from twenty to forty and was wearing a loose, vivid skirt and a buttoned-up blouse, making her stomach stand out with the skin stretched like a drum. There was something vaguely familiar about her, Harry thought. And from the size of her pupils Harry was able to conclude there had been something more stimulating than marijuana on her breakfast menu that day.

"Looking for something else?" she asked. She had observed that they hadn't shown any interest in buying marijuana.

"No—" Harry started to say.

"Acid. You want LSD, don't you." She leaned forward and spoke with urgency and passion.

"No, we don't want any acid," Andrew said in a low, firm voice. "We're looking for something else. Understand?"

She sat gazing at them. Andrew made a move to go on, but then she jumped up, apparently unaffected by the large stomach, and took his arm. "OK, but we can't do that here. You'll have to meet me in the pub over there in ten minutes."

Andrew nodded, and she turned and hurried down the street with her large bump, a small puppy running at her heels.

"I know what you're thinking, Harry," Andrew said, lighting up a cigar. "It wasn't nice to trick Mother Kindheart into believing we would buy some heroin. The police station's a hundred meters up the street and we could find what we need on Evans White there. But I have a hunch this'll be quicker. Let's go and have a beer and see what happens."

Half an hour later Mother Kindheart entered the near-empty pub with a man who seemed at least as hunted as she was. He resembled the Klaus Kinski version of Count Dracula: pale, lean, dressed in black with dark bags under his eyes.

"There you go," Andrew whispered. "You can hardly accuse him of not testing the stuff he sells."

Mother Kindheart and the Kinski clone made straight for them. The latter did not appear to want to spend any more time in daylight than was absolutely necessary and skipped the small talk.

"How much?"

Andrew sat demonstratively with his back to them. "I prefer there to be as few people present as possible before we get down to brass tacks, mister," he said without turning.

Kinski tossed his head and Mother Kindheart left with a peeved expression. She probably worked on a percentage basis, and Harry assumed the trust between her and Kinski was as it always was with junkies: non-existent.

"I've got nothing on me, and if you're cops I'll cut your balls off. Show me the bread first, then we can get out of here." He spoke fast, he was nervous and his eyes jumped about.

"Is it far?" Andrew asked.

"It's a short walk, but a lo-ong trip." What was meant to be a smile was a brief glimpse of teeth before it was gone.

"Good on ya, mate. Sit down and shut up," Andrew said, showing him his police badge. Kinski froze. Harry stood up and patted the back of his belt. There was no reason to check whether Harry really had a weapon.

"What is this amateur dramatics stuff? I've got nothing on me, I told you, didn't I?" He slumped defiantly into the chair opposite Andrew.

"I take it you know the local sheriff and his assistant? And they probably know you. But do they know you've started selling *horse*?"

The man shrugged. "Who said anything about *horse*? I thought it was grass we—"

"Of course. No one said anything about junk, and it's unlikely anyone will so long as you give us some information."

"You're kidding, aren't you. Would I risk being beheaded for snitching just because two out-of-town cops who don't even have anything on me come bursting in and—"

"Snitching? We met here, unfortunately couldn't agree on the price of the goods and that was that. You've even got a witness that we met here on normal business. Do as we tell you and you'll never see us again, and nor will anyone else here."

Andrew lit a cigar, peered through narrow slits at the poor junkie on the other side of the table, blew smoke into his face and continued.

"Should we not get what we're after, however, we might put on our badges when we leave here and perform a couple of arrests, which wouldn't exactly increase your popularity in the local community. I don't know if cutting the balls off snitches is used up here—after all, potheads are peaceful folk as a rule. But they know the odd trick or two, and it wouldn't surprise me if right out of the blue the sheriff didn't stumble across your whole stock, quite by chance. Potheads aren't so happy about competition from the hard stuff, you know, at least not from junkie snitches. And I'm sure you know all about the penalties for dealing in large quantities of heroin, don't you."

More blue cigar smoke in Kinski's face. It's not every day you have the chance to blow smoke into an asshole's face, Harry thought.

"OK," Andrew said, after no reply was forthcoming. "Evans White. Tell us where he is, who he is and how we can get hold of him. Now!"

Kinski looked around. His large, hollow-cheeked skull turned on the thin neck, making him look like a vulture hovering over some carcass, checking anxiously to see if the lions were returning.

"That all?" he asked. "Nothing else?"

"Nothing else," Andrew said.

"And how do I know you won't be back asking for more?"

"You don't."

He nodded as though he had known it was the only answer he would get.

"OK. He's no big fish yet, but from what I've heard he's on the way up. He's worked for Madam Rousseau, the grass queen up here, but now he's trying to set up his own business. Grass, acid and perhaps a bit of morphine. The grass is the same as the rest that's sold here, local production. But he must have connections in Sydney and delivers grass there in exchange for good, cheap acid. Acid's what it's all about now."

"Where can we get hold of Evans?" Andrew asked.

"He's in Sydney quite a bit, but I saw him in town a couple of days ago. He's got a kid with a chick from Brisbane who used to hang out here. I don't know where she is now, but the kid's definitely in the block of flats where he lives when he's in Nimbin."

He explained where the block was.

"What sort of fella is White?" Andrew pressed.

"What can I say?" He scratched the beard he didn't have. "A charming arsehole, isn't that what they're called?"

Andrew and Harry didn't know if that was what they were called, but nodded anyway.

"He's straight enough to deal with, but I wouldn't want to be his girl, if you know what I mean."

They shook their heads to say they didn't know what he meant.

"He's a playboy, not exactly known for making do with one chick at a time. There are always arguments with his women, they scream and shout, so it's not unusual for one of them to sport a shiner once in a while."

"Hm. Do you know anything about a blonde-haired Norwegian girl called Inger Holter? She was found murdered by Watson's Bay in Sydney last week."

"Really? Never heard of her." He clearly wasn't an avid newspaper reader, either.

Andrew stubbed out his cigar and he and Harry got up.

"Can I rely on you keeping your traps shut?" Kinski asked with a doubtful glare.

"Of course," Andrew said, striding toward the door.

"What was the meal with our Swedish witness like?" Andrew asked after they had made a courtesy stop at the police station, a building that looked like any other house on the street, except for a little sign on the lawn announcing its purpose.

"Good. Quite spicy, but good," Harry answered pertly.

"Come on, Harry. What did you talk about?"

"Lots. Norway and Sweden."

"I see. Who won?"

"She did."

"What's Sweden got that Norway hasn't?" Andrew asked.

"First things first: a couple of good film directors. Bo Widerberg, Ingmar Bergman—"

"Ah, film directors," Andrew snorted. "We've got them, too. Edvard Grieg, on the other hand, is one of yours."

"Wow," Harry said. "I didn't know you were a connoisseur of classical music. In addition."

"Grieg was a genius. Take, for example, the second movement of the symphony in C minor where—"

"Sorry, Andrew," Harry said, "I grew up with two-chord punk and the closest I've been to a symphony is Yes and King Crimson. I don't listen to music from previous centuries, OK? Everything before 1980 is Stone Age. We have a band called the Dumdum Boys who—"

"The C minor symphony was first performed in 1981," Andrew said. "Dumdum Boys? That's a very pretentious moniker."

Harry gave up and learned about Grieg all the way to the White residence.

11

A Dealer

Evans White regarded them through half-open eyes. Strands of hair hung over his face. He scratched his groin and belched deliberately. He didn't seem at all surprised to see them. Not because he was expecting them, but probably because he didn't think visits were anything special. After all, he was sitting on the region's best acid, and Nimbin was a small place where rumors traveled fast. Harry imagined that a man like White did not bother with tiny amounts and certainly not from his home, but that was hardly likely to deter people from showing up for the odd wholesale purchase.

"You've come to the wrong place. Try in town," he said, closing the screen door.

"We're from the police, Mr. White." Andrew held up his badge. "We'd like to talk to you."

Evans turned his back on them. "Not today. I don't like cops. Come another time with an arrest warrant, a search warrant or whatever, then we'll see what we can do for you. Until then goodbye."

He slammed the inner door as well.

Harry leaned against the doorframe and shouted: "Evans White! Can you hear me? We are wondering whether this is you in the photo, sir. And if so, whether you knew the blonde woman sitting beside you. Her name's Inger Holter. She's dead now."

Silence for a while. Then the door hinges creaked. Evans peered out.

Harry placed the photo against the netting.

"She didn't look so good when Sydney police found her, Mr. White."

In the kitchen newspapers were scattered across the worktop, the sink was overflowing with plates and glasses, and the floor had not seen soapy water for a few months. Nevertheless, Harry could see at a glance that the place did not show any signs of real decay, and that it wasn't the home of a junkie on his uppers. There were no week-old leftovers, there was no mold, there was no stink of piss and the curtains weren't drawn. Furthermore, there was a kind of basic order in the room which made Harry realize Evans White still had a grip on things.

They found themselves chairs, and Evans fetched a stubby from the fridge which he put straight to his mouth. The belch resounded round the kitchen and was followed by a contented chuckle from Evans.

"Tell us about your relationship with Inger Holter, Mr. White," Harry said, waving away the smell of the belch.

"Inger was a nice, attractive and very stupid girl with some notion that she and I could be happy together." Evans studied the ceiling. Then he sniggered contentedly again. "I think, in fact, that sums it up very neatly."

"Have you any idea how she could have been killed or who could have done it?"

"Yes, we have newspapers up in Nimbin, too, so I know she was strangled. But who did it? A strangler, I suppose." He threw his head back and grinned. A curl fell over his brow, his white teeth glistened in the tanned face and the laughter lines around his brown eyes stretched back toward ears hung with pirate rings.

Andrew cleared his throat. “Mr. White, a woman whom you knew well and with whom you had an intimate relationship has just been murdered. What you might or might not feel about that is not our business. However, as you are no doubt aware, we are looking for a murderer, and unless you try to help us this very minute we will be forced to have you taken to the police station in Sydney.”

“I’m going to Sydney anyway so if that means you’ll pay for my plane ticket, fine by me.”

Harry didn’t know what to think. Was Evans White as tough as he was trying to make out, or was he suffering from deficient mental faculties? Or an inadequately developed soul, a typically Norwegian concept? Harry wondered. Did courts anywhere else in the world judge the quality of a soul?

“As you wish, Mr. White,” Andrew said. “Plane ticket, free board and lodging, free solicitor and free PR as a murder suspect.”

“Big deal. I’ll be out again within forty-eight hours.”

“And then we’ll offer you a round-the-clock tail, a free wake-up service, maybe even the odd free raid thrown in as well. And who knows what else we can cook up.”

Evans knocked back the rest of the beer and sat fiddling with the label on the bottle. “What do you gentlemen want?” he said. “All I know is that one day she was suddenly gone. I was going to Sydney, so I tried to ring her, but she wasn’t at work or at home. The day I arrive in Sydney I read in the newspaper she’s been found murdered. I walk around like a zombie for two days. I mean to say, m-u-r-d-e-r-e-d? What are the statistical chances of ending your life being throttled to death, eh?”

“Not high. But have you got an alibi for the time of the murder? It’d be good . . .” Andrew said, taking notes.

Evans started with horror. “Alibi? What do you mean?

Surely you can't suspect me, for Christ's sake. Or are you telling me the cops have been on the case for a week and still don't have any real leads?"

"We're looking at all the evidence, Mr. White. Can you tell me where you were for the two days before you arrived in Sydney?"

"I was here, of course."

"Alone?"

"Not completely." Evans grinned and chucked the empty stubby. It flew through the air in an elegant parabola before landing noiselessly in the rubbish bin by the worktop. Harry nodded acknowledgment.

"May I ask who was with you?"

"You already have. But fine, I've nothing to hide. It was a woman called Angelina Hutchinson. She lives in the town here."

Harry noted that down.

"Lover?" Andrew asked.

"Sort of," Evans answered.

"What can you tell us about Inger Holter? Who was she?"

"Agh, we hadn't known each other for that bloody long. I met her on Fraser Island. She said she was headed down to Byron Bay. It's not far from here, so I gave her my phone number in Nimbin. A few days later she rang me and asked if she could stop over one night. She was here for more than a week. After that we met in Sydney when I was there. That must have been two or three times. As you know, we didn't exactly become an old married couple. And besides she was already beginning to be a drag."

"A drag?"

"Yes, she had a soft spot for my son, Tom-Tom, and let her imagination run away about a family and a house in the country. That didn't suit me, but I let her jabber on."

"Jabber on about what?"

Evans squirmed. "She was the kind that's hard-faced when you meet her, but she's as soft as butter if you tickle her under the chin and tell her you love her. Then she can't do enough for you."

"So she was a considerate young lady?"

Evans clearly didn't like the path this conversation was following. "Maybe she was. I didn't know her that well, as I said. She hadn't seen her family in Norway for a while, had she, so maybe she was starved for . . . affection, someone being there for her, know what I mean? Who bloody knows? As I said, she was a stupid, romantic chick, there was no evil in her . . ."

Evans's voice faltered. The kitchen fell silent. Either he's a good actor or he does have human emotions after all, Harry thought.

"If you didn't see any future in the relationship, why didn't you split up with her?"

"I was already on my way. Standing in the doorway about to say bye, sort of. But she was gone before I could do anything. Just like that . . ." He snapped his fingers.

Yes, his voice has thickened, no doubt about it, Harry thought.

Evans gazed down at his hands. "Quite a way to depart, wasn't it."

12

Quite a Big Spider

They drove up steep mountain roads. A signpost indicated the way to the Crystal Castle.

"The question is: is Evans White telling the truth?" Harry said.

Andrew avoided an oncoming tractor.

"Let me share a crumb of my experience with you, Harry. For over twenty years I've been talking to people with a variety of reasons for lying or telling the truth. Guilty and innocent, murderers and pickpockets, bundles of nerves and cold fish, blue-eyed baby faces, scarred villain faces, sociopaths, psychopaths, philanthropists . . ." He searched for more examples.

"Point taken, Andrew."

". . . Aboriginals and whites. They've all told their stories with one objective: to be believed. And do you know what I've learned?"

"That it's impossible to say who's lying and who isn't?"

"Exactly, Harry!" Andrew began to warm to the topic. "In traditional crime fiction every detective with any self-respect has an unfailing nose for when people are lying. It's bullshit! Human nature is a vast impenetrable forest which no one can know in its entirety. Not even a mother knows her child's deepest secrets."

They turned into a car park in front of a large green garden with a narrow gravel path winding between a fountain, flower beds and exotic species of tree. A huge house presided over the garden and was obviously the Crystal Castle that the Nimbin sheriff had pointed out to them on a map.

A bell above the door announced their arrival. This was clearly a popular place, for the shop was packed with tourists. An energetic woman greeted them with a radiant smile and welcomed them with such enthusiasm it was as if they were the first people she had seen here in months.

"Is this your first time here?" she asked, as though her crystal shop were a habit-forming affair people flocked to regularly once they had been hooked. And for all they knew that is exactly how it might have been.

"I envy you," she said after they confirmed it was. "You're about to experience the Crystal Castle for the first time! Take that corridor there. On the right is our wonderful vegetarian cafe with the most exquisite meals. After you've been there, go left, into the crystal and mineral room. That's where the real action is! Now, go, go, go!"

She waved them off. After such a build-up, naturally it was an anticlimax to discover that the cafe was basically a standard outlet selling coffee, tea, lettuce with yogurt and lettuce sandwiches. In the designated crystal and mineral room there was an exhibition of glittering crystals, Buddha figures with crossed legs, blue and green quartz and uncut stones in an elaborate light display. The room was filled with a faint aroma of incense, soporific pan-pipe music and the sound of running water. Harry considered the shop nice enough, though a touch camp, and unlikely to take your breath away. What might cause respiratory difficulties, however, were the prices.

"Ha ha," Andrew laughed, on seeing some of the price tags. "The woman's a genius."

He pointed to the generally middle-aged and evidently well-off customers in the shop. "The flower-power generation has grown up. They have adult jobs, adult incomes, but their hearts are somewhere on an astral planet."

They walked back to the counter. The energetic woman was still wearing her radiant smile. She took Harry's hand and pressed a blue-green stone in his palm.

"You're Capricorn, aren't you? Put this stone under your pillow. It will remove all the negative energy in the room. It costs sixty-five dollars, but you really should have it, I think, so let's say fifty."

She turned to Andrew.

"And you must be a Leo?"

"Oh no, ma'am, I'm a policeman." He discreetly held up his badge.

She blanched and stared at him in horror. "How awful. I hope I haven't done anything wrong."

"Not as far as I know, ma'am. I presume you're Margaret Dawson, formerly White? If so, may we have a word with you in private?"

Margaret Dawson quickly pulled herself together and called one of the girls to take charge of the till. Then she accompanied Andrew and Harry to the garden where they sat around a white wooden table. A net was stretched out between two trees. At first Harry thought it was a fishing net, but upon closer inspection it proved to be an enormous spider's web.

"Looks like rain," she said, rubbing her hands.

Andrew cleared his throat.

She bit her lower lip.

"I'm sorry, Officer. This makes me so nervous."

"That's OK, ma'am. Quite a web you've got there."

"Oh, that. That's Billy's, our mouse spider. He's probably asleep somewhere."

Harry unconsciously tucked his legs under him. "Mouse spider? Does that mean it eats . . . mice?" he asked.

Andrew smiled. "Harry's from Norway. They aren't used to big spiders."

"Oh, well, I can put your mind at rest. The big ones aren't dangerous," Margaret Dawson said. "However, we do have a lethal little creature called a redback. It likes towns best, though, where it can hide in the crowd, so to speak. In dark cellars and damp corners."

"Sounds like someone I know," Andrew said. "But back to business, ma'am. Your son."

Now Mrs. Dawson really did blanch.

"Evans?"

Andrew eyed Harry.

"To our knowledge, he hasn't been in trouble with the police before, Mrs. Dawson," Harry said.

"No, no, he hasn't. Thank God."

"We actually drove by because your place was on our route back to Brisbane. We were wondering if you knew anything about an Inger Holter."

She ran the name through her memory. Then she shook her head.

"Evans doesn't know a lot of girls. The ones he does know he brings here to meet me. After having a child with . . . with this terrible girl whose name I'm not sure if I want to remember, I forbade . . . I said I thought he should wait a bit. Until the right one came along."

"Why should he wait?" Harry asked.

"Because I said so."

"Why did you say so, ma'am?"

"Because . . . because it's not the right moment—" she glanced at the shop to signal that her time was precious—"and because Evans is a sensitive boy who can be easily hurt. There's been a lot of negative energy in his life, and he needs a woman he can trust one hundred percent. Not these . . . tarts that just muddle his thinking."

Gray cloud cover had settled over her pupils.

"Do you see your son often?" Andrew asked.

"Evans comes here as much as he can. He needs the peace. He works so hard, poor thing. Have you tried any of the herbs he sells? Now and then he brings a few along and I put them in the tea in the cafe."

Andrew cleared his throat again. From the corner of his eye, Harry noticed a movement between the trees.

"We'd better be off, ma'am. One last question, though."

"Yes?"

Andrew seemed to have something stuck in his throat—he kept coughing and coughing. The web had started to sway.

"Have you always had such blonde hair, Mrs. Dawson?"

13

Bubbur

It was late when they landed in Sydney. Harry was dead on his feet and longing for his hotel bed.

"A drink?" Andrew suggested.

"Don't you need to get home?" Harry asked.

Andrew shook his head. "I won't meet anyone there except myself at the moment."

"At the moment?"

"Well, for the last ten years. I'm divorced. Wife lives in Newcastle with the girls. I try to see them as often as I can, but it's quite a distance and the girls will soon be big enough to have their own plans for the weekend. Then I'll discover, I suppose, that I'm not the only man in their lives. They're good-looking little devils, you see. Fourteen and fifteen. Shit, I should chase away every admirer that darkens the door."

Andrew beamed. Harry couldn't help but like this unaccustomed version of a colleague.

"Well, that's the way it goes, Andrew."

"That's right, mate. How 'bout you?"

"Well. No wife. No children. No dog. All I have is a boss, a sister, a father and a couple of guys I still call pals even though years pass between their calls. Or mine."

"In that order?"

"In that order." They laughed.

"Come for one. At the Albury?"

"That sounds like work," Harry said.

"Precisely."

Birgitta smiled as they entered. She finished serving a customer and came over to them. Her eyes were focused on Harry.

"Hi," she said.

All Harry wanted to do was curl up on her lap and go to sleep.

"Two double gin and tonics, in the name of the law," Andrew said.

"I'd prefer a grapefruit juice," Harry said.

She served them and leaned across the bar.

"Thanks for yesterday," she whispered in Swedish to Harry. In the mirror behind her he saw himself sitting with an idiotic grin on his face.

"Hey, hey, no Scandinavian turtle-doving here now, thank you very much. If I'm paying for the drinks we speak in English." Andrew shot them a stern look. "And now I'll tell you young ones something. Love is a greater mystery than death." He paused for dramatic effect. "Uncle Andrew's going to tell you about an ancient Australian legend, to wit, the story of the giant snake Bubbur and Walla."

They bunched up closer, and Andrew licked his lips with relish as he lit a cigar.

"Once upon a time there was a young warrior called Walla who had fallen in love with a beautiful young woman called Moora. And she with him. Walla had successfully completed his tribe's initiation rites, he was a man and could therefore marry whichever of the tribe's women he liked, provided he had not been married before and she wanted him. And Moora did. Walla could hardly tear himself away from his beloved, but the tradition was that he had to go on a hunting expedition from which the spoils would be a kind of dowry for the bride's parents, then the wedding could take place. One fine morning, the dew glistening on the leaves, Walla set out. Moora gave him a white cockatoo feather, which he wore in his hair.

"While Walla was away Moora went out to collect honey for the feast. However, it was not so easy to find, and she had to go further from the camp than she was wont to do. She came to a valley with huge rocks. A strange silence hung over the valley, there was not a bird or an insect to be heard. She was about to leave when she spotted a nest with some big white eggs, the biggest she had ever seen. 'I'll take them to the feast,' she thought and stretched out a hand.

"At that moment she heard something slither over the rocks, and before she had time to run or open her mouth, an enormous yellow-and-brown snake coiled itself around her waist. She fought, but could not free herself, and the snake was beginning to exert pressure. Moora looked up at the blue sky above the valley and tried to call Walla's name, but she did not have enough air in her lungs to utter a sound. The snake's grip tightened, and in the end all the life was squeezed out of Moora, and all the bones in her body were crushed. Then the snake slithered back into the shadows it had come from—where it was impossible to see it because the colors merged with the light-dappled trees and rocks of the valley.

"Two days passed before they found her crushed body among the rocks. Her parents were inconsolable and her mother wept and asked her husband what they would say to Walla when he returned home."

Andrew gazed at Harry and Birgitta through shiny eyes.

"The campfire was no more than embers when Walla returned from hunting the following dawn. Even though it had been a strenuous trek, his steps were light and his eyes bright and happy. He went to Moora's parents, who were sitting mute by the fire. 'Here are my gifts to you,' he said. And he had brought back a good catch: a kangaroo, a wombat and emu thighs.

"'You've arrived in time for the funeral, Walla, you who would have been our son,' Moora's father said. Walla looked as if he had been slapped and could barely conceal his pain and grief, but being the hardy warrior he was, he restrained the tears and asked coldly: 'Why have you not already buried her?' 'Because we didn't find her until today,' the father said. 'Then I'll accompany her and demand her spirit. Our Wirinun can heal her broken bones, then I will return her spirit and breathe life into her.' 'It's too late,' said the father. 'Her spirit has already left to go where all women's spirits go. But her killer is still alive. Do you know your duty, my son?'

"Walla departed without a word. He lived in a cave with the other unmarried men of the tribe. He did not speak to them either. Several months passed. Walla sat on his own and refused to take part in the singing and dancing. Some thought he had been hardening his heart to try and forget Moora. Others thought he was planning to follow Moora to the women's kingdom of death. 'He will not succeed,' they said. 'There is one place for women and one for men.'

"A woman came to the fire and sat down. 'You're wrong,' she said. 'He's deep in thought, planning how he can avenge the death of his woman. Do you suppose all you have to do is grab a spear and kill Bubbur, the great yellow-and-brown snake? You've never seen it, but I saw it once when I was young, and that was the day my hair turned gray. It was the most frightening sight imaginable. Mark my words, Bubbur can only be defeated in one way, and that is with bravery and cunning. And I think this young warrior has those attributes.'

"The next day Walla went to the fire. His eyes gleamed

and he seemed almost excited as he asked who wanted to accompany him to collect rubber. 'We have rubber,' they said, surprised to note Walla's good mood. 'You can have some of ours.' 'I want fresh rubber,' he said. He laughed at their startled faces and said: 'Join me and I'll show you what I'm going to use it for.' Curious, they joined him, and after they had collected the rubber, he led them to the valley with the huge rocks. There he built a platform in the highest tree and told the others to retreat to the valley entrance. With his best friend, he climbed the tree, and from there they shouted Bubbur's name as the echoes rang through the valley and the sun rose in the sky.

"Then it appeared—an enormous yellow-and-brown head swinging to and fro, searching for the source of the sound. Around it a teeming mass of small yellow-and-brown snakes, obviously hatched from the eggs Moora had seen. Walla and his friend kneaded the rubber into small balls. When Bubbur saw them in the tree it opened its jaws, flicked out its tongue and stretched up for them. The sun was now at its zenith and Bubbur's red-and-white jaws glistened. As Bubbur launched its attack Walla hurled the largest ball of rubber down the snake's open mouth and instinctively it sank its fangs into it.

"Bubbur rolled around on the ground but was unable to get rid of the rubber stuck in its mouth. Walla and his friend managed to perform the same trick with the smaller snakes, and soon they were rendered harmless with their jaws sealed. Then Walla called the other men, and they showed no mercy, all the snakes were killed. After all, Bubbur had killed the tribe's most beautiful daughter, and Bubbur's progeny would one day grow up to be as big as their mother. From that day forward the feared yellow-and-brown Bubbur snake has been a rarity in Australia. But our fear of it has made it longer and fatter for every year that has passed."

Andrew drained the last of his gin and tonic.

"And the moral is?" Birgitta asked.

"Love is a greater mystery than death. And you have to watch out for snakes."

Andrew paid for the drinks, gave Harry a pat of encouragement and left.

MOORA

14

A Dressing Gown

He opened his eyes. The city outside his window droned and growled as it woke up, and the curtain waved lazily at him. He lay looking at an absurdity hanging on the wall on the other side of the spacious room—a picture of the Swedish royal couple. The Queen with her calm, secure smile and the King looking like someone was holding a knife to his back. Harry knew how he felt—he had himself been persuaded to play the title role in *The Frog Prince* at primary school.

From somewhere came the sound of running water, and Harry rolled over onto the other side of the bed to smell her pillow. A jellyfish tentacle—or was it a long, red hair?—lay on the sheet. He was reminded of a headline on *Dagbladet*'s sports page: ERLAND JOHNSEN, MOSS FC—FAMOUS FOR HIS RED HAIR AND LONG BALLS.

He considered how he felt. Light. As light as a feather, in fact. So light he was afraid the fluttering curtains would lift him out of bed and whistle him through the window where he would float over Sydney in the rush hour and discover that he wasn't wearing any clothes. He concluded that the lightness was due to draining himself of various bodily fluids in the night with such a vengeance that he must have lost several kilos in weight.

"Harry Hole, Oslo Police Station—famous for his weird ideas and empty balls," he muttered.

"Pardon?" came a voice in Swedish.

Birgitta was standing in the room in an unusually hideous dressing gown with a white towel wrapped around her head like a turban.

"Oh, good morning, thou ancient, thou free and mountainous North, thou quiet, thou joyful beauty! I greet thee. I was just looking at the picture of the rebel king on the wall over there. Do you think he would rather have been a farmer digging the soil? That's how it seems."

She studied the picture. "We can't all find the right niche in life. What about you then?" She plonked herself down on the bed beside him.

"A serious question for so early in the morning. Before I answer, I demand you remove that dressing gown. Without wishing to appear in any way negative, I think, as a spontaneous reaction, your dressing gown qualifies for inclusion in my top ten 'Ugliest-garment-I've-ever-seen' list."

Birgitta laughed. "I call it the passion killer. It performs a useful function when pig-headed strangers become too brash."

"Have you checked to see if that color has a name? Perhaps you're sitting on some unknown tint, a kind of undiscovered gap on the palette somewhere between green and brown?"

"Don't try and talk your way out of answering my question, you stubborn Norwegian buck!" She hit him over the head with a pillow, but after a brief wrestling match she ended up underneath. Harry held her hands tight while bending and trying to open her dressing-gown belt with his mouth. Birgitta screamed when she realized what he was up to and freed a knee which she planted firmly on his chin. Harry groaned and rolled over onto his side. In a flash she placed her knees on his arms and sat on him.

"Answer me!"

"All right, all right, I give in. Yes, I've found my niche in life. I'm the best copper you can imagine. Yes, I would rather catch bad boys than dig the soil—or go to gala dinners and stand on a balcony waving to the masses. And, yes, I know it's perverse."

Birgitta kissed him on the mouth.

"You could have cleaned your teeth," Harry said through pinched lips.

As she leaned back and laughed, Harry seized the opportunity. He lifted his head, grabbed the belt with his teeth and pulled. The dressing gown slipped open and he rolled her over. Her skin was hot and moist from the shower.

"Police!" she screamed, wrapping her legs around him. Harry felt his pulse pounding right through his body.

"Help," she whispered, and nibbled his ear.

Afterward they lay gazing at the ceiling.

"I wish . . ." Birgitta began.

"Yes?"

"Oh, nothing."

They got up and dressed. Harry saw from his watch that he was already late for the morning meeting. He stood by the front door with his arms around her.

"I think I know what you wish," Harry said. "You wish I would tell you something about myself."

Birgitta rested her head against his neck. "I know you don't like doing it," she said. "I have a feeling that anything I know about you I've had to force out of you. Your mother was a kind, clever woman, half Sami, and you miss her. Your father's a teacher and doesn't like what you're doing, but doesn't say so. And the person you love above all else on earth, your sister, has 'a touch of' Down's syndrome. I like to know this sort of thing about you. But I want you to tell me things because you want to tell me them."

Harry stroked her neck. "Do you want to know something real? A secret?"

She nodded.

"Sharing secrets binds people together though," Harry whispered into her hair. "And that's not always what people want."

They stood in the hall without speaking. Harry took a deep breath.

"All my life I've been surrounded by people who love me. I've been given everything I asked for. In short, I have no explanation for why I've turned out as I have." A puff of wind brushed Harry's hair, so gently that he had to close his eyes. "Why I have become an alcoholic."

He said it with brutal harshness. Birgitta clung to him without moving.

"It takes quite a bit for a civil servant in Norway to be given the boot. Incompetence is not enough, laziness is a non-concept and you can abuse your boss as much as you like, no problem. To tell the truth, you can do just about anything—legislation protects you against most things. Except for drinking. If you turn up for work in an inebriated state more than twice in the police force, that's grounds for immediate dismissal. For a time there it was easier to count the days I wasn't drunk."

He relaxed his grip and held her in front of him. He wanted to see how she was reacting. Then he drew her into him again.

"Nevertheless, I got by somehow and those who guessed what was going on turned a blind eye. Someone should have reported me, but loyalty and solidarity are strong in the police. One evening a colleague and I were going to a flat on Holmenkollen Ridge to interview a guy about a drugs murder. He wasn't even a suspect, but while we were outside ringing the doorbell we saw his car come steaming out of the garage and we jumped in ours and gave chase.

We put the blue light on the roof and were doing 110 kph down Sørkedalsveien. The road curved left and right, we hit a couple of curbs and my colleague asked if he shouldn't take over at the wheel. I was so intent on catching our man that I just dismissed the suggestion."

What happened later he only knew from reports. In Vinderen a car had pulled out from the petrol station. Driven by a young boy who had just passed his test and gone to the garage to buy cigarettes for his father. The two policemen shunted his car through the fence onto the train lines, dragging the bus shelter where two minutes earlier five or six people had been standing and came to a halt on the platform on the other side of the rails. Harry's colleague was hurled through the windscreen and found twenty meters further down the line. He had struck a fence post head first. The force had been so great the post was bent at the top. They had had to take fingerprints to be absolutely sure of his identity. The boy in the other car was paralyzed from the neck down.

"I went to visit him in a place called Sunnås," Harry said. "He's still dreaming about driving a car again one day. They found me in the wreckage with a cracked skull and internal bleeding. I was on life support for several days."

His father had visited him every day with his sister. They had sat on either side of the bed holding his hand. Because serious concussion had disturbed his vision, he wasn't allowed to read or watch TV. So his father had read to him. Sat close to the bed and whispered in his ear so as not to wear him out while reading from Sigurd Hoel and Kjartan Fløgstad, his father's favorite authors.

"I had killed a man and destroyed someone else's life, yet I was lying cocooned in love and attentive devotion. And the first thing I did when I was moved to a ward was bribe the man in the next bed to get his brother to buy me a bottle of whiskey."

Harry paused. Birgitta's breathing was calm and even.

"Are you shocked?" he asked.

"I knew you were an alcoholic the first moment I saw you," Birgitta answered. "My father's one."

Harry didn't know what to say.

"Tell me more," she said.

"The rest is . . . the rest is about the Norwegian police. Perhaps it's better not to know."

"We're a long way from Norway now," she said.

Harry gave her a quick squeeze.

"You've heard enough for one day," he said. "To be continued in the next issue. I must be off. Is it all right if I come to the Albury and get under your feet tonight as well?"

Birgitta smiled a sad smile—and Harry knew he was getting more involved than he should.

15

Statistical Significance

"You're late," Watkins stated as Harry arrived in the office. He placed a set of photocopies on his desk.

"Jet lag. Anything new?" Harry asked.

"You've got a bit of reading here. Yong Sue's dug up some old rape cases. He and Kensington are having a bopeep right now."

Yong laid a transparency on the overhead projector.

"This year in Australia more than five thousand rapes have been reported. Obviously, trying to find a pattern from such a collection is hopeless without using statistics. Cold, concise statistics. Keyword number one is statistical significance. In other words, we're looking for a system that cannot be explained by statistical chance. Keyword number two is demography.

"I searched first for reports on unsolved murders and rapes over the last five years containing the words 'strangle' or 'suffocate.' I found twelve murders and a few hundred rapes. Next, I whittled down the number by adding that the victims should be blondes aged between sixteen and thirty-five and living on the east coast. Official statistics and data concerning hair color released by the Passport Office show that this group constitutes less than five percent of the female population. Yet I was left with seven murders and over forty rapes."

Yong placed another transparency on the OHP showing percentages and a bar chart. He allowed the others to read, without making any comment. A long silence followed. Watkins was the first to speak.

"Does that mean . . . ?"

"No," Yong said. "It doesn't mean we know anything we didn't know before. The numbers are too vague."

"But we can imagine," Andrew said. "We can, for example, imagine that there is a person out there raping blonde women systematically and killing them a little less systematically. And who likes putting his hands round a woman's throat."

Suddenly everyone started speaking at once and Watkins held up his hands for silence.

Harry was the first to speak up. "Why hasn't this connection been discovered before? We're talking about seven murders and forty to fifty rapes with a possible link here."

Yong Sue shrugged. "Rape is unfortunately an everyday event in Australia as well, and perhaps it isn't given the priority you think it should be given."

Harry nodded. He felt no cause to swell his chest with pride on Norway's account.

"Furthermore, most rapists find their victims in the town or region where they live, and they don't flee the area afterward. That's why there's no systematic collaboration between the various states in standard rape cases. The problem in the cases that form my statistics is the geographical spread."

Yong pointed to the list of place names and dates.

"One day in Melbourne, a month later in Cairns and the week after in Newcastle. Rapes in three different states in under two months. Sometimes wearing a balaclava, sometimes a mask, at least once a nylon stocking and a few times the women haven't seen the rapist at all. The crime scenes are everything from dark backstreets to parks. The victims have been dragged into cars, or their homes have been broken into at night. In summary, there is no pattern here except that the victims are blonde, have been strangled and no one has been able to give the police a description of the man. Well, there is one other thing. When he carries out the murder he's extremely clean. Alas. He probably washes the victims, removes any traces of himself: fingerprints, semen, clothing fibers, hair, skin under the victim's nails and so on. But apart from that there are none of the things we generally associate with a serial killer: no signs of grotesque, ritual acts or calling cards for the police saying 'I was here.' After the three rapes in two months it's been quiet for a whole year. Unless he's behind some of the other rapes reported. But we can't know that."

"What about the killings?" Harry asked. "Shouldn't that have rung some bells?"

Yong shook his head. "As I said, geographical spread. If the Brisbane police find a body that has been sexually abused, Sydney's not the first place they'll look. Anyway, the murders are spread over so much time it would be difficult for anyone to see a clear connection. After all, strangulation isn't unusual in rape cases."

"Don't you have a fully functional federal police force in Australia?" Harry asked.

Smiles all round the table. Harry changed the subject.

"If it's a serial killer—" Harry started.

"—then he often has a pattern, a theme," Andrew finished. "But there isn't one here, is there?"

Yong shook his head. "Some officer at some point over the years must have considered the idea that a serial killer was on the loose. He probably took out old files from the archives and compared them, but the variations have been too wide to support the suspicion."

"If it is a serial killer, wouldn't he have a more or less conscious desire to be caught?" Lebie asked.

Watkins cleared his throat. This was his special area.

"That's the way it's presented in crime fiction," he said. "The murderer's actions are a cry for help; he leaves small coded messages and evidence as the result of an unconscious desire for someone to stop him killing. And sometimes that is how it is. But unfortunately most serial killers are like most people; they don't want to be caught. And if this really is a serial killer he hasn't given us much to go on. There are a number of things I don't like . . ."

He scrunched up his face and revealed a top set of yellow teeth.

"First of all, there doesn't seem to be any pattern to the killings, apart from the fact that the victims are blondes and he throttles them. That might suggest he views murders as isolated events, like a piece of art that has to be different from what went before, or there's an underlying pattern here we can't see yet. But it could also mean the murders are unplanned, so in some cases it becomes a necessity, for example if the victim has seen his face, resisted, screamed for help or something unforeseen has happened."

"Perhaps he only murdered when he couldn't get it up?" Lebie suggested.

"Perhaps we ought to let some psychologists have a closer look at these cases," Harry said. "They might be able to come up with a profile that could help us."

"Perhaps," Watkins said. He seemed to have his mind on other matters.

"What's second of all, sir?" Yong asked.

"What?" Watkins was back.

"You said, 'first of all.' What's the second thing you don't like?"

"His sudden inactivity," Watkins said. "Of course, that may be for purely practical reasons. Like he's traveling or he's ill. But it could also be because he's got a feeling some-one's going to suspect a link somewhere. So he stops for a while. Just like that!" He snapped his fingers. "In which case, we've got a really dangerous man on our hands. One who's disciplined and cunning and isn't driven by the kind of self-destructive passion that can only escalate and in the end betray most serial killers. A smart, calculating murderer whom we're unlikely to catch until he's unleashed a veritable bloodbath. If we ever do."

"What do we do now?" Andrew asked. "Do we tell all blondes under pensionable age to stay at home in the evenings?"

"Doing that would make him go underground and we'd never find him then," Lebie said. He had taken out a penknife and was painstakingly cleaning his nails.

"On the other hand, are we going to leave all the blondes in Australia to their doom, as bait for this bloke?" Yong said.

"There's no point telling women to stay indoors," Watkins said. "If he's on the prowl for a victim, he'll find one. He broke into a couple of houses, didn't he. Forget it. We'll have to smoke him out."

"How though? He operates right across the bloody country, and no one knows when he'll strike next. The guy rapes and kills at random." Lebie was talking to his nails.

"That's not correct," Andrew answered. "To have survived for so long there's nothing random about it. There is a pattern. There's always a pattern. Not because you plan it, but because all humans are creatures of habit, there's no difference between you and me and the rapist. It's just a question of finding what this particular creature's habits are."

"The man's out of his mind," Lebie said. "Aren't all serial killers schizophrenic anyway? Don't they hear voices telling them to kill? I agree with Harry. Let's get a shrink in."

Watkins was scratching his neck. He seemed bemused.

"A psychologist can probably tell us a lot about a serial killer, but it's not at all certain that that's what we're after here," Andrew said.

"Seven murders. I call that serial killing," Lebie said.

"Listen," Andrew said, leaning over the table and holding up his big, black hands. "For a serial killer the sexual act comes second to killing. Raping without killing has no meaning. But for our man raping is paramount. In cases where he kills there is consequently a practical reason, as Inspector Watkins says. Perhaps the victim can expose him—she's seen his face." Andrew paused. "Or they know who he is." He placed his hands down in front of him.

The fan was creaking away in the corner, but the air was stuffier than ever.

"Statistics are all well and good," Harry said, "but we mustn't let ourselves get carried away. Inger Holter's murder may be an isolated act. Some people died of common pneumonia during the Black Death, didn't they. Let's assume that Evans White is not a serial killer. The fact that there's another guy running round killing blondes doesn't mean that Evans White can't have taken the life of Inger Holter."

"Complicated explanation, but I take your point, Holy," Watkins said and summed up: "OK, folks, we're looking for a rapist and a possible—I repeat—*possible* serial killer. I'll leave it to McCormack to decide whether to ramp up the investigation. In the meantime we'll have to continue what we're doing now. Kensington, anything new to report?"

"Holy didn't make the morning meeting, so for his sake I'll repeat myself. I spoke to Robertson, Inger Holter's wonderful landlord, and asked him if the name Evans White rang any bells. And the fog must have lifted temporarily because in fact the name did. We're going over this afternoon. Otherwise, the sheriff of Nimbin rang. This Angelina Hutchinson confirmed that she'd been at Evans White's house for the two nights before Inger Holter was found."

Harry swore.

Watkins clapped his hands. "OK, back to work, boys. Let's nail this bastard."

The words came without much conviction.

16

A Fish

Harry had once heard that dogs have an average short-term memory of three seconds, but with repeated stimuli it can be expanded by a considerable amount. The phrase "Pavlov's dog" comes from the Russian physiologist Ivan Pavlov's experiments with dogs in which he examined conditioned reflexes in the nervous system. He provided a special stimulus every time he put food out for the dogs over a prolonged period. Then one day he gave the stimulus without putting food out. The dogs' pancreas and stomach produced the juice to digest the food nonetheless. Not so surprising perhaps, but at any rate it got Pavlov a Nobel Prize. It had been proved that after repeated stimuli the body could "remember."

When Andrew, for the second time in very few days, sent Robertson's Tasmanian Devil rocketing into the hedge with a well-directed kick, there was therefore reason to believe that this kick would stay longer in the mind than the first. The next time Robertson's dog heard unfamiliar footsteps outside the gate—instead of its evil little brain brewing up a storm, its ribs would perhaps start aching.

Robertson received them in the kitchen and offered them a beer. Andrew accepted, but Harry asked for a glass of mineral water. However, Robertson was unable to accommodate, so Harry thought he would make do with a smoke.

"If you don't mind," Robertson said as Harry took out a packet of cigarettes. "Smoking's banned in my house. Cigarettes harm your body," he said, knocking back half of the bottle of beer.

"So you take your health seriously, do you," Harry said.

"Sure do," Robertson said, ignoring the sarcasm. "In this house we don't smoke or eat fish or meat. We breathe in fresh air and eat what nature provides."

"Does that apply to the dog as well?"

"My dog hasn't eaten meat or fish since it was a puppy. It's a genuine lacto-vegetarian," he said, with pride.

"That accounts for its bad moods," Andrew muttered.

"It's our understanding that you know one Evans White, Mr. Robertson. What can you tell us?" Harry said, taking out his notebook. He wasn't intending to jot anything down, but it was his experience that people felt their statement was more important if you pulled out a notebook. Unconsciously, they were more thorough, took the time to check that everything was correct and they were more precise with facts such as times, names and places.

"Officer Kensington rang to find out who Inger Holter's visitors had been while she lived here. I told him that I'd been in her room and seen the photo pinned to the wall, and I remembered I'd seen the young guy with the child on his lap."

"Really?"

"Yes, the guy was here twice to my knowledge. The first time they locked themselves in her room and stayed there for almost two days. She was very, erm . . . noisy. I started worrying about the neighbors and put on loud music so as not to embarrass them. Inger and this bloke, that is. Although they didn't seem to be too bothered about it. The second time he was only here for two shakes of a lamb's tail, then he stormed out."

"Did they have a row?"

"I suppose you could say that, yes. She called after him that she'd tell the bitch what a bastard he was. And that she'd tell some man about his plans."

"Some man?"

"She said a name, but I don't remember what it was."

"And this bitch. Who could it have been?" Andrew asked.

"I try not to meddle in tenants' private lives, Officer."

"Excellent beer, Mr. Robertson. Who's the bitch?" Andrew said, ignoring the previous remark.

"Well, that's the point." Robertson hesitated as his eyes jumped nervously from Andrew to Harry. He essayed a smile. "I suppose she's important to the case, don't you think?" The question was left hanging in the air, but not for long. Andrew banged down the stubby. And leaned into Robertson's face.

"You've been watching too much TV, Robertson. In the real world I don't discreetly push a hundred-dollar note across the table, you don't whisper a name and we don't each go our separate ways without another word. In the real world I ring for a police car, it steams out here with sirens blaring, they handcuff you, march you off, however ashamed you are, to the car with all the neighbors watching. Then we accompany you to the station and lock you up as a suspect overnight, unless you've coughed up a name or your solicitor's made an appearance. In the real world, in the worst-case scenario, you're accused of holding back information to cover up a murder. That makes you an automatic accessory to a crime and carries a penalty of six years' imprisonment. So what's it going to be, Mr. Robertson?"

Robertson had gone pale around the gills and his mouth had opened and shut a couple of times without emitting a sound. He resembled a fish in a tank that had just realized that it wasn't going to be fed, it was the food.

"I . . . I didn't mean to imply that—"

"For the last time, who's the bitch?"

"I think it's her in the photo . . . the woman who was here . . ."

"Which photo?"

"She's standing behind Inger and the bloke in the photo in her room. She's the little brown one with the headband. I recognized her because she was here a couple of weeks ago asking after Inger. I called her and they stood on the doorstep talking. Their voices gradually got louder and louder and they really laid into each other. Then the door slammed, and Inger ran upstairs to her room crying. I haven't seen her since."

"Would you mind, please, bringing me the photo, Mr. Robertson? I have a copy in my office."

Robertson had become helpfulness itself and shot up to Inger's room. When he was back, it took Harry no more than a fleeting glimpse to see which of the women in the photo Robertson meant.

"I thought there was something familiar about the face when we met her," Harry said.

"Isn't that Mother Kindheart?" Andrew exclaimed in surprise.

"I bet her real name is Angelina Hutchinson."

The Tasmanian Devil was not to be seen anywhere when they left.

"Have you ever wondered why everyone calls you *Officer*, as if you were a local bobby on the beat, Detective?"

"It must be because of my confidence-inspiring personality. *Officer* sounds like a kind uncle, doesn't it?" Andrew said contentedly. "And now I don't have the heart to correct them."

"You're just one big cuddly bear, you are," Harry laughed.

"Koala bear," Andrew said.

"Six years' imprisonment," Harry said. "You liar."

"First thing that came into my head," Andrew said.

17

Terra Nullius

It was pouring in Sydney. The rain was hammering down on the tarmac, spraying against house walls and in barely a minute forming into rivers running alongside curbs. People dived for shelter in squelching shoes. Some had obviously listened to the morning weather forecast and were carrying umbrellas. Now they were springing up like large, colorful toadstools in the streets. Andrew and Harry were in the car waiting at the traffic lights in William Street by Hyde Park.

"Do you remember the Aboriginal guy in the park right by the Albury that night?" Harry asked.

"Green Park?"

"He greeted you but you didn't greet him back. Why not?"

"I didn't know him."

The lights turned to green and Andrew jumped on the gas.

The Albury wasn't busy when Harry entered.

"You're early," Birgitta said. She was putting clean glasses on the shelves.

"I thought the service would be better before the rush."

"We serve anyone and everyone here." She pinched Harry's cheek. "What do you want?"

"Just a coffee."

"It's on the house."

"Thank you, sweetheart."

Birgitta laughed. "Sweetheart? That's what my father calls my mother." She sat down on a stool and leaned over the bar toward Harry. "And actually I ought to be nervous when a guy I've known for less than a week starts using terms of affection with me."

Harry breathed in her aroma. Scientists still know very little about how the olfactory cortex in the brain converts impulses from receptors into conscious senses of smell. But Harry wasn't thinking so much about the hows, he just knew that when he smelled her, all sorts of things started happening in his head and body. Like his eyelids closing halfway, like his mouth spreading into a broad grin and his mood soaring.

"Relax," he said. "'Sweetheart' belongs to the more innocuous pet-name category."

"I didn't even know that innocuous pet names existed."

"Yes, they do. There's 'love' for example. 'Sweetie.' Or 'honey.' "

"And what are the dangerous ones?"

"Well, schnookiepooks is quite dangerous," Harry said.

"Wha-at?"

"Schnookiepooks. Muffiewuff. You know, fluffy-bear-type words. The important thing is that they're pet names that don't have a hackneyed or impersonal sound to them. They have to be more tailor-made, intimate words. And they're generally pronounced through the nose, so they have that nasal sound people use with children. Then there's reason to feel claustrophobic."

"Have you got any more examples?"

"What's happened to the coffee?"

Birgitta whacked him with the cloth. Then she poured some coffee into a big mug. She was standing with her back to him, and Harry felt an urge to reach over and touch her hair.

She gave him his coffee then went to serve another customer as business began to pick up. His attention was attracted by the sound of the TV suspended over the shelves in the bar. The news was on, and eventually Harry understood that it was about an Aboriginal group demanding certain territorial rights.

" . . . with regard to the new Native Title legislation," the newsreader said.

"So justice has prevailed . . ." he heard a voice behind him say.

Harry turned. At first he didn't recognize the long-legged, powdered woman with the coarse features and the blonde wig towering above him. But then he identified the fat nose and the gap between the teeth.

"The clown!" he exclaimed. "Otto . . ."

"Otto Rechtnagel, His Highness, in person, Handsome Harry. That's the trouble with these high heels. I actually prefer my men to be taller than me. May I?" He parked himself on the bar stool beside Harry.

"What's your poison?" Harry asked, trying to catch Birgitta's eye.

"Relax, she knows," said Otto.

Harry offered him a cigarette, which he took without a word of thanks and placed in a pink holder. Harry held out a match, and Otto, hollow-cheeked and provocative, observed him while dragging on the cigarette. The short dress clung to his slim, nylon-clad thighs. Harry had to concede that the guise was a minor masterpiece. Otto in drag was more woman than many he had met. Harry took his eyes away and pointed to the TV screen.

"What do you mean by justice prevailing?"

"Haven't you heard about Terra Nullius? Eddy Mabo?"

Harry shook his head twice. Otto pursed his lips and out came two thick smoke rings, slowly ascending into the air.

"Terra Nullius is a funny little concept. The English hit upon it when they came here and saw that there wasn't much cultivated land in Australia. And just because the Aboriginal people didn't stand over potato fields half the day, the English considered them to be of lower status. However, the Aboriginal tribes knew a thing or two about nature; they went wherever there was food, in whichever season, and lived a life of apparent plenty. But because they weren't settlers, the English determined that no one owned the land. It was Terra Nullius. And according to the Terra Nullius principle the English could just issue property deeds to the new settlers without taking any account of what the Aboriginal people might have to say. They hadn't laid claim to their own land."

Birgitta placed a large margarita in front of Otto.

"A few years back, Eddy Mabo, a bloke from the Torres Strait Islands, challenged the Establishment by disputing the Terra Nullius principle and asserting that the land at that time had been illegally taken from the Aboriginals. In 1992 the High Court accepted his view and stated that Australia had belonged to the Aboriginal people. The court ruling determined that where Indigenous inhabitants had lived or occupied an area before the whites came and still did today, they could demand these areas back. Naturally, that created a terrible hoo-ha with loads of whites screaming blue murder because they were afraid they would lose their land."

"And what's the situation now?"

Otto took a deep swig from the salt-rimmed cocktail glass, pulled a face as if he had been served vinegar and wiped his mouth carefully with a slighted expression.

"Well, the ruling's there. And the Native Title laws

exist. But they're interpreted in a way that doesn't seem to be too despotic. It's not the case that some poor farmer suddenly finds his property is being confiscated. So the worst panic has gradually passed."

Here I am sitting in a bar, Harry thought, listening to a transvestite lecturing on Australian politics. He felt at home, a bit like Harrison Ford in the bar scene in *Star Wars*.

The news was interrupted by a commercial break with smiling Australians in flannel shirts and leather hats. They were advertising a brand of beer whose greatest quality was that apparently it was "proudly Australian."

"Well, here's to Terra Nullius," Harry said.

"Cheers, Handsome. Oh, I almost forgot. Our new performance will be at St. George's Theatre on Bondi Beach. I *urge* you and Andrew to come and see it. Bring a friend if you like. OK with me if you save all your applause for my numbers."

Harry bowed his head and thanked Otto for the three tickets he was holding with his little finger outstretched.

18

A Pimp

Crossing Green Park on his way from the Albury to King's Cross, Harry involuntarily looked for the gray Aboriginal man, but this evening there were just a couple of white drunks sitting on the bench in the pale light from the park lamps. The clouds from earlier in the day had drifted away and the sky was high and starry. In the road he passed two men who were clearly having an argument—they stood on opposite sides of the pavement shouting at each other, so Harry had to walk through the middle. "You didn't say you were going to stay out all night!" screeched one in a reedy, tear-filled voice.

Outside a Vietnamese restaurant a waiter stood leaning against the doorframe smoking. He looked as if he'd had a long day already. The queue of cars and people slowly oozed along Darlinghurst Road in King's Cross.

On the corner of Bayswater Road Andrew stood chewing a bratwurst.

"There you are," he said. "On the dot. Germanic to the core."

"Germany's—"

"Germans are Teutons. You come from a northern Germanic tribe. You even look it. You're not denying your own tribe, are you?"

Harry was tempted to reply with the same question, but refrained.

Andrew was in a bubbly mood. "Let's kick off with someone I know," he said.

They agreed to start the search for the proverbial needle as close to the middle of the haystack as they could get—among the prostitutes in Darlinghurst Road. They were not hard to find. Harry already recognized a few of them.

"Mongabi, my man, how's business?" Andrew stopped and warmly greeted a dark-skinned man wearing a tight suit and bulky jewelery. A gold tooth glistened when he opened his mouth.

"Tuka, you raging stallion! Can't complain, you know."

He looks like a pimp, if anyone does, Harry thought.

"Harry, say hello to Teddy Mongabi, the baddest pimp in Sydney. He's been doing this for twenty years and still stands with his girls on the street. Aren't you getting a bit long in the tooth for this now, Teddy?"

Teddy threw up his arms and grinned. "I like it down here, Tuka. This is where it's happening, you know. If you sit in an office it isn't long before you lose your perspective and control. And control is everything in this game, you know. Control of the girls and control of the punters. People are like dogs, you know. A dog you don't have under control is an unhappy dog. And unhappy dogs bite, you know."

"If you say so, Teddy. Listen, I'd like to have a word with one of your girls. We're on the lookout for a bad boy. He could have been up to some of his tricks here, too."

"Fine, who'd you like to talk to?"

"Is Sandra here?"

"Sandra'll be here any moment. Sure you don't want anything else? Apart from a chat, I mean."

"No thanks, Teddy. We'll be at the Palladium. Can you tell her to drop by?"

Outside the Palladium there was a doorman encouraging the crowd to enter with salacious enticements. He brightened up when he saw Andrew, who exchanged two words with the doorman and they were waved past the ticket office. A narrow staircase led down into the cellar of the dimly lit strip club where a handful of men sat round tables waiting for the next performance. They found a table some way back in the room.

"Seems like you know everyone round here," Harry said.

"Everyone who needs to know me. And I need to know. Surely you have this weird symbiosis between police and the underworld in Oslo, too, don't you?"

"Course. But you seem to have a warmer relationship with your contacts than we do."

Andrew laughed. "I guess I feel a certain affinity. If I hadn't been in the police force I might have been in this business, who knows."

A black miniskirt teetered down the stairs on high stilettos. Beneath the short fringe she peered around with heavy, glazed eyes. Then she came over to their table. Andrew pushed out a chair for her.

"Sandra, this is Harry Holy."

"Really?" she said, with broad, red lips held in a crooked smile. One canine was missing. Harry shook a cold, corpse-like hand. There was something familiar about her. Had he seen her in Darlinghurst Road one night? Perhaps she had been wearing different makeup or different clothes?

"So what's this about? Are you after some villains, Kensington?"

"We're looking for one villain in particular, Sandra. He likes to choke girls. Using his hands. Ring a bell?"

"A bell? Sounds like fifty percent of our customers. Has he hurt anyone?"

"Probably only those who were able to identify him," Harry said. "Have you seen this guy?" He held up the photo of Evans White.

"No," she answered without looking, and turned to Andrew. "Who's this then, Kensington?"

"He's from Norway," Andrew said. "He's a policeman and his sister was working at the Albury. She was raped and murdered last week. Twenty-three years old. Harry's taken compassionate leave and come here to find the man who did it."

"I'm sorry." Sandra looked at the photo. "Yes," she said. Nothing else.

Harry got excited. "What do you mean?"

"I mean, yes, I've seen him."

"Have you, er . . . met him?"

"No, but he's been in Darlinghurst Road several times. I have no idea what he was doing here, but his face is familiar. I can ask around a bit."

"Thank you . . . Sandra," Harry said. She sent him a quick smile.

"I have to go to work now, boys. See you, I guess." With that, the miniskirt went the same way it had come.

"Yes!" Harry shouted.

"Yes? Because someone's seen the bloke in King's Cross? Making an appearance in Darlinghurst Road is not forbidden. Nor is shagging prostitutes, if that's what he did. Not very forbidden, anyway."

"Don't you feel it, Andrew? There are four million inhabitants in Sydney, and she's seen the one person we're looking for. Of course, it doesn't prove anything, but it's a sign, isn't it? Can't you feel we're getting warmer?"

The muzak was switched off and the lights were lowered. The customers in the establishment directed their attention to the stage.

"You're pretty sure about this Evans White, aren't you."

Harry nodded. "Every fiber in my body tells me it's Evans White. I've got a gut instinct, yes."

"Gut instinct?"

"Intuition isn't hocus-pocus when you think about it, Andrew."

"I'm thinking about it now, Harry. And I can't feel anything in my gut. Explain to me how this gut of yours works, if you wouldn't mind."

"Well . . ." Harry looked at Andrew to check he wasn't pulling his leg. Andrew returned the gaze with a genuinely interested expression. "Intuition is just the sum of all your experience. The way I see it, everything you've experienced, everything you know, you think you know and didn't know you knew is there in your subconscious lying dormant, as it were. As a rule you don't notice the sleeping creature, it's just there, snoring and absorbing new things, right. But now and then it blinks, stretches and tells you, hey, I've seen this picture before. And tells you where in the picture things belong."

"Wonderful, Holy. But are you sure your sleeping creature sees all the details in this picture? What you see depends on where you're standing and the angle you're looking from."

"What do you mean?"

"Take the sky. The sky you see in Norway is just the same as the one you see in Australia. But because now you're down under, you're standing on your head compared with being at home, aren't you. So you see the stars upside down. If you don't know you're standing upside down you get confused and make mistakes."

Harry looked at Andrew. "Upside down, eh?"

"Yep." Andrew puffed on his cigar.

"At school I learned that the sky you see is quite different from the one we see. If you're in Australia the globe covers the view of the stars we see at night in Norway."

"OK then," Andrew said, unruffled. "Nevertheless, it's a question of where you view things from. The point is that everything is relative, isn't it. And that's what makes it so bloody complicated."

From the stage came a hissing sound and white smoke. The next moment it changed to red and violins were heard from the speakers. A woman wearing a plain dress and a man in trousers and a white shirt stepped out of the smoke.

Harry had heard the music before. It was the same as the drone he had heard in his neighbor's headphones on the plane, all the way from London. But it was only now he understood the text. A woman's voice was singing that they called her the wild rose and she didn't know why.

The girlish timbre was in sharp contrast to the man's deep, somber voice:

"Then I kissed her goodbye,
Said all beauty must die,
I bent down and planted a rose between her teeth . . ."

Harry was dreaming about stars and yellow-and-brown snakes when he was awoken by a light click of his hotel-room door. For a moment he lay still, aware only of how contented he was. It had started raining again, and the drainpipes outside his window were singing. He got up, naked, opened the door wide and hoped his incipient erection would be noticed. Birgitta laughed with surprise and leapt into his arms. Her hair was soaking wet.

"I thought you said three," Harry said, pretending to be offended.

"The customers wouldn't leave," she said, lifting her freckly face to him.

"I'm wildly, uncontrollably, head over heels in love with you," he whispered, gripping her face between his hands.

"I know," she said.

Harry stood by the window, drinking orange juice from the minibar and examining the sky. The clouds had drifted away again, and someone had stuck a fork in the velvet sky several times so that the divine light behind shone through the holes.

"What do you think of transvestites?" Birgitta asked from the bed.

"You mean, what do I think of Otto?"

"As well."

Harry thought. "I think I like his arrogant style. The lowered eyelids, the displeased expression. The world-weariness. What should I call it? It's like a melancholy cabaret in which he flirts with all and sundry. A superficial, self-parodying flirtation."

"And you like that?"

"I like his couldn't-give-a-stuff attitude. And that he stands for everything the majority hates."

"And what is it that the majority hates?"

"Weakness. Vulnerability. Australians boast that they're a liberal nation. Perhaps they are as well. But my understanding is that their ideal is the honest, uncomplicated, hard-working Australian with a good sense of humor and a touch of patriotism."

"True blue."

"What?"

"They call it being true blue. Or fair dinkum. It means someone or something is genuine, decent."

"And behind the facade of jovial decency it's easy to hide so much bloody crap. Otto, on the other hand, with all his outlandish garb, representing seduction, illusion and falsity, strikes me as the best example of sincerity I've met here. Naked, vulnerable and genuine."

"That sounds very PC, if you ask me. Harry Holy, the gay man's best friend." Birgitta was in teasing mode.

"I argued the point well though, didn't I?"

He lay down on the bed, looked at her and blinked his innocent, blue eyes. "I'm bloody glad I'm not in the mood for another round with you, frøken. As we've got to get up so early in the morning, I mean."

"You just say things like that to get me going," Birgitta said, as they launched themselves at each other once more.

19

A Pleasant Prostitute

Harry found Sandra in front of Dez Go-Go. She was standing by the curb scanning her little queendom in King's Cross, her legs tired from balancing on high heels, her arms crossed, a cigarette between her fingers and the Sleeping Beauty eyes that are both inviting and repelling at once. In short, she looked like a prostitute in any part of the world.

"Morning," Harry said. Sandra gazed at him without a sign of recognition. "Remember me?"

She raised the corners of her mouth. It might have been intended as a smile. "Sure, love. Let's go."

"I'm Holy, the policeman."

Sandra peered at him. "So it bloody is. At this hour my contact lenses are beginning to go on strike. Must be all the exhaust fumes."

"Can I buy you a coffee?" Harry asked politely.

She shrugged. "Not much going on here anymore, so I may as well call it a night."

Teddy Mongabi suddenly appeared in the strip-club door chewing a matchstick. He nodded briefly to Harry.

"How did your parents take it?" Sandra asked when the coffee came. They were sitting in Harry's breakfast place,

Bourbon & Beef, and the waiter remembered Harry's regular order: Eggs Benedict, hash browns, flat white. Sandra took her coffee black.

"Excuse me?"

"Your sister . . ."

"Oh, yes, right." He lifted the cup to his mouth to gain time.

"Mm, yes, as well as can be expected. Thank you for asking."

"It's a terrible world we live in."

The sun had not yet cleared the rooftops in Darlinghurst Road, but the sky was already azure with a few circular puffs of cloud here and there. It looked like wallpaper for a child's room. But it didn't help, because the world was a terrible place.

"I talked to some of the girls," Sandra said. "The bloke's name in the picture is White. He's a dealer. Speed and acid. Some of the girls buy from him, but none of them has had him as a customer."

"Perhaps he doesn't have to pay to have his needs covered," Harry said.

Sandra snorted. "Need for sex is one thing. Need to buy sex is quite another. For lots of men that's the kick. There's plenty we can do for you that you don't get at home, believe you me."

Harry glanced up. Sandra was staring straight at him and the glaze in her eyes was gone for a moment.

He believed her.

"Did you check the dates we talked about?"

"One of the girls says she bought acid off him the night before your sister was found."

Harry put down the cup of coffee, spilling it, and leaned across the table. He spoke quickly and softly. "Can I talk to her? Is she reliable?"

Sandra's broad, red mouth parted in a smile. There was a black cavity where the tooth was missing. "As I said, she bought acid, which is forbidden in Australia. And is she reliable? She's an acidhead . . ." She hunched her shoulders. "I'm only telling you what she told me. But she doesn't have the world's clearest concept of what day a Wednesday or a Thursday is, let's put it like that."

The mood at the morning meeting was irritable. Even the fan's growl was deeper than usual.

"Sorry, Holy. We're dropping White. No motive, and that woman of his says he was in Nimbin at the time of the murder," Watkins said.

Harry raised his voice. "Listen, Angelina Hutchinson is on speed and God knows what else. She's pregnant, probably by Evans White. He's her pusher, for Christ's sake! God and Jesus rolled into one! She'll do whatever he tells her. We spoke to the landlord and the woman hated Inger Holter, and with good reason. The Norwegian girl tried to steal her golden goose."

"Perhaps we'd better have a closer look at the Hutchinson woman," Lebie said quietly. "At least she has a clear motive. Perhaps she's the one who needs White as an alibi and not the other way round."

"White's lying, isn't he. He was seen in Sydney the day before Inger Holter was found." Harry had gotten up and walked the two paces the conference room allowed.

"By a prostitute on LSD and we don't even know if she'll make a statement," Watkins pointed out, turning to Yong. "What did the airlines say?"

"The Nimbin police themselves saw White in the main street three days before the murder. Neither Ansett Airlines nor Qantas has had White on the passenger lists between that time and the murder."

"Doesn't mean a thing," Lebie growled. "If you sell dope you don't travel under your own name. Anyway, he could have caught the train. Or driven if he'd had the time."

Harry had some steam up now. "I repeat. American statistics show that in seventy percent of all murder cases the victim knows the murderer. Yet we're focusing the investigation on a serial killer we all know we have as much chance of catching as winning the pools. Shouldn't we do something with better odds? After all, we have a guy who has quite a bit of circumstantial evidence stacked against him. The point is that now we have to shake him. Act while the trail's still hot. Bring him in and wave a charge in his face. Push him into making a mistake. Right now he has us where he wants us: in . . . a . . . a . . ." He searched in vain for the English word for *bakevja.* Rut.

"Hm," Watkins said, thinking aloud. "Course it won't look too good if someone we had right under our noses turns out to be guilty, and we did nothing."

At that moment the door opened and Andrew entered. "G'day, folks, sorry I'm late. But someone has to keep the streets safe. What's up, boss? You've got a frown on you like the Jamison Valley."

Watkins sighed.

"We're wondering whether to redistribute some of the resources here. Drop the serial-killer theory for a while and put all our energies into Evans White. Or Angelina Hutchinson. Holy seems to think her alibi's not up to much."

Andrew laughed and plucked an apple from his pocket. "I'd like to see a pregnant girl of forty-five kilos squeeze the life out of a sturdy Scandinavian woman. And then fuck her afterward."

"Just a thought," muttered Watkins.

"And as far as Evans White's concerned, you can forget it." Andrew shone the apple on his sleeve.

"Oh yes?"

"I've just been talking to a contact. He was in Nimbin buying some grass on the day of the murder, having heard about White's wonderful products."

"And?"

"No one told him White didn't do business from home, so he went to his flat only to be chased away by a raving lunatic with a rifle under his arm. I showed him the photo. Sorry, but there's no doubt that Evans White was in Nimbin on the day of the murder."

The room fell silent. Just the whirr of the fan, and the crunch as Andrew took a large bite out of his apple.

"Back to the drawing board," said Watkins.

Harry had arranged to meet Birgitta in the Opera House at five for a coffee before she went to work. When they arrived the cafe was closed. A notice said it was something to do with a ballet performance.

"There's always something," Birgitta said. They stood against the railing and looked across the harbor to Kirribilli on the other side. "I want the rest of the story."

"He was called Stiansen, my colleague. Ronny. Thuggish name in Norway, but he wasn't a thug. Ronny Stiansen was a nice, kind boy who loved being a policeman. Mostly, at any rate. The funeral took place while I was still in hospital. My boss at the police station visited me later. He passed on the Chief of Police's best wishes, and perhaps I should have smelled a rat then. But I was sober and my mood was rock bottom. The nurse had discovered the alcohol I'd had smuggled in and shifted my neighbor to another ward, so I hadn't had a drink for two days. 'I know what you're thinking,' said my boss. 'But stop it. You've got a job to do.' He thought I was considering suicide. He was mistaken. I was thinking about how I could get hold of some booze.

"My boss isn't the type to beat about the bush. 'Stiansen's dead. There's nothing you can do to help him now,' he said. 'All you can do is help yourself and your family. And us. Have you read the newspapers?' I answered that I hadn't read anything—my father had been reading books to me and I had asked him not to say a word about the accident. My boss said that was fine. That made it much easier. 'You see, it wasn't you driving the car,' he said. 'Or to put it another way, there wasn't a drunk from Oslo Police HQ sitting behind the wheel.' He asked me if I understood. Stiansen was driving. Of the two of us he was the one whose blood test showed he was stone-cold sober.

"He produced some old newspapers and I could see with my somewhat blurred vision that they had written that the driver had been killed instantaneously while the colleague in the passenger seat had been seriously injured. 'But I was in the driver's seat,' I said. 'I doubt it. You were found in the rear seat,' the boss said. 'Remember you had serious concussion. My guess is you can't remember anything about the drive at all.' Of course I knew where this was heading. The press was interested only in the driver's blood test, and so long as that was clean no one would bother about mine. The incident was bad enough for the force already."

Birgitta had a deep frown between her eyes and looked shaken.

"But how could you tell Stiansen's parents that he had been driving? These people must be totally without feeling. How . . . ?"

"As I said, loyalty within the police is strong. In some cases the force can come before family considerations. But maybe on this occasion Stiansen's family had been given a version that was easier to digest. In the boss's version Stiansen had taken a calculated risk to chase a potential drug dealer and murderer, and accidents can happen to anyone on duty. After all, the boy in the other car was inexperienced and another driver in the same situation would have reacted more quickly, and wouldn't have driven in front of us. Remember we had the siren on."

"And were doing 110 kilometers an hour."

"In a 50 kph area. Well, the boy couldn't be blamed of

course. The point was how to present the case. Why should the family be told their son was a passenger? Would it be any better for the parents if their son was thought to be someone who passively allowed a drunken colleague to drive the car? The boss went through the arguments over and over again. My head ached so much I thought it was going to explode. In the end I leaned over the edge of the bed and was throwing up as the nurse charged in. The next day the Stiansen family came. The parents and a younger sister. They brought flowers and hoped I would soon be on the road to recovery. The father said he blamed himself because he hadn't been strict enough with his son about speeding. I cried like a baby. Every second was like a slow execution. They sat with me for over an hour."

"God, what did you say to them?"

"Nothing. They did all the talking. About Ronny. About all the plans he'd had, about what he was going to be and do. About his girlfriend, who was studying in America. He had mentioned me. Said I was a good police officer and a good friend. Someone you could trust."

"What happened then?"

"I was in hospital for two months. The boss dropped by now and again. Once he repeated what he'd said before. 'I know what you're thinking. Stop it.' And this time he was right. I just wanted to die. Maybe there was a trace of altruism in keeping the truth hidden; lying in itself was not the worst part. The worst part was that I'd saved my own skin. This may sound odd, and I've mulled it over often enough, so let me explain.

"In the fifties there was a young university lecturer called Charles Van Doren who was famous all over the USA for his appearances on a game show. Week after week he beat off all the challengers. The questions were at times unbelievably difficult and everyone was speechless with admiration that this guy could apparently answer all of them. He received marriage proposals in the post, he had his own fan club and his lectures at the university were packed, of course. In the end he announced publicly that the producers had given him all the questions beforehand.

"When asked why he had exposed the scam he told them about an uncle who had admitted to his wife, Van Doren's aunt, that he had been unfaithful. It had caused quite a stir in the family, and afterward Van Doren had asked his uncle why he'd told her. The affair had taken place many years before, after all, and he hadn't had any contact with the woman subsequently. The uncle had answered that being unfaithful hadn't been the worst part. It was the getting away with it that he couldn't hack. And so it was for Charles Van Doren as well.

"I think people feel a kind of need for punishment when they can no longer accept their own actions. At any rate I yearned for it: to be punished, to be whipped, to be tortured, to be humiliated. Anything so long as I felt accounts were settled. But there was no one to punish me. They couldn't even give me the boot; officially I'd been sober, hadn't I. On the contrary, I received recognition from the Chief of Police in the press because I had been seriously injured on active service. So I punished myself instead. I gave myself the worst punishment I could think of: I decided to live and I decided to stop drinking."

"And afterward?"

"I got to my feet again and started working. Worked longer days than all the others. Trained. Went on long walks. Read books. Some on law. Stopped meeting bad friends. Good ones too, by the way. The ones I had left after all the boozing. I don't know why in fact, it was like a big cleanup. Everything in my old life had to go, good as well as bad. One day I sat down and rang round all those I thought I had known in my former life and said: 'Hi, we can't meet anymore. It was nice knowing you.' Most accepted it. A couple were even glad, I suppose. Some maintained I was walling myself in. Well, they may have been right. For the last three years I've spent more time with my sister than anyone else."

"And the women in your life?"

"That's another story and at least as long. And as old. After the accident there's been no one worth the breath. I suppose I've become a lone wolf preoccupied with my own concerns. Who knows, I might simply have been more charming when I was drunk."

"Why did they send you here?"

"Someone high up must think I'm useful. Probably it's a kind of acid test to see how I function under pressure. If I manage this without making an arsehole of myself it may open certain possibilities for me back home, I've gleaned."

"And do you think that's important?"

Harry shrugged. "There's not a lot that's important."

A hideous, rusty boat flying a Russian flag was under way, and further out in Port Jackson they saw white sails banking but looking as if they were lying still.

"What are you going to do now?" she asked.

"Not a lot I can do here. Inger Holter's coffin has been sent home. The funeral director rang me from Oslo today. I was told the embassy had organized the transport. They talked about a 'cadaver.' A beloved child has many names, but it's strange for the deceased to have so many."

"So when are you going to go?"

"As soon as all of Inger Holter's contacts that we know of have been eliminated from the case. I'll talk to McCormack tomorrow. I'll probably go before the weekend. If nothing concrete comes to light. Otherwise this could become a long, drawn-out affair, and we've agreed that the embassy should keep us in the loop."

She nodded. A group of tourists was standing next to them and the whirr of cameras mingled with the cacophony of the Japanese language, seagulls' screams and the throb of passing boats.

"Did you know that the person who designed the Opera House turned his back on the whole thing?" Birgitta said out of nowhere. As the waves around the budget overshoot on the Sydney Opera House rose to their peak, the Danish architect Jørn Utzon dropped the whole project and resigned in protest. "Just imagine walking away from something you've started. Something you really believed would be good. I don't think I could ever do that."

They had already decided that Harry would accompany Birgitta to the Albury rather than her catch the bus. But they didn't have a lot to say and walked in silence along Oxford Street toward Paddington. Distant thunder rumbled, and Harry gazed up in amazement at the pure, blue sky. On a corner stood a gray-haired, distinguished man, impeccably dressed in a suit with a placard hanging from his neck saying: "The secret police have taken my work, my home, and they have ruined my life. Officially I don't exist, they have no address or telephone number and they aren't listed in the state budget. They think they can't be charged. Help me to find the crooks and have them convicted for their misdeeds. Sign here or make a donation." He held up a book with pages of signatures.

They passed a record shop, and on impulse Harry went in. Behind the counter stood a man wearing glasses. Harry asked if he had any records by Nick Cave.

"Sure, he's Australian," said the man, removing his glasses. He had an eagle tattooed on his forehead.

"A duet. Something about a wild rose . . ." Harry started to say.

"Yeah, yeah, I know the one you mean. 'Where the Wild Roses Grow' from *Murder Ballads.* Shit song. Shit album. You'd be better off buying one of his good records."

The man put his glasses back on and disappeared behind the counter.

Harry was amazed again and blinked in the gloom.

"What's so special about the song?" Birgitta asked as they came out onto the street.

"Nothing, obviously." Harry laughed. The guy in the shop had put him back in a good mood. "Cave and this woman sing about a murder. They make it sound beautiful, almost like a declaration of love. But it is indeed a shit song." He laughed again. "I'm beginning to like this town."

They walked on. Harry glanced up and down the street. They were almost the only mixed-sex couple in Oxford Street. Birgitta held his hand.

"You should see the gay pride parade during Mardi Gras," Birgitta said. "It goes down Oxford Street here. Last year they said over half a million people came from all over Australia to watch and take part. It was crazy."

Gay street. Lesbian street. It was only now that he noticed the clothes exhibited in the shop windows. Latex. Leather. Tight tops and tiny silk panties. Zips and rivets. Exclusive, though, and stylish, not the sweaty, vulgar stuff that permeated the strip clubs in King's Cross.

"There was a gay man who lived nearby when I was growing up," Harry recounted. "He must have been forty or so, lived alone, and everyone in the neighborhood knew he was gay. In the winter we threw snowballs at him, shouted 'buttfucker' then ran like mad, convinced he would give us one up the backside if he caught us. But he never came after us, just pulled his hat further down over his ears and walked home. One day, suddenly, he moved. He never did anything to me, and I've always wondered why I hated him so much."

"People are afraid of what they don't understand. And hate what they're afraid of."

"You're so wise," Harry said and Birgitta punched him in the stomach. He fell onto the pavement screaming, she laughed and begged him not to make a scene, and he got up and chased her up Oxford Street.

"I hope he moved here," Harry said afterward.

* * *

Having left Birgitta (he was worried that he had begun to think of every separation from her, short or long, as leave-taking), he queued at a bus stop. A boy with a Norwegian flag on his rucksack was in front of him. Harry was wondering if he should make his presence known when the bus arrived.

The bus driver groaned when Harry gave him a twenty-dollar note.

"S'pose you didn't have a fifty, did ya?" he said sarcastically.

"If I'd had one, I'd have given it to you, you stupid bastard," he said in eloquent Norwegian while smiling innocently. The bus driver glowered ferociously at him as he handed out the change.

He had decided to follow the route Inger took to walk home on the night of the murder. Not because it hadn't been walked by others—Lebie and Yong had visited the bars and restaurants on the route and shown the photo of Inger Holter, without any success, of course. He had tried to take Andrew along with him, but he had dug his heels in and said it was a waste of valuable time better spent in front of the TV.

"I'm not kidding, Harry. Watching TV gives you confidence. When you see how stupid people generally are on the box it makes you feel smart. And scientific studies show that people who feel smart perform better than people who feel stupid."

There was little Harry could say to such logic, but Andrew had at any rate given him the name of a bar in Bridge Road where he could pass on Andrew's greetings to the owner. "Doubt he's got anything to tell you but he might knock fifty percent off the coke," Andrew had said with a cheerful grin.

Harry got off the bus at the town hall and ambled in the

direction of Pyrmont. He looked at the tall blocks and the people walking around them the way city folk do, without being any the wiser as to how Inger Holter had met her end that night. At the fish market he went into a cafe and ordered a bagel with smoked salmon and capers. From the window he could see the bridge across Blackwattle Bay and Glebe on the other side. They had started setting up an outdoor stage in the open square, and Harry saw from the posters it was to do with Australia Day, which was that weekend. Harry asked the waiter for a coffee and started to wrestle with the *Sydney Morning Herald*, the kind of paper you can use to wrap up a whole cargo of fish, and it is a real job to get through even if you only look at the pictures. But there was still an hour's daylight left and Harry wanted to see what creatures emerged in Glebe after the onset of darkness.

20

Cricket

The owner of the Cricket was also the proud owner of the shirt Allan Border wore when Australia beat England four times during the 1989 Ashes series. It was exhibited behind glass and a wooden frame above the poker machine. On the other wall there were two bats and a ball used in a 1979 series when Australia drew with Pakistan. After someone had pinched the stumps from the South Africa game, which used to hang over the exit, the owner had deemed it necessary to nail his treasures down—whereupon one pad belonging to the legendary Don Bradman was shot to pieces by a customer who was unable to wrest it from the wall.

When Harry entered and saw the combination of treasures on the walls and the ostensible cricket fans forming the clientele of the Cricket, the first thing that struck him was that he ought to revise his perception of cricket as a toffs' sport. The customers were neither groomed nor particularly sweet-smelling, and nor was Borroughs behind the bar.

"Evenin'," he said. His voice sounded like a blunt scythe against a whetstone.

"Tonic, no gin," Harry said and told him to keep the change from the ten-dollar bill.

"A lot for a tip, more like a bribe," Borroughs said, waving the note. "Are you a policeman?"

"Am I so easy to spot?" Harry asked with a resigned expression.

"Apart from the fact you sound like a bloody tourist, yeah."

Borroughs put down the change and turned away.

"I'm a friend of Andrew Kensington," Harry said.

Borroughs swiveled round as fast as lightning and picked up the money.

"Why didn't you say that straightaway?" he mumbled.

Borroughs couldn't remember having seen or heard about Inger Holter, which in fact Harry already knew as he and Andrew had spoken about him. But as his old tutor in the Oslo Police Force, "Lumbago" Simonsen, always said: "Better to ask too many times than too few."

Harry looked around. "What have you got here?" he asked.

"Kebab with Greek salad," Borroughs answered. "Today's special, seven dollars."

"Sorry, let me rephrase," Harry said. "I mean, what kind of people do you serve? What's your clientele like?"

"I reckon it's what you'd call the underclass." He gave a forbearing smile. It said a lot about Borroughs' adult working life and his dream to turn the bar into something.

"Are they regulars?" Harry asked, nodding to a dark corner of the room and the five men drinking beer at a table.

"Yup. Most here are. We're not exactly on the tourist map."

"Would you mind if I asked them a few questions?" Harry asked.

Borroughs hesitated. "Those blokes aren't exactly mummy's boys. I don't know how they earn their cash, and I don't intend to ask them, either. But they don't work nine to five, let's put it that way."

"No one likes innocent young girls being raped and strangled in the district, do they. Not even people with a foot on either side of the law. It frightens people away and isn't good for business whatever you're selling."

Borroughs rubbed and polished a glass. "I'd tread carefully if I were you."

Harry nodded to Borroughs, and walked slowly toward the corner table so they would have time to see him. One of them got up before he came too close. He folded his arms and revealed a tattooed dagger on a bulging forearm.

"This corner's taken, blondie," he said in a voice so gruff that it seemed to be only air.

"I have a question—" Harry started, but the gruff man was already shaking his head. "Just one. Does anyone here know this man, Evans White?" Harry held up the photo.

Until now the two who were facing him had just been staring at him, more bored than outright hostile. At the mention of White's name, they examined him with renewed interest, and Harry noted that the necks of the two men facing the other way were twitching.

"Never heard of him," the gruff man said. "We're in the middle of a personal . . . conversation here, mate. See you."

"That conversation wouldn't involve the turnover of substances that are illegal according to Australian law, would it?" Harry asked.

Long silence. He had adopted a perilous strategy. Undisguised provocation was a tactic you could resort to if you had decent backup or good escape routes. Harry had neither. He just thought it was time things started happening.

One neck stood up. And up. It had almost reached the ceiling when it turned and showed its ugly, pockmarked front. A silky moustache underlined the oriental features of the man.

"Genghis Khan! Good to see you. I thought you were dead!" Harry exclaimed, putting out his hand.

Khan opened his mouth. "Who are you?"

It sounded like a death rattle. Any death-metal band would have killed for a vocalist with that kind of a bass gurgle.

"I'm a policeman and I don't believe—"

"Ayy-dii." Khan peered down at Harry from the ceiling.

"Pardon?"

"The badge."

Harry was aware the situation demanded more than his plastic card with a passport photo issued by Oslo Police Force.

"Has anyone told you that you have the same voice as the singer in Sepultura . . . what's his name now?"

Harry put a finger under his chin and looked as if he was racking his brains. The gruff man was on his way around the table. Harry pointed to him.

"And you're Rod Stewart, aren't you? Aha, you're sitting here and planning Live Aid 2 and s—"

The punch hit Harry in the teeth. He stood swaying with a hand to his mouth.

"May I take it that you don't think I have a future as a stand-up?" Harry inquired. He studied his fingers. There was blood, spit and something soft which he could only assume was pulp from the inside of his tooth.

"Shouldn't pulp be red?" he asked Rod, holding up his fingers.

Rod scrutinized Harry skeptically before leaning over and looking closer at the white bits.

"That's the bone, from under the enamel," he opined. "Old man's a dentist," he explained to the others. Then he took a step back and struck again. For a moment everything went black for Harry, but he still found himself standing when daylight returned.

"See if you can find some pulp now," Rod said with curiosity.

Harry knew it was stupid, the summation of all his experience and common sense told him it was stupid, his aching jaw said it was stupid, but unfortunately his right hand thought it was a brilliant idea and at that moment it was in charge. It hit Rod on the tip of the chin and Harry heard the crunch of Rod's jaw closing before he staggered back two paces, which is the inevitable consequence of a perfectly placed uppercut.

A blow of this kind is transferred along the jawbone to the cerebellum, or small brain, an apt term in this case, Harry thought, where an undulating movement accounts for a number of minor short circuits, but also, if you're lucky, instant loss of consciousness and/or long-term brain damage. In Rod's case, the brain seemed to be unsure what it would be, a loss of consciousness or just a concussion.

Genghis Khan didn't intend to wait for the outcome. He grabbed Harry by the collar, lifted him up to shoulder height and tossed him away like a bag of flour. The couple who had just had today's special for seven dollars got more meat than they had bargained for and jumped back when Harry landed with a crash on their table. Christ, hope I faint soon, Harry thought as he felt the pain and saw Khan advancing toward him.

The clavicle is a fragile bone and very exposed. Harry took aim and lashed out with his foot, but the treatment he had been given by Rod must have affected his vision because he kicked thin air.

"Pain!" Khan promised, raising his arms above his head. He didn't need a sledgehammer. The blow hit Harry in the chest and immediately paralyzed all coronary and respiratory functions. Accordingly he neither saw nor heard the dark-skinned man coming in and grabbing the ball Australia had used against Pakistan in 1979, a rock-hard Kookaburra weighing 160 grams and measuring 7.6 centimeters in diameter. His arm whipped through the air with phenomenal power and the ball whirred straight toward its target.

Unlike Rod's cerebellum, Khan's didn't entertain any

doubt, as the missile hit him in the forehead just below his hairline. It was instant g'night. Khan started to topple, then he fell like a skyscraper rocked by an explosion.

Now, however, the other three round the table had stood up and they looked incensed. The new arrival stepped forward with his arms raised in a low, nonchalant guard. One of the men rushed at him, and Harry, who, through the haze, appeared to recognize the newcomer, guessed right: the dark man swayed back, stepped in and executed two well-aimed left jabs, as if to test the distance, then the right powered up from below in a crunching uppercut. Fortunately it was so cramped at the end of the room that they couldn't all go for him at once. With the first man down for the count, the second launched his attack, a touch more cautious, holding his arms in a way that suggested he had a belt of some hue in a martial art hanging on the wall at home. The first tentative attack was met by the newcomer's guard, and as he whirled round to complete the obligatory karate kick, the man had moved. The kick met open space.

However, the swift left-right-left combination sent the karate exponent crashing against the wall. The dark-skinned man danced after him and hit him with a straight left, knocking his head back with a sickening crunch. He trickled floorward like food leftovers thrown against the wall. The cricketer hit him one more time on his way down, though it was hardly necessary.

Rod was sitting on a chair following the events through glazed eyes.

There was a click as the third man's flick knife snapped into position. As he advanced on the dark man with hunched back and arms out to the sides, Rod puked over his shoes—a sure sign he had a concussion, Harry observed with pleasure. He felt a bit nauseous himself, especially when he saw Andrew's first opponent had taken the cricket bat off the wall and was closing in on the boxer from behind. The knifeman was standing next to Harry now, but was unaware of him.

"Behind you, Andrew!" Harry yelled, hurling himself at the man's knife arm. He heard the dry thud of the bat as it made contact and tables and chairs were knocked over, but he had to concentrate on the knifeman, who had slipped out of his grasp and was now circling, him, sweeping his arms theatrically, an insane grin on his lips.

With his eyes fixed on the knifeman, Harry fumbled on the table behind him for something he could use. He could still hear the sound of the cricket bat in action from the bar area.

The knifeman laughed as he approached, tossing the knife from one hand to the other.

Harry lunged forward, stabbed and withdrew. The knifeman's right arm fell down by his side and the knife clattered to the floor. He gazed at his shoulder in amazement, at a protruding kebab skewer with a piece of mushroom on it. The right arm seemed paralyzed, and he pulled cautiously at the skewer with his left hand to check it really was there, still with the same dazed expression on his face. I must have hit a bundle of muscles or nerves, Harry thought as he let loose a punch.

All he felt was that he hit something hard, and a flash of pain ran up his arm. The knifeman stumbled backward, looking up at Harry with wounded eyes. A thick line of dark blood oozed from one nostril. Harry was clutching his right hand. He raised his fist to strike again, but changed his mind.

"Punching is so bloody painful. Couldn't you just give in?" he asked.

The knifeman nodded and slumped down beside Rod, who still had his head between his legs.

When Harry turned, he saw Borroughs standing in the middle of the floor with a gun pointing at Andrew's first opponent, and Andrew himself lying between overturned tables, lifeless. Some of the customers had left, some stood rubbernecking, but most were still in the bar watching TV. There was a Test match on.

As the ambulances arrived to deal with the injured, Harry ensured they dealt with Andrew first. They carried him out with Harry at his side. Andrew was bleeding from one ear and there was a wheeze to his breathing, but at least he had come around.

"I didn't know you played cricket, Andrew. Great throwing arm, but was it necessary to go at it so hard?"

"You're right. I totally misjudged the situation. You had everything under control."

"Well," Harry said, "I have to be quite honest and admit I didn't."

"OK," Andrew said, "I'll be quite honest and say I've got a terrible headache and I regret I turned up at all. It would've been fairer if you'd been lying here. And I do mean that."

The ambulances came and went, and only Harry and Borroughs were left in the bar.

"I hope we didn't destroy too much of the furniture and fittings," Harry said.

"No, it's not so bad. Anyway, my customers appreciate a bit of live entertainment once in a while. But you'd better look over your shoulder from now on. The boss of those boys won't be pleased when he gets to hear about this," Borroughs said.

"Really?" Harry said. He had an inkling that Borroughs was trying to tell him something. "And who's the boss?"

"I didn't say a word, but the bloke in the photo is not a million miles off."

Harry nodded slowly. "Then I'd better be on my guard. And armed. Mind if I take an extra skewer with me?"

21

A Drunk

Harry found a dentist in King's Cross, who took one look at him and decided quite a bit of preparatory work would have to be done to build up a front tooth that had broken off in the middle. He carried out a temporary repair and accepted a fee Harry hoped Oslo's Chief of Police would be charitable enough to reimburse.

At the police station he was informed the cricket bat had broken three of Andrew's ribs and given him a concussion. He was unlikely to be leaving his sickbed this week.

After lunch Harry asked Lebie if he would join him on a couple of hospital visits. They drove to St. Etienne Hospital, where they had to register their names in the visitors' book—a thick, weighty tome that lay open in front of an even weightier nun presiding behind the glass window with crossed arms, but she just directed them in, shaking her head.

"She doesn't speak English," Lebie explained.

They entered a reception area where a smiling young man immediately logged their names on the computer and allocated them room numbers and explained where they were to go.

"From the Middle Ages to the Computer Age in ten seconds," Harry whispered.

They exchanged a few words with a yellow-and-blue Andrew, but he was in a bad mood and told them to clear off after five minutes. On the floor above they found the knifeman in a single room. He was lying in bed with his arm in a sling and a swollen face, and regarded Harry with the wounded look from the night before.

"What do you want, you bastard cop?" he said.

Harry sat down on a chair beside the bed. "I want to know whether Evans White ordered someone to murder Inger Holter, who was given the order and why."

The knifeman tried to laugh, but instead began to cough. "I have no idea what you're talking about, cop, and I don't think you do, either."

"How's the shoulder?" Harry asked.

The knifeman's eyeballs seemed to grow in his skull. "You just try . . ."

Harry pulled the skewer from his pocket. A thick, blue blood vessel appeared on the man's forehead.

"You're kidding."

Harry said nothing.

"You're out of your bloody minds! Surely you can't imagine you can get away with this! If they so much as find a mark on my body after you've left, your fuckin' crap job will be down the pan, you bastard!"

The knifeman had worked himself up into a falsetto.

Harry placed a finger on his lips. "Do yourself a favor. Shh. Do you see that burly, bald-headed guy by the door? It's not so easy to see the likeness, but in fact he's the cousin of the man whose skull you boys smashed with the bat yesterday. He asked for special permission to join me today. His job is to tape up your gob and hold you down while I loosen the bandage and stick this beauty the one place where there'll be no mark. Because there's already a hole, isn't there."

He gently squeezed the knifeman's right shoulder. Tears appeared in the man's eyes and his chest heaved violently.

His eyes jumped from Harry to Lebie and back again. Human nature is a wild, impenetrable forest, but Harry thought he saw a firebreak in the forest when the knifeman opened his mouth. He was undoubtedly telling the truth.

"You can't do anything to me that Evans White can't do ten times worse if he finds out I've grassed him up. But let me just say this: you're barking up the wrong tree. You've got things seriously wrong."

Harry looked at Lebie. He shook his head. Harry considered for a moment, then he got up and put the skewer on the bedside table.

"Get well soon."

"Hasta la vista," the knifeman said, aiming an imaginary gun with his index finger.

At the hotel there was a message for Harry in reception. He recognized the main Sydney Police Station number and rang straight away from his room. Yong Sue answered.

"We've been through all the records again," he said. "And carried out closer checks. Some misdemeanors are removed from official records after three years. That's the law. We're not allowed to register limitation misdemeanors. However, if it's a sexual offense then . . . well, let me put it this way, we keep them noted in a highly unofficial backup file. I've dug up something interesting."

"Uh-huh?"

"The official record of Inger Holter's landlord, Hunter Robertson, was unblemished. But when we burrowed deeper we discovered he'd been fined twice for flashing. Indecent exposure."

Harry tried to imagine indecent exposure.

"How indecent?"

"Playing with his sexual organs in a public place. Doesn't have to mean anything, of course, but there's more. Lebie drove past, but no one was at home, just an ill-tempered cur barking inside the door. However, a neighbor came out. Seems he had an arrangement with Robertson to let the dog out and feed it every Wednesday night, and he has the key. So, of course, Lebie asked if he'd unlocked the door and let the dog out the Wednesday night before they found Inger. He had."

"So?"

"Robertson said in his statement that he'd been at home all night before Inger was found. I thought you'd want to know."

Harry could feel his pulse beginning to race.

"What are you going to do now?"

"A police car will pick him up early, before he goes to work tomorrow."

"Hm. When and where did these awful misdeeds take place?"

"Let me see. I think it was in a park. Here it is. Green Park, it says here. It's a small—"

"I know it." He thought quickly. "I reckon I might go for a walk. Seems like there's a regular clientele hanging round there. Perhaps they know something."

Harry was given the dates for the indecent exposure offenses, which he noted down in a little black Sparebanken Nor almanac his father gave him every year for Christmas.

"Just out of interest, Yong. What's decent exposure?"

"Being eighteen years old, drunk and mooning at a passing police patrol on Independence Day in Norway."

He was so gobsmacked he couldn't utter a word.

Yong was sniggering at the other end.

"How . . . ?" Harry began.

"It's unbelievable what you can do with a couple of passwords and a Danish colleague in the adjacent office." Yong was laughing fit to burst.

Harry could feel a gasket beginning to blow.

"I hope you don't mind." Yong suddenly sounded concerned that he had gone too far. "I haven't told anyone else."

He seemed so contrite that Harry couldn't be angry.

"One of the police officers was a woman," Harry said. "She complimented me on my tight buttocks afterward."

Yong laughed with relief.

The photocells in the park considered it was dark enough and the lamps switched themselves on as Harry walked toward the bench. He recognized the gray man sitting there at once.

"Evening."

The head lying with its chin on the chest was slowly raised, and two brown eyes looked at Harry—or, to be more precise, *through* Harry—and fixed themselves on a very distant point.

"Fig?" he asked in a croaky voice.

"I beg your pardon?"

"Fig, fig," he repeated, waving two fingers in the air.

"Oh, fag. You want a cigarette?"

Harry flicked two cigarettes from the packet and took one himself. They sat in silence for a moment, enjoying the smoke. They were sitting in a green lung in the middle of a large city, yet Harry had the feeling he was in a deserted remote area. Perhaps it was because night had fallen, accompanied by the electric sound of invisible grasshopper legs being rubbed against one another. Or perhaps it was the feeling of something ritualistic and timeless, this smoking together, the white policeman and the black man with the broad, outlandish face descended from this vast continent's Indigenous population.

"Do you want to buy my jacket?"

He studied the man's jacket, which was a kind of windcheater made of thin material in vibrant red and black.

"The Aboriginal flag," he explained to Harry, showing him the back of the jacket. "My cousin makes them."

Harry politely refused the offer.

"What's your name?" the Aboriginal man asked.

"Harry."

"That's an English name. I've got an English name, too. It's Joseph. With a 'p' and an 'h.' In fact, it's a Jewish name. The father of Jesus, dig? Joseph Walter Roderigue. My tribal name's Ngardagha. N-gar-dag-ha."

"Spend a lot of time in the park, do you, Joseph?"

"Yes, a lot." Joseph clicked back into his middle-distance look and was gone. He pulled a large juice bottle from his jacket, offered Harry a drink and took a swig himself before screwing on the top. His jacket slid open and Harry saw the tattoos on his chest. "Jerry" was written above a large cross.

"Fine tattoo you've got, Joseph. May I ask who Jerry is?"

"Jerry's my son. My son. He's four." Joseph splayed his fingers as he counted up to four.

"Four. I understand. Where's Jerry now?"

"Home." Joseph waved his hand in a way to suggest a direction where home was. "Home with his mother."

"Listen, Joseph. I'm after a man. His name's Hunter Robertson. He's white, quite small and doesn't have much hair. Sometimes he comes to the park. Sometimes he exposes . . . himself. Do you know who I mean? Have you seen him, Joseph?"

"Yeah, yeah. He's coming," Joseph said, rubbing his nose, as if he considered Harry was talking about an everyday event. "Just wait. He's coming."

22

Two Flashers

A church bell rang in the distance as Harry lit his eighth cigarette and inhaled deep into his lungs. Sis had said he should stop smoking the last time he took her to the cinema. They had seen *Robin Hood: Prince of Thieves* with the worst cast Harry had seen this side of *Plan 9 from Outer Space*. But it didn't bother Sis that Kevin Costner's Robin Hood answered the Sheriff of Nottingham in broad American. In general there was very little that bothered Sis; she squealed with delight when Costner cleaned up Sherwood Forest and sniffled when Marian and Robin finally found each other.

Afterward they had gone to a cafe where he had bought her a hot chocolate. She had told him how good she felt in her new flat in the Sogn Residential Centre, even though a couple of those living in her corridor were "daft in the head." And she wanted Harry to stop smoking. "Ernst says it's dangerous. You can die from it."

"Who's Ernst?" Harry had asked, but was met with a fit of giggles. Then she turned serious again. "You mustn't smoke, Harald. You mustn't die, do you hear?" She had the "Harald" and the "do you hear?" from her mother.

The Christian name *Harry* was a result of his father getting his way. Olav Hole, a man who usually ceded to his wife in all things, had raised his voice and insisted that the boy should be called after his grandfather who had been a seaman and apparently a fine fellow. His mother had yielded in a moment of weakness, to use her words, which she had regretted bitterly afterward.

"Has anyone ever heard of anyone called Harry ever making it in anything?" she had said. (When Harry's father was in a teasing mood he had quoted her because of all the *any*s and *ever*s.)

Anyway, Harry's mother called him Harald after her uncle but everyone else called him Harry. And, after she had died, Sis had started to call him Harald. Perhaps it was Sis's way of trying to fill the gap left by her. Harry didn't know; so many strange things went on in the girl's head. For example, she had smiled with tears in her eyes and cream on her nose when Harry had promised her he would stop, if not immediately then at least in time.

Now he was sitting and imagining the smoke curling upward like a huge snake into his body. Bubbur.

Joseph twitched. He had been asleep.

"My forefathers were Crow people," he said without preamble and straightened up. "They could fly." The sleep seemed to have sobered him up. He rubbed his face with both hands.

"Wonderful thing, being able to fly. Have you got a tenner?"

Harry had only a twenty-dollar note.

"That'll do," Joseph said, snaffling it.

As though it had been a temporary break in the weather, the clouds drifted in again across Joseph's brain and he mumbled on in some unintelligible language redolent of what Andrew had been speaking to Toowoomba. Hadn't Andrew called it Creole? In the end, the drunken man's chin had fallen back onto his chest.

* * *

Harry had just decided to finish his cigarette and leave when Robertson turned up. Harry had half expected him to appear in a coat, which he imagined was standard issue for a flasher, but Robertson was wearing only jeans and a T-shirt. He peered left and right and walked with a strange bouncing gait as if he were singing inside and adapting his movement to the rhythm. He didn't recognize Harry until he had reached the benches, and there was little in Robertson's face to suggest he was overly pleased about the reunion.

"Evening, Robertson. We've been trying to get hold of you. Sit down."

Robertson glanced around and shifted weight from one foot to the other. He looked as if he most wanted to make a break for it, but in the end sat down with a sigh of despair.

"I've told you everything I know," he said. "Why are you harassing me?"

"Because you have a track record of harassing others."

"Harassing others? I haven't bloody harassed anyone!"

Harry studied him. Robertson was a hard man to like, but with the best—or worst—will in the world Harry couldn't make himself believe he was sitting next to a serial killer. A fact that served to make him quite grumpy, because it meant he was wasting his time.

"Do you know how many girls can't sleep because of you?" Harry said, trying to put as much contempt into his tone as he was able. "How many cannot forget and have to live with the image of a depraved wanker mentally raping them? You've got into their minds, made them feel vulnerable and frightened to go out in the dark; you've humiliated them and made them feel used."

Robertson had to laugh. "Is that the best you can come up with, Officer? What about all the sex lives I've ruined? And the fears they have, reducing them to a life on tranquilizers? By the way, I reckon your colleague should watch out. The one who said I could be sentenced to six years for being an accessory if I didn't stand up straight and make a statement to you yobbos. I've spoken to my solicitor now, and he's going to take the matter up with your boss, just so you know. So don't you try and pull the wool over my eyes again."

"OK, we can do this in two ways, Robertson," Harry said, noticing that he didn't have the same authority in the role of brutish policeman that Andrew would have had. "You can tell me what I want to know here and now or—"

"—or we can go down to the station. Thank you, I've heard that one before. Please, haul me in, then my solicitor can come and get me within the hour, and you and your colleague will be reported for hounding civilians into the bargain. Be my guest!"

"That wasn't quite what I had in mind," Harry answered quietly. "I imagined more a discreet leak, impossible to uncover naturally, to one of Sydney's news-hungry, out-and-out sensationalist Sunday papers. Can you visualize it? *Inger Holter's landlord, see picture, previous indecent exposure conviction, in police spotlight*—"

"Conviction! I was fined. Forty dollars!" Hunter Robertson's voice had gone falsetto.

"Yes, I know, Robertson, it was a minor misdemeanor," Harry said with feigned sympathy. "So minor that it's been easy to keep it hidden from the local community. Such a shame they read Sunday newspapers where you live, isn't it? And at work . . . What about your parents? Can they read?"

Robertson crumpled. The air went out of him like a punctured beach ball, reminding Harry of a beanbag, and he knew he'd obviously touched a sore spot when he mentioned the parents.

"You heartless bastard," Robertson whispered in a hoarse, pained voice. "Where do they make people like you?" and after a while: "What do you want to know?"

"First of all I want to know where you were the evening before Inger was found."

"I've already told the police I was at home alone and—"

"This conversation is over. I hope the editors find a nice picture of you."

He got up.

"OK, OK. I wasn't at home!" Robertson screeched. He leaned back and closed his eyes.

Harry sat down again.

"When I was a student and lived in a bedsit in one of the town's finer areas a widow lived across the street," Harry said. "At seven o'clock, seven on the dot, every Friday evening she opened the curtains. I lived on the same floor and my bedsit looked straight into her living room. Especially on Fridays, when she turned on the enormous chandelier. If you saw her on any other day of the week she was a graying old lady with glasses and a cardigan, the type of lady you see on the tram and queuing at the chemist's all the time.

"But on Fridays at seven, when the performance started, you would have anything on your mind but grumpy, coughing old ladies with a stick. She wore a silk dressing gown with a Japanese pattern and black high-heeled shoes. At half past seven she received a male visitor. At a quarter to eight she had taken off the dressing gown and was sporting her black corset. At eight she was half out of the corset and humping away on the chesterfield. At half past eight the visitor had gone, the curtains were drawn and the performance was over."

"Interesting," said Robertson, flatly.

"What was interesting was that there was never any trouble. If you lived on my side of the street, you couldn't avoid seeing what went on, and lots of people in the block must have been following the performances. But it was never talked about, as far as I know, it was never reported to the police and there were no complaints. The other interesting thing was the regularity of it. At first I thought that had something to do with the partner, when he was available, he might have been working, or married, or something like that. But soon I realized she changed partners without changing the timetable. And then it dawned on me: she obviously knew what any TV programmer knows: once you have attracted an audience with a fixed slot it's very damaging if you change the time of broadcasting. And it was the audience that spiced up her sex life. Understand?"

"I understand," Robertson answered.

"A superfluous question, of course. Now, why did I tell this story? It struck me that our comatose friend here, Joseph, was so sure you would come tonight I checked my calendar and most dates fitted. Tonight's a Wednesday, the night Inger went missing was a Wednesday and the two times you were caught flashing were Wednesdays as well. You have fixed slots, don't you."

Robertson didn't answer.

"Therefore my next question is: why haven't you been reported recently? After all, it's four years since the last incident. And men exposing themselves to small girls in the park is not something people generally appreciate."

"Who said it was small girls?" Robertson snapped. "And who said it wasn't appreciated?"

If Harry had been able to whistle he would have done so under his breath. He suddenly remembered the couple arguing nearby earlier in the evening.

"So you do it for men," he said, almost to himself. "For the gays in the district. That explains why you have to keep it quiet. Have you got a crowd of regulars as well?"

Robertson shrugged. "They come and go. But they certainly know when and where they can see me."

"And when you were reported?"

"Just casual passersby. We're more careful now."

"So I could find a witness willing to state you were here the night Inger disappeared?"

Robertson nodded.

They sat in silence listening to Joseph's light snoring.

"There's something else that doesn't quite fit," Harry said at length. "It's been at the back of my mind, but I couldn't put my finger on it until I heard that every Wednesday your neighbor feeds your dog and lets it out."

Two men walked past slowly and stopped on the edge of the light cast by the streetlamp.

"So I asked myself: why's he feeding it when Inger's on her way back from the Albury with some meat leftovers? At first I dismissed the idea, thinking you'd probably talked about it. Perhaps the meat was for the day after. But then I recalled something that should have struck me straightaway: your dog doesn't eat . . . at least isn't allowed to eat meat. In which case, what was Inger doing with it? She'd told people at the bar it was for the dog. Why would she lie?"

"I don't know."

Harry noticed Robertson checking his watch. Must be showtime soon.

"One last thing. What do you know about Evans White?"

Robertson turned and looked at him with watery, light blue eyes. Was that a tiny glint of fear?

"Very little," he said.

Harry gave up. He hadn't made much progress. Bubbling away inside, he could feel an urge to hunt, to give chase and to arrest, but this scenario kept slipping further away all the time. In a few bloody days he would be on his way back to Norway. Strangely enough, though, this thought didn't make him feel any better.

"About the witnesses," Robertson said. "I would appreciate it if you'd . . ."

"I don't want to ruin your show, Robertson. I know that those coming will derive some benefit." He peered into his cigarette packet, took out one, and put the rest in Joseph's jacket pocket as he got up to go. "I certainly appreciated the widow's weekly performance."

23

Black Snake

As usual the Albury was in full swing. They were blasting out "It's Raining Men." On the stage three of the boys were wearing knee-high boots and not much else, and the audience was cheering and singing along. Harry watched more of the show before going to Birgitta's bar.

"Why don't you sing along, Handsome?" said a familiar voice. Harry turned. Otto wasn't in drag tonight; however, a pink, open-neck silk shirt and a hint of mascara and lipstick showed that he had still taken pains with his appearance.

"I haven't got the voice for it, Otto. Sorry."

"Bah, you Scandinavians are all alike. Can't let go until you've poured so much booze down you you're useless for . . . yeah, you know what I mean."

Harry smiled at the lowered eyelids. "Don't flirt with me, Otto. I'm a lost cause."

"Hopeless hetero, eh?"

Harry nodded.

"Let me buy you a drink anyway, Handsome. What d'you fancy?" He ordered a grapefruit juice for Harry and a Bloody Mary for himself. They toasted and Otto downed half the cocktail in one go.

"The only thing that helps with love's sorrows," he said,

draining the rest, shivering, ordering another and eyeing Harry. "So, you've never had sex with a man? Perhaps we'll have to do something about that one day."

Harry could feel his earlobes getting hot. How could this gay clown make him, a fully grown man, so embarrassed that he looked like a Brit after six hours on a Spanish beach?

"Let's make a tasteless and wonderfully vulgar wager," Otto said, his eyes glinting with amusement. "I bet one hundred dollars that this soft, slim hand of yours will have felt my vitals before you return to Norway. Do you dare to accept the bet?"

Otto clapped his hands at the sight of Harry's scarlet face.

"If you insist on handing out money, fine by me," Harry said. "But my understanding, Otto, was that you were suffering from love's sorrows. Shouldn't you be at home thinking about other things rather than tempting straight men?" He regretted what he had said at once. He had never liked being teased.

Otto withdrew his hand and shot him a wounded glare.

"Sorry, I was just blabbing. I didn't mean it," Harry said.

Otto shrugged. "Anything new in the murder case?" he asked.

"No," Harry said, relieved they had changed the subject. "Looks as if we may have to search beyond her circle of acquaintances. Did you know her, by the way?"

"Everyone who hangs out here knew Inger."

"Did you ever talk to her?"

"Well, I suppose I must have exchanged a few words with her. She was a bit complicated for my taste."

"Complicated?"

"She turned the heads of quite a few hetero customers. Dressed provocatively, sent long stares and smiled a bit too long if that could get her extra tips. That kind of thing can be dangerous."

"Do you think any of the customers might have . . . ?"

"I just mean you might not have to look too far, Officer."

"What are you implying?"

Otto cast his eyes around and finished his drink. "I'm all mouth, Handsome." He made to go. "Now I'll do what you suggested. Go home and think about other things. Wasn't that what the doctor prescribed?"

He waved to one of the stole-clad boys behind the bar, who brought him a brown paper bag.

"Don't forget the show!" Otto called over his shoulder as he left.

Harry was sitting on a stool at Birgitta's bar discreetly watching her work. He followed her quick hands pulling pints, changing money and mixing drinks, the way she moved behind the bar because all the distances were second nature: from the beer tap to the counter to the till. He saw her hair slide in front of her face, the quick flick to remove it and her occasional gaze across the customers to spot new orders—and Harry.

The freckled face lit up, and he felt his heart throbbing in his chest, heavy, wonderful.

"Friend of Andrew's came in a while ago," she said, walking over to Harry. "He visited him in hospital and wanted to say hello. He asked for you. Think he's still sitting here somewhere. Yes, there he is."

She pointed to a table and Harry recognized the elegant black man at once. It was Toowoomba, the boxer. He went over to his table.

"Am I disturbing you?" he asked, and was met with a broad smile.

"Not at all. Sit down. I was sitting here to see if an old mate of mine would show up."

Harry sat down.

Robin "The Murri" Toowoomba continued to smile. For some reason one of those embarrassing pauses sprang up that no one admits is embarrassing, but which actually is.

Harry said hurriedly: "I was talking to one of the Crow people today. What tribe do you belong to?"

Toowoomba regarded him with surprise in his eyes. "What do you mean, Harry? I'm from Queensland."

Harry could hear how foolish his question sounded. "Sorry, that was a stupid question. My tongue has a tendency to move faster than my brain today. I didn't mean to . . . I don't know a great deal about your culture. I was wondering if you came from a particular tribe . . . or something like that."

Toowoomba patted him on the shoulder. "I'm just teasing you, Harry. Relax." He laughed quietly and Harry felt even more stupid.

"You react like most whities," Toowoomba said. "What else can you expect? It goes without saying that you're full of prejudice."

"Prejudice?" Harry could feel himself getting irritated. "Have I said anything—"

"It's not what you say," Toowoomba said. "It's what you unconsciously expect of me. You imagine you've said something wrong, and it doesn't occur to you that I'm intelligent enough to take into account that you're a foreigner. I don't suppose you would be personally offended if Japanese tourists in Norway didn't know everything about your country? Such as your king being called Harald." Toowoomba winked. "It's not just you, Harry. Even white Australians are hysterically cautious about saying something wrong. That's what's so paradoxical. First of all, they take our people's pride, and when it's gone they're scared to death of treading on it."

He sighed and opened his large white palms. Like turning a flounder, Harry thought.

Toowoomba's warm, deep voice seemed to vibrate on its frequency, rendering it unnecessary to speak loudly to drown all the noise around them.

"But you tell me something about Norway, Harry. I've read it's supposed to be very beautiful there. And cold."

Harry talked. About fjords, mountains and people living between the two. About unions, suppression, Ibsen, Nansen and Grieg. And about the country to the north that saw itself as enterprising and forward-looking, but seemed more like a banana republic. Which had forests and harbors when the Dutch and English needed timber, which had waterfalls when electricity was invented and which, best of all, discovered oil outside its front door.

"We've never made Volvo cars or Tuborg beer," Harry said. "We've just exported our nature and avoided thinking. We're a nation with golden hair up our arses," Harry said, not even trying to select an appropriate English idiom.

Then he told him about Åndalsnes, a tiny settlement up in Romsdalen Valley, surrounded by high mountains which were so beautiful that his mother had always said that that was where God had started when He was creating the world, and that He had spent so long on Romsdalen that the rest of the world had to be done posthaste to be finished by Sunday.

And fishing with his father on the fjord early in the morning, in July, and lying on the shore and smelling the sea—while the gulls screamed and the mountains stood like silent, immovable guards around their little kingdom.

"My father's from Lesjaskog, a little settlement further up the valley, and he and my mother met at a village dance in Åndalsnes. They always talked about moving back to Romsdalen when they retired."

Toowoomba nodded and drank beer, and Harry sipped at another grapefruit juice. He could feel the acidity in his stomach.

"I wish I could tell you where I come from, Harry. It's

just that people like me have no real connection to a place or a tribe. I grew up in a hut under a freeway outside Brisbane. No one knows which tribe my father came from. He came and went so fast that no one had time to ask. And my mother doesn't give two hoots where she comes from, so long as she can scrape together enough money for a bottle of wine. Being a Murri will have to do."

"And what about Andrew?"

"Hasn't he told you?"

"Told me what?"

Toowoomba withdrew his hands. A deep frown settled between his eyes. "Andrew Kensington's even more rootless than I am."

Harry didn't question him any further, but after another beer Toowoomba returned to the topic.

"I suppose I ought to let him tell you this himself, because Andrew had a very special upbringing. You see, he belongs to the family-less generation of Aboriginals, the Stolen Generation."

"What do you mean?"

"It's a long story. Everything revolves around a bad conscience. Ever since the end of the nineteenth century the politics surrounding Indigenous peoples has been governed by the authorities' bad conscience about the terrible treatment we've received. Just a shame that good intentions don't always lead to good results. If you want to govern a nation you have to understand it."

"And the Aboriginal people haven't been understood?"

"There have been different phases, different policies. I belong to the forcibly urbanized generation. After the Second World War the authorities considered they had to change earlier policies and try to assimilate rather than isolate Indigenous inhabitants. They tried to do that by controlling where we lived and even who we married. Many were sent to towns to adapt to European urban culture.

The results were catastrophic. Within a very short time we topped all the wrong statistics: alcoholism, unemployment, marital break-ups, prostitution, criminality, violence, drugs—you name it, we were there. Aboriginals were and have always been Australia's social losers."

"And Andrew?"

"Andrew was born before the war. At that time the authorities' policy was to 'protect' us as though we were some kind of endangered species. Therefore opportunities for owning land or looking for work were limited. But the most bizarre legislation was the law allowing authorities to remove a child from an Aboriginal mother if there was a suspicion that the father was not Aboriginal. I may not have the world's most pleasant story about my origins, but at least I have one. Andrew has nothing. He has never seen his parents. When he was born the authorities collected him and put him in a children's home. All he knows is that after they had robbed his mother, she was found dead in a bus shelter in Bankstown, fifty kilometers north of the children's home, and no one knew how she had got there or what the causes of her death were. The white father's name was withheld until Andrew no longer cared."

Harry struggled to absorb all of this. "Was that really legal? What about the UN and the Universal Declaration of Human Rights?"

"None of that came until after the war. And don't forget that Aboriginal politics had the best of intentions. The goal was to preserve the culture, not to destroy it."

"What happened to Andrew then?"

"They realized he was academic and sent him to a private school in England."

"I thought Australia was too egalitarian to send children to private schools."

"All this was administered and paid for by the authorities. I suppose the intention was that Andrew should stand as a shining example of a political experiment that had otherwise caused so much pain and so many human tragedies. On his return, he went to Sydney University. That was when they started to lose control of him. He ended up in trouble, had a reputation for being violent and his grades suffered. My understanding is there was an unhappy love affair somewhere in the picture, a white woman who left him because her family was not very enthusiastic, but Andrew has never shown much interest in talking about it. It was, nevertheless, a difficult period in his life, and it could easily have been worse than it was. While he was in England he learned to box—he claimed that was how he had survived boarding school. In Sydney he took up boxing again and when he was offered the chance to travel with Jim Chivers he dropped out of university and got away for a while."

"I've just seen him box," Harry said. "He hasn't forgotten much."

"In fact, he'd only thought of boxing as a break from his studies, but he was successful with Chivers, the press began to show some interest and he carried on. When he boxed his way through to the final of the Australian championships, there were even a couple of professional agents from the USA over to have a look at him. However, something happened in Melbourne the night before the final. They were at a restaurant, and it was claimed that Andrew tried it on with the girlfriend of the other finalist. His name was Campbell, and he was with a nice-looking North Sydney girl who later became Miss New South Wales. There was a fight in the kitchen and everyone there, Andrew, Campbell's trainer, the agent and another bloke, smashed everything in sight.

"They found Andrew hanging over the washbasin with a split lip, cuts to his forehead and a sprained wrist. No one was reported—that's probably why the rumor spread he'd made a pass at Campbell's girlfriend. At all events, Andrew had to withdraw from the final, and afterward his boxing career seemed to flag. To be fair, he did knock out a couple of good boxers in some tournaments, but the press had lost interest and the professional agents never showed up again.

"Bit by bit he stopped boxing at tournaments—another rumor had it he had started drinking, and after one tournament on the west coast he was asked to leave the Chivers team, apparently because he had inflicted serious injuries on some amateurs. After that he disappeared. It's been difficult to get out of him exactly what he was doing, but at any rate he was drifting aimlessly around Australia for a couple of years until he went back to university."

"So boxing came to an end?" Harry said.

"Yes," Toowoomba replied.

"What happened then?"

"Well." Toowoomba signaled that he wanted the bill. "Andrew was probably more motivated when he went back to studying and for a while things went well. But it was the early 1970s, hippies, party time and free love, and he may well have been taking various substances which weren't helpful to his studies, and his exam results were so-so."

He chuckled to himself.

"So one day Andrew woke up, got out of bed, looked at himself in the mirror and took stock. He had a terrible hangover, a black eye—God knows where from—probably a growing addiction to certain chemical compounds, and was over thirty without any qualifications. Behind him lay a ruined career as a boxer and before him, to put it mildly, an uncertain future. So what do you do then? You apply to Police College."

Harry laughed.

"I'm just quoting Andrew," Toowoomba said. "Unbelievably, he got in despite his record and advanced age—maybe because the authorities wanted more Aboriginal police officers. So Andrew had his hair cut, removed the ring from his ear, dropped the chemicals, and you know the rest. Of course, he's a no-hoper as far as climbing up the career ladder is concerned, but he's reckoned to be one of the best detectives in the Sydney force nevertheless."

"Still quoting Andrew?"

Toowoomba laughed. "Naturally."

From the stage bar they could hear the finale of the evening's drag show and "Y.M.C.A.," the Village People version, a surefire winner.

"You know a lot about Andrew," Harry said.

"He's a bit like a father to me," Toowoomba said. "When I moved to Sydney I had no plans, other than to get as far away from home as possible. I was literally picked up off the street by Andrew who started training me and a couple of other boys who had also lost their way. It was Andrew who made me apply to university as well."

"Wow, another university-qualified boxer."

"English and History. My dream is to teach my own people one day." He said that with pride and conviction.

"And in the meantime you knock the shit out of drunken seamen and country bumpkins?"

Toowoomba smiled. "You need capital to make your way in this world, and I have no illusions about earning anything as a teacher. But I don't just box amateurs; I've put my name forward for the Australian championships this year."

"To get the title Andrew didn't?"

Toowoomba raised his glass to a toast. "Maybe."

After the show the bar began to thin out. Birgitta had said she had a surprise for Harry, and he was impatiently waiting for closing time.

Toowoomba was still sitting at the table. He had paid, and was now twirling his beer glass. Harry had an indefinable feeling that Toowoomba wanted something; he didn't only want to tell old stories.

"Have you got any further with the case you're here for, Harry?"

"I don't know," Harry answered. "Now and then you feel like you're searching with a telescope and the solution's so close to you it's no more than a blur on the lens."

"Or you're standing upside down."

Harry watched him drain his glass.

"I have to go, but let me tell you a story first which might help to redress your ignorance of our culture. Have you heard about the black snake?"

Harry nodded. Before he'd left for Australia he'd read something about reptiles you should be wary of. "If memory serves the black snake is not very impressive in size, but all the more venomous for that."

"That's right, but according to the fable it wasn't always like that. A long time ago, in the Dreamtime, the black snake was innocuous. However, the iguana was poisonous and much bigger than it is today. It ate humans and animals, and one day the kangaroo called all the animals to a meeting to find a way to overcome the ferocious killer—Mungoongali, the great chief of the iguanas. Ouyouboolooey—the black snake—the fearless, little snake immediately accepted the task."

He continued in a low, calm voice while keeping his eyes fixed on Harry.

"The other animals laughed at the little snake and said they would need someone bigger and stronger to fight Mungoongali. 'Just you wait and see,' said Ouyouboolooey, and slithered off to the iguana chief's camp. When he got there he greeted the huge brute and said he was only a little snake, not particularly good to eat, just searching for a place where he could be left in peace, away from the other animals that teased and tormented him. 'Make sure you're not in my way or it will be the worse for you,' Mungoongali said, not appearing to pay much attention to the black snake.

"The next morning Mungoongali went hunting, and Ouyouboolooey slithered after him. There was a man sitting by a campfire. He had hardly blinked before Mungoongali had run at him and smashed his head with one powerful, well-aimed blow. Then the iguana put the man onto its back and carried him to its camp, where it unloaded the poison sac and started to consume the fresh human meat. As quick as lightning, Ouyouboolooey jumped out, took the poison sac and disappeared into the bushes. Mungoongali chased after the little snake, but couldn't find him. The other animals were still in the meeting when Ouyouboolooey returned.

"'Look at this,' he screamed and opened his jaws for all to see the poison sac. All the animals flocked around him and congratulated him on saving them from Mungoongali. After the others had gone home, the kangaroo went over to Ouyouboolooey and said he should spit the poison into the river so that they could sleep safe and sound in the future. But Ouyouboolooey answered by biting the kangaroo, who fell to the ground, paralyzed.

"'You've always despised me, but now it's my turn,' said Ouyouboolooey to the dying kangaroo. 'As long as I have this poison you will never be able to come near me again. None of the other animals will know I still have the poison. They will think that I, Ouyouboolooey, am their savior and protector while I avenge myself on them one by one in my own good time.' With that he pushed the kangaroo into the river and it sank from view. He himself slithered back into the bushes. And that's where you'll find him today. In the bushes."

Toowoomba put his lips to his glass, but it was empty and he got up.

"It's late."

Harry got up, too. "Thanks for the story, Toowoomba. I'll be heading back soon, so if I don't see you, good luck at the championships. And with your future plans."

Toowoomba held out his hand, and Harry wondered if

he was ever going to learn. His hand felt like a piece of battered steak afterward.

"Hope you find out what the blur on the lens is," Toowoomba said. He had already gone by the time Harry realized what he was talking about.

24

The Great White

The watchman gave Birgitta a torch.

"You know where to find me, Birgitta. Make sure you don't get eaten," he said, limping back into his office with a smile.

Birgitta and Harry walked along the dark, winding corridors of the large building that is Sydney Aquarium. It was almost two o'clock in the morning, and Ben, the night-watchman, had let them in.

A casual question from Harry—why all the lights were off—had led to a detailed explanation from the old watchman.

"Of course it saves electricity, but that's not the most important reason—the most important reason is that we're telling the fish it's night. I think so, anyhow. Before, we used to turn off the lights with a standard switch, and you could hear the shock when all of a sudden everything went pitch black. A whoosh went through the whole aquarium as hundreds of fish dashed to hide or swam off in blind panic."

Ben hushed his voice to a stage-like whisper and imitated the fish with zigzag hand movements.

"There was a lot of splashing and waves, and some fish, mackerel for example, went stir-crazy and smacked into the glass and killed themselves. So we started using dimmers, which gradually reduce the light in line with daylight hours, aping nature. After that there was a lot less illness among the fish as well. The light tells your body when it's day and night, and personally I feel the fish need a natural daily rhythm to avoid stress. They have a biological clock the same way we do, and you shouldn't mess about with it. I know that some barramundi breeders in Tasmania, for example, give the fish extra light in the autumn. Trick them into thinking it's still summer to make them spawn more."

"Ben likes to talk a lot when he's warmed to a topic," Birgitta explained. "He's almost as happy talking to people as he is to his fish." She had worked for the last two summers as a spare hand at the aquarium and had become good friends with the watchman, who claimed he had been working at the aquarium ever since it opened.

"It's so peaceful here at night," Birgitta said. "So quiet. Look!" She shone the torch on the glass wall where a black-and-yellow moray fish glided out of its cave revealing a row of small, sharp teeth. Further down the corridor she lit up two speckled stingrays slipping through the water behind the green glass with slow-motion winglike movements. "Isn't that beautiful?" she whispered with gleaming eyes. "It's like ballet without the music."

Harry felt as though he were tiptoeing through a dormitory. The only sounds were their steps and a faint but regular gurgle from the aquariums.

Birgitta stopped by one high glass wall. "This is the aquarium's saltie, Matilda from Queensland," she said, directing the cone of light at the glass. There was a dried-out tree trunk lying on a reconstructed riverbank inside. And in the pool a floating piece of wood.

"What's a saltie?" Harry asked, trying to catch sight of

something living. At that moment the piece of wood opened two shimmering, green eyes. They lit up in the dark like reflectors.

"It's a crocodile that lives in salt water, in contrast to the freshie. Freshies live off fish and you don't need to be afraid of them."

"And salties?"

"You should definitely be afraid of them. Many so-called dangerous predators attack humans only when they feel threatened, are afraid or you've encroached on their territory. A saltie, however, is a simple, uncomplicated soul. It just wants your body. Several Australians are killed every year in the swamplands to the north."

Harry leaned against the glass. "Doesn't that lead to . . . a . . . er, certain antipathy? In some parts of India they wiped out the tiger under the pretext it was eating babies. Why have these man-eaters not been exterminated?"

"Most people here have the same relaxed kind of attitude to crocodiles as they do to traffic accidents. Almost, anyway. If you want roads, you've got to accept deaths, right? Well, if you want crocodiles, it's the same thing. These animals eat humans. That's life."

Harry shuddered. Matilda had closed her eyelids in a similar way to the headlamp covers on some models of Porsche. Not a ripple in the water betrayed the fact that the wood lying half a meter from him behind the glass was in reality more than a ton of muscle, teeth and ill temper.

"Let's go on," he suggested.

"Here we have Mr. Bean," Birgitta said, shining the torch on a small, light brown, flounder-like fish. "This is a fiddler ray, it's what we call Alex in the bar, the man Inger called Mr. Bean."

"Why Fiddler Ray?"

"I don't know. They called him that before I started there."

"Funny name. It obviously likes lying still on the bottom."

"Yes, and that's why you've got to be careful when you're in the water. It's poisonous, you see, and it'll sting you if you tread on it."

They descended a staircase that wound down to one of the big tanks.

"The tanks aren't actually aquariums in the true sense of the word, they've just enclosed a part of Sydney Harbour," Birgitta said as they entered.

From the ceiling a greenish light fell over them in undulating stripes, and made Harry feel as if he were standing under a mirrorball. It was only when Birgitta pointed the torch upward that he saw they were surrounded by water on all sides. They were standing in a glass tunnel under the sea, and the light was coming from outside, filtered through the water. A huge shadow glided past them, and he instinctively recoiled.

"Mobulidae," she said. "Devil rays."

"My God, it's enormous!" Harry breathed.

The whole skate was one single billowing movement, like a massive waterbed, and Harry felt sleepy just looking at it. Then it turned onto its side, waved to them and floated into the dark watery world like a black bedsheet spook.

They sat on the floor and from her rucksack Birgitta took a rug, two glasses, a candle, and an unlabeled bottle of red wine. Present from a friend working at a vineyard in Hunter Valley, she said, opening it. Then they lay side by side on the rug looking up into the water.

It was like lying in a world turned upside down, like seeing into an inverted sky full of fish all the colors of the rainbow and strange creatures invented by someone with an overactive imagination. A blue, shimmering fish with an inquiring moon-face and thin, quivering ventral fins hovered in the water above them.

"Isn't it wonderful to see how much time they take, how apparently meaningless their activities are?" whispered Birgitta. “Can you feel them slowing time down?” She placed a cold hand on Harry’s neck and squeezed softly. “Can you feel your pulse almost stopping?”

Harry swallowed. “I don’t mind time going slowly. Not right now,” he said. “Not for the next few days.”

Birgitta squeezed harder. “Don’t even talk about it,” she said.

“Sometimes I think, ‘Harry, you’re not so bloody stupid after all.’ I notice, for example, that Andrew always talks about the Aboriginal people as ‘them.’ That’s why I’d guessed a lot of Andrew’s story before Toowoomba told me specific details. I’d more or less surmised that Andrew hadn’t grown up with his own family, that he doesn’t belong anywhere but floats along on the surface and sees things from the outside. Like us here, observing a world which we cannot take part in. After the chat with Toowoomba I realized something else: at birth Andrew didn’t receive that gift of natural pride you have with being part of a people. That’s why he had to find his own. At first I thought he was ashamed of his brothers, but now I know he’s grappling with his own shame.”

Birgitta grunted. Harry went on.

“Sometimes I think I’ve got something, only in the next minute to be thrown into confusion once again. I don’t like being confused; I have no tolerance for it. That’s why I wish either I didn’t have this ability to capture details, or I had a greater ability to assemble them into a picture that made some sense.”

He turned to Birgitta and buried his face in her hair.

“It’s a bad job on God’s part to give a man with so little intelligence such a good eye for detail,” he said, trying to place something that had the same scent as Birgitta’s hair. But it was so long ago he had forgotten what it was.

“So what can you see?” she asked.

"Everyone's trying to point my attention to something I don't understand."

"Like what?"

"I don't know. They're like women. They tell me stories that mean something else. What's between the lines may be blindingly obvious, but, as I say, I don't have the ability to see. Why can't you women just say things as they are? You overestimate men's ability to interpret."

"Is it my fault now?" she exclaimed with a smile and smacked him. The echo rolled down the underwater tunnel.

"Shh, don't wake the Great White," said Harry.

It took Birgitta quite a while to spot that he hadn't touched his wineglass.

"A little glass of wine can't hurt, can it?" she said.

"Yes, it can," Harry answered. "It can hurt." He pulled her toward him with a smile. "But let's not talk about that." Then he kissed her, and she took a long, trembling breath, as though she had been waiting for this kiss for an eternity.

Harry woke with a start. He didn't know where the green light in the water had come from, whether it was the moon over Sydney or searchlights on land, but now it was gone. The candle had burned out, and it was pitch-black. Yet he had a feeling he was being watched. He located the torch beside Birgitta and switched it on—she was wrapped in her half of the rug, naked and with a contented expression. He shone the light on the glass.

At first he thought it was his own reflection he could see, then his eyes became accustomed to the light and he felt his heart register a last pounding beat before it froze. The Great White was beside him, watching him with cold, lifeless eyes. Harry breathed out and condensation formed on the glass in front of the pale, watery face, the apparition of a drowned man that was so large it seemed to fill the whole tank. The teeth protruded from the jaw, looking as if they had been drawn by a child, a zigzag line of triangles, white daggers, arranged at random in two gumless rows.

Then it floated up and above him, all the while with its dead eyes fixed on him, stiffened into a look of hatred, a white corpse-like body gliding past the torch beam in slow, undulating movements, seemingly never-ending.

25

Mr. Bean

"So you're leaving soon?"

"Yup." Harry sat with a cup of coffee in his lap, not knowing quite what to do with it. McCormack got up from his desk and started pacing by the window.

"So you think we're still a long way from cracking the case, do you? You think there's some psychopath out there in the masses, a faceless murderer who kills on impulse and leaves no clues. And that we'll have to hope and pray he makes a mistake next time he strikes?"

"I didn't say that, sir. I just don't think I've got anything to offer here. Plus, I had a call to say they need me in Oslo."

"Fine. I'll inform them you've acquitted yourself well here, Holy. I understand you're being considered for promotion at home."

"No one said anything to me, sir."

"Take the rest of the day off and see some of Sydney's sights before you go, Holy."

"I'll just eliminate this Alex Tomaros from our inquiries first, sir."

McCormack stood gazing out of the window at an overcast and stifling hot Sydney.

"I long for home too, Holy. Across the beautiful sea."

"Sir?"

"Kiwi. I'm a Kiwi, Holy. My parents came here when I was ten. Folk are nicer to each other over there. That's how I remember it, anyway."

"We don't open for several hours yet," said the grumpy woman at the door with a broom in her hand.

"That's all right. I've got an appointment with Mr. Tomaros," Harry said, wondering whether she would be convinced by a Norwegian police badge. It proved to be unnecessary. She opened the door just wide enough for Harry to enter. There was a smell of stale beer and soap, and strangely enough the Albury seemed smaller now that he saw it empty and in daylight.

He found Alex Tomaros, alias Mr. Bean, alias Fiddler Ray, inside his office behind the bar. Harry introduced himself.

"How can I help you, Mr. Holy?" He spoke quickly and with an unmistakable accent, the way foreigners, even when they have lived in a country for years, often do.

"Thank you for agreeing to meet at such short notice, Mr. Tomaros. I know other officers have been here and asked you a whole load of things, so I won't detain you any longer than necessary. I—"

"That's fine. As you see, I have quite a bit to do. Accounts, you know . . ."

"I understand. From your statement I saw that you were doing accounts on the evening Inger Holter went missing. Was there anyone here with you?"

"If you'd read my statement thoroughly I'm sure you'd have seen I was on my own. I'm always on my own . . ." Harry studied Tomaros's arrogant face and slavering mouth. I believe you, he thought. ". . . doing accounts. Completely and utterly. If I'd wanted, I could have swindled this place out of hundreds of thousands of dollars without anyone noticing a thing."

"Technically, then, you don't have an alibi."

Tomaros removed his glasses. "Technically, I rang my mother at two and said I'd finished and was on my way home."

"Technically, there's a great deal you could have done between one, when the bar closed, and two, Mr. Tomaros. Not that I'm saying you're under suspicion or anything."

Tomaros stared at him without blinking.

Harry flicked through his empty notepad and pretended to be looking for something.

"Why did you ring your mother, by the way? Isn't it a bit unusual to ring someone at two o'clock in the morning with that kind of message?"

"My mother likes to know where I am. The police have spoken to her too, so I don't know why we have to go through this again."

"You're Greek, aren't you?"

"I'm an Australian and have lived here for twenty years. My mother's an Australian national now. Anything else?" He was controlling himself well.

"You showed a personal interest in Inger Holter. How did you react when she rejected you?"

Tomaros licked his lips, and he was about to say something but paused. The tongue appeared again. Like a snake's, Harry thought. A poor little black snake everyone despises and believes is harmless.

"Miss Holter and I talked about having dinner together, if that's what you're alluding to. She's the only person here I've asked out. You can check with any of the others. Cathrine and Birgitta, for example. I set great store by having a good relationship with my employees."

"*Your* employees?"

"Well, technically, I'm—"

"The bar manager. Well, Mr. Bar Manager, how did you like her boyfriend making an appearance here?"

Tomaros's glasses had started misting up. "Inger had a good relationship with many of the customers, so it was impossible for me to know which of them was her boyfriend. So she had a boyfriend? Good for her . . ."

Harry didn't need to be a psychologist to see through Tomaros's attempt to sound indifferent.

"You had no idea, then, who she was on intimate terms with, Tomaros?"

He rolled his shoulders. "There was the clown, of course, but his inclinations were elsewhere . . ."

"The clown?"

"Otto Rechtnagel, a regular here. She used to give him food for—"

"The dog!" Harry shouted. Tomaros jumped in his chair.

Harry got up and smacked a fist into his palm.

"That's it! Otto was given a bag yesterday. It was leftovers for the dog! I remember now, he said he had a dog. Inger told Birgitta she was taking leftovers for the dog on the evening she went missing, and all the time we assumed they were for the landlord's dog. But the Tasmanian Devil's a vegetarian. Do you know what the leftovers were? Do you know where Rechtnagel lives?"

"Good God, how should I know?" Tomaros said, horrified. He had pushed his chair right back against the bookcase.

"OK, listen to me. Keep quiet about this conversation, don't even mention it to your beloved mother, otherwise I'll be back to cut your head off. Do you understand, Mr. Bea—Mr. Tomaros?"

Alex Tomaros just nodded.

"And now I need to make a phone call."

* * *

The fan creaked abjectly, but no one in the room noticed. Everyone's attention was focused on Yong, who had placed a transparency showing a map of Australia on the overhead projector. On the map he had put small red dots with dates next to them.

"These are the times and places of the rapes and murders which we feel our man is responsible for," he said. "We've tried before to find some geographical or temporal pattern without any success. Now it looks as if Harry's found one for us."

Yong put another transparency over the first with the same map. This one had blue dots, which covered almost all the red ones beneath.

"What's this?" Watkins asked tetchily.

"This is taken from the list of shows performed by the Australian Travelling Show Park, a circus, and indicates where they were on the relevant dates."

The fan continued its lament, but otherwise the conference room was utterly still.

"Holy Dooley, we've got 'im!" Lebie shouted.

"The chances of this being a coincidence are, statistically speaking, about one in four million," Yong smiled.

"Wait, wait, who is it we're looking for now?" Watkins interjected.

"We're looking for this man," Yong said, placing a third transparency on the overhead. Two sad eyes set in a pale, slightly bloated face with a tentative smile looked at them from the screen. "Harry can tell you who this is."

Harry got up.

"This is Otto Rechtnagel, a professional clown, forty-two years old, who has been on the road with the Australian Travelling Show Park for the last ten years. When the circus isn't working he lives alone in Sydney and performs freelance. At the moment he's started up a small troupe giving shows in town. He's got a clean record as far as we can see, has never been in the spotlight in connection with any sexual offenses and is considered a convivial, quiet fellow, though somewhat eccentric. The crunch is that he knew the deceased, he was a regular at the bar where Inger Holter worked and they had become good friends over time. She was probably on her way to Rechtnagel's the night she was killed. With food for his dog."

"Food for his dog?" Lebie laughed. "At half past one in the morning? I think our clown had something else on his mind."

"And right there you've put your finger on the bizarre side of the case," Harry said. "Otto Rechtnagel has maintained a facade as a hundred percent, card-carrying homosexual since the age of ten."

This information occasioned mumbling round the table.

Watkins groaned. "Do you believe that a homosexual man like this could have killed seven women and raped six times as many?"

McCormack had entered the room. He had been briefed. "If you've been a happy homo with exclusively homo friends for the whole of your life, it's perhaps not so surprising that you become anxious the day you discover that the sight of a shapely pair of tits makes John Thomas twitch. Christ, we're living in Sydney, the only town in the world where people are closet heteros."

McCormack's booming laugh drowned the braying of Yong, who was laughing so much his eyes had become two narrow slits in his face.

Watkins didn't let himself get carried away by all this good humor. He scratched his head. "Nonetheless, there are a couple of things here that don't stack up. Why would someone who has been so cold and calculating right through suddenly reveal himself like this? Why invite a victim home in this way? I mean, he couldn't know if Inger had told others where she was going. If she had, she would have led us directly to him. Besides, it looks like the other victims were chosen at random. Why would he suddenly break the pattern and choose a girl he knows?"

"The only thing we know about this poor bastard is that he has no clear pattern," Lebie said, blowing at one of his rings. "However, it seems as if he likes variety. Except that the victims have to be blondes"—he polished the ring on his shirtsleeve—"and that they are often strangled afterward."

"One in four million," Yong repeated.

Watkins sighed. "OK, I give in. Perhaps we're simply having our prayers answered. Perhaps he has finally committed the all-important mistake."

"What are you going to do now?" McCormack asked.

Harry spoke up. "Otto Rechtnagel is unlikely to be at home, he's got a performance with his circus troupe on Bondi Beach tonight. I suggest we go and watch the show and arrest him straight afterward."

"I can see our Norwegian colleague has a sense for the dramatic," McCormack said.

"If the performance has to be interrupted the media will be onto it straightaway, sir."

McCormack nodded slowly. "Watkins?"

"Fine by me, sir."

"OK, haul him in, boys."

26

Another Patient

Andrew had pulled the duvet up to his chin and looked as if he was already lying in state. The swellings on the side of his face had acquired a spectrum of entertaining colors, and when he tried to smile at Harry his face distorted in pain.

"Jeez, does it hurt so much to smile?" Harry said.

"Everything hurts. Thinking hurts."

There was a bouquet of flowers on his bedside table.

"From a secret admirer?"

"If you like. His name's Otto. And tomorrow Toowoomba's coming, and today you're here. It's good to feel loved."

"I've brought something for you, too. You'll have to smoke it when no one's watching." Harry held up a long, dark cigar.

"Ah, a Maduro. Of course. From my dear Norwegian *rubio*." Andrew beamed and allowed himself a careful laugh.

"How long have I known you now, Andrew?"

Andrew stroked the cigar as if it were a pussy cat. "Must be about a week now, mate. We'll soon be like brothers."

"And how long does it take to *really* know someone?"

"Well, Harry, it doesn't necessarily take very long to get to know the beaten tracks through the big, dark forest. Some people have fine, straight paths and streetlamps and road signs. They seem to tell you everything. But that's where you should be careful you don't take anything for granted. Because you don't find the forest's animals on illuminated paths, you find them in the bushes and the scrub."

"And how long does it take to know them?"

"Depends on who's there. And the forest. Some forests are darker than others."

"And what's your forest like?"

Andrew put the cigar in the drawer of his bedside table. "Dark. Like a Maduro cigar." He looked at Harry. "But of course you've found that out . . ."

"I've spoken to a friend of yours who's cast a bit more light over who Andrew Kensington is, yes."

"Well, then you know what I'm talking about. About not letting yourself be deceived by the illuminated paths. But you have a couple of dark patches yourself, so I don't need to explain this to you."

"Meaning?"

"Let's just say that I recognize a man who's given things up. Drinking, for example."

"I suppose everyone does," Harry mumbled.

"Everything you do leaves traces, doesn't it. The life you've lived is written all over you, for those who can read."

"And you can read?"

Andrew placed his large fist on Harry's shoulder. He had perked up remarkably quickly, Harry thought.

"I like you, Harry. You're my pal. I think you know what things are about, so don't look in the wrong place. I'm just one of the many millions of lonely souls trying to live on the face of this earth. I'm trying to acquit myself without making too many mistakes. Now and then I may even be on top of things enough to try and do some good. That's all. I'm not important here, Harry. Finding out about me won't lead you anywhere. Shit, *I'm* not even particularly interested in finding out too much about myself."

"Why not?"

"When your forest is so dark you don't know it yourself, it's wise not to go on trips of discovery. You can soon find yourself treading on thin air."

Harry nodded and sat looking at the flowers in the vase. "Do you believe in chance?" he asked.

"Well," Andrew said, "life consists of a connected series of quite improbable chance occurrences. When you buy a lottery ticket and get number 822531, for example, the odds of you getting that number are one in a million."

Harry nodded again. "What bothers me," he said, "is that I've had that lottery number too many times in a row."

"Really?" Andrew sat up in bed with a groan. "Tell Uncle Andrew."

"On my arrival in Sydney the first thing that happens is I hear you weren't actually going to be assigned to this case at all, but you insisted on being given the Inger Holter murder and, furthermore, asked specifically to work with me, the foreigner. Back then I should have asked myself a few questions. The next thing you do is introduce me to one of your friends under the pretext of watching a semi-entertaining circus number to kill some time. Out of four million inhabitants in Sydney I meet this one guy on the first evening. One guy! One in four million. The same guy pops up again, by the way, we even make a very intimate wager of a hundred dollars, but the point is he pops up in the bar where Inger Holter worked and it transpires he knew her! One in four million again! And while we're trying to home in on a *probable* murderer, Evans White to be precise, you suddenly unearth a contact who has *seen* White, one of eighteen million people on this continent, a contact who happens to be in Nimbin of all places on the very night of the murder!"

Andrew seemed to have fallen into a deep reverie. Harry went on.

"So, of course, it's natural for you to give me the address

of the pub where Evans White's gang *happen* to be regulars, so that under pressure they can confirm the story everyone wants me to believe: that White is not involved."

Two nurses had come in and one of them grabbed hold of the bed end. The other said in a friendly but firm tone: "I regret to say visiting time is over now. Mr. Kensington has to have an EEG test and the doctors are waiting."

Harry leaned over to Andrew's ear. "I'm at best a man of middling intelligence, Andrew. But I know there's something you're trying to tell me. I just don't know why you can't say it straight out. Or why you need me. Has someone got a hold on you, Andrew?"

He ran alongside the bed as the nurses swung it through the door and continued down the corridor. Andrew had slumped back onto his pillow and closed his eyes.

"Harry, you said that Whitefellas and Aboriginals had more or less the same story about the first people to live on this earth because we'd drawn the same conclusions about things of which we know nothing, that we had some innate thought processes. On the one hand, that's probably the most stupid thing I've ever heard, but on the other I hope you're right. In which case it's just a question of closing our eyes and see—"

"Andrew!" Harry hissed into his ear. They had stopped by a lift and one of the nurses held the door.

"Don't play bloody games with me, Andrew, do you hear?! Is it Otto? Is Otto Bubbur?"

Andrew opened his eyes. "How—?"

"We're going to arrest him this evening. After the show."

"No!" Andrew half sat up in bed, but a nurse pressed him carefully but firmly back down.

"The doctor has told you to lie still, Mr. Kensington. Remember, you have a serious concussion." She turned to Harry. "This is as far as you go."

Andrew struggled to get up again. "Not yet, Harry! Give

me two days. Not yet. Promise me you'll wait two days! Sister, go to hell!" He smacked away the hand trying to push him down.

Harry stood by the headboard holding the bed. He stooped and whispered with a fiery intensity, almost spitting out the words, "For the time being, none of the others is aware that Otto knows you, but of course it's just a question of time before they find out. They'll start wondering about your role in all of this, Andrew. I can't delay this arrest without a bloody good reason."

Andrew grabbed Harry's shirt collar. "Look closer, Harry. Use your eyes! See . . ." he started, then gave up and sank back on the pillow.

"See what?" Harry persisted, but Andrew had closed his eyes and was waving him to stop. He suddenly looks so old and small, Harry thought. Old, small and black in a big, white bed.

A nurse brusquely pushed Harry away, and the last he saw before the lift doors shut was Andrew's large, black hand, still waving.

27

An Execution

A thin veil of cloud had drifted in front of the afternoon sun over the ridge behind Bondi Beach. The sands and sea were beginning to empty, and coming toward them was a steady stream of the types that populate Australia's famous, glamorous beach: surfers with sun-creamed lips and noses, waddling bodybuilders, girls in cut-off jeans on Rollerblades, sunburned B-list celebrities and silicone-enhanced bathing nymphs; in short, the beautiful people, the young and—at least on the surface—the successful. Campbell Parade, the boulevard where the "in" fashion boutiques and small, plain but expensive restaurants stand shoulder to shoulder, was at this time of day a seething mass of people. Open sports cars moved slowly in the traffic, revving their engines with impatient rutting cries while the drivers observed the activity on the pavements through mirror sunglasses.

Harry thought about Kristin.

He was thinking about the time he and Kristin had gone Interrailing and got off the train in Cannes. It had been peak tourist season and there hadn't been a single reasonably priced room in the whole town. They had been away from home so long that they were scraping the bottom of their piggy bank, and their travel budget certainly couldn't stretch to an overnight stay at any of the numerous luxury hotels. So they inquired when the next train left for Paris, stowed their rucksacks in a left-luggage locker at the station and went down to La Croisette. They promenaded to and fro looking at the people and animals, all equally beautiful and rich, and the crazy yachts, each with their own crew, cabin cruiser moored to the stern as a commuter vehicle and helicopter pad on the roof, which made them swear then and there to vote Socialist for the rest of their lives.

In the end, all the promenading made them so sweaty they had to have a swim. Towels and bathing costumes were in the rucksacks, so they were forced to swim in their underwear. Kristin had run out of clean knickers and was wearing a pair of Harry's sturdy pants. They plunged into the Mediterranean, among expensive tangas and bulky jewelery, giggling happily in their white Y-fronts.

Harry remembered lying on the sand afterward and watching Kristin standing in a loose T-shirt and removing the wet, heavy pants. He enjoyed the sight of her glowing skin with droplets of water glittering in the sun, of the T-shirt riding up to reveal a long, suntanned thigh, of her gently curved hip, of the Frenchmen's long stares, he liked how she looked at him, catching him in the act, how she smiled and held his eyes as she lingeringly pulled up her jeans, how she put a hand under her T-shirt to raise the zip, but left it there, leaned back and closed her eyes . . . then ran her red tongue provocatively around her lips, teetered and fell, hard, on top of him with a snort of laughter.

Afterward they ate at an exorbitantly expensive restaurant with a view of the sea, and as the sun set they were sitting entwined on the sand with Kristin shedding a few tears with the beauty of it and they agreed they would book into the Carlton Hotel and sneak off without paying, and perhaps skip the two days they had planned to be in Paris.

That summer was always the first thing he thought about

when his mind turned to Kristin. It had been so intense, and afterward it was easy to say that there had been separation in the air. But Harry couldn't remember thinking about it at the time.

That autumn Harry did his military service, and before Christmas Kristin had met a musician and gone to London.

Harry, Lebie and Watkins were sitting at a pavement cafe on the corner of Campbell Parade and Lamrock Avenue. The table was in the shade, it was late afternoon, but not so late that their sunglasses looked out of place. Their jackets in the heat were less satisfactory, but the alternative was shirtsleeves and gun holsters. They didn't say much, they just waited.

In the middle of the promenade, between the beach and Campbell Parade, was St. George's Theatre, a beautiful yellow building where Otto Rechtnagel was soon to perform.

"Have you used a Browning Hi-Power before?" Watkins asked.

Harry shook his head. They had shown him how to load and put the safety catch on when he was being equipped at the Firearms Desk, and that was all. It wasn't a problem; Harry didn't exactly imagine that Otto would pull out a machine gun and mow them all down.

Lebie checked his watch. "Time we got going," he said. Sweat was wreathed around his head.

"OK, final run-through: while everyone's on the stage and bowing after the finale, Harry and I enter by the side door. I've arranged that the caretaker will leave it open. He's also put up a nameplate on Rechtnagel's dressing-room door. We stand outside until Rechtnagel comes, and we arrest him there. Smack on the handcuffs, no weapons unless there's an emergency. Out the back door, where we have a police car waiting for us. Lebie will be in the crowd with a walkie-talkie and will call us when Rechtnagel's on his way. Also if Rechtnagel should smell a rat and try to make an escape through the crowd to the main entrance. Let's take up our positions and say a quiet prayer that they have air-conditioning."

The small, intimate auditorium of St. George's Theatre was full and the atmosphere was excited as the curtain rose. In fact, though, the curtain didn't rise, it fell. The clowns stood looking up at the ceiling where the curtain had come loose, then they discussed the matter gesticulating wildly, running around helter-skelter, pushing the curtain off the stage, tripping over one another and apologizing to the audience with doffed caps. All of which was greeted by laughter and good-humored shouts. In the house there seemed to be quite a number of friends and acquaintances of the performers. The stage was cleared and converted into a scaffold scene, and Otto entered to the accompaniment of a heavy funeral march played on one drum.

Harry saw the guillotine and immediately realized this was a variation of the same number he had seen in the Powerhouse. Obviously the Queen was in for it tonight, for Otto was wearing a red ball gown with an immensely long, white wig and white-powdered face. The executioner also had a new costume: a tight-fitting black outfit with large ears and webbing under his arms, which made him look like a devil.

Or a bat, Harry reflected.

The blade of the guillotine was raised, a marrow was placed beneath and the blade fell. With a thud it hit the block as if the marrow hadn't been there at all. The executioner triumphantly held the two halves in the air as the audience cheered and whistled. After some heartrending scenes, during which the Queen wept and begged for mercy and vainly tried to ingratiate herself with the man in black, she was dragged to the guillotine with her legs flailing around under her dress, to the audience's great delight.

The guillotine was raised again and the drumroll started, getting louder and louder as the lights were lowered.

Watkins leaned over. "So blondes get killed on the stage, too?"

The drumroll continued. Harry looked around: people were on the edge of their seats; some were bent forward with gaping mouths, others had their hands over their ears. Generations of people had sat like that for more than a hundred years, allowing themselves to be delighted and terrified by the same show. As if in answer to his thoughts, Watkins leaned over again.

"Violence is like Coca-Cola and the Bible. A classic."

Still the drumroll continued, and Harry noticed this was taking time. It hadn't taken so long for the blade to fall before, had it? The executioner was worried; he shuffled forward and peered up at the top of the guillotine, as if there were something wrong. Then all of a sudden, without anyone doing anything apparently, the blade whizzed down. Harry stiffened involuntarily, and a gasp went through the auditorium as the blade hit the neck. The drum stopped at once, and the head fell to the floor with a thud. A deafening silence followed, before a scream rent the air from somewhere in front of Watkins and Harry. Alarm spread around the theater and Harry squinted through the gloom to see what was going on. All he could see was the executioner backing away.

"Oh my God!" Watkins whispered.

A sound emanated from the stage, as though someone was clapping. Then Harry saw. From the neckband of the beheaded Queen a spine protruded like a white worm, slowly nodding the head up and down. Blood was spurting from the gaping hole and splashing onto the stage.

"He knew we were coming!" Watkins whispered. "He

knew we were onto him! He even dressed up as one of his fucking rape victims!" He leaned into Harry's face. "Shit, shit, shit, Holy!"

Harry didn't know what was making him feel so queasy, whether it was the blood, the tasteless collocation of "fucking" with "rape victims," or simply the man's evil breath.

A red pool had formed which the executioner skidded in as he, apparently still in shock, ran forward to pick up the head. He fell to the floor with a bang, and two of the clowns ran onto the stage screaming at each other.

"Get the lights on!"

"Up with the curtain!"

Two of the other clowns ran on with the stage curtain and all four stood looking at one another and the high ceiling. A shout was heard from behind the stage, there was a flash from the lighting rig and a loud bang, and the theater descended into total darkness.

"This stinks, Holy. Come on!" Watkins grabbed Harry's arm and made to move.

"Sit down," Harry whispered, pulling him back into his seat.

"What?"

The lights came on, and the stage, which only a few seconds before had been a mess of blood, heads, guillotines, clowns and curtains, was empty, apart from the executioner and Otto Rechtnagel who stood at the edge of the stage with the Queen's blonde head under his arm. They were met with a roar of wild cheering from the audience, to which they responded with deep bows.

"Well, bugger me," said Watkins.

28

The Hunter

In the interval Watkins permitted himself a beer. “That number almost did it for me,” he said. “I’m still bloody trembling. Perhaps we should get the bastard now. This waiting is making me nervous.”

Harry shrugged. “Why? He’s not going anywhere, and he doesn’t suspect anything. Let’s stick to the plan.”

Watkins discreetly pressed the walkie-talkie to check he was in contact with Lebie, who, to be on the safe side, had stayed seated in the auditorium. The police car was already in position at the back door.

Harry had to concede that the finessing of the guillotine number was effective, but he was still pondering why Otto had exchanged Louis XVI for the blonde woman no one would have identified. Perhaps he had counted on Harry using the free tickets and being present. Was this his way of playing with the police? Harry knew that it was not unusual for serial killers to feel more and more confident as time passed without an arrest. Or was he begging for someone to stop him? And of course there was a third possibility—they had quite simply modified the trick.

A bell rang.

“Here we go again,” Watkins said. “I hope no one else will be killed this evening.”

* * *

Some way into the second act Otto appeared dressed as a hunter and crept across the stage with a pistol in his hand while peering up into trees that had been rolled in on wheels. From the foliage came some birdsong which Otto tried to imitate as he took aim at the branches. The crack of a gun was heard, a small puff of smoke rose and something black fell and hit the stage with a thump. The hunter ran over and to his surprise lifted up a black cat! Otto took a deep bow and left the stage to scattered applause.

"Didn't understand that one," Watkins whispered.

Harry might have appreciated the performance if he hadn't been tense. However, as it was, he sat following his watch more than the events on the stage. Besides, several of the numbers contained political satire of a more local flavor and went over his head, but the audience greatly appreciated them. At the end, the music piped up, the lights came on and all the performers appeared onstage.

Harry and Watkins apologized to the row of people who had to stand to let them out, and hurried to the door at the side of the stage. As agreed, it was open and they went into a corridor that ran in a semicircle behind. At the furthest end they found the door with *Otto Rechtnagel, Clown* on it and waited. The music and the stamping from the auditorium were making the walls shake. Then came a brief crackle from Watkins's walkie-talkie. He picked it up.

"Already?" he said. "The music's still playing. Over." His eyes widened. "What?! Repeat! Over."

Harry knew something had gone wrong.

"Stay where you are and keep an eye on the stage door. Over and out!" Watkins slipped the walkie-talkie back into his inside pocket and took the gun from his shoulder holster.

"Lebie can't see Rechtnagel onstage."

"Perhaps he can't recognize him. They use quite a bit of makeup when they—"

"The bugger's not on the stage," he repeated, tugging the dressing-room door handle, but it was locked. "Shit, Holy. I can feel this ain't good. Fuck!"

The corridor was narrow, so Watkins pressed his back against the wall and kicked the lock on the door. After three kicks it gave with a shower of splinters. They lurched into an empty dressing room full of white steam. The floor was wet. The water and the steam were coming from a half-open door clearly leading to a bathroom. They stood on either side of the door; Harry had also taken out his gun, and was fumbling to find the safety catch.

"Rechtnagel!" Watkins shouted. "Rechtnagel!"

No answer.

"I don't like this," he snarled under his breath.

Harry had seen too many detective programs on TV to like it much, either. Running water and unanswered shouts had a tendency to presage less than edifying sights.

Watkins pointed to Harry with his forefinger and the shower with his thumb. Harry felt like signaling back with his middle finger, but acknowledged it was his turn now. He kicked open the door, took two paces into a baking hot steam bath and was saturated in a second. Before him he glimpsed a shower curtain. He pushed it aside with the muzzle of his gun.

Nothing.

He burned his arm as he switched off the water, and swore loudly in Norwegian. His shoes squelched as he maneuvered himself into a better position to see through the receding steam.

"Nothing here!" he yelled.

"Why's there so much bloody water then?"

"There's something blocking the drain. Just a moment."

Harry put his hand into the water where he thought the blockage might be. He rummaged around, but then his fingers met something soft and smooth jammed in the drain.

He grabbed it and pulled it out. Nausea rose in his throat; he swallowed and struggled to breathe, but it felt as if the steam he was inhaling was suffocating him.

"What's up?" Watkins asked. He was standing in the doorway and looking down at Harry crouching in the shower.

"I think I've lost a bet and I owe Otto Rechtnagel a hundred dollars," Harry said quietly. "At least what's left of him."

Later Harry recalled the rest of what happened at St. George's Theatre through a mist, as though the steam from Otto's shower had spread and invaded everywhere: into the corridor where it blurred the outline of the caretaker trying to open the props-room door, in through the keyholes leaving a reddish filter over the sight that met them when they broke open the door and saw the guillotine dripping blood, into the auditory channels where it made the sound of screams strangely muted and fuzzy, as they were unable to prevent the other performers from entering and seeing Otto Rechtnagel scattered across the room.

The extremities had been slung into the corners like the arms and legs of a doll. The walls and floor were spattered with real, viscous blood that would coagulate and go black in no time at all. A limbless torso lay on the guillotine block, flesh and blood with wide-open eyes, a clown's nose and mouth and cheeks smeared with lipstick.

The steam had adhered to Harry's skin, mouth and palate. As if in slow motion he saw Lebie emerge from the mist, come over and whisper into his ear: "Andrew's done a runner from the hospital."

29

Birgitta Undresses

Someone must have lubricated the fan. It was whirring blithely without a sound.

"The only person the officers in the car saw coming out of the back door was this black executioner figure, is that right?"

McCormack had summoned everyone to his office.

Watkins nodded. "It is, sir. We'll have to wait to hear what the performers and the caretakers saw—they're being interviewed now. Either the murderer was in the auditorium and got in through the open stage door or he entered by the back door before the police car was in position."

He sighed.

"The caretaker says the back door was locked during the performance, so in that case the murderer must have had a key, been let in or have sneaked in unnoticed with the performers and then hidden somewhere. Then he knocked on the dressing-room door after the cat number while Otto was getting ready for the finale. He probably drugged him—the boys in Forensics have found traces of diethyl ether—let's hope so anyway, either in the dressing room or afterward in the props room. Whatever, the bloke must be a real cold-hearted bastard. After cutting him up he takes the severed sexual organs, returns to the dressing room and turns on the taps so that anyone trying to get hold of him would hear water and think Otto was having a shower."

McCormack cleared his throat. "What about this guillotine? There are simpler ways to kill a man . . ."

"Well, sir, I would guess the guillotine was a spontaneous idea. He could hardly have known it would be moved to the props room in the interval."

"A very, very sick man," Lebie said to his nails.

"What about the doors? They were all locked, weren't they? How did they get into the props room?"

"I spoke to the caretaker," Harry said. "As troupe leader Otto had a bunch of keys in his room. They've gone."

"And what about this . . . devil's costume?"

"It was in the box next to the guillotine, with the loose head and the wig, sir. The killer put it on after the murder and used it as a disguise. Also very cunning. And hardly likely to have been planned."

McCormack rested his head in his hands.

"What was that, Yong?"

Yong had been on the computer while the others were talking.

"Let's forget the devil in black clothes for a while," he said. "Logic tells us that the killer's someone in the troupe."

Watkins snorted loudly.

"Let me finish, sir," Yong said. "We're looking for someone who knows the show, so he knew that Otto didn't have any more to do after the cat number and therefore wouldn't be needed onstage until the finale, about twenty minutes later. A member of the troupe wouldn't have had to sneak in, either, which I doubt an outsider would have managed unobserved. Presumably at least one of you would have noticed if he'd used the door at the side of the stage."

The others could only nod.

"Anyway, I've checked, and discovered that there are

three other members of the troupe who were in the Australian Travelling Show Park. Which means that this evening there are three other people who could have been at the crime scenes we discussed on the relevant dates. Maybe Otto was simply an innocent who knew too much? Let's start looking where we have a chance of finding something. I suggest we kick off with the troupe instead of a phantom of the opera who is probably over the hills and far away already."

Watkins shook his head. "We can't ignore the obvious—an unknown person who leaves the scene of a crime wearing an outfit stored beside a murder weapon. It's impossible for him *not* to have anything to do with the murder."

Harry agreed. "I think we can forget the other actors in the troupe. First of all, nothing's changed the fact that Otto may have raped and killed all the girls. There can be a whole host of reasons for someone wanting to murder a serial killer. The individual may be involved in some way, for example. Perhaps he knew Otto was going to be arrested by the police and didn't want to risk a confession and being dragged down in its wake. Second, it's not certain the murderer knew in advance how much time he had—he may have forced Otto to tell him when he would be onstage again. And third, listen to your feelings!" He closed his eyes. "You can feel it, can't you? The guy in the bat costume is our man. Narahdarn!"

"What?" said Watkins.

McCormack chuckled. "Seems as if our Norwegian friend has stepped into the void left by our very own Detective Kensington," he said.

"Narahdarn," Yong repeated. "The Aboriginal symbol of death, the bat."

"There's something else that worries me," McCormack continued. "The bloke can slip out the rear door unnoticed and be ten steps away from the busiest streets in Sydney where he can be sure to disappear in seconds. Yet he takes the time to put on a costume which is bound to attract attention. But which also means we have no description of him. You almost get the feeling he knew the police car was there to keep an eye on the door. And, if so, how is that possible?"

Silence.

"How's Kensington doing in hospital, by the way?" McCormack took out a lozenge and started sucking.

The room was silent. The fan was blowing noiselessly.

"He's not there anymore," Lebie said at length.

"Crikey, that was a short convalescence!" McCormack said. "Well, never mind, we need all available units as quickly as possible now because I can tell you this: chopped-up clowns create bigger headlines than raped girls. And as I've told you before, boys, those who think we don't need to give a stuff about the newspapers are mistaken. Newspapers have got chiefs of police dismissed and appointed before in this country. So unless you want me thrown out on my ear you know what has to be done. But go home and sleep first. Yes, Harry?"

"Nothing, sir."

"OK. G'night."

Things were different. The curtains in the hotel weren't drawn, and in the glow of the neon lights in King's Cross Birgitta undressed in front of him.

He lay in bed as she stood in the middle of the room dropping garment after garment, all the while holding his gaze with a serious, almost sorrowful expression. Birgitta was long-legged, slim and as white as snow in the pale light. From the half-open window could be heard the sounds of an intense nightlife—cars, motorbikes, gambling machines playing barrel-organ music and pulsating disco music. And beneath all this—like human crickets—the sound of loud conversations, indignant screams and boisterous laughter.

Birgitta undid her blouse, not consciously or sensually lingering over it, but slowly. She just undressed.

For me, Harry thought.

He had seen her naked before, but this evening it was different. She was so beautiful that he felt his throat constrict. Before, he hadn't understood her bashfulness, why she didn't take off her T-shirt and panties until she was under the blanket and why she covered herself with a towel when she went from the bed to the bathroom. But gradually he had realized that it wasn't about being embarrassed or ashamed of her body, but about revealing herself. It was about first building up time and feelings, building a little nest of security, it was the only way that would give him the *right*. That was why things were different tonight. There was something ritualistic about the undressing, as though with her nakedness she wanted to show him how vulnerable she was. Show him that she dared because she trusted him.

Harry could feel his heart pounding, partly because he was proud and happy that this strong, beautiful woman was giving him her proof of trust, and partly because he was terrified that he might not be worthy of it. But most of all because he felt that all he thought and felt was on the outside, for all to see in the glow of the neon sign, red then blue and then green. By undressing she was also undressing him.

When she was naked she stood still and all her white skin seemed to illuminate the room.

"Come on," he said in a voice that was thicker than he had intended, and folded the sheet to the side, but she didn't move.

"Look," she whispered. "Look."

30

Genghis Khan

It was eight o'clock in the morning, and Genghis Khan was still asleep as the nurse let Harry into the single hospital room. He opened his eyes as Harry scraped the chair moving it close to the bed.

"Morning," Harry said. "I hope you slept well. Do you remember me? I was the one on the table with breathing difficulties."

Genghis Khan groaned. He had a broad white bandage around his head and looked a great deal less dangerous than when he had been leaning over Harry at the Cricket.

Harry took a cricket ball from his pocket.

"I've just been talking to your solicitor. He said you're not going to report my colleague."

Harry tossed the ball from his right hand to his left.

"Considering you were on the point of killing me, I would have taken it very amiss if you'd reported the guy who saved my bacon. But this solicitor of yours clearly thinks you have a case. First of all, he says you did *not* assault me, you just *removed* me from the vicinity of your friend on whom I was in the process of inflicting *serious* injury. Secondly, he asserts it was chance that allowed you to escape with no more than a fractured skull instead of death from this cricket ball."

He threw the ball into the air and caught it again in front of the pale Warrior Prince's face.

"And do you know what? I agree. A ball slung straight in the face from a distance of four meters—it was a sheer, utter miracle you survived. Your solicitor rang me at work today wanting to know the precise course of events. He thinks there are grounds for compensation, at least if you have long-term damage. Your solicitor belongs to that breed of vulture that allocates itself a third of the reparations, but he's probably told you that, hasn't he? I asked him why he hadn't managed to persuade you to sue. He thought it was just a question of time. So now I'm wondering: is it just a question of time, Genghis?"

Genghis shook his head warily. "No. Please go now," came a weak gurgle.

"But why not? What have you got to lose? If you were to become incapacitated there are big bucks in a case like this. Remember, you're not suing a poor, private individual, you're suing the state. I've checked and seen that you've even managed to keep your nose more or less clean. So who knows, a jury might uphold your claim and make you a millionaire. But you don't even want to try?"

Genghis didn't answer, just stared at Harry with his slanting, sorrowful eyes beneath the white bandage.

"I'm getting sick of sitting in this hospital, Genghis, so I'll make this brief. Your assault on me resulted in two broken ribs and a punctured lung. Since I was not in uniform, did not show ID and wasn't working under the auspices of the police department, and Australia is beyond my area of jurisdiction, the authorities have declared that from a legal point of view I was acting as a private person and not as a civil servant. In other words, I can decide whether I report you for violent assault or not. Which brings us back to your *relatively* clean record. You see, there is a matter of a conditional sentence for grievous bodily harm hanging over your head, is that not correct? Add six months to this and we're up to a year. A year, or you could tell me . . ." he went up to the ear that was sticking out from Genghis Khan's bandaged head like a pink mushroom and shouted, ". . . WHAT THE HELL'S GOING ON!"

Harry dropped back on his chair.

"So what do you say?"

31

A Fat Lady

McCormack stood with his back to Harry, his arms crossed and a hand propping up his chin while staring out of the window. The thick mist had erased the colors and frozen movement so that the view was more like a blurred black-and-white picture of the town. The silence was broken by a tapping noise. Harry eventually realized it was McCormack's fingernails drumming on the teeth in his upper jaw.

"So Kensington knew Otto Rechtnagel. And you were aware of that all along."

Harry shrugged. "I know I should have said before, sir. But I didn't feel—"

"—it was your business to say who Andrew Kensington knew or didn't know. Fair enough. But now Kensington's done a runner, no one knows where he is and you suspect mischief?"

Harry nodded confirmation to his back.

McCormack watched him in the window reflection. Then he swiveled round in a semi-pirouette to stand face-to-face with Harry.

"You seem a bit . . ." he completed the pirouette and had his back to him again, ". . . restless, Holy. Is something bothering you? Is there anything else you'd like to tell me?"

Harry shook his head.

Otto Rechtnagel's flat was in Surry Hills; to be exact, on the road between the Albury and Inger Holter's room in Glebe. A mountain of a woman was blocking their way up the stairs when they arrived.

"I saw the car. Are you the police?" she asked in a high-pitched, shrill voice, and continued without waiting for an answer. "You can hear the dog yourselves. It's been like that since this morning."

They heard the hoarse barking from behind the door marked *Otto Rechtnagel.*

"It's sad about Mr. Rechtnagel, it is, but now you've got to take his dog. It's been barking non-stop and it's driving us all out of our minds. You shouldn't be allowed to keep dogs here. Unless you do something we'll be forced to . . . er, well, you know what I mean."

The woman rolled her eyes and thrust out two podgy arms. There was an immediate tang of sweat and compensatory perfume. Harry disliked her intensely.

"Dogs know," Lebie said, running two fingers over the balustrade and examining his forefinger with disapproval.

"What do you mean by that, young man?" the fat woman asked, dropping her arms to her sides and still looking as if she had no intention of moving.

"It knows its master is dead, ma'am," Harry said. "Dogs have a sixth sense about things like that. It's grieving."

"Grieving?" She eyed them suspiciously. "A dog? What rubbish."

"What would you do if someone cut off the arms and legs of your master, ma'am?" Lebie looked at the woman. Her jaw dropped.

After the landlady had made way they took out the various keys they had found in Otto's trouser pockets in the dressing room. The barking had changed to growling; Otto Rechtnagel's dog had probably heard the approach of strangers.

The bull terrier was standing in the hall as the door opened, its legs positioned ready for action. Lebie and Harry stood motionless, signaling to the comical white dog that the ball was in its court. The growling changed to half-hearted barking, then it gave up the whole idea and slunk into the living room. Harry followed.

Daylight flooded in through the large windows in the living room which was lavishly over-furnished: a solid red sofa covered with huge colorful cushions, sizable paintings on the walls and a low but vibrant green glass table. In the corners of the room there were two china leopards.

On the table was a lampshade which did not belong there.

The dog had its nose in a wet patch in the middle of the floor. A pair of men's shoes were hanging above it in the air. There was a stench of urine and excrement. Harry followed the shoe and sock up the foot and saw the black skin between where the sock stopped and the trousers began. He let his gaze wander further up the trousers, to the enormous hands limply hanging down and had to force his eyes upward to the white shirt. Not because he hadn't seen a man hanging before, but because he had recognized the shoes.

The head rested against one shoulder, and the end of the cable with a gray lightbulb dangled from his chest. The cable had been tied around a solid hook in the ceiling—perhaps a chandelier had hung from there at some point—and wound round Andrew's neck three times. His head was almost touching the ceiling. Dreamy, dimmed eyes stared out and a bluish-black tongue protruded from his mouth as though he had made a defiant gesture at death. Or life. An overturned chair lay on the floor.

"Fuck," Harry muttered under his breath. "Fuck, fuck, fuck." He fell into a chair, the energy knocked out of him. Lebie entered and a short cry escaped his lips.

"Find a knife," Harry whispered. "And ring for an ambulance. Or whatever it is you usually ring for."

From where Harry was sitting daylight was behind Andrew's back, and the swaying body was just an alien, black silhouette against the window. Harry begged his Maker to put another man at the end of the cable before he got to his feet again. He promised not to say a word to anyone about the miracle. He would even pray, if it would help.

He heard steps in the hallway and Lebie screaming from the kitchen: "Get out, you fat cow!"

After they had buried Harry's mother he had gone five days without feeling anything, other than that he ought to have felt something. He was therefore surprised when he slumped back among the cushions on the sofa and his eyes filled and sobs forced their way up his throat.

Not that he hadn't cried at other times. He had felt a lump in his throat as he sat alone in the room at the Bardufoss barracks reading the letter from Kristin that said "this is the best thing that has happened to me in the whole of my life." It was not clear from the context whether she meant leaving him or meeting the English musician she would be traveling with. He had only known it was one of the worst things that had happened to him in the whole of his life. Yet the sobs had stopped there, some way up his throat. Like nausea and *almost* vomiting.

He got to his feet and looked up. Andrew had not been replaced. Harry went to take a few steps across the floor, to pull up a chair to have something to stand on when they cut him down, but was unable to move. He remained motionless until Lebie came in with a kitchen knife. When Lebie started sending him strange looks Harry realized that hot tears were running down his cheeks.

Jeez, is that all? Harry thought, perplexed.

Without saying a word, they cut Andrew down, laid him on the floor and searched his pockets. There were two bunches of keys, one big and one small, as well as a loose key Lebie immediately confirmed fitted in the front-door lock.

"No signs of external violence," Lebie said, after a quick inspection.

Harry unbuttoned Andrew's shirt. He had a crocodile tattooed on his chest. Harry also pulled up Andrew's trouser legs and checked.

"Nothing," he said. "Not a thing."

"We'll have to wait and see what the doctor says," Lebie said.

Harry felt tears coming again and barely managed to shrug his shoulders.

32

Chatwick

As Harry had suspected, there was feverish activity at the office.

"It's on Reuters," Yong said. "Associated Press's sending over a photographer, and they've rung from the mayor's office saying NBC's going to fly in a TV crew to do a story."

Watkins shook his head. "Six thousand people die in a tidal wave in India and are mentioned in a single newsflash. One homosexual clown has a few limbs cut off and it's a world event."

Harry asked them to come into the conference room. He closed the door.

"Andrew Kensington's dead," he said.

Watkins and Yong stared at him in disbelief. In brief, direct terms Harry told them how they had found Andrew hanging from the ceiling in Otto Rechtnagel's flat.

He looked them straight in the eye and his voice was unwavering. "We didn't ring you because we wanted to be sure there wouldn't be any leaks. Perhaps we ought to keep a lid on this for the time being."

It struck him that it was easier to speak about this as a police matter. He could be objective and he knew how to deal with it. A body, a cause of death and a course of events, which they would try to keep under wraps. It kept Death—the stranger he didn't know how to confront—at arm's length for the moment.

"OK," Watkins said, flustered. "Careful now. Let's not jump to any hasty conclusions."

He wiped the sweat off his top lip. "I'll get McCormack. Shit, shit, shit. What have you done, Kensington? If the press gets a sniff of this . . ." And Watkins was gone.

The three left behind sat listening to the fan's lament.

"He worked with us here in Homicide now and then," Lebie said. "He wasn't really one of us, I suppose, nevertheless he was . . ."

"A kind man," Yong said, studying the floor. "A kind man. He helped me when I was new here. He was . . . a kind man."

McCormack agreed they should keep it under their hats. He was not at all happy, pacing up and down, heavier on his feet than usual, and his bushy eyebrows gathered like a gray trough of low pressure above his nose.

After the meeting Harry sat in Andrew's chair and flicked through his notes. He didn't glean much, just a few addresses, a couple of phone numbers that turned out to be for garage workshops and some incomprehensible doodles on a sheet of paper. The drawers were as good as empty, just office equipment. Then Harry examined the two bunches of keys they had found on him. One had Andrew's initials on the leather holder, so he assumed they were his private keys.

He picked up the phone and rang Birgitta. She was shocked, asked some questions, but left the talking to Harry.

"I don't understand," Harry said. "A guy I've known for little more than a week dies and I cry like a baby, while I couldn't shed so much as a tear for my mother for five days.

My mother, the greatest woman in the world! Where's the logic to it?"

"Logic?" Birgitta said. "I doubt it has much to do with logic."

"Well, I just wanted to let you know. Keep it to yourself. Will I be getting a visit after you finish work?"

She hesitated. She was expecting a phone call from Sweden tonight. From her parents.

"It's my birthday," she said.

"Many happy returns."

Harry rang off. He sensed an old foe growling in his stomach.

Lebie and Harry headed toward Andrew Kensington's home in Chatwick.

"The number where the man hunts the bird . . ." Harry began.

The sentence hung in the air between two sets of traffic lights.

"You were saying . . . ?" Lebie said.

"Nothing. I was just thinking about the show. I'm mystified by the bird number. It didn't seem to have any point. A hunter who thinks he's hunting a bird and suddenly discovers the prey is a cat, so a hunter is hunted. OK, but so what?"

After half an hour's drive they reached Sydney Road, a nice street in a pleasant district.

"Jeez, is this right?" Harry said as they saw the house number they had been given by the HR department. It was a large brick house with a double garage, a well-tended lawn and a fountain at the front. A gravel path led to an impressive mahogany door. A young boy opened it after they had rung. He nodded gravely when they mentioned Andrew, pointed to himself and covered his mouth with a hand to show them he was mute. Then he took them round the back and pointed to a small, low brick building on the other side of the enormous garden. Had it been an English estate one might have called it the gatekeeper's cottage.

"We are going to go in," Harry said and noticed that he was overarticulating. As if there was something wrong with the boy's hearing as well. "We're . . . we were colleagues of Andrew. Andrew's dead."

He held up Andrew's bunch of keys with the leather holder. For a moment the boy looked at the keys in bewilderment, gasping for air.

"He died suddenly last night," Harry said. The boy stood in front of them with his arms hanging by his sides and his eyes slowly moistening. Harry realized the two of them must have known each other well. He'd been told Andrew had lived at this address for almost twenty years, and it occurred to him the boy had probably grown up in the big house. An involuntary image appeared to Harry: the little boy and the black man playing with a ball in the garden, the boy being given money to run and buy an ice cream. Perhaps he had been raised with well-intentioned advice and semi-true stories about the policeman in the cottage, and, when he was old enough, he would have found out how to treat girls and throw a straight left without dropping his guard.

"Actually, that's wrong. We were more than colleagues. We were friends, we were friends too," Harry said. "Is it all right if we go in?"

The boy blinked, pinched his mouth and nodded.

The first thing that struck him on entering the small bachelor pad was how clean and tidy it was. In the frugally furnished sitting room, there were no newspapers lying around on the coffee table in front of the portable TV, and in the kitchen no dishes waiting to be washed. In the hall, shoes and boots were lined up with laces inside. The strict order reminded him of something.

In the bedroom, the bed was made immaculately, white sheets tucked in so tightly at the side that getting under the blankets required an aerobatic maneuver. Harry had already cursed this arrangement in his hotel bedroom. He peeped into the bathroom. Razor and soap were laid out in military order next to aftershave, toothpaste, toothbrush and shampoo on the vanity shelf over the sink. That was all. No extravagant toiletries either, Harry observed—and suddenly became aware of what this meticulousness reminded him of: his own flat after he stopped drinking.

Harry's new life had in fact started there, with the simple exercise of discipline, based on everything having its place, shelf or drawer and being returned there after use. Not so much as a Biro was left out, not a blown fuse in a fuse box. In addition to the practical application there was of course a symbolic significance: rightly or wrongly, he used the level of chaos in his flat as a thermometer for the state of the rest of his life.

Harry asked Lebie to go through the wardrobe and the chest of drawers in the bedroom, and waited until he had gone out to open the cupboard beside the mirror. They were on the top shelf, neatly stacked in rows and pointing at him, like a warehouse of miniature missiles: a couple of dozen vacuum-packed disposable syringes.

Genghis Khan had not been lying when he said Andrew was a junkie. For that matter, Harry had been in no doubt either when they found Andrew in Otto's flat. He knew that in a climate that generally necessitates short sleeves and T-shirts a police officer cannot walk around with a forearm covered with needle holes. Therefore he had to insert the syringe where the marks wouldn't be seen, such as, for example, on the back of his legs. Andrew's calves and the backs of his knees were full of them.

* * *

Andrew had been a customer of the guy with the Rod Stewart voice for as long as Genghis could remember. He reckoned Andrew was the type who could consume heroin and continue to function almost as normal both socially and professionally. "That's not as unusual as many like to think," Genghis had said.

"But when Speedy discovered round and about that this bloke was a police officer he got paranoid and wanted to shoot him. Thought he was an undercover cop. But we talked him out of it. The bloke had been one of Speedy's best customers for years. Never any haggling, always had his money ready, kept arrangements, no chat, never any shit. I've never seen an Aboriginal deal with dope so well. Bloody hell, I've never seen *anyone* deal with dope so well!"

Nor had he seen or heard any rumors about Andrew talking to Evans White.

"White hasn't got anything to do with the customer side down here anymore. He's a wholesaler, that's all. He pushed stuff in King's Cross for a while—I have no idea why, he earns enough as it is. Apparently he stopped—had some trouble with a couple of prostitutes, I heard."

Genghis had spoken openly. More openly than was necessary to save his hide. In fact, he had seemed to find it amusing. He must have reckoned there was no great danger of Harry going after them as long as they had at least one of his colleagues on their books.

"Say hello and tell the bloke he's welcome back. We don't hold grudges," Genghis had grinned at length. "Whoever they are, they always come back, you know. Always."

33

A Pathologist

The caretaker at St. George's Theatre was in the lunch room and remembered Harry from the previous night. He seemed relieved.

"F-finally someone who's not going to dig and ask questions about what it looked like. We've had journalists buzzing round here the wh-whole day," he said. "Plus those forensic fellas of yours. But they've got enough work to do of their own; they don't b-bother us."

"Yes, they have quite a job on their hands."

"Yeah. I didn't sleep much last night. Wife had to give me one of her s-sleeping pills. You shouldn't have to experience that sort of thing. S'pose you're used to it, though."

"Well, that was slightly stronger fare than usual."

"I don't know if I'll ever be able to go into that r-room again."

"Oh, you'll get over it."

"No, listen to me, I can't even bloody call it the p-props room, I say *that room*." The caretaker shook his head in desperation.

"Time heals," Harry said. "Trust me, I know a bit about that."

"I hope you're right, Officer."

"Call me Harry."

"Coffee, Harry?"

Harry said please and laid the bunch of keys on the table between them.

"Ah, there they are," the caretaker said. "The bunch of keys Rechtnagel borrowed. I was f-frightened they wouldn't turn up and we would have to change all the locks. Where did you find them?"

"At Otto's place."

"What? But he used the keys last night, didn't he? His dressing-room door . . ."

"Don't worry about it. I wonder if there was anyone else apart from the performers behind the stage yesterday."

"Oh yes. Let's see now. The l-lighting engineer, two stagehands and the sound manager were there, of course. No costume or makeup people, this isn't a b-big production. Well, that's about it. During the show there were only the stagehands and the other performers. And me."

"And you didn't see anyone there?"

"Not a soul," the caretaker answered without any hesitation.

"Could anyone have got in another way apart from the back door or the stage door?"

"Well, there's a corridor at the side of the gallery. Now the g-gallery was closed yesterday, but the door was open because the lighting engineer was sitting up there. Have a word with him."

The lighting engineer's prominent eyes bulged like those of a deep-sea fish that had just been brought to the surface.

"Yes, hang on. There was a bloke sitting there before the interval. If we can see in advance that there's not going to be a full house we sell only stall tickets, but there was nothing odd about him sitting there. The gallery isn't locked even if the tickets are actually for the stalls. He was on his own, in the back row. I remember I was surprised he would want to sit there, so far from the stage. Mm, there wasn't a lot of light, but, yes, I did see him. When I returned after the break, he was gone, as I said."

"Could he have got behind the stage through the same door as you?"

"Well." The lighting engineer scratched his head. "I assume so. If he went into the props room he could have avoided being seen by anyone. Thinking about it now, I would say the man didn't actually look very well. Yeah. I knew there was something at the back of my mind, nagging at me, something that didn't quite fit—"

"Listen," Harry said, "I'm going to show you a photo—"

"By the way, there was something else about the man—"

"This is all great," Harry interrupted him, "I'd like you to imagine the man you saw yesterday, and when you see the photo you mustn't think, just say the first thing that occurs to you. Afterward, you'll have more time and maybe change your mind, but for now I want your instinctive reaction. OK?"

"OK," said the lighting engineer and closed his protuberant eyes, making him look like a frog. "I'm ready."

Harry showed him the photograph.

"That's him!" he said, quick as a flash.

"Take a bit more time and tell me what you think."

"There's no doubt. That's what I was trying to tell you, Officer, the man was black . . . an Aboriginal. That's your man!"

Harry was worn out. It had already been a long day, and he was trying not to think about the rest. When he was ushered into the autopsy room by an assistant, Dr. Engelsohn's small, plump figure was bent over a large, fat woman's body on a kind of operating table illuminated by huge overhead lamps. Harry didn't think he could face any more fat women today.

Grumpy Engelsohn looked like a mad professor. The little hair he had stuck out in all directions and blond bristles were scattered randomly across his face.

"Yes?"

Harry realized the man had forgotten the phone conversation of some two hours before.

"My name's Harry Holy. I rang you about the initial results of the autopsy on Andrew Kensington."

Even though the room was full of strange smells and solutions Harry could still detect the unmistakable odor of gin on his breath.

"Oh, yes. Of course. Kensington. Sad case. I spoke with him several times. When he was alive, mind you. Now he's as silent as a clam in that drawer."

Engelsohn motioned behind him with his thumb.

"Listen, Mr. . . . what was it again? . . . Holy, yes! We've got a queue of bodies here all hassling me to be first. Well, not the bodies, no, the detectives. But all of them will have to sit tight and wait their turn. Those are the rules here, no queue-jumping, understand? So when Big Chief McCormack himself rings this morning and says we have to prioritize a suicide, then I start wondering. I didn't manage to ask McCormack, but perhaps you, Mr. Horgan, can tell me what on earth makes this Kensington so special?"

He shook his head in a toss of contempt and breathed more gin over Harry.

"Well, we're hoping that's what you can tell us, Doctor. Is he special?"

"Special? What do you mean by *special*? That he's got three legs, four lungs or nipples on his back, or what?"

Harry was exhausted. What he needed least of all now was a drunken pathologist trying to be awkward because he felt someone had stepped on his toes. And university-qualified people had a tendency to have more sensitive toes than others.

"Was there anything . . . unusual?" Harry ventured, trying another formulation.

Engelsohn regarded him with misty eyes. "No," he said. "There was nothing unusual. Nothing unusual at all."

The doctor continued to look at him with his head rocking from side to side, and Harry knew there was more to come. He had just inserted a dramatic pause which, to his alcohol-soaked brain, probably did not seem as long as it did to Harry.

"For us it's not unusual," the doctor continued at length, "for a body to be full to the brim with dope. Or, as in this case, with heroin. What *is* unusual is that he's a policeman, but as we get so few of your colleagues on our tables I couldn't say *how* unusual that is."

"Cause of death?"

"Didn't you say you were the one to find him? What do you think you die of if you're hanging from the ceiling with a cable round your neck? Whooping cough?"

Inside Harry, the fuse was beginning to burn, but for the time being he held the mask.

"So he died of suffocation, not an overdose?"

"Bingo, Horgan."

"OK. Next question is time of death."

"Let's say somewhere between midnight and two in the morning."

"You can't be more precise?"

"Would you be happier if I said five minutes past one?" The doctor's already ruddy cheeks were even redder now. "OK, let's say five minutes past one."

Harry breathed in deep a couple of times. "I apologize if I'm expressing myself . . . if I seem rude, Doctor. My English is not always—"

"—as it should be," Engelsohn completed.

"Exactly. You are undoubtedly a busy man, Doctor, so I won't delay you any further. I hope, however, you can confirm that you have taken on board what McCormack said about the autopsy report not going through the usual official channels but directly to him."

"That's not possible. My instructions are clear, Horgan. You can pass on my regards to McCormack and tell him that from me."

The mad little professor faced Harry with his legs akimbo and arms crossed, sure of his ground. There was a glint of battle in his eyes.

"Instructions? I don't know what status instructions have in the Sydney Police Force but where I come from instructions are there to tell people what to do," Harry said.

"Forget it, Horgan. Professional ethics is obviously not a subject you're familiar with in your dealings, so I doubt we'll be able to have a fruitful discussion about that. What do you think? Shall we draw a line under this now and say goodbye, Mr. Horgan?"

Harry didn't move. He was looking at a man who believed he had nothing to lose. An alcoholic, middle-aged and middle-range pathologist who no longer had any prospects of promotion or getting to the top and who therefore had no fear of anyone or anything. Because what could they actually do to him? For Harry this had been one of the longest and the worst days of his life. And now he'd had enough. He grabbed the lapels of the white coat and lifted him up.

The seams nearly burst.

"What I think? I think we should give you a blood test and then talk about professional ethics, Dr. Engelsohn. I think we should talk about how many people can testify that you were rat-arsed when you carried out the autopsy on Inger Holter. Then I think we should talk about someone who can give you the boot, not just from this job but any job that requires medical qualifications. What do you think, Dr. Engelsohn? What do you think about my English now?"

Dr. Engelsohn thought Harry's English was just perfect, and upon mature reflection took the view that just this once the report could perhaps go through non-official channels.

34

Frogner Lido's Top Board

McCormack was sitting with his back to Harry again and looking out of the window. The sun was going down, but still you could catch a glimpse of the temptingly blue sea between the skyscrapers and the dark green Royal Botanic Gardens. Harry's mouth was dry and he had a headache coming on. He had delivered a reasoned and almost unbroken monologue for over three-quarters of an hour. About Otto Rechtnagel, Andrew Kensington, heroin, the Cricket, the lighting engineer, Engelsohn; in brief, everything that had happened.

McCormack sat with his fingertips pressed together. He hadn't said anything for a long while.

"Did you know that way out there, in New Zealand, live the most stupid people in the world? They live alone on an island, with no neighbors to bother them, just a load of water. Yet that nation has participated in just about all the major wars there have been in the twentieth century. No other country, not even Russia during the Second World War, has lost so many young men proportionate to the population. The surplus of women is legendary. And why all this fighting? To help. To stand up for others. These simpletons didn't even fight on their own battlefields, no sir, they boarded boats and planes to travel as far as possible to die. They helped the Allies against the Germans and the Italians, the South Koreans against the North Koreans and the Americans against the Japanese and the North Vietnamese. My father was one of those simpletons."

He turned from the window and faced Harry.

"My father told me a story about an artillery gunner on his boat during the Battle of Okinawa against the Japanese in 1945. The Japanese had mobilized kamikaze pilots, and they attacked in formation using tactics they called 'falling like walnut-tree leaves over water.' And that was exactly what they did. First came one plane, and if it was shot down, two others appeared behind it, then four and so on in an apparently endless pyramid of diving planes. Everyone on board my father's boat was scared out of their wits. It was total insanity, pilots willing to die to make sure their bombs landed where they were intended. The only way they could be stopped was by mounting the densest possible flak, a wall of antiaircraft missiles. A tiny hole in the wall and the Japanese were on top of them. It was calculated that if a plane wasn't shot down within twenty seconds after it had appeared within shooting range it was too late. In all probability it would succeed in crashing into the ship. The gunners knew they *had* to hit every time, and sometimes the aerial assaults could last all day. My father described the regular pom-pom-pom of the cannons and the increasingly high-pitched wails of the planes as they dived. He said he'd heard them every night since.

"The last day of the battle he was standing on the bridge when they saw a plane emerging from the barrage and heading straight for their ship. The artillery hammered away as the plane closed in, looming larger from second to second. At the end they could clearly see the cockpit and the outline of the pilot inside. The shells from the plane began to strafe the deck. Then the antiaircraft shells hit home and the guns raked the wings and fuselage. The tail broke off, and gradually, in slow motion, the plane disintegrated into its basic parts and in the end all that was left was a small chunk attached to the propeller, which struck the deck with a trail of fire and black smoke. The other gunners were already swinging into action against new targets when a bloke in the turret directly below the bridge, a young corporal my father knew because they both came from Wellington, clambered out, waved to Dad with a smile and said: 'It's hot today.' Then he jumped overboard and was gone."

Perhaps it was the light, but Harry suddenly had the impression McCormack looked old.

"It's hot today," McCormack repeated.

"Human nature is a vast, dark forest, sir."

McCormack nodded. "So I've heard, Holy, and it may be true. I saw you had time to get to know each other, you and Kensington. I've also heard that Andrew Kensington's doings on this case ought to be investigated. What's your opinion, Holy?"

"I don't know what you mean, sir."

McCormack got up and started pacing in front of the window, a procedure Harry was now familiar with.

"I've been a policeman all my life, Holy, but still I look at my colleagues around me and wonder what it is that makes them do it, fight other people's wars. What drives them? Who wants to go through so much suffering for others to have what they perceive as justice? They're the stupid ones, Holy. We are. We're blessed with a stupidity so great that we believe we can achieve something.

"We get shot to pieces, we're obliterated and one day we jump into the sea, but in the meantime, in our endless stupidity, we believe someone needs us. And if one day you should still see through the illusion, it's already too late because we've *become* police officers, we're in the trenches and there's no way back. We can just wonder what the hell happened, when it was exactly that we made the wrong decision. We're doomed to be do-gooders for the rest of our lives and doomed to fail. But, happily, truth is a relative business. And it's flexible. We bend and twist it until it has space in our lives. Some of it, anyway. Now and then catching a villain is enough to gain some peace of mind. But everyone knows it's not healthy to deal with the extinction of vermin for any length of time. You get to taste your own poison.

"So, what is the point, Holy? The man's been in the flak turret all his life, and now he's dead. What more is there to say? Truth is relative. It's not so easy to understand what extreme stress can do to a person, for those who haven't experienced it themselves. We have forensic psychiatrists who try to draw a line between those who are sick and those who are criminal, and they bend and twist the truth to make it fit into their world of theoretical models. We have a legal system which, at its best, we hope can remove the occasional destructive individual from the streets, and journalists who would like to be seen as idealists because they make their names by exposing others in the belief that they're establishing some kind of justice. But the *truth*?

"The truth is that no one lives off the truth and that's why no one cares about the truth. The truth we make for ourselves is just the sum of what is in someone's interest, balanced by the power they hold."

His eyes held Harry's.

"So who cares about the truth with regard to Andrew Kensington? Who would benefit if we sculpted an ugly, distorted truth with sharp, dangerous bits sticking out that doesn't fit anywhere? Not the Chief of Police. Not the politicians on the town council. Not those fighting for the Aboriginal cause. Not the police officers' trade union. Not our embassies. No one. Or am I wrong?"

Harry felt like answering that Inger Holter's parents

would, but refrained. McCormack stopped by the portrait of a young Queen Elizabeth II.

"I'd be obliged if what you've told me remains between us two, Holy. I'm sure you appreciate that things are best left like this."

Harry picked a long, red hair off his trouser leg.

"I've discussed this with the mayor," McCormack said. "So that it won't seem conspicuous, the Inger Holter case will be prioritized for a little while longer. If we can't dig up any more, soon enough people will be happy to live with the notion that it was the clown who killed the Norwegian girl. Who killed the clown may be more problematical, but there's a lot to suggest a crime of passion, jealousy, maybe a rejected secret lover, who knows? In such cases people can accept that the perpetrator gets away. Nothing is ever confirmed, of course, but the circumstantial evidence is clear, and after a few years the whole matter is forgotten. A serial killer on the loose was just one theory the police were toying with at some point but later dropped."

Harry made to leave. McCormack coughed.

"I'm writing your report, Holy. I'll send it to your Chief of Police in Oslo after you've gone. You're leaving tomorrow, aren't you?"

Harry gave a brief nod and was gone.

The gentle evening breeze did not relieve his headache. And his personal gloom did not make the image any more pleasant. Harry wandered aimlessly through the streets. A small animal crossed the path through Hyde Park. At first he thought it was a large rat, but as he passed by he saw a furry little rascal peering up at him with shiny reflections from the park lamps in its eyes. Harry had never seen an animal like it, but assumed it would have to be a possum. The animal didn't appear to be frightened of him, quite the contrary, it sniffed the air inquisitively and made some bizarre wailing sounds.

Harry crouched down. "Are you wondering what you're actually doing in this big city too?" he said.

The animal cocked its head by way of an answer.

"What do you think? Shall we go home tomorrow or not? You to your forest, and me to mine?"

The possum ran off, it didn't want to be persuaded to go anywhere. It had its home here in the park, among the cars, the people and the litter bins.

In Woolloomooloo he walked past a bar. The embassy had rung. He had said he would ring back. What was Birgitta thinking? She didn't say much. And he hadn't asked much. She'd said nothing about her birthday, perhaps because she'd known he would come up with some idiotic idea. Go over the top. Give her a much too expensive present or say something superfluous for the sole reason that it was the last evening and deep down he felt bad because he was going. "What's the point?" she might have thought.

Like Kristin when she came back from England.

They had met on the terrace outside Frogner Kafé and Kristin had told him she would be home for two months. She was tanned and gentle and smiled her old smile over a glass of beer, and he had known exactly what he was going to say and do. It was like playing an old song on the piano you thought you'd forgotten—his head was empty, but his fingers knew their way. The two of them had gotten drunk, but that was before getting drunk was the be-all and end-all, so Harry could remember the rest as well. They had caught the tram to town, and Kristin had smiled her way past the queue at the Sardines club for both of them. In the night, sweaty from dancing, they had taken a taxi back up to Frogner, climbed over the fence into the lido, and on the top diving board, ten meters above the deserted park, they had shared a bottle of wine Kristin had brought in her bag, looking out over Oslo and telling each other what they wanted to be, which was always different from what they had said the previous time. Then they had held hands, run and jumped off the edge. As they fell he'd heard her shrill scream in his ears like a wonderful, out-of-control fire alarm. He had been lying on the edge of the pool laughing when she climbed up out of the water and came toward him with her dress clinging to her body.

The next morning they had woken up wrapped around each other in his bed, sweaty, hungover and aroused, and he had opened the balcony door and returned to the bed with a swaying post-booze erection, which she had welcomed with glee. He had fucked her stupid, clever and with passion, and the sounds of children playing in the backyard had been drowned when the fire alarm went off again.

It was only afterward that she'd posed the enigmatic question.

"What's the point?"

What was the point if there couldn't be anything between them? If she was going back to England, if he was so selfish, if they were so different and would never get married, have children and build a house together? If it wasn't *going* anywhere?

"Aren't the last twenty-four hours good enough reason in themselves?" Harry had said. "What if they find a lump in your breast tomorrow, what's the point then? If you're in your house with your children and a black eye, hoping your husband has gone to sleep before you go to bed, what's the point then? Are you really so sure you can capture happiness with your master plan?"

She had called him an immoral, shallow hedonist and said there was more to life than bonking.

"I know you want all that other shit," Harry had said, "but do you need to be one step along the road to marital nirvana? When you're in an old people's home you'll have forgotten the color of the dinner service you got as a wedding present, but I swear you'll remember the diving board and making love by the pool afterward."

She was the one who really should have been the bohemian of the two of them, but the last words she said as she marched out, slamming the door, was that he didn't understand a thing and it was time he grew up.

"What's the point?" Harry shouted, and a passing couple in Harmer Street turned.

Didn't Birgitta know what the point was, either? Was she afraid of things getting out of hand because he was leaving tomorrow? Was that why she preferred to have a birthday party on the phone to Sweden? Of course he should have asked her straight out, but as before, what was the point?

Harry could feel how tired he was and knew he wasn't going to get any sleep. He turned and went back to the bar. There were neon lights on the ceiling with dead insects inside and poker machines along the walls. He found a table by the window, waited for service and decided not to order if no one came. He just wanted to sit down.

The man came over and asked Harry what he wanted, and Harry gave the drinks menu a long, hard look before ordering a Coke. In the window he saw his double reflection, and wished Andrew could have been here now so that he had someone to discuss the case with.

Had Andrew been trying to tell him that Otto Rechtnagel had murdered Inger Holter? And, if so, why? How had Harry managed *not* to understand what Andrew wanted him to understand? The introduction, the cunning reports, the obvious lie about the eyewitness in Nimbin having seen White—had all of this been to divert his attention from White and make him *see*?

Andrew had ensured that he'd been put on the case and

teamed up with a foreigner whom he reckoned he would be able to control. But why hadn't Andrew stopped Rechtnagel himself? Had Otto and Andrew been lovers, was that why? Was Andrew the source of Otto's heartbreak? If so, why kill Otto just as they were going to arrest him? Harry rebuffed a drunken woman who staggered to his table and wanted to sit down.

And why kill himself after the murder? Andrew could have got away with it. Or could he? The lighting engineer had seen him, Harry knew about his friendship with Otto and he didn't have an alibi for the time of the murder.

Right, perhaps it was time for the closing credits after all. Shit.

The dogs were barking in Harry's stomach.

Andrew had taken insane risks to catch up with Otto before Harry and the others got their hands on him. Harry's throbbing headache had worsened, and now it felt as though someone was using his head as an anvil. In the shower of sparks behind his eyes he tried to hold on to one thought at a time, but there were new ones coming all the while, each one nudging out the last. Perhaps McCormack had been right—perhaps it had just been a hot day for a dysfunctional soul. Harry couldn't face thinking about the alternative—that there was more. That Andrew Kensington had worse things to hide and more to escape from than occasionally enjoying a man.

A shadow fell over him, and he looked up. The waiter's head was obscuring the light, and in the silhouette Harry thought he could see Andrew's bluish-black tongue sticking out.

"Anything else, sir?"

"I see you have a drink called Black Snake . . ."

"Jim Beam and Coke."

The dogs went wild down below.

"Fine. A double Black Snake without any Coke."

35

An Old Enemy Awakes

Harry was lost. In front of him were some steps, behind him was water and more steps. The level of chaos was rising, the masts in the bay were veering from one side to the other, and he had no idea how he had ended up here. He decided to climb. "Onward and upward," to quote his father.

It wasn't easy, but with the house walls as a support he struggled up the steps. Challis Avenue, a sign said, but that didn't mean a thing to him, so he continued straight on. He tried to look at his watch, but couldn't find it. The streets were dark and empty, so Harry presumed it was late. After ascending even more steps he reckoned that had to be the end of them and turned left into Macleay Street. He must have walked a long way, for the soles of his feet were sweaty. Or had he been running? A tear in the left knee of his trousers suggested a possible fall.

He passed some bars and restaurants, but all of them were closed. Even if it was late it must be possible to have a drink in a big city like Sydney. He walked off the pavement and flagged down a taxi with a light on the roof. It braked, then changed its mind and drove on.

Shit, do I look that bad? Harry wondered with a chuckle.

Further along the street he began to meet people, he

heard an increasing hubbub of voices, cars and music, and rounding the corner he suddenly recognized where he was again. Talk about luck, he was in King's Cross! Darlinghurst Road lay before him, brash and noisy. Now all options were open. In the first bar he was refused entry, he was allowed into a little Chinese dive, and there they served him whiskey in a tall plastic glass. It was cramped and dark inside, with an unbearable racket from all the gambling machines, so he reemerged on the street after knocking back the contents of the glass. He held on to a post watching the cars float past and trying to suppress a faint memory of having spewed on the floor of a bar earlier in the evening.

Standing there, he felt a tap on his back. He swiveled round and saw a large red mouth opening and a cavity from a missing canine.

"I heard about Andrew. I'm sorry," it said. Then it chewed gum. It was Sandra.

Harry tried to say something, but his diction must have been poor, for Sandra sent him an uncomprehending look.

"Are you free?" he asked at length.

Sandra laughed. "Yes, but I don't think you're up to it."

"Is that necessary?" Harry managed to say after some effort.

Sandra looked around. Harry caught a glimpse of a shiny suit in the shadows. Teddy Mongabi was not far away.

"Listen, I'm working now. Perhaps you should go home and have a nap, so we can talk tomorrow."

"I can pay," Harry said, taking out his wallet.

"Put it away!" Sandra said, pushing his wallet back. "I'll come with you and you'll have to pay me something, but not here, OK?"

"Let's go to my hotel, it's just round the corner, the Crescent Hotel," Harry said.

Sandra shrugged. "Whatever."

On the way there they passed a bottle shop where Harry bought two bottles of Jim Beam.

The night porter at the Crescent studied Sandra from top to toe as they came into the reception area. He seemed to be on the point of saying something, but Harry beat him to it.

"Haven't you ever seen an undercover policewoman before?"

The night porter, a young besuited Asian, smiled tentatively.

"Well, forget you ever saw her and give me my room key, please. We have work to do."

Harry doubted the porter would buy his slurred pretext, but he gave Harry his key without any objections.

In the room, Harry opened the minibar and removed all the booze.

"I'll have this," Harry said, picking out the miniature bottle of Jim Beam. "You can have the rest."

"You must really like whiskey," Sandra said, opening a beer.

Harry looked at her and seemed confused. "Must I?"

"Most people like to vary their poison. For a change, isn't that right?"

"Oh yes? Do you drink?"

Sandra hesitated. "Not really. I'm trying to cut down. I'm on a diet."

"Not really," Harry repeated. "So you don't know what you are talking about. Did you see *Leaving Las Vegas* with Nicolas Cage?"

"Eh?"

"Forget it. It was supposed to be about an alkie who decided to drink himself to death. I could believe that, no sweat. The problem was that the guy drank anything. Gin, vodka, whiskey, bourbon, brandy . . . the whole shebang. Fair enough if there are no alternatives. But this guy was standing in the world's best-stocked booze hall in Las Vegas, had loads of money and no preferences. No bloody preferences! I have never met an alkie who doesn't care what he drinks. Once you've found your poison you stick to it, don't you? He even won an Oscar."

Harry leaned back, emptied the mini-bottle and went to open the balcony door.

"Take a bottle from the bag and come here. I want us to sit on the balcony with a view of the town. I've just experienced déjà vu."

Sandra grabbed two glasses and the bottle and sat beside him with her back to the wall.

"Let's forget for a moment what the bastard did when he was alive. Let's drink a toast to Andrew Kensington." Harry filled their glasses.

They sat drinking in silence. Harry started laughing.

"Take Richard Manuel, musician with the Band. He had serious problems, not just with drinking but with . . . well, life. In the end he couldn't hack it, hanged himself in a hotel room. In his house they found two thousand bottles, all the same brand—Grand Marnier. That was all. D'you see? Fucking orange liqueur! There you have a man who had found his poison. Nicolas Cage—pah! It's a strange universe we live in . . ."

He thrust out a hand to Sydney's starry night sky, and they drank some more. Harry's eyes had started to blink when Sandra placed a hand on his cheek.

"Listen, Harry, I have to go back to work. I think you're ready for bed."

"What does a whole night cost?" Harry poured himself more whiskey.

"I don't think—"

"Stay here. Let's drink up, then we'll do it. I promise to come quickly." Harry sniggered.

"No, Harry. I'm going now." Sandra got up and stood with her arms crossed. Harry struggled to his feet, lost his balance and took two backward steps toward the balcony railing. Sandra caught him, he put his arms around her slender shoulders, leaned on her heavily and whispered: "Can't you keep an eye on me, Sandra? Just tonight. For Andrew's sake. What am I saying? For my sake."

"Teddy'll start wondering where I—"

"Teddy will get his money and keep his mouth shut. Please?"

Sandra paused, then sighed and said: "All right, but let's get these rags off you first, Mr. Holy."

She maneuvered him onto the bed, removed his shoes and pulled down his trousers. Miraculously, he managed to unbutton his shirt himself. Sandra's black miniskirt was over her head in a flash. She was even thinner without clothes, her shoulders and hips jutted out, and her ribs were like a washboard beneath her small breasts. When she went to switch off the room light Harry saw that she had bruising on her back and behind her thighs. She lay beside him and stroked his hairless chest and stomach.

Sandra smelled faintly of sweat and garlic. Harry stared at the ceiling. He was amazed that in his present state he had any sense of smell at all.

"The smell," he asked. "Is that you or the men you've had tonight?"

"Both, I assume," Sandra replied. "Does it bother you?"

"No," Harry answered without knowing for sure whether she meant the smell or the other men.

"You're pretty stewed, Harry. We don't need to—"

"Feel," Harry said, taking her hot, clammy hand and putting it between his legs.

Sandra laughed. "Strewth. And there was my mother telling me men who drink have only got big gobs."

"With me it's vice versa," Harry said. "Booze paralyzes my tongue, but inflates my dick. It's true. I don't know why, it's always been like that."

Sandra sat on him, pulled her flimsy panties to the side and drew him in without any fuss.

He watched her as she bounced up and down. She met his gaze, sent him a brief smile and looked away. It was the kind of smile you get when you're on the tram and inadvertently stare at someone for too long.

Harry closed his eyes, listened to the rhythmic creak of the bed and thought that it wasn't exactly true. Booze does paralyze everything. The sensitivity that made him think it would be quick, as he had promised, was gone. Sandra toiled away undaunted as Harry's thoughts slipped out from under the sheets, out of the bed and out of the window. He traveled beneath an upside-down starry sky across the sea until he reached a white stripe of sand on the coast.

As he came lower he saw the sea crashing onto a beach, and even lower, a town he had visited before and there was a girl he knew lying on the sand. She was asleep, and he landed gently beside her so as not to wake her. Then he lay down and closed his eyes. When he awoke the sun was setting and he was alone. On the promenade behind him people he thought he recognized were taking a stroll. Hadn't some of them been in films he had seen? Some wore sunglasses and were walking tiny, emaciated dogs on a lead by the tall hotel fronts that loomed on the other side of the street.

Harry padded down to the water's edge and was about to go into the water when he saw it was full of sea nettles. They lay on the surface stretching out long, red threads, and in the soft, jelly-like mirror reflection he could make out contours of faces. A motorboat was pounding against the sea, coming closer and closer, and suddenly Harry was awake. Sandra was shaking him.

"There's someone here!" she whispered. Harry heard someone pounding on the door.

"Bloody receptionist!" he said, jumping up with a pillow in front of him and opening the door.

It was Birgitta.

"Hi!" she said, but her smile froze when she saw Harry's tormented expression.

"What's the matter? Is there something wrong, Harry?"

"Yes," Harry said. "There is something wrong." His head was throbbing and every beat of his pulse made his mind go blank. "Why are you here?"

"They didn't ring. I waited and waited and then I rang home, but no one picked up. They probably misunderstood the time and rang while I was at work. Summer time and all that. They must have been confused by the time difference. Typical Dad."

She spoke quickly and was obviously trying to act as if it were the most natural thing in the world to stand in a hotel corridor in the middle of the night, chatting about trivia with a man who evidently was not going to let her in.

They stood looking at each other.

"Have you got someone in there?" she asked.

"Yes," Harry said. The slap sounded like a dry twig breaking.

"You're drunk!" she said. Tears were in her eyes.

"Listen, Birgitta—"

She shoved him hard and sent him flying backward into the room, and followed him in. Sandra already had her miniskirt in place; she was sitting on the bed trying to put on her shoes. Birgitta doubled up as if she had sudden abdominal pains.

"You whore!" she screamed.

"Right first time," Sandra replied drily. She was taking the scene with a great deal more calm than the other two, but still heading for a sharp exit.

"Grab your things and get out!" Birgitta shouted in a strangulated voice, throwing the handbag on the chair at Sandra. It hit the bed and disgorged its contents. Harry stood in the middle of the floor, naked and uncertain on his feet, and saw to his surprise a Pekinese sitting on his bed. Beside the fluffy object was a hairbrush, cigarettes, keys, a lump of shimmering, green kryptonite and the biggest selection of condoms Harry had ever seen. Sandra rolled her eyes, grabbed the Pekinese by the scruff of the neck and stuffed it back in the bag.

"What about the wonga, sweetie?" she said.

Harry didn't move, so she picked up his trousers and took out the wallet. Birgitta had collapsed on a chair and for a moment all that could be heard was Sandra's low, concentrated counting and Birgitta's half-stifled sobs.

"I'm outta here," Sandra said when she was happy and on her way.

"Wait!" Harry said, but it was too late. The door was slammed shut.

"Wait?!" Birgitta said. "Did you say wait?" she screamed, getting out of the chair. "You whoremonger, you bloody piss-artist. You've no right—"

Harry tried to put his arm round her, but she punched him away. They faced each other like two wrestlers. Birgitta seemed to be in some kind of trance; her eyes were glazed and blind with hatred and her mouth trembling with fury. It occurred to Harry that if she'd ever wanted to kill him she would have done it there and then, without any hesitation.

"Birgitta, I—"

"Drink yourself to death and get out of my life!" She turned on her heel and stormed out. The whole room shook as she slammed the door.

The phone rang. It was reception. "What's going on, Mr. Holy? The lady in the adjacent room to you has rung and—"

Harry cradled the receiver. A sudden, uncontrollable fury rose in him, and he cast around for something to smash. He snatched the whiskey bottle from the table and was about to launch it at the wall, but changed his mind at the last moment.

Lifelong training in self-control, he thought, opening the bottle and putting it to his mouth.

36

Room Service

There was a rattle of keys and Harry was woken by the door opening.

"No room service now. Please come back later!" Harry shouted into the pillow.

"Mr. Holy, I represent the management of this hotel."

Harry turned over. Two besuited individuals had entered the room. They stood at a respectful distance from the bed, but seemed very determined nonetheless. Harry recognized one as the receptionist from the previous night. The other continued.

"You have breached hotel rules, and I regret to say we are obliged to ask you to settle your account as soon as possible and leave the premises, Mr. Holy."

"Hotel rules?" Harry could feel he was about to spew.

The suit coughed. "You brought into your room a woman who, we suspect, was a . . . well, a prostitute. Not only that, you woke half the residents on this floor with your commotion. We are a respectable hotel and cannot condone this sort of behavior. I'm sure you understand, Mr. Holy."

Harry grunted by way of answer and turned his back on them.

"Fine, Mr. Management Representative. I'm leaving today anyway. Let me sleep in peace until I check out."

"You should already have checked out, Mr. Holy," said the receptionist.

Harry squinted at his watch. It was a quarter past two.

"We have been trying to wake you."

"My plane . . ." Harry said, bundling his legs out of the bed. After two attempts he had terra firma beneath his feet and stood up. He had forgotten he was naked, and the receptionist and the manager retreated in fright. Harry felt dizzy, the ceiling did a couple of circuits and he had to sit down on the edge of the bed again. Then he threw up.

BUBBUR

37

Two Bouncers

The waiter at Bourbon & Beef removed his untouched Eggs Benedict and sent the customer sympathetic looks. He had come here every morning for a week, read the paper and eaten his breakfast. Some days he had looked tired, true enough, but the waiter had never seen him in such a state as today. Furthermore, it had been almost half past two when he arrived.

"Hard night, sir?"

The customer sat with his suitcase beside him at the table staring into the middle distance, red-eyed and unshaven.

"Yeah. Yup, it was a hard night. I did . . . a lot."

"Good on ya. That's what King's Cross is for. Anything else, sir?"

"No thanks. I've got a plane to catch . . ."

The waiter listened with regret. He had begun to like the calm Norwegian who seemed a little lonely, but was friendly and gave handsome tips.

"Yes, I can see the suitcase. If that means it's the last time you'll be in for a while, this one's on me. Are you sure I can't offer you a bourbon, a Jack Daniel's? One for the road, as it were?"

The Norwegian looked up at him in surprise. As though

the waiter had just suggested something the customer had not managed to think of himself and which had been the obvious move all along.

"Make it a double, please."

Kristin had moved back to Oslo a few years later. Via friends Harry had gathered that she had a little girl of two, but that the English guy had been left in London. Then one evening he saw her at Sardines. Moving closer, he saw how changed she was. Her skin was pale and her hair hung limp. When she noticed him her face cracked into a kind of terror-stricken smile. He said hi to Kjartan beside her, a "musician friend" he thought he recognized. She spoke quickly and nervously about all sorts of inconsequential things, not letting Harry slip in the questions she knew he had. Then she talked about her future plans, but her eyes had no spark and the wildly gesticulating arms of the Kristin he remembered were replaced with slow, apathetic movements.

At one point Harry thought she was crying, but by then he was so drunk that he couldn't say for certain.

Kjartan had gone, returned and mumbled something in her ear, freeing himself from her embrace with a condescending smile to Harry. Then everyone had gone, and Harry and Kristin were left sitting in the empty room among cigarette packets and shards of glass until they were thrown out. It is not easy to say who supported whom through the door or who had suggested a hotel, but at any rate they ended up in the Savoy, where they made short work of the minibar and crawled into bed. Harry had dutifully made an ineffectual attempt to penetrate her, but it was too late. Of course it was too late. Kristin lay with her head buried in the pillow and wept. Harry had sneaked out when he woke and caught a taxi to the Postcafé, which opened an hour earlier than the other waterholes. Where he sat musing on just how late it was.

* * *

The owner of Springfield Lodge was called Joe, an overweight, easygoing guy who with thrift and prudence had run his small, slightly down-at-heel establishment in King's Cross for nearly twenty years. It was neither better nor worse than any other hotel at the lower end of the price range in this district, and he had few, if any, complaints. One of the reasons for this was that, as mentioned before, Joe was an easygoing guy. Another was that he always insisted on guests viewing the room first and he knocked off five dollars if they paid for more than one night. A third and perhaps conclusive reason was that he managed to keep the place fairly free of backpackers, drunks, drug addicts and prostitutes . . .

Even those turned away found it difficult not to like Joe. For at Springfield Lodge no one was met with glares or orders to get out; there was no more than a regretful smile and an apology that the hotel was full, there might be a cancellation in the following week and they were welcome to drop by again. Thanks to Joe's considerable ability to read faces and his swift, sure categorization of applicants, he performed this task without a moment's hesitation, and therefore seldom had any bother with argumentative types. Only on very rare occasions had Joe committed a blunder sizing up a potential customer, and he bitterly regretted it.

He recalled a couple of these incidents as he quickly summed up the contradictory impressions given by the tall, blond man before him. His plain quality clothing suggested he had money but didn't feel forced to part with it. The fact that he was a foreigner was a big plus; it was usually Australians who created problems. Backpackers with sleeping bags often meant wild parties and missing towels, but this man had a suitcase, and it seemed in good condition, which suggested he wasn't constantly on the move. True, he hadn't shaved but then it wasn't so long since his hair had seen the insides of a barber's shop. Moreover, his nails were clean and manicured, and his pupils were of relatively normal dimensions.

The upshot of all these impressions and the fact that the man had just placed a VISA card on the counter together with ID as a Norwegian policeman was that his usual "I'm sorry but" got stuck in his throat.

For there was no doubt the man was drunk. Smashed, even.

"I know you know I've had a few," said the man in surprisingly good, slurred English when he noticed Joe's hesitation. "Let's assume I go crazy in the room. Let's assume that. Break the TV and the bathroom mirror and throw up over the carpet. That sort of thing's happened before. Would a deposit of a thousand dollars cover it? In any case, I intend to keep myself so drunk I'll hardly be able to make much noise, annoy other guests or show my face in the corridors or reception."

"I'm afraid we're fully booked this week. Maybe—"

"Greg at Bourbon & Beef recommended this place and told me to pass on his regards to Joe. Is that you?"

Joe studied the man.

"Don't you make me regret this," he said, giving him the key to Room 73.

"Hello?"

"Hi, Birgitta, this is Harry. I—"

"I've got a visitor, Harry. Not a good time."

"I just wanted to say I didn't mean to—"

"Listen, Harry. I'm not angry and there's no damage done. Fortunately, hurt is limited when you've known a guy for scarcely a week, but I'd rather you didn't contact me anymore. OK?"

"Well, no, actually it isn't—"

"As I said, I've got a visitor, so I wish you luck with the rest of your stay and hope you return to Norway safe and sound. Bye."

. . .

"Bye."

Teddy Mongabi hadn't liked Sandra spending the night with the Scandinavian policeman. He thought it reeked of trouble. When he saw the man walking up Darlinghurst Road with rubber knees and drooping arms, his first instinct had been to step back and melt into the crowd. However, his curiosity overcame him and he crossed his arms and barred the way for the crazy Norwegian. The man tried to move past him, but Teddy grabbed his shoulder and spun him round.

"Don't you say hello to old friends, mate?"

The mate regarded him through dulled eyes. "The pimp . . ."

"I hope Sandra lived up to expectations, Officer."

"Sandra? Now let me see . . . Sandra was good. Where is she?"

"She's off this evening. But perhaps I can tempt the officer with something else?"

Harry lurched to find his balance.

"Right. Right. Come on, pimp. Tempt me."

Teddy laughed. "This way, Officer." He supported the drunken policeman down the stairs to the club and sat him at a table with a view of the stage. Teddy flicked his fingers and a scantily clad lady appeared straightaway.

"Two beers please, Amy. And ask Peri to dance for us."

"Next performance isn't until eight, Mr. Mongabi."

"Call it an extra performance. Now, Amy!"

"Right, Mr. Mongabi."

The police officer had a foolish grin on his face. "I know

who's coming," he said. "The murderer. The murderer's coming."

"Who?"

"Nick Cave."

"Nick Who?"

"And the blonde singer. She probably wears a wig as well. Listen . . ."

The pounding disco music had been switched off and the policeman held both forefingers in the air ready to conduct a symphony orchestra, but no sound came.

"I heard about Andrew," Teddy said. "Too awful for words. Just awful. My understanding was that he hanged himself. Why on earth would such a cheerful man—"

"Sandra wears a wig," the policeman said. "It fell out of her bag. That was why I didn't recognize her when I met her. Right here! Andrew and I were sitting over there. I'd seen her a couple of times in Darlinghurst before, but then she was wearing a wig. A blonde wig. Why doesn't she wear it anymore?"

"Aha, the police officer prefers blondes. Then I think I may have something you'll like . . ."

"Why?"

Teddy shrugged. "Sandra? Well, she was given a bit of a shaking by some bloke recently. Sandra maintained it was something to do with the wig and decided to give it a miss for a while. In case he showed up again."

"Who?"

"I don't know, Officer. And if I did, I wouldn't say. In our line of work discretion is a virtue. Which I'm sure you also appreciate. I'm so bad at names, but isn't your name Ronny?"

"Harry. I have to talk to Sandra." He struggled to his feet and almost knocked over the tray of beer Amy was carrying. He slumped across the table. "Have you got a phone number, pimp?"

Teddy waved Amy away. "On principle we don't give clients the addresses or phone numbers of our girls. For safety reasons. You understand, don't you?" Teddy was regretting not following his first instincts—he should have kept away from the drunken and difficult Norwegian.

"I understand. Gimme the number."

Teddy smiled. "As I said, we don't give—"

"Now!" Harry grabbed the lapels of the shiny gray suit jacket and blew a mixture of whiskey breath and vomit stench into Teddy's face. An ingratiating string arrangement oozed from the speakers.

"I'll count to three, Officer. If you haven't let go by then I'll call for Ivan and Geoff. That will mean an aerial exit through the back door. Outside the back door there's a flight of steps. Twenty steep concrete steps."

Harry grinned and tightened his grip. "Is that supposed to frighten me, you bloody pimp bastard? Look at me. I'm so pissed I can't feel a thing. I'm fuckin' indestructible, man. Geoff! Ivan!"

Shadows stirred behind the bar. As he turned his head to look, Teddy jerked himself free from Harry's grip. He shoved and Harry reeled backward. He took his chair and the table with him as he crashed to the floor. Instead of getting up he stayed where he was, chuckling, until Geoff and Ivan arrived and sent Teddy an inquiring look.

"Get him out the back door," Teddy said, watching as the policeman was picked up like a rag doll and thrown over the shoulder of a black bruiser in a dinner jacket.

"I don't bloody know what's wrong with people today," Teddy said, straightening his crease-free suit jacket.

Ivan led the way and opened the door.

"What the hell's this bloke had?" Geoff said. "He's laughing so much he's shaking."

"Have to see how long he laughs then," Ivan said. "Put him down here."

Geoff lowered Harry to his feet, and he stood swaying in front of the two men.

"Can you keep a secret, mister?" Ivan said with a bashful smile. "I know this is a gangster cliché, but I hate violence."

Geoff sniggered.

"Cut it out, Geoff. I really do. Just ask anyone who knows me. He can't stand it, they'll tell you. Ivan can't sleep, gets depressed. The world is a tough enough place for any poor sod without us making things worse by breaking arms and legs, isn't it. So. So just go home, and we won't make any more trouble here. OK?"

Harry nodded and fumbled in his pockets for something.

"Even though you're the gangster this evening," Ivan said. "You!"

He poked a forefinger in Harry's chest.

"You!" Ivan repeated and shoved a bit harder. The blond police officer teetered perilously.

"You!"

Harry stood rocking on his heels and waving his arms. He hadn't turned to see what was behind him, he seemed to know already. A smile spread across his face as his glazed eyes met Ivan's. He fell backward and groaned as he hit the first steps. Not a sound emerged the rest of the way down.

38

A Bloke Called Speedy

Joe heard the scratching at the front door, and peering through the glass at the new guest, bent double, he knew he'd made one of his rare mistakes. When he opened the door the guest collapsed against him. Had it not been for Joe's low center of gravity they both would have taken a tumble. Joe managed to get Harry's arm across his shoulder and drag him to a chair in reception where he could examine him closer. Not that the blond drunk had been a pretty sight when he checked in, but now he really did look bad. He had a deep gash on one elbow—Joe could see red flesh gleaming through—one cheek was swollen and blood was dripping from his nose onto filthy trousers. His shirt was torn and his chest rattled whenever he breathed. But at least he did—breathe.

"What happened?" Joe said.

"Fell down some stairs. No damage done, just need to rest a bit."

Joe was no doctor, but judging from the breathing sounds he reckoned a rib or two had gone. He found some antiseptic ointment and plasters, patched up the guest as best he could and finally pushed some cotton wool up one nostril. Harry shook his head when Joe tried to give him a painkiller.

"Painkiller stuff in my room," he gasped.

"You need a doctor," Joe said. "I'll—"

"No doctor. I'll be fine in a couple of hours."

"Your breathing doesn't sound good."

"Never has. Asthma. Give me a couple of hours in bed and I'll be out of your hair."

Joe sighed. He knew he was about to make mistake number two.

"Forget it," he said. "You need more than a couple of hours. Anyway, it's not your fault that steps are so bloody steep in Sydney. I'll pop up in the morning."

He helped the guest to his room, settled him on the bed and removed his shoes. On the table there were three empty and two unopened bottles of Jim Beam. Joe was teetotal, but had lived long enough to know that you couldn't discuss anything with an alcoholic. He opened one of the bottles and put it on the bedside table. The bloke would be feeling awful when he woke up at all events.

"Crystal Castle. Hello."

"Hello, may I speak to Margaret Dawson?"

"Speaking."

"I can help your son if you tell me he killed Inger Holter."

"What?! Who is this?"

"A friend. You have to trust me, Mrs. Dawson. If not, your son's lost. Do you understand? Did he kill Inger Holter?"

"What is this? Is this supposed to be a joke? Who is Inger Holter?"

"You're Evans's mother, Mrs. Dawson. Inger Holter also had a mother. You and I are the only ones who can help your son. Tell me he killed Inger Holter! Do you hear me?!"

"I can hear you've been drinking. Now I'm going to ring the police."

"Say it!"

"I'm putting the phone down now."

"Say it . . . Bloody cow!"

Alex Tomaros put his arms behind his head and leaned back in the chair as Birgitta came into the office.

"Sit down, Birgitta."

She sat on the chair in front of Tomaros's modest desk, and Alex used the opportunity to study her more closely. He thought she looked tired. She had black bags under her eyes, seemed irritated and was even paler than normal.

"I was interviewed by a policeman a few days ago, Birgitta. A certain Mr. Holy, a foreigner. In the course of the conversation it emerged that he'd been speaking to some of the staff here and had information of . . . er, an indiscreet kind. We're all interested, naturally, in the person who killed Inger Holter being found, but I would just like to draw your attention to the fact that any similar statements in the future will be interpreted as . . . disloyal. And I don't need to tell you that, trade being tough right now, we cannot afford to pay people we don't feel we can trust."

Birgitta said nothing.

"A man rang earlier today and I happened to pick up the phone. He did try to distort his voice by slurring, but I recognized the accent. It was Mr. Holy again, and he asked to speak to you, Birgitta."

Birgitta's head shot up. "Harry? Today?"

Alex took off his glasses. "You know I have a soft spot for you, Birgitta, and I admit I've taken this . . . er, leak a bit personally. I had hoped that in time we might become good friends. So, don't be stupid and destroy everything."

"Did he ring from Norway?"

"I wish I could confirm that he had, but sad to say it sounded like an extremely local line. You know very well that I have nothing to hide, Birgitta, nothing with any relevance for this case at any rate. And that's what they're after, isn't it? It won't help Inger if you blab about all the other stuff. So, can I rely on you, my dear Birgitta?"

"What is all the other stuff, Alex?"

He appeared surprised. "I thought Inger might have told you. About the drive."

"What drive?"

"After work. I thought Inger was giving me quite a lot of encouragement and things got somewhat out of hand. All I was going to do was drive her home and I didn't mean to frighten her, but she took my little joke a bit too literally, I'm afraid."

"I have no idea what you're talking about, Alex, and I'm not sure I want to, either. Did Harry say where he was? Was he going to ring back?"

"Hey, hey, wait a moment. You're on first-name terms with the man and your cheeks color up whenever I mention him. What's actually going on here? Is there something between you two, or what?"

Birgitta rubbed her hands in anguish.

He leaned across the desk and put out a hand to pat her on the head, but she slapped it away with an irritated gesture.

"Cut that out, Alex. You're an idiot, and I've told you that before. Be less of an idiot the next time he calls, please. And ask where I can get hold of him, right?" She got up and stomped out.

Speedy could scarcely believe his eyes when he entered the Cricket. Borroughs, behind the bar, shrugged his shoulders.

"He's been sitting there for two hours," he said. "He's seriously tanked."

Right in the corner at their regular table sat the man

who was the indirect cause of two of his pals ending up in the hospital. Speedy felt the new HK .45 ACP pistol in his calf holster and walked over to the table. The man's chin had fallen onto his chest and he seemed to be asleep. A half-empty whiskey bottle was on the table in front of him.

"Hi," Speedy shouted.

The man slowly raised his head and sent him an imbecilic smile.

"I've been waiting for you," he slurred.

"You're sitting at the wrong table," said Speedy, and stood his ground. He had a busy evening ahead of him and couldn't risk being delayed by this idiot. Customers could come in at any moment.

"I want you to tell me something first," said the man.

"Why should I?" Speedy felt the pistol pressing against his trouser leg.

"Because this is where you keep shop, because you just came in the door and therefore this is the time of the day when you're at your most vulnerable because you have the goods on you and because you don't want me to search you in front of all these witnesses. Stay where you are."

It was only now that Speedy saw the muzzle of the Hi-Power which the man was holding in his lap and nonchalantly pointing straight at him.

"What do you want to know?"

"I want to know how often Andrew Kensington bought off you and when he made his last purchase."

"Have you got a tape recorder on you, cop?"

The cop smiled. "Relax. Testimonies made under threat of a gun don't count. The worst that can happen is that I shoot you."

"OK, OK."

Speedy could feel himself beginning to sweat. He weighed up the distance to his calf holster.

"Unless what I've heard is lies, he's dead. So it can't hurt, can it. He was cautious, he didn't want too much. He bought twice a week, one bag each time. Fixed routine."

"When was the last time he bought before playing cricket here?"

"Three days before. He was going to buy the next day."

"Did he ever buy from others?"

"Never. That I do know. This kind of thing is personal—a confidential matter, so to speak. Besides, he was a policeman and could hardly risk exposure."

"So when he was here he was almost out of junk? Yet several days later he had enough for an overdose that would probably have killed him if a cable hadn't done it for him. How do you get that to tally?"

"He ended up in hospital. It was the need for junk that made him leg it. Who knows, maybe he had some in reserve anyway."

The cop sighed, exhausted. "You're right," he said, putting the pistol in the inside pocket of his jacket and grabbing the glass in front of him. "Everything in this world is permeated with these *maybe*s. Why can't someone just cut through the crap and say this is how it is, full stop, two and two are whatever they are and that's that. It would make life easier for a whole lot of people, believe me."

Speedy started to raise his trouser leg, but changed his mind.

"And what happened to the syringe?" the cop mumbled as though to himself.

"What?" said Speedy.

"We never found a syringe at the crime scene. Maybe he flushed it down the toilet. As you said—a cautious man. Even when he was about to die."

"Are you sharing?" Speedy asked, taking a seat.

"It's your liver," the cop said, sliding the bottle over.

39

The Lucky Country

Harry ran through the smoke into the tight passage. The band was playing so loud everything around him was vibrating. There was a sour smell of sulphur, and the clouds were hanging so low that he was banging into them with his head. Through the wall of noise one sound could still be heard, an intense grinding which had found an unoccupied frequency. It was the grinding of teeth on teeth and chains being dragged along the tarmac. A pack of dogs bayed behind him.

The passage became narrower and narrower, and in the end he had to run with his arms out in front so as not to get wedged between the high red walls. He looked up. From windows way above the brick walls small heads protruded. They were waving green and gold flags and singing to the deafening music.

"This is the lucky country, this is the lucky country, we live in the lucky country."

Harry heard gnashing behind him. He screamed and fell. To his surprise everything around him was dark, and instead of a rough landing on tarmac he continued to fall. He must have tumbled into a pit. And either Harry was moving very slowly or the pit was very deep because he was still in motion. The music at the surface became more and more distant, and as his eyes adapted to the darkness he saw that the sides of the pit had windows through which he could see into other people.

Jeez, am I going to fall right the way through the earth? Harry wondered.

"You're Swedish," said a woman's voice.

Harry looked around, and as he did so, the light and the music returned. He was standing in an open square, it was night, and a band was playing on a stage behind him. He was facing a shop window, a TV shop window, to be more precise, with a dozen different sets tuned to a variety of channels.

"So you're out celebrating Australia Day as well, are you?" said another voice, a man's this time, in a familiar language.

Harry turned. A couple were smiling encouragement. He ordered his mouth to maintain the smile, hoping the order would be obeyed. A certain facial tension suggested he still had control over this bodily function. Others he had had to give up on. His subconscious had rebelled and at this very moment there was a battle for his sight and hearing. His brain was working at full capacity to find out what was happening, but it wasn't easy, because it was being bombarded all the time by distorted and sometimes absurd information.

"We're Danish, by the way. My name's Poul and this is my wife, Gina."

"Why do you think I'm Swedish?" Harry heard himself say. The Danish couple looked at each other.

"You were talking to yourself. Weren't you aware of that? You were watching TV and wondering whether Alice would fall right the way through the earth. And she did, didn't she? Ha ha!"

"Oh yes, she did," Harry said, completely baffled.

"It's not like a Scandinavian midsummer's night, is it. This is just laughable. You can hear rockets going off, but you can't see a thing because of the mist. For all we know, the rockets might have set fire to some of the skyscrapers. Ha ha! Can you smell the powder? It's the dampness that causes it to settle on the ground. Are you a tourist here as well?"

Harry had a think. It must have been a really good think, because when he was ready to answer the Danes had gone.

He redirected his attention to the TV screens. Burning trees on one screen and tennis on another. In a news program they were showing pictures of windsurfers, a woman weeping and parts of a yellow wetsuit with massive bite marks. On the adjacent TV set blue-and-white police tape fluttered in the wind at the edge of the forest as uniformed officers went back and forth with bags. Then a large, pale face filled the screen. It was a bad photo of an unattractive, young blonde girl. There was a sad expression in her eyes as though she were upset she wasn't more attractive.

"Attractive," Harry said. "Strange business. Did you know that . . . ?"

Lebie passed behind a police officer who was being interviewed on camera.

"Shit," Harry shouted. "Bloody hell!" He banged his palm on the shop window. "Turn up the sound! Turn up the volume in there! Someone . . ."

The picture had changed to a weather map of the east coast of Australia. Harry pressed his nose against the glass until it was squashed, and in the reflection of one unused screen he saw the face of John Belushi.

"Was that something I was imagining, John? Remember I'm under the influence of a very strong hallucinogenic drug right now."

"Let me in! I have to talk to her."

"Go home and sleep it off. We don't let drunks . . . Hey!"

"Let me in! I'm telling you I'm a friend of Birgitta's. She works at the bar."

"We know that, but our job is to keep people like you out, do you understand, blondie?"

"Ow!"

"Go quietly now, or I'll be forced to break your arm, you . . . Ow! Bob! Bob!"

"Sorry, but I'm sick of being manhandled. Have a nice evening."

"What is it, Nicky? Is it him over there?"

"Let him go. Shit! He just wriggled out of my hold and punched me in the guts. Give me a hand, will you?"

"This town's falling apart at the seams. Think I'm gonna move back to bloody Melbourne. Did you see the news? Another girl raped and strangled. They found her this afternoon in Centennial Park."

40

Skydiving

Harry woke with a splitting headache. The light hurt his eyes, and no sooner had he registered that he was lying under a blanket than he had to throw himself to the side. The vomit came in quick spurts and the contents of his stomach splashed on the stone floor. He fell back on the bench and felt the gall sting his nose as he asked himself the classic question: where on earth am I?

The last thing he could remember was that he had gone into Green Park, and the stork had looked accusingly at him. Now he seemed to be in a circular room with some benches and a couple of big wooden tables. Along the walls hung tools, spades, rakes and a garden hose, and in the middle of the floor there was a drain.

"Good morning, white brother," said a deep voice he recognized. "*Very* white brother," he said as he approached. "Stay where you are."

It was Joseph, the gray Aboriginal man from the Crow people.

He turned on a tap by the wall, took the hose and sprayed the vomit down the drain.

"Where am I?" Harry asked, to start somewhere.

"In Green Park."

"But . . ."

"Relax. I've got the keys here. This is my second home." He peered through a window. "It's a nice day outside. What's left of it."

Harry looked up at Joseph. He seemed to be in a sensationally good mood for a bum.

"The parkie and I have known each other a while, and we have a kind of special arrangement," Joseph explained. "Sometimes he pulls a sickie and I take care of what has to be done—pick up litter, empty bins, cut the grass, that sort of thing. In return I can kip here now and again. Sometimes he leaves me some tucker as well, but not today, I'm afraid."

Harry tried to think of something other than "but" to say, but gave up. Joseph, on the other hand, was in a talkative mood.

"If I'm honest, what I like best about this deal is that it gives me something to do. It fills the day and makes me think about other things, kind of. Sometimes I even think I'm making myself useful."

Joseph beamed and waggled his head. Harry couldn't comprehend that this was the same person who'd been sitting in a comatose state on the bench just a short time ago and with whom he had been vainly trying to communicate.

"I couldn't believe it when I saw you yesterday," Joseph said. "That you were the same person who'd been sitting so sober and upright and I had bummed ciggies off a few days before. And yesterday it was bloody impossible to talk to you. Ha ha!"

"Touché," Harry said.

Joseph left and returned with a bag of hot chips and a cup of Coke. He watched Harry gingerly consuming the simple but astonishingly effective meal.

"The precursor to Coca-Cola was discovered by an

American chemist who wanted to concoct a remedy for hangovers," Joseph said. "But he reckoned he'd failed and sold the recipe on for eight dollars. If you ask me no one has found anything better."

"Jim Beam," Harry answered between mouthfuls.

"Yes, apart from Jim. And Jack and Johnnie and a couple of other blokes. Ha ha. How do you feel?"

"Better."

Joseph put two bottles on the table. "Hunter Valley's cheapest red wine," he said. "Will you have a glass with me, whitie?"

"Thanks, Joseph, but red wine's not my . . . Have you got anything else? A brown something, for example?"

"Think I keep a stock, do you?"

Joseph seemed a bit affronted that Harry had refused his generous offer.

Harry got up with difficulty. He attempted to reconstruct the gap in his memory between pointing his gun at Rod Stewart and their literally falling around each other's necks and sharing some acid. He was unable to pinpoint what had led to such utter bliss and mutual attraction, except the self-explanatory—Jim Beam. However, he was able to remember that he had punched the bouncer at the Albury.

"Harry Hole, you are a pathetic piss-artist," he muttered.

They went outside and flopped down on the grass. The sun stung his eyes and the alcohol from the previous day stung in the pores of his skin, but otherwise it was in fact not bad at all. A light breeze was blowing, and they lay on their backs gazing at the white puffs of cloud drifting across the sky.

"It's jumping weather today," Joseph said.

"I have no intention of jumping," Harry said. "I'm going to lie perfectly still or tiptoe around at the very worst."

Joseph squinted into the light. "I wasn't thinking of that kind of jumping, I was thinking of sky-jumping, skydiving."

"Wow, are you a skydiver?"

Joseph nodded.

Harry shielded his eyes and looked up at the sky. "What about the clouds? Aren't they a problem?"

"Not at all. They're cirrus clouds, feather clouds, about fifteen thousand feet up."

"You surprise me, Joseph. Not that I know what a skydiver should look like, but I wouldn't have imagined that he's . . ."

"A drunk?"

"For example."

"Ha ha. That's two sides of the same coin."

"Do you mean that?"

"Have you ever been alone in the air, Harry? Have you flown? Have you jumped from a great height and felt the air trying to hold you up, to catch you and caress your body?"

Joseph was already well on his way down the first bottle, and his voice had assumed a warmer tone. His eyes gleamed as he described the beauty of free fall to Harry.

"It opens all your senses. Your whole body screams that you can fly. 'And I haven't got any wings,' it shouts to you, trying to drown the wind whistling past your ears. Your body is convinced it's going to die and goes into full-alarm mode—opens all its senses to the max to see if any of them can find a way out. Your brain is the world's biggest computer, it registers everything: your skin feels the temperature rising as you fall, your ears notice the increase in pressure and you become aware of every furrow and hue in the map below. You can even *smell* the planet as it comes nearer. And if you can push mortal fear to the back of your mind, Harry, for an instant you're an angel. You're living a life in forty seconds."

"And if you can't?"

"You don't push it away, just to the back of your mind. Because it has to be there, like a clear, strident note, like cold water on your skin. It's not the fall but the mortal fear that opens your senses. It starts as a shock, an adrenaline rush through your veins as you leave the plane. Like an injection. Then it mingles with your blood and makes you feel happy and strong. If you close your eyes you can see it as a wonderful poisonous snake lying there and watching you with its snake eyes."

"You're making it sound like dope, Joseph."

"It *is* dope!" Joseph was gesticulating wildly now. "That's just what it is. You want the fall to last forever, and if you've been skydiving for a while, you notice that pulling the ripcord becomes harder and harder. In the end you're scared that one day you'll overdose, that you won't pull it, and so you stop jumping. And that's when you know you're hooked. Abstinence eats away at you, life appears meaningless, trivial, and in the end you find yourself squeezed behind the pilot of a small, ancient Cessna, taking an eternity to climb to ten thousand feet and consuming all your savings."

Joseph took a deep breath and closed his eyes.

"In a nutshell, Harry, they're two sides of the same coin. Life becomes a living hell, but the alternative is even worse. Ha ha."

Joseph raised himself on his elbows and took a slug of wine.

"I'm a flightless bird. Do you know what an emu is, Harry?"

"An Australian ostrich."

"Clever boy."

When Harry closed his eyes he heard Andrew's voice. Because, of course, it was Andrew lying next to him on the grass and sermonizing about what was important and what was less important.

"Have you heard the story about why the emu can't fly?"

Harry shook his head.

"OK, stick with me, Harry. In the Dreamtime the emu had wings and could fly. He and his wife lived by a lake where their daughter had married Jabiru, a stork. One day Jabiru and his wife had been out fishing and brought home a wonderfully big catch; they ate almost everything and in their haste forgot to leave the best bits for her parents, as they usually did. When the daughter took the remains of the fish to her father, Emu, he was furious. 'Don't I always give you the best bits when I've been hunting?' he said. He grabbed his club and a spear, and flew to Jabiru to give him a sound beating.

"Jabiru, however, was not of a mind to let himself be beaten without offering any resistance, so he took a huge branch and knocked the club away. Then he hit his father-in-law first on the left and then on the right, breaking both wings. Emu crawled to his feet and slung the spear at his daughter's husband. It pierced his back and exited through his mouth. Beside himself with pain, the stork flew to the marshes where it transpired the spear was useful for catching fish. Emu went to the dry plains, where you can see it running around with the stumps of broken wings, unable to fly."

Joseph put the bottle to his lips, but there were only a few drops left. He eyed the bottle with an aggrieved expression and replaced the cork. Then he opened the second.

"Is that more or less the same as your story, Joseph?"

"Well, er . . ."

The bottle gurgled, and he was ready.

"I worked as a parachute instructor up in Cessnok for eight years. We were a great bunch, excellent working atmosphere. No one got rich, neither us nor the owners; the club was driven by sheer enthusiasm. Most of the money we earned as instructors was spent on our own jumps. I was a good instructor. Some thought I was the best. Nonetheless they stripped me of my license because of one unfortunate incident. They maintained I was drunk during one skydive with a course participant. As though I would have spoiled a jump by drinking!"

"What happened?"

"What do you mean? Do you want the details?"

"You a bit busy?"

"Ha ha. OK, I'll tell you."

The bottle glistened in the sun.

"OK, this is how it was. It was an improbable convergence of ill-starred circumstances that did it, not a stiffener or two. First of all, there was the weather. As we took off there was a layer of cloud at about eight thousand feet. That's no problem if the clouds are so high because you mustn't pull the rip cord before four thousand feet. The important thing is that students see the ground after the parachute has been released, so they don't go crazy and head for Newcastle. They have to be able to see the ground signals to know where they should steer according to wind and terrain to land safely in the drop zone, right? When we took off it was true there were a few clouds coming in, but they still seemed some way off. The problem was that the club used an ancient Cessna held together with gaffer tape, prayers and goodwill. It took more than twenty minutes to reach ten thousand feet, the height at which we would jump. After takeoff the wind picked up, and when we passed the clouds at eight thousand feet, it blew a second layer of cloud in beneath us, which we didn't see. Understand?"

"Didn't you have contact with the ground? Couldn't they tell you about the low clouds?"

"Radio, yes. Ha ha. That was another matter that was hushed up afterward. You see, the pilot always played the Stones in the cockpit at full blast when we reached ten thousand feet, to get the students going, make them aggressive instead of shit-scared. If they did send us a message from the ground we never received it."

"Didn't you even make a final check with them before jumping?"

"Harry, don't make this story more complicated than it already is. All right?"

"All right."

"The second thing that went wrong was the mess with the altimeter. It has to be set to zero before the plane takes off so that it shows the height relative to the ground. The moment we were due to jump I discovered I had left my altimeter down below, but the pilot always had full parachute equipment with him, so I borrowed his. He was as afraid as the rest of us that the plane would suddenly fall apart one day. We were already at ten thousand feet so we had to move fast. I had to hurry onto the wing and didn't have time to check my altimeter against the student's—which of course I had checked was set to zero on the ground. I assumed the pilot's meter would be more or less accurate, even though he didn't set it to zero every time we took off. That didn't bother me too much—when you've done more than five thousand jumps, as I had, you can judge the height visually to a reasonable degree of accuracy by looking down.

"We were standing on the wing, and the student had three good jumps behind him, so I wasn't concerned. No problem with the exit, we jumped with arms and legs splayed and he was floating fine, quite stable, as we raced through the first cloud cover. I had a shock when I saw the second layer beneath us, but I thought we would just perform the activities we had and see how high we were as we approached. The student did some regulation ninety-degree turns and horizontal moves before returning to the standard X-shape. My altimeter was showing six thousand feet when the student went to pull his rip cord, so I signaled he should wait. He looked at me, but it isn't so easy to read the facial expressions of a bloke with his cheeks and lips flapping round his ears like wet linen on a clothes line in a gale."

Joseph paused and nodded contentedly.

"Wet linen on a clothes line in a gale," he repeated. "Not bad at all. Cheers."

The bottle was tilted up.

"I read five thousand feet on my altimeter as we hit the second layer," he continued, after regaining his breath. "A thousand to go before we pulled. I grabbed hold of the student and kept an eye on the altimeter in case the cloud was thick and we had to pull the chutes in the cloud, but we were out again in a flash. My heart stopped when I saw the ground racing toward us; trees, grass, tarmac, it was like zooming in with a camera. I pulled for both of us at once. Had either of the main chutes failed there wouldn't have been time to activate the reserve chute. Turned out the low cloud was at something closer to two thousand feet. People below went pretty pale when they saw us emerging from the cloud without chutes. On top of that, the idiot of a student panicked after his chute opened and managed to steer himself into a tree. That didn't matter in itself, but he was left hanging four meters above the ground, and instead of waiting for help to arrive, he unhooked himself, fell and broke his leg. He made an official complaint saying I'd smelled of alcohol, and the club committee took a decision. I was given a lifetime suspension."

Joseph finished off bottle number two.

"What happened then?"

"This." He tossed the bottle away. "Social security, bad colleagues and bad wine." He had begun to slur. "They broke my wings, Harry. I'm from the Crow tribe; I'm not made to live like an emu."

The shadows in the park had huddled together; now they were beginning to lengthen. Harry woke up with Joseph standing over him.

"I'm off home now, Harry. You might want a couple of things from the pavilion before I hop it."

"Oh shit, yes. My gun. And my jacket."

Harry got up. It was time for a drink. After Joseph had

locked up they stood shuffling their feet and sucking their teeth.

"So you reckon you'll be heading back to Norway soon, do you?" Joseph said.

"Any day now, yes."

"Hope you catch the plane this time."

"Thought I'd ring the airline this afternoon. And my workplace. They're probably wondering what's happened to me."

"Oh shit," Joseph said, smacking his forehead. He took out his keys again. "I reckon there's too much tannin in the red wine I drink. It corrodes the brain cells. I can never remember whether I've switched off the light or not, and the parkie gets pretty angry if he comes and finds the light's been left on."

He unlocked the door. The light was off.

"Ha ha. You know how it is when you know a place inside out, you switch off the light automatically, you don't even think about it. And then you can't bloody remember whether you've done it or not . . . isn't that crazy, Harry?"

Harry's back had stiffened and he stared at Joseph.

41

A Baroque Sofa

The caretaker at St. George's Theatre shook his head with incredulity and poured more coffee for Harry.

"I've never seen the l-like. It's full here every single night. When they do the guillotine number people go berserk, scream and carry on. Now it's even on the poster: 'Deadly guillotine—as seen on TV and in the press. It's killed before . . .' Christ, it's become the star of the show. Strange business."

"Strange business indeed. So they've found a replacement for Otto Rechtnagel and perform the same show?"

"More or less, yes. They've never had anywhere near as much s-success before."

"What about the number with the cat that gets shot?"

"They dropped that one. Didn't seem to appeal."

Harry squirmed. The sweat was pouring down the inside of his shirt. "Mm, never quite understood why they had that number . . ."

"It was Rechtnagel's idea. I had a go at being a c-clown in my youth, so I like to keep an eye on what's happening onstage when the circus is in t-town, and I remember that number wasn't part of the show until the rehearsal the previous day."

"Yes, I had a feeling Otto was behind it."

Harry scratched his shaven chin.

"I've got a problem gnawing away at me. I wonder if you can help. I might be barking up the wrong tree, but listen to this theory and tell me what you think. Otto knows I'm in the auditorium, he knows something I don't know which he has to try and tell me, but he can't say it openly. For a variety of different reasons. Perhaps because he himself is involved. So this number is cooked up for me. He wants to tell me that the person I'm hunting is a hunter himself, that he's someone like me, a colleague. I know that sounds a bit weird, but you know how eccentric Otto could be. What do you think? Does that sound like him?"

The caretaker studied Harry for some time.

"Officer, I think you should help yourself to a bit more c-coffee. That number wasn't trying to tell you anything. It's a c-classic Jandy Jandaschewsky number. Anyone in a circus can t-tell you that. Nothing more, nothing less. Sorry if that ruins things for you, but—"

"On the contrary," Harry said, relieved. "In fact, that's what I'd hoped to hear. Now I can safely exclude that theory. Was there more coffee, did you say?"

He asked to see the guillotine, and the caretaker took him to the props room.

"I still get shivers down my spine whenever I walk in here, but now at least I sleep at n-night," the caretaker said, unlocking the door. "The room's been scrubbed down since."

A cold rush of air came out as the door opened.

"Togs on," said the caretaker, pressing the light switch. The guillotine towered over the room with a rug over it, like a reclining diva.

"Togs on?"

"Oh, just an in-joke. We usually say that at St. George's when we enter a d-dark room. Yup."

"Why's that?" Harry raised the rug and felt the blade of the guillotine.

"Oh, it's an old yarn dating back to the 1970s. The boss here at that time was a Belgian, Albert Mosceau, a hot-blooded man, but those of us who worked under him liked him well enough, he was a genuine theater person, bless his soul. People say, as you know, that theater types are terrible philanderers and l-libertines, and that may be true, well, I'm just saying how it is. Anyway, in those days we had a famous, handsome actor in the company, n-no names mentioned, who was an old goat. The women swooned, and the men were jealous. Now and then we used to do a tour of the theater for people who asked, and one day the guide came with a class of k-kids to the props room. He switched on the light—and there he was on the baroque sofa we used for Tennessee Williams's *The Glass Menagerie*, rooting one of the canteen ladies.

"Now the guide could of course have saved the day, for the famous actor, no names mentioned, was lying on his front. But the guide was a stripling who hoped to become an actor himself one day and was, like most theater people, a vain galoot. So he wasn't wearing glasses even though he was very short-sighted. Anyway, to cut to the chase, he didn't see that things were happening on the sofa and he must have thought the sudden thronging at the door was because he was such a damned good talker, or something like that. As the guide continued waffling on about Tennessee Williams, the old goat swore, making sure not to show his face though, just his hairy arse. But the guide recognized the voice and exclaimed: 'Goodness, is that you there, Bruce Lieslington?'"

The caretaker chewed his lower lip.

"Oooh dear."

Harry laughed and held up his palms. "It's OK. I've forgotten the name already."

"Anyway, next day Mosceau called a meeting. He explained what had happened and said he considered it a very serious matter. 'We can't have this kind of publicity,' he said. 'So I'm sorry to say that, with immediate effect, there will be a b-ban on this kind of g-g-guided tour.'"

The caretaker's laughter resounded against the walls of the props room. Harry had to smile. Only the reclining diva in steel and wood was as silent and unapproachable.

"Now I understand the 'togs on.' What happened to the luckless guide? Did he become an actor in the end?"

"Unfortunately for him and fortunately for the stage, no. But he stayed in the industry and today he's the lighting engineer here at St. George's. Oh yes, I forgot, you've met him . . ."

Harry breathed in slowly. Down below there was a growling and jerking at the chains. Shit, shit, shit, it was so hot!

"Yes, that's right. He probably wears contact lenses now, doesn't he?"

"Nope. He claims he works better if he sees the s-stage in a blur. Says he can concentrate on the totality instead of getting hung up on details. He's a really strange b-bloke."

"Strange bloke indeed," said Harry.

"Yes?"

"Sorry to ring so late, Lebie. This is Harry Holy."

"Holy? Christ, what time is it in Norway now?"

"No idea. Listen, I'm not in Norway. There was some trouble with the plane."

"What was that?"

"It left early, let me put it like that, and it hasn't been easy to get another seat. I need some help."

"Spit it out."

"You have to meet me in Otto Rechtnagel's flat. Bring a crowbar if you're no good with picklocks."

"OK. Right away?"

"That'd be nice. Appreciate it, mate."

"Was sleeping badly anyway."

"Hello?"

"Dr. Engelsohn? I have a question about a body. My name's—"

"I don't give a damn who you are, it's . . . three o'clock in the morning, and you can ask Dr. Hansson, who's on duty. Goodnight."

"Are you deaf? I said Goo—"

"This is Holy. Don't ring off again, please."

. . .

"*The* Holy?"

"I'm glad that you seem to have remembered my name at last, Doctor. I've discovered something interesting in the flat where Andrew Kensington was found dead. I have to see him—that is, I have to see the clothes he was wearing when he died. You do still have them, don't you?"

"Yes, but—"

"Meet me outside the mortuary in half an hour."

"My dear Mr. Holy, I really can't see that—"

"Don't make me repeat myself, Doctor. How would you like to be struck off by the Australian Medical Association, sued by relatives, and then there are the newspaper headlines . . . shall I go on?"

"Well, I can't get there in half an hour."

"There's very little traffic at this time of night, Doctor. I have a suspicion you'll make it."

42

A Visitor

McCormack went into the office, closed the door behind him and took up a stance by the window. Sydney's summer weather certainly was changeable; it had rained all night. McCormack was over sixty, had passed police retirement age and had, as pensioners are wont to do, started to talk to himself.

Mostly it was minor everyday observations he doubted others apart from himself really knew how to appreciate. Such as: "Looks like it's going to clear up today as well, yep." He stood rocking back and forth on his heels looking across his town. Or: "First to arrive again today, oh yes."

Only as he was hanging his jacket in the wardrobe behind the desk did he notice the sounds coming from the sofa. A man was levering himself up into a sitting position.

"Holy?" McCormack stared in amazement.

"Sorry, sir. Hope it was all right to borrow your sofa . . ."

"How did you get in?"

"I never had time to return my ID, so the night porter let me in. The door to your office was open, and since it was you I wanted to talk to I had a nap here."

"You should be in Norway. Your boss called. You look terrible, Holy."

"What did you tell him, sir?"

"You were staying for Kensington's funeral. As the Norwegian representative."

"But how . . . ?"

"You'd given your phone number here to the airline, so when they rang half an hour before departure because you hadn't shown up, I got the picture. A call to the Crescent Hotel and a confidential conversation with the hotel manager supplied the rest. We've been trying to get hold of you without any luck. I understand how it is, Holy, and I suggest we don't make any more fuss. Everyone knows there's a reaction after such events. The important thing is you've got yourself together and we put you on a plane."

"Thank you, sir."

"No worries. I'll ask my secretary to speak to the airline."

"Just a couple of things before you do, sir. We've been doing a bit of work overnight, and the final results won't be known until Forensics turn up and check it. I'm pretty sure about the outcome, though, sir."

The old fan, despite the lubrication, had finally given up the ghost and been replaced by a new, bigger and quieter one. Harry could confirm the world was continuing, even in his absence.

Of those present only Watkins and Yong did not know the details now, but Harry took it from the top anyway.

"We didn't give it a moment's thought when we found Andrew because it was the middle of the day. It didn't even occur to me when I found out the time of death. It was only later that it struck me the light was off when we arrived at Rechtnagel's flat. If things happened the way we had assumed, this would have been the course of events: Andrew switched off the light by the door, groped his way to the chair in a heroin haze—the room is pitch-black at two in the morning—balanced on the wobbly chair and put the loop over his head."

In the ensuing silence it was obvious that even with new technology it was hard to manufacture a fan that didn't make an irritating noise, however low the buzz.

"That doesn't sound right," Watkins said. "Perhaps it wasn't pitch-black, perhaps the streetlamps or something else lit the room from outside?"

"Lebie and I were there at two in the morning and checked. The sitting room was as dark as a grave."

"Could the light have been on when you arrived without your noticing?" Yong asked. "After all, it was the middle of the day. An officer may have turned off the light later."

"We cut Andrew down with a knife," Lebie said. "I would have got an electric shock, so I checked the light was off."

"OK," Watkins said. "Let's assume he chose to hang himself in the dark, so Kensington is a bit of an unusual bloke. What else is new?"

"But he didn't hang himself in the dark," Harry said.

McCormack coughed from the back of the room.

"Here's what we found in Rechtnagel's flat," Harry said, holding up a lightbulb. "See the brown stain? That's scorched rayon." He held up a white garment. "And this is the shirt Andrew was wearing when we found him. Drip-dry. Sixty percent rayon. Rayon melts at 260 degrees Celsius. A lightbulb is about 450 degrees on the surface. Can you see the brown stain over the breast pocket? That's where the bulb was touching the shirt when we found him."

"Impressive physics, Holy," Watkins said. "Now tell us what you think happened."

"One of two things," Harry said. "Someone was there before us, saw Andrew hanging from the cable, switched off the light and left. The snag is, the only two registered keys for the flat were found on Otto and Andrew."

"The flat has a snap lock, doesn't it?" Watkins said. "Maybe this person unlocked the door and put the key in Andrew's poc— . . . no, then Andrew wouldn't have been able to get in." He blushed.

"You may still have a point," Harry said. "My theory is that Andrew didn't have a key to the flat. He was let in by someone who was already there or who arrived at the same time, someone who had the other key. This person was present when Andrew died. Afterward he put the key in Andrew's pocket so that it would look as if he had entered the flat alone. The fact that the key isn't on the ring with the others suggests that. Then he switched off the light and closed the door after him as he left."

Silence.

"Are you saying Andrew Kensington was murdered?" Watkins asked. "If so, how?"

"I think Andrew was forced to inject himself with heroin, an overdose, probably at gunpoint."

"Why couldn't he have done that before he arrived?" Yong asked.

"Firstly, I don't believe that a controlled, seasoned addict like Andrew would suddenly give himself an overdose by accident. Secondly, Andrew didn't have enough of his own supplies for an overdose."

"So why hang him?"

"Giving an overdose is not an exact science. It's not always easy to say how a hardened body will react. Perhaps he would have survived long enough for someone to find him alive. Though probably it was more to drug him up, so that he wouldn't resist when he was stood on the chair with the cable round his neck. Ah, speaking of the cable. Lebie?"

Lebie maneuvered the toothpick to the corner of his mouth with a bit of tongue-and-lip gymnastics.

"We got the boys in Forensics to check the cable. Ceiling-lamp cables are rarely washed, right, and we thought it would be easy to get fingerprints. But it was as clean as a . . . er . . ." Lebie fluttered a hand.

"As something very clean?" Yong suggested helpfully.

"Right. The only prints to be found were our own."

"So, unless Andrew wiped the cable before hanging himself," Watkins concluded, "and slipped his head into the loop without using his fingers, someone else did it for him. Is that what you're saying?"

"Looks like it, boss."

"But if this bloke's as smart as you make out why did he switch off the light as he left?" Watkins splayed his palms and scanned the faces at the table.

"Because," Harry said, "it's an automatic reaction. He does it without thinking. The way people do, leaving their flats. Or a flat they have a key to, where they have been used to coming and going as they like."

Harry leaned back in his chair. He was sweating like a pig, unsure how much longer he could wait for another drink.

"I think the man we're looking for is Otto Rechtnagel's secret lover."

Lebie stood beside Harry in the lift.

"Going out for lunch?" he asked.

"Thought I would," Harry said.

"Mind if I join you?"

"Not at all."

Lebie was good company if you didn't want to talk much.

They found a table at Southern's in Market Street. Harry ordered a Jim Beam. Lebie looked up from the menu.

"Two barramundi salads, black coffee and nice, fresh bread, please."

Harry eyed Lebie with surprise. "Thank you, but I think I'll pass this time," he said to the waiter.

"The order stands," Lebie smiled. "My friend will change his mind when he tastes the barramundi here."

The waiter left and Harry watched Lebie. He had placed both hands on the table with fingers spread, looking from one to the other as if comparing.

"When I was young I hitched up the coast to Cairns, along the Great Barrier Reef," he said to the smooth backs of his hands. "At a hostel for backpackers I met two German girls who were traveling round the world. They had hired a car and driven all the way from Sydney and told me in great detail about all the places they had been, how long for and why they had been there and how the rest of the trip was planned. It was clear not much had been left to chance. Perhaps that's the German mindset. So, when I asked if they'd seen any kangaroos on the trip they laughed and assured me they had. It was of course implicit that they had ticked that off on their 'things-to-do' list. 'Did you stop and feed them?' I asked, but they looked at each other dumbfounded, and then at me. 'No, ve did not!' 'Why not? They're quite cute, you know.' 'Aber, zey vere dead!' "

Harry was so astonished at Lebie's long monologue that he forgot to smile.

The waiter came and put the Jim Beam in front of Harry. Lebie looked at the glass.

"The day before yesterday I saw a girl who was so pretty I felt like stroking her cheek and saying something nice to her. She was twenty-odd, wore a blue dress and was barelegged. *Aber, she was dead.* As you know, she was blonde, had been raped and had bruising around her neck from strangulation.

"And last night I dreamt these meaninglessly young and pointlessly beautiful girls were filling up all the roadside verges around the whole of Australia—from Sydney to Cairns, from Adelaide to Perth, from Darwin to Melbourne. And all for one solitary reason. We had closed our eyes because we couldn't face the truth. We hadn't done enough. We had allowed ourselves to be weak and human."

Harry knew where Lebie was heading. The waiter came with the fish.

"You're the one who's come closest to him, Harry. You've had your ear to the ground, and you may recognize the vibrations of his feet if he approaches again. There will always be a hundred good reasons to get drunk, but if you're chucking up in a hotel room, you're no use to anyone. He isn't human. So we can't be human. We have to show our powers of endurance, we have to show our powers of resistance." Lebie spread out his serviette. "But we have to eat."

Harry put the whiskey glass to his mouth and watched Lebie as he slowly drained it. Then he put the empty glass on the table, grimaced and grabbed the knife and fork. The rest of the meal passed in silence.

43

A Big Fish

Sandra was standing in her usual spot. She didn't recognize him until he was close.

"Nice to see you again," she said, her eyes distant with small pupils.

They walked over to Bourbon & Beef, where the waiter immediately ran over and held the chair out for her.

Harry asked Sandra what she would like, and ordered a Coke and a double whiskey.

"Christ, I thought he'd come to turf me out," she said, relieved.

"I'm a kind of regular," Harry explained.

"How's your girlfriend?"

"Birgitta?" Harry was quiet. "I don't know. She won't talk to me. Feeling terrible, I hope."

"Why do you hope she's feeling terrible?"

"I hope she loves me, of course."

Sandra emitted a rasping laugh. "And how are you, Harry Holy?"

"Terrible." Harry smiled sadly. "But I may feel a lot better if I can trap a murderer."

"And you think I can help you?" she said, lighting a cigarette. Her face was, if possible, even paler and more drawn than before, and her eyes were red-rimmed.

"We're look-alikes," Harry said, pointing to their reflections in the blackened window beside the table.

Sandra said nothing.

"I remember, if a bit unclearly, that Birgitta threw your bag on the bed and the contents fell out. At first I thought you kept a Pekinese in your bag." Harry paused. "Tell me, what do you need a blonde wig for?"

Sandra stared out of the window. That is, she was staring at the window, possibly at their reflections.

"A customer bought it for me. He wanted me to wear it when he was with me."

"Who . . . ?"

Sandra shook her head. "Forget it, Harry. I'm not saying. There aren't many rules in my profession, but keeping your mouth shut about punters is one of them. And it's a good rule."

Harry sighed. "You're frightened," he said.

Sandra's eyes flashed. "Don't try it, Harry. You won't get anything from me, OK?"

"You don't need to tell me who it is, Sandra. I know. I just wanted to check first if you were frightened of saying."

"*I know*," Sandra aped, clearly furious. "And how do you know then?"

"I saw the stone roll out of your bag, Sandra. The green crystal. I recognized the sign painted on it. He gave it to you. It's from his mother's shop, the Crystal Castle."

She rested her big black eyes on him. Her red mouth had stiffened into an ugly sneer. Harry placed a careful hand on her arm.

"Why are you so frightened of Evans White, Sandra? Why won't you give him to us?"

Sandra tore her arm away. She turned back to the window. Harry waited. She sniffled and Harry passed her the handkerchief which, unaccountably, he had in his pocket.

"There are plenty of other people who feel terrible, you

know," she whispered at length. Her eyes were redder still as she turned to him. "Do you know what this is?" She drew up the sleeve of her dress and showed him a white forearm with nasty, red marks, some of them encrusted.

"Heroin?"

"Morf. Morphine," Sandra said. "Not many people in Sydney can manage it, so most end up on heroin anyway. But I'm allergic to heroin. My body can't take it. I've tried it and I almost died. So my poison is morphine. And last year there was only one person in King's Cross able to supply it in sufficient quantity. And he takes his payment through a kind of role play. I make myself up and don a white wig. OK by me, I don't give a shit what kicks he gets out of it, so long as I get what I need. Anyway, there are bigger sickos than those who want you to dress up as their mother."

"Mother?"

"I think he hates his mother. Or loves her more than is normal. One of the two, I don't know for sure, he won't talk about it, and Christ knows I don't want to, either!" She gave a hollow laugh.

"Why do you think he hates her?"

"The last few times he was rougher than usual. He bruised me."

"Round your neck?"

Sandra shook her head. "He tried. Soon after the murder of the Norwegian girl was in the paper, the strangling. He put his hands round my throat and told me to lie still and not to be frightened. I didn't give it any more thought afterward."

"Why not?"

Sandra shrugged. "People are influenced by what they read and see. Take *9½ Weeks,* for example, when it was on at the cinema. Suddenly there were loads of punters who wanted us to crawl around naked on the floor while they sat watching."

"Shit film," Harry said. "What happened?"

"He put his hands round my throat and ran his thumbs over my voice box. Nothing violent. But I took off the wig and said I wasn't up for that game. He came to his senses and said that was fine. It had just come over him. Didn't mean anything."

"And you believed him?"

Sandra rolled her shoulders. "You don't know how a bit of independence can affect the way you see things," she said, finishing the whiskey.

"Don't I?" Harry said, eyeing the still untouched Coke bottle with disapproval.

McCormack was drumming his fingers with impatience. Harry was sweating even though the fan was on full. Otto Rechtnagel's neighbor had had a lot to say when Yong turned up. Much too much. Sadly, nothing of what she said had been of any interest. Yong seemed to have found it hard to behave as a good listener in her less than convivial company.

"Fat arse," he answered with a smile when Watkins asked him what kind of an impression she had made on him.

"Anything new about the girl in Centennial Park?" McCormack said.

"Not much," Lebie said. "But she wasn't the apple of Mummy's eye—she took speed and she had just started work at a strip joint in King's Cross. She was on her way home when she was murdered. We have two witnesses who say they saw her going into the park."

"Anything else?"

"Not so far, sir."

"Harry," said McCormack, wiping away the sweat, "what's your theory?"

"The latest," mumbled Watkins, just loud enough for everyone to hear.

"Well," Harry began, "we never found the witness who Andrew said had seen Evans White in Nimbin on the day Inger Holter was murdered. What we know now is that White is more than usually captivated by blondes, he had an unstable childhood and it might be interesting to examine his relationship with his mother. He's never had a steady job or a fixed abode and for that reason following his movements is tricky. It's not impossible that he may have had a clandestine relationship with Otto Rechtnagel, and it's not inconceivable that he joined Otto on his travels. He may have rented a room in a hotel and found his victims wherever he came across them. This is all theory, of course."

"Maybe Otto's the serial killer," Watkins speculated. "Maybe someone else killed him and Kensington and had nothing to do with the other murders?"

"Centennial Park," Lebie said. "That's our serial killer. I would bet everything I own. Not that I have a lot to lose there . . ."

"Lebie's right," Harry said. "He's still out there somewhere."

"OK," said McCormack. "I can hear our friend Holy's using expressions like *not impossible* and *not inconceivable* to launch his theories now, which may be wise. We have nothing to gain by being cocky. Furthermore, it should be clear to all of us now that we're dealing with a very intelligent man. And very confident. He handed out the ready-made answers we were after, gave us the murderer on a silver platter and assumes now these answers have calmed our fevered brows and that we regard the case as solved, since the perpetrator died by his own hand. By fingering Kensington he knew, of course, that we would decide to hush the matter up—which you have to admit is clever thinking."

McCormack glanced at Harry as he said the latter.

"Our advantage lies in the fact that he thinks he's safe. People who think they're safe are often reckless. Now, however, it's time we decided how we're going to tackle this matter. We have a new suspect and we cannot afford another blunder. The problem is that if we make too much of a splash we risk frightening off the big fish. We have to have stomachs of steel and stand quite still, until we can see the big fish clearly beneath us, so clear that it's unmistakable and so close we can't miss. Then, and only then, can we throw the harpoon."

He gazed at each in turn. Everyone nodded to confirm the boss's indisputable good sense.

"And to do this we need to work defensively, quietly and systematically."

"Disagree," said Harry.

The others turned to him.

"There is, you see, another way to catch fish without making a splash," Harry said. "A piece of string and a hook with some bait we know he'll go for."

44

A Box Jellyfish

The wind drove dust clouds ahead as it whirled up along the gravel road and over the low stone wall around the cemetery and into the small gathering of mourners. Harry had to squeeze his eyes shut to avoid getting dust particles in them, and the wind caught shirts and jacket tails, making those assembled look from a distance as if they were dancing on Andrew Kensington's grave.

"Hellish wind," Watkins whispered during the priest's recitations.

Harry stood thinking about Watkins's choice of words, hoping he was wrong. It was of course difficult to say where the wind was coming from, but it was certainly in a hurry. And if it was here to take Andrew's soul with it, no one could say it was taking its job lightly. The pages of hymn books were fluttering, the green soil-laden tarpaulin beside the grave flapped and those who didn't have hats to hold on to watched comb-overs and other hairstyles unravel.

Harry wasn't listening to the priest, he was looking through scrunched-up eyes across the grave. Birgitta's hair was flying backward like a red jet of flame. She met his stare with a blank expression. A gray-haired old woman sat trembling on a chair with a stick in her lap. Her skin was yellow, and her age could not conceal her distinctly English equine face. The wind had knocked her hat skew-whiff. Harry had worked out that she was Andrew's foster-mother, but she was so old and fragile she had scarcely registered Harry's condolences outside the church—she'd just nodded, mumbling an incomprehensible sentence over and over again. Behind her stood a small, barely visible black woman with a girl in each hand.

The priest threw earth into the grave in Lutheran manner. Harry had been told that Andrew had belonged to the Anglican Church, which, alongside the Catholic Church, was by far the biggest in Australia, but Harry, who had been to only a few funerals, couldn't see that this service was much different from those in Norway. Even the weather was the same. When they had buried his mother, turbulent, blue-gray clouds had chased each other above the cemetery, but fortunately they had been in too much haste to rain on them. There had been sun the day they buried Ronny. At that time, though, Harry was in the hospital with blinds drawn because the light gave him a headache. Just like today, police officers had constituted the majority of the funeral gathering. Perhaps they had sung the same hymn at the end: "Nearer, My God, to Thee!"

The gathering dissolved, people began to move toward their cars and Harry walked behind Birgitta. She stopped so that he could catch up with her.

"You look ill," she said without an upward glance.

"You don't know what I look like when I'm ill," he said.

"Don't you look ill when you're ill? All I'm saying is you *look* ill. *Are* you ill?"

A gust of wind blew, and Harry's tie lifted and covered his face.

"Perhaps I'm a little ill," he said. "Not *very* ill. You look like a jellyfish with all that hair flapping in . . . my face." Harry took a red strand out of his mouth.

Birgitta smiled. “You should thank your lucky stars I’m not a box jellyfish,” she said.

“A what?” Harry said.

“A box jellyfish,” Birgitta said. “It’s very common in Australia. Its sting is worse than an ordinary jellyfish’s, you could say . . .”

“Box jellyfish?” Harry heard a familiar voice behind him say. He turned. It was Toowoomba.

“How are you?” Harry said and explained that it was Birgitta’s hair blowing into his face that had prompted the comparison.

“Well, if it had been a box jellyfish, it would have left red stripes across your face, and you would have been screaming like a man being given twenty lashes,” Toowoomba said. “And within a few seconds you would have collapsed, the poison would have paralyzed your respiratory organs, you would have had difficulty breathing, and if you hadn’t got immediate help, you would have died an extremely painful death.”

Harry held his palms up in defense. “Thanks, there have been enough deaths for today.”

Toowoomba nodded. He was wearing a black silk smoking jacket with a bow tie. He noticed Harry’s gaze.

“It’s the only thing I have remotely resembling a suit. Besides, I inherited it from him.” He nodded toward the grave. “Not recently, but a number of years ago. Andrew said he’d grown out of it. Rubbish, of course. He didn’t want to admit it, but I knew he’d bought it to wear at the banquet after the Australian championships. He probably hoped the outfit would experience with me what it never experienced with him.”

They walked along the gravel road as cars slowly passed.

“May I ask you a personal question, Toowoomba?” Harry said.

“I reckon so.”

"Where do you think Andrew will end up?"

"What do you mean?"

"Do you think his soul will go up or down?"

Toowoomba wore a serious expression. "I'm a simple man, Harry. I don't know much about that kind of thing, and I don't know much about souls. But I do know a couple of things about Andrew Kensington, and if there's something up there, and if it's beautiful souls they want that's where his belongs." He smiled. "But if there's anything down there, I think that's where he'd prefer to be. He hated boring places."

They chuckled quietly.

"But since this is a personal question, Harry, I'll give you a personal answer. I think Andrew's parents and my own had a point. They had a sober view of death. Although it's true to say many tribes believed in a life after death, some believed in reincarnation, the soul wandering from human to human, and some believed souls could return as spirits. Some tribes believed the souls of the dead could be seen in the firmament as stars. And so on. But the common thread was that they believed humans, sooner or later, after all these stages, died a proper, final, definitive death. And that was that. You became a pile of stones and were gone. For some reason I like the thought of that. These perspectives of eternity leave you so weary, don't you think?"

"I think it sounds like Andrew left you more than the smoking jacket, that's what I think," Harry said.

Toowoomba laughed. "Can you hear that so easily?"

"His master's voice," Harry said. "The man should have been a priest."

They stopped by a dusty little car, which was obviously Toowoomba's.

"Listen, I might need someone who knew Andrew," Harry said, reacting to a hunch. "The way he thought. Why he did what he did."

He straightened up, and their eyes met.

"I think someone killed Andrew," Harry said.

"Bullshit!" Toowoomba burst out. "You don't think, you *know*! Everyone who knew Andrew knows he would never willingly leave a party. For him, life was the biggest party. I don't know anyone who loved life more than him. Whatever it did to him. If he was going to check out there would have been plenty of opportunities—and reasons—before."

"Then we agree," Harry said.

"You can usually reach me on this number," Toowoomba said, scribbling on a matchbox. "It's a mobile phone number."

Toowoomba was going north and clattered off in his old white Holden. Birgitta and Harry stood watching, then Harry suggested hitching a ride with one of his colleagues into town. But it seemed most of them had gone. Then a magnificent old Buick pulled up in front of them, the driver rolled down the window and stuck out a red face with a striking nose. It was like the kind of potato where several tubers had grown into one, and, if possible, even redder than the rest of his face with its fine network of thin veins.

"Going to town, folks?" the nose asked, and told them to hop in.

"My name's Jim Connolly. This is my wife, Claudia," he said, after they had settled onto the broad backseat. A tiny, dark face with a beaming smile turned to them from the front seat. She looked Indian, and was so small they could barely see her above the headrest.

Jim observed Harry and Birgitta in the rearview mirror. "Friends of Andrew? Colleagues?"

He steered the jalopy carefully down the gravel road while Harry explained the connections.

"Right, so you're from Norway and you're from Sweden. That's a long way away, that is. Well, almost everyone here comes from somewhere far away. Take Claudia, for example, she's from Venezuela, where they have all the Miss Universes, you know. How many titles have you had, Claudia? Including your own. Ha ha." He laughed so much his eyes disappeared beneath laughter lines, and Claudia joined in.

"I'm Australian," Jim continued. "My great-great-great-grandfather came here from Ireland. He was a murderer and a thief. Ha ha ha. Some time back people didn't like to admit they were descendants of convicts, even though it was nearly two hundred years ago. But I've always been proud of it. They were the ones plus a bunch of sailors and soldiers who founded this country. And a fine country it is, too. We call it the lucky country down here. Yeah, yeah, things change. Now I hear it's 'in' to trace your forefathers back to the convicts. Ha ha ha. Too bad about Andrew, wasn't it?"

Jim was like a verbal machine gun, and Harry and Birgitta couldn't manage to chip in much before he took over again. And the faster he spoke, the slower he drove. Like David Bowie on Harry's old cassette player. Years ago he'd been given a battery-powered recorder by his father, and the louder you turned up the volume the slower the tape went.

"Andrew and I used to box together on the Jim Chivers roadshows. You know, Andrew never had his nose broken. No sirree, no one ever sullied his pugilistic virtue. They've got pretty flat noses, these Aboriginal guys, p'raps that's why no one ever gave it a thought. But Andrew was fit and healthy on the inside. He had a healthy heart and a healthy nose. Well, as healthy as a heart can be after you've been kidnapped by the authorities at birth. And his heart wasn't as healthy after the row during the Australian championships in Melbourne. I suppose you heard about that, did you? He lost quite a lot then." They were doing less than forty now.

"The champion, Campbell, well, his girl, she was after Andrew, on her knees she was, but she'd probably been so stunningly beautiful all her life that she'd never experienced rejection. If she had, everything would have been very different. But when she knocked on Andrew's hotel door that night and he politely asked her to leave, she couldn't cope with it; she went straight back to her boyfriend and told him Andrew had groped her. They rang his room and told him to go down to the kitchen. Rumors are still circulating about the fight down there. Andrew's life went into a siding after that. But they never got his nose. Ha ha ha. Are you a couple?"

"Not exactly," Harry composed himself enough to say.

"That's not how it looks," Jim said, watching them in the mirror. "Perhaps you just don't know it yourselves yet, but even though you look a bit weighed down by the gravity of circumstances today, there's a glow there. Correct me if I'm wrong, but you look like Claudia and I did when we were young and in love, the way we were for the first twenty or thirty years. Ha ha ha. Now we're just in love. Ha ha ha."

Claudia looked at her husband with sparkling eyes.

"I met Claudia at one of the roadshows. She was performing as a contortionist. She can fold herself up like an envelope even today. So I don't know what I'm doing with this big Buick. Ha ha ha. I wooed her every day for more than a year before she so much as allowed me to kiss her. And afterward she told me she had fallen in love the first time she saw me. That alone was sensational, bearing in mind that this nose of mine had already taken a lot of beatings. Then she went and played the prude for one whole, long, awful year. Women scare the wits out of me sometimes. What do you say, Harry?"

"Well," Harry said, "I know what you mean."

He looked at Birgitta. She put on a weak smile.

After spending three-quarters of an hour covering a distance that normally takes twenty minutes, they pulled in at the town hall, where Harry and Birgitta thanked him for the lift and jumped out. The wind had picked up in the town as well, and they stood in the gusts palpably not knowing quite what to say.

"A very unusual couple," Harry said.

"Yes," Birgitta said. "They're happy."

The wind whirled and shook a tree in the park, and Harry imagined he saw a hirsute shadow dart for cover.

"What do we do now?" Harry said.

"You come home with me."

"OK."

45

Payback

Birgitta poked a cigarette into Harry's mouth and lit it.

"Well earned," she said.

Harry reflected. He didn't feel too bad. He pulled the sheet over him.

"Are you embarrassed?" Birgitta laughed.

"I just don't like your lustful eyes on me. You may not want to believe it, but in fact I'm not a machine."

"Really?" Birgitta playfully nibbled his lower lip. "You could have fooled me. That piston of—"

"All right, all right. Do you have to be so vulgar now that life has become so blissful, sweetheart?"

She cuddled up to him, resting her head on his chest.

"You promised another story," she whispered.

"Indeed." Harry took a deep breath. "Let me see. So this is the start. I was in the eighth year and a new girl joined the parallel class. Her name was Kristin, and it took only three weeks for her and my best pal, Terje, who had the whitest teeth in the school and played guitar in a band, to become officially declared boyfriend and girlfriend. The problem was she was the girl I had been waiting for all my life." He paused.

"So what did you do?"

"Nothing. Went on waiting. In the meantime I became Kristin's pal—she could chat about everything under the sun with me, she felt. She could confide when things between her and Terje weren't working, without realizing that her pal was quietly exultant, waiting for the moment to strike."

He grinned.

"Christ, how I hated myself."

"I'm shocked," mumbled Birgitta, affectionately stroking his hair.

"A friend invited a gang of us to his grandparents' unoccupied farmhouse the same weekend that Terje's band had a gig. We drank homemade wine and Kristin and I sat on the sofa chatting late into the night. After a while we decided to explore the house and went up to the loft. There was a locked door, but Kristin found a key hanging on a hook and unlocked it. We lay side by side on the duvet of a very undersized four-poster. In the hollows of the bed linen there was a layer of something black, and I jumped when I saw it was dead flies. There must have been thousands of them. I saw her face close to mine, surrounded by dead flies on the white pillow, bathed in a bluish light from the moon, so big and round outside the window, which made her skin seem transparent."

"Pah!" Birgitta said and rolled on top of him. His eyes lingered on hers.

"We talked about everything and nothing. Lay quite still listening to nothing. In the night a car drove past on the road and the light from the headlamps swept across the ceiling and all kinds of strange shadows stole through the room. Kristin finished with Terje two days later."

He turned on his side with his back to Birgitta. She snuggled up to him.

"What happened next, Valentino?"

"Kristin and I met in secret. Until it was no longer secret."

"How did Terje take it?"

"Well. Sometimes people react in textbook manner. Terje told his friends to choose: him or me. I think it was a landslide victory. In favor of the boy with the whitest teeth in the school."

"That must have been terrible. Were you lonely?"

"I don't know what was worst. Or who I pitied most. Terje or myself."

"At least you and Kristin had each other."

"True, but some of the magic had gone. The ideal girl was gone, you see."

"What do you mean?"

"I had a girl who had left a boy for his best friend."

"And for her you were the boy who had unscrupulously used his best friend to get in with her."

"Exactly. And that would always be there. Under the surface maybe, but nevertheless smoldering away with unspoken, mutual contempt. As though we were accomplices responsible for a scandalous murder."

"So you had to make do with a relationship that wasn't perfect. Welcome to reality!"

"Don't get me wrong. I think our common sins in many ways bound us closer together. I think we really did love each other for a while. Some days were . . . perfect. Like drops of water. Like a beautiful painting."

Birgitta laughed. "I like you when you talk, Harry. Your eyes seem to light up when you say things like that. As if you're back there. Do you long to go back?"

"To Kristin?" Harry wondered. "I may long to go back to the time we were together, but to Kristin? People change. The person you long for may no longer exist. Bloody hell, we all change, don't we. Once something has been experienced, it's too late, you can't get back the feeling of experiencing the same thing for the first time. It's sad, but that's the way it is."

"Like being in love for the first time?" Birgitta said quietly.

"Like being in love . . . for the first time," Harry said, caressing her cheek. Then he took another deep breath.

"There's something I have to ask you, Birgitta. A favor."

The music was deafening and Harry had to lean in to hear what he was saying. Teddy was effusing about his new shooting star, Melissa, who was nineteen years old and, right now, setting the place on fire, which, Harry had to admit, was no exaggeration.

"Rumors. That's what does it, you know," Teddy said. "You can advertise and market as much as you like, but ultimately there's only one thing that sells, the rumor mill."

And rumors had obviously done their job because for the first time in ages the club was nearly full. After Melissa's cowboy and lasso number the men were on their chairs, and even the female minority was applauding politely. "See," Teddy said. "That's not because she's found a novelty number, it's classic striptease, God knows it is. We've had a dozen girls here doing the same number and no one raised an eyebrow. The reason this is different: innocence and emotion."

From experience, however, Teddy knew that such waves of popularity were sadly a passing phase. On the one hand, the public was always on the lookout for something new; on the other, this industry had a nasty tendency to consume its own offspring.

"Good striptease requires enthusiasm, you know," Teddy shouted over the disco rhythms. "Not many of these girls can maintain the enthusiasm, however hard they work at it. Four shows, every fuckin' day. You lose interest and forget the crowds. I've seen it happen too many times before. Doesn't matter how popular you are, a trained eye can see when a star is extinguished."

"How?"

"Well, they're dancers, aren't they. They have to listen to the music, get inside it, you know. When they're 'edgy' and a tiny bit ahead of the beat, it's not what you might think, a sign that they're overenthusiastic. Quite the opposite, it's a sign they're fed up and want to get it over with asap. Also, often subconsciously, they cut down on the movements so that it becomes more suggestive than complete. It's the same with people who have told the same joke too many times; they start leaving out the small but vital details that make you laugh at the punchline. That's the kind of thing it's difficult to do anything about—body language doesn't lie, and it transmits itself to the audience, you know. The girls are aware of the problem and to spice up the show, to help it take off, they have a few drinks before going onstage. Occasionally a few too many. And then . . ." Teddy held a finger against one nostril and sniffed.

Harry nodded. Familiar story.

"They discover powder, which unlike alcohol gives them a buzz and they've heard it also helps to keep them slim. Soon they have to take more to get the high they need to give of their best every evening. Soon they have to take it just to perform the shows. And soon the effects are visible, they notice they're losing concentration and begin to hate the drunken, cheering audience. Then one night they march off the stage. Furious, and in tears. They argue with the manager, take a week's holiday then come back. But they can't *feel* the atmosphere anymore, can't feel the inner sense that helped them to time things right. Audiences vote with their feet and in the end it's time to go on the street and move on."

Yes, Teddy had his finger on the pulse. But all of that lay in the future. Now it was time to milk the cow, and right now it was standing on the stage with large eyes and udders full to bursting and was probably—all things considered—a very happy cow.

"You wouldn't believe who comes here to check out these

new talents of ours," Teddy chuckled, brushing his lapel. "Some of them come from your very own profession, if I can put it like that. And they're not exactly boys on the bottom rung, either."

"Bit of striptease doesn't hurt anyone, does it."

"We-ell," Teddy drawled. "Don't know about that. So long as they settle up for the damage afterward, I suppose the odd graze doesn't hurt."

"What do you mean by that?"

"Not a lot. Enough of that. What brings you to these parts, Officer?"

"Two things. The girl who was found in Centennial Park turned out to be a little less naive than first impressions indicated. The blood samples showed she was full of amphetamines and on closer investigation the trail led here. In fact, we discovered she had been on the stage here earlier the night she went missing."

"Barbara, yes. Tragic, wasn't it." Teddy did his best to assume a grieving exterior. "Not much of a stripper, but an absolutely great girl. Have you found anything?"

"We were hoping you might be able to help us, Mongabi."

Teddy ran a hand nervously through his slicked-back hair.

"Sorry, Officer. She wasn't in my stable. Talk to Sammy. He'll be in later."

A pair of enormous satin-clad tits obscured the view between them for a moment, then they were gone and a colorful cocktail was standing on the table beside Harry.

"You said you came here for two things, Officer. What was the second?"

"Oh, right. A purely private matter, Mongabi. I was wondering if you had seen my friend over there before?" Harry pointed to the bar. A tall black figure in a smoking jacket waved to them. Teddy shook his head.

"Are you absolutely sure, Mongabi? He's quite well

known. Before too long he's going to be an Australian boxing champion."

There was a pause. Teddy Mongabi's eyes went shifty.

"What is it you would like to . . . ?"

"Heavyweight, goes without saying." Harry found the straw among the umbrellas and slices of lemon in the fruit juice and sucked.

Teddy forced a smile. "Listen, Officer, am I mistaken or were we just having a cozy conversation?"

"Indeed we were. But not everything in life is cozy, is it. Cozy Time is over."

"Listen, Officer Holy, I don't think what happened recently was any nicer than you do. I'm sorry about it. Even though you should bear your part of the guilt, you know. When you came in here and sat down tonight, I thought it was with a common understanding that all that was behind us. I believe we can agree on a number of things. You and I, we speak the same language, Officer."

There was a second's silence as the disco music suddenly stopped. Teddy hesitated. There was a loud gurgle as the last of the fruit juice disappeared up the straw.

Teddy swallowed. "For example, I know that Melissa has no special plans for the rest of the evening." He sent Harry an imploring look.

"Thank you, Mongabi, I appreciate the thought. But I simply don't have the time right now. I have to finish this business first, and then I'm off."

He pulled a black police truncheon from his jacket.

"We're so damn busy I don't even know if I have the time to kill you properly," Harry said.

"What the hell . . . ?"

Harry got up. "I hope Geoff and Ivan are on duty tonight. My friend was *so* looking forward to meeting them, you know."

Teddy struggled to his feet.

"Close your eyes," Harry said, and struck.

46

Bait

"Yuh?"

"Hello, is that Evans?"

"Maybe. Who's asking?"

"Hi, this is Birgitta. Inger's friend. We met at the Albury a couple of times. I've got long, blonde, slightly reddish hair. Do you remember me?"

"Of course I remember you. How are you doing? How did you get hold of my number?"

"I'm fine. Bit up and down. You know. Bit depressed because of Inger and all that, but I won't bother you with it. I got your number from Inger, in case we had to contact her when she was in Nimbin."

"I see."

. . .

"Yes, the thing is I know you have something I need, Evans."

"Uh-huh?"

"Stuff."

"I understand. Hate to disappoint you, but I doubt I have what you're after. Listen . . . er, Birgitta—"

"You don't understand, I *have* to meet you!"

"Easy now. For what you need there are hundreds of other suppliers, and this is not a secure line, so I suggest you don't say anything you shouldn't. I'm sorry I can't help you."

"What I need starts with 'm,' not 'h.' And you're the only person who has it."

"Rubbish."

"OK, maybe there are a few others, but I don't trust any of them. I'm buying for several people. I need a lot and I pay well."

"I'm a bit tied up now, Birgitta. Don't ring here again, please."

"Wait! I can . . . I know a few things. I know what you like."

"Like?"

"What you . . . really like. What your kick is."

. . .

. . .

"Sorry, I just had to get someone out of the room. This is a real pain in the arse. So. What do you think I like, Birgitta?"

"I can't say it on the phone, but . . . but I have blonde hair, and I . . . I like it, too."

"Jeez. Girlfriends! You never cease to amaze me. I thought Inger would've kept her mouth shut about that sort of thing."

"When can I meet you, Evans? This is urgent."

. . .

"I'll be in Sydney day after tomorrow, but perhaps I should consider an earlier flight . . . ?"

"Yes!"

"Hm."

"When can we—?"

"Shh, Birgitta, I'm thinking."

. . .

"OK, listen carefully. Walk down Darlinghurst Road tomorrow evening at eight. Stop by Hungry Jack's on the left. Look for a black Holden with tinted glass. If it isn't there before half past eight you can go. And make sure I can see your hair."

47

Data

"The last time? Well, Kristin rang me out of the blue one night. She was a bit drunk, I think. She gave me an ear-bashing for something, don't remember what. For destroying her life, probably. She had a tendency to think people around her were always destroying things she had planned so carefully."

"That's how it is with girls who have spent too much time growing up alone and playing with dolls, you know."

"Maybe. But, as I said, I don't remember. I was hardly ever sober myself."

Harry sat up in the sand on his elbows and scanned the sea. The waves rose, the tips went white and the foam hung in the air for a second before it fell, glittering in the sun like crushed glass, and crashed against the cliffs beyond Bondi Beach.

"But I saw her once more. She visited me at the hospital after the accident. Initially, when I opened my eyes, I thought I was dreaming, seeing her beside my bed, pale, almost transparent. She was just as beautiful as the first time I saw her."

Birgitta pinched him in the side.

"Am I laying it on too thick?"

"Not at all, just go on." She was lying on her stomach and giggling.

"What is this? You're supposed to get a bit jealous when I'm talking about an old flame. But the more I go into details about my romantic past the more you seem to like it."

Birgitta peered at him over her sunglasses.

"I like finding out that my macho cop has had an emotional life. Even though it was some time ago."

"Some time ago? What do you call this then?"

She laughed. "This is the mature, carefully considered holiday romance which doesn't become too intense but has enough sex for it to be worth the effort."

Harry shook his head. "That's not true, Birgitta, and you know it."

"Yes, it is, but it's fine, Harry. It's fine for *now*. Continue the story. If the details become too intimate, I'll tell you. Anyway, I'll get my own back when I tell you about my ex-boyfriend." She wriggled in the hot sand with a contented expression. "Ex-boyfriends, I mean."

Harry brushed the sand off her white back.

"Are you sure you don't get sunburned? With this sun and your skin—"

"You're the one who rubbed in the suntan lotion, herr Hole!"

"I was just wondering if it was a high enough factor. OK, forget it. I just didn't want you to get burned."

Harry stared at her light-sensitive skin. When he had asked for a favor she had said yes straightaway—without any hesitation.

"Relax, Daddy, and tell the story."

The fan wasn't working.

"Shit, it was brand bloody new!" said Watkins, hitting the back as he switched it on and off. To no avail. It was no more than a piece of silent aluminum and dead electricity.

McCormack growled.

"Forget it, Larry. Ask Laura for a new one. It's D-Day today and we have more important things on our minds. Larry?"

Watkins, irritated, moved the fan away.

"Everything's ready, sir. We'll have three cars in the area. Miss Enquist will be equipped with a radio transmitter so that we can plot where she is at any given moment, as well as a microphone, so that we can hear and assess the situation. The plan is she takes him home to her flat where Holy, Lebie and myself are positioned in the bedroom wardrobe, on the balcony and in the corridor respectively. If anything happens in the car, or they drive somewhere else, the three cars will follow."

"Tactics?"

Yong straightened his glasses. "Her job is to get him to say something about the murders, sir. She'll put him under pressure by saying she'll go to the police with what Inger Holter told her about his sexual habits. If he feels secure that she can't escape he may lift the lid."

"How long can we wait before we go in?"

"Until we have substantial evidence on tape. In a worst-case scenario, until he lays his hands on her."

"Risk?"

"This isn't without risk, of course, but strangling someone isn't a quick process. We're only seconds away at any stage."

"What if he's got a weapon?"

Yong shrugged. "From what we know that would be uncharacteristic behavior, sir."

McCormack had gotten up and started pacing to and fro in the small room. He reminded Harry of a fat old leopard he had seen in the zoo when he was young. The cage was so small the front part of the body began to turn before the rear had finished the previous turn. Back and forth. Back and forth.

"What if he wants sex before anything is said or anything has happened?"

"She'll refuse. Say she's changed her mind, she only said it to persuade him to get her some morphine."

"And then we let him go on his way?"

"We don't do any splashing unless we know we can catch him, sir."

McCormack sucked his top lip under his bottom lip. "Why's she doing this?"

Silence.

"Because she doesn't like rapists and murderers," Harry said after a long pause.

"Apart from that."

There was an even longer silence.

"Because I asked her to," Harry said at length.

"Can I disturb you, Yong?"

Yong Sue looked up from his computer with a smile. "Sure, mate."

Harry slumped onto a chair. The busy officer typed away, keeping one eye on the screen and one eye on him.

"Nice if this stayed between us, Yong, but I've lost my belief."

Yong stopped typing.

"I think Evans White's a wild goose chase," Harry continued.

Yong looked bewildered. "Why?"

"It's a bit difficult to explain, but there are a couple of things I can't get out of my mind. Andrew was trying to tell me something at the hospital. And before, too."

Harry broke off. Yong motioned him to go on.

"He was trying to tell me the solution was closer to home than I thought. I believe the guilty party is someone Andrew, for some reason, couldn't arrest himself. He needed an outsider. Such as me—a Norwegian who drops in and has to catch the next flight back. I reckoned that was how it was when I thought Otto Rechtnagel was the murderer, that because he was a close friend, Andrew wanted someone else to stop him. There was something that grated though, for me, deep down. Now I realize he wasn't the person Andrew wanted me to nab, it was someone else."

Yong cleared his throat. "I haven't mentioned this before, Harry, but I was surprised when Andrew came up with this witness who had seen Evans White in Nimbin on the same day Holter was murdered. Now, in retrospect, it's struck me that Andrew might have had another motive for removing the focus from Evans White: the guy had a hold on him. Evans White knew Andrew was on heroin and could have had him kicked out of the force and put in prison. I don't like the idea, but have you considered the possibility that Andrew and White may have struck a little deal? That Andrew would make sure we gave White a wide berth?"

"This is beginning to get complicated, Yong, but—well, yes, I have considered that possibility. And rejected it. Don't forget it was Andrew who enabled us to identify and find Evans White from the photo."

"Hm." Yong scratched the back of his head with a pencil. "We would have managed that without him, but it would have taken longer. Do you know the chances of a murder victim's partner being the culprit in any given case? Fifty-eight percent. Andrew knew we would invest substantial resources into finding Inger Holter's secret lover after you'd translated that letter. So if he really wanted to protect White and keep him hidden at the same time he might just as well have helped. For appearances' sake. You found it remarkable, for example, that he could immediately recognize a few walls in a place he had been just the once, drugged up and a hundred years ago, didn't you."

"You might be right, Yong, I don't know. Anyway, I don't think there's much point sowing too many seeds of doubt now that the guys know what to do. When it comes to the crunch, perhaps Evans White is our man after all. But if I really believed that, I would never have asked Birgitta to take part in this."

"So who do you think is our man?"

"Who do I think it is *this* time, you mean?"

Yong smiled. "Something like that."

Harry rubbed his chin. "I've already rung the alarm bells twice, Yong. Wasn't it the third time the boy cried 'Wolf' that they stopped reacting? That's why I have to be a hundred percent sure this time."

"Why have you come to me with this, Harry? Why not one of the bosses?"

"Because you can do a couple of things for me, make discreet inquiries and find some data I need, without anyone else in the building getting wind of it."

"No one else should know?"

"I know it sounds dodgy. And I know you have more to lose than most, but you're the only person who can help me, Yong. What do you say?"

Yong sent Harry a long stare.

"Will it help to find the murderer, Harry?"

"I hope so."

48

The Plan

"Bravo, come in."

The radio crackled.

"Radio works as it should," Lebie said. "How's it going in there?"

"Fine," Harry answered.

He was sitting on the made bed studying a photograph of Birgitta on the bedside table. It was a confirmation photo. She looked young, serious and strange, with curls in her hair and no freckles because the picture was overexposed. She didn't look good. Birgitta had said she kept the photo there for encouragement on bad days, as proof that she had progressed despite everything.

"What's the timetable?" Lebie called.

"She finishes work in fifteen minutes. They're at the Albury attaching the mike and transmitter now."

"Are they driving her to Darlinghurst Road?"

"Nope. We don't know where White is in the area. He might see her alighting from a car and get suspicious. She's going to walk from the Albury."

Watkins came in from the corridor.

"Seems great. I can stand round the corner behind the gateway without them seeing me and follow them. We'll have visual contact with her the whole way, Holy. Where are you, Holy?"

"In here, sir. I heard you. Good to hear that, sir."

"Radio, Lebie?"

"I've got contact, sir. Everyone's in position. Just waiting."

Harry had gone through it over and over again. From all sides. Argued with himself, tried every angle and in the end decided he didn't care whether she might interpret it as an awful cliché, a childish form of expression or an easy way out. He unpacked the wild rose he had bought and put it in the glass of water beside the photo on the bedside table.

He hesitated. Perhaps it would distract her? Perhaps Evans White would start asking questions if he saw a rose beside her bed? He ran a forefinger over one of the thorns. No. Birgitta would appreciate the encouragement; the sight of the rose would make her feel stronger.

He checked his watch. It was eight o'clock.

"Hey, let's get this over with!" he shouted to the sitting room.

49

A Walk in the Park

Something was wrong. Harry couldn't hear what they were saying, but he could hear the crackle of the radio from the sitting room. And there was too much of it. Everyone knew exactly what they had to do in advance, so if it was all going to plan it shouldn't be necessary to talk so much on the radio.

"Fuck, fuck, fuck," Watkins said. Lebie removed the headphones and turned to Harry.

"She didn't show up," he said.

"What?"

"She left the Albury at exactly quarter past eight. It shouldn't take more than ten minutes to walk from there to King's Cross. That was twenty-five minutes ago."

"I thought you said she would be under surveillance the whole time!"

"From the meeting place, yes. Why would anyone—?"

"What about the mike? She was wired up when she left, wasn't she?"

"They lost contact. They had it and then there was nothing. Not a peep."

"Have we got a map? Which route did she take?" He spoke softly and quickly. Lebie took the street atlas from his bag and gave it to Harry, who found the page showing Paddington and King's Cross.

"Which way would she have gone?" Lebie asked on the radio.

"The simplest. Down Victoria Street."

"Here it is," Harry said. "Round the corner of Oxford Street and down Victoria Street, past St. Vincent's Hospital, across Green Park on the left, to the crossroads, up to where Darlinghurst Road starts and two hundred meters along to where Hungry Jack's is. Couldn't be any bloody simpler!"

Watkins took the radio mike. "Smith, send two cars up Victoria Street to find the girl. Tell the people at the Albury to lend a hand. One car stays outside Hungry Jack's in case she appears. Be quick and don't make any fuss. Report back as soon as you know anything." He threw the mike down. "Fuck, fuck, fuck! What the hell is going on? Has she been run over? Robbed? Raped? Shit, shit, shit!"

Lebie and Harry exchanged glances.

"Could White possibly have driven up Victoria Street, spotted her and picked her up there?" Lebie suggested. "He has seen her before after all, at the Albury, and may have recognized her."

"The radio transmitter," Harry said. "It must still be working!"

"Bravo, bravo! Watkins here. Are you getting any signals from her transmitter? . . . Yes? . . . Direction of the Albury? Then she isn't far away. Quick, quick, quick! Great! Out!"

The three men sat in silence. Lebie shot Harry a glance.

"Ask if they've seen White's car," Harry said.

"Bravo, come in. Lebie here. What about the black Holden? Has anyone seen it yet?"

"Negative."

Watkins jumped up and began to pace the floor while swearing under his breath. Harry had been crouched down ever since he came into the sitting room and only noticed now that his thigh muscles were quivering.

The radio crackled.

"Charlie, this is Bravo. Come in."

Lebie pressed the loudspeaker button. "Charlie here, Bravo. Speak."

"Stolz here. We've found the bag with the transmitter and microphone in Green Park. The girl's vanished into thin air."

"In the bag?" Harry said. "Wasn't it supposed to have been taped to her body?"

Watkins squirmed. "Probably I forgot to say, but we discussed what would happen if he got into a clinch with her . . . er, held her and, well, you know. Made a move. Miss Enquist agreed it would be safer to keep the equipment in the bag."

Harry already had his jacket on.

"Where are you going?" Lebie asked.

"He was waiting for her," Harry said. "Maybe he followed her from the Albury. She didn't even have a chance to scream. My guess is he used a cloth with diethyl ether. Same as Otto Rechtnagel got."

"In the street?" Lebie said with a skeptical tone.

"Nope. In the park. I'm on my way now. Somebody I know there."

Joseph kept blinking. He was incredibly drunk.

"I think they stood there smooching, Harry."

"You've said that four times now, Joseph. What did he look like? Where were they going? Did he have a car?"

"Mikke and I, we commented, when he dragged her past, that she was even drunker than we were. I think Mikke envied her that. Hee hee. Say hello to Mikke. He's from Finland."

Mikke was lying on the other bench and was well gone.

"Look at me, Joseph. Look at me! I have to find her. Do you understand? The guy's probably a murderer."

"I'm trying, Harry. I'm really trying. Shit, I wish I could help you."

Joseph squeezed his eyes shut and groaned as he banged his forehead with his fist.

"The light's so bloody bad in this park I didn't see much. I think he was quite big."

"Fat? Tall? Blond? Dark? Lame? Glasses? Beard? Hat?"

Joseph rolled his eyes in answer. "D'ya have a fig, mate. Makes me think better, you know."

But all the cigarettes in the world could not blow away the alcoholic mist wreathing Joseph's brain. Harry gave him the rest of the packet and told him to ask Mikke what he remembered when he came round. Not that he reckoned there would be much.

When Harry returned to Birgitta's flat it was two in the morning. Lebie was sitting by the radio and watched Harry with sympathetic eyes.

"Gave it a burl, did ya? No good, eh?"

Burl? It was beyond Harry, but he nodded in agreement.

"No good," he said, crashing down into a chair.

"What was the mood like at the station?" Lebie asked.

Harry fumbled for a cigarette before realizing he had given them to Joseph.

"One notch from chaos. Watkins is close to going off the rails, and cars are racing round Sydney like headless chickens, with their sirens on in full-pursuit mode. The only thing they know about White is he left his flat in Nimbin early today and caught the four o'clock flight to Sydney. Since then no one's seen him."

He bummed a cigarette off Lebie and they smoked in silence.

"Nip home and get yourself a few hours' sleep, Sergey.

I'll stay here tonight in case Birgitta turns up. Leave the radio on, so it can keep me posted."

"I can sleep here, Harry."

Harry shook his head. "Get yourself home. I'll ring you if there is anything."

Lebie put a Sydney Bears cap on his polished skull. He loitered by the door.

"We'll find her, Harry. I can feel it in my bones. So hang in there, mate."

Harry looked at Lebie. It was hard to say whether Lebie believed what he said.

As soon as he was alone he opened the window and gazed across the rooftops. It had turned cooler, but the air was still mild and mingling with the smell of town, people and food from all corners of the earth. It was one of the planet's most beautiful summer nights in one of the planet's most beautiful towns. He looked up at the starry sky. An infinity of small, flashing lights that seemed to pulsate with life if he watched for long enough. All this meaningless beauty.

He tested his feelings. He couldn't afford to give way to them. Not yet, not now. First, the good feelings. Birgitta's face between his hands, the traces of laughter in her eyes. The bad feelings. Those were the ones he had to keep at arm's length, but he entertained them, as if to form an impression of the power they had.

He felt as though he were sitting in a submarine at the bottom of a very deep ocean. The sea was pressing in; around him the creaks and bangs had already started. He could only hope the hull would hold, that a lifetime's training in self-discipline would finally reveal its worth. Harry thought of the souls that became stars when their earthly shells died. He managed to restrain himself from searching for one star in particular.

50

The Rooster Factor

After the accident Harry had repeatedly asked himself whether he would have exchanged fates if he had been able. So that he would have been the person who had bent the fence post in Sørkedalsveien, who had been given a ceremonial funeral with full police honors and grieving parents, who had a photograph in a corridor at Grønland Police Station and who in time had become a pale but dear memory to colleagues and relatives. Was it not a tempting alternative to the lie he had to live, which in many ways was even more humiliating than accepting the guilt and shame?

But Harry knew he would not have swapped his fate. He was happy to be alive.

Every morning he woke in the hospital, his mind dizzy from pills and void of thoughts, it was with a sense that something had gone terribly wrong. As a rule it took a couple of drowsy seconds before his memory reacted, told him who and where he was and reconstructed the situation for him with relentless horror. His next thought was that he was alive. That he was still on course, it wasn't over yet.

After being discharged he was given a session with a psychiatrist.

"In point of fact, you're a bit late," the psychiatrist said.

"Your subconscious has probably already chosen how it wants to work with what's happened, so we can't influence its first decision. It may, for example, have chosen to repress events. But if it has made such a choice we can try to make it change its mind."

All Harry knew was that his subconscious told him it was a good thing to be alive, and he wasn't willing to take the risk that a psychiatrist might make him change his mind, so that was the first and last time he went to see him.

In the days that followed he taught himself it was also a bad strategy to fight against everything he felt at once. Firstly, he wasn't sure what he felt—at least he didn't have the whole picture, so it was like challenging a monster he hadn't even seen. Secondly, his chances of winning were better if he divided the war up into small skirmishes where he might gain some perspective of the enemy, find his weak points and over time break him down. It was like inserting paper into a shredder. If you inserted too much at once, the machine panicked, coughed and died with a clunk. And you had to start again.

A friend of a colleague, whom Harry had met at a rare dinner engagement, was a local council psychologist. He had sent Harry a quizzical look when Harry elucidated on his method for combating emotions.

"War?" he'd said. "Shredder?" He had appeared to be genuinely concerned.

Harry opened his eyes. The first morning light was seeping in through the curtains. He looked at his watch. Six o'clock. The radio crackled.

"This is Delta. Charlie, come in."

Harry jumped up from the sofa and grabbed the microphone.

"Delta, this is Holy. What's up?"

"We've found Evans White. We got an anonymous tip-off from a woman who had seen him in King's Cross, so we sent three patrol cars and picked him up. He's being questioned now."

"What's he said?"

"He denied everything until we played him the tape of his conversation with Miss Enquist. He told us he'd driven by Hungry Jack's three times after eight o'clock, in a white Honda. But he gave up when he didn't see her and drove back to a flat he's renting. Later he went to a nightclub, and that was where we found him. By the way, the tip-off asked after you."

"I thought as much. Her name's Sandra. Have you searched his flat?"

"Yeah. Nada. Zilch. And Smith says he saw the same white Honda drive past him three times outside Hungry Jack's."

"Why didn't he drive the black Holden as arranged?"

"White says he lied about the car to Miss Enquist in case someone was trying to set him up, so that he could do a couple of circuits and check the coast was clear."

"All right. I'm on my way now. Ring the others and wake them up, will you?"

"They drove home two hours ago, Holy. They'd been up all night and Watkins told us—"

"I don't give a shit what Watkins said. Call them."

They had put back the old fan. It was hard to say if it had benefited from its break; at any rate it creaked in protest at being brought out of retirement.

The meeting was over, but Harry was still sitting in the conference room. His shirt had large, wet patches under his arms, and he had placed a phone on the table in front of him. He closed his eyes and mumbled something to himself. Then he lifted the receiver and dialed the number.

"Hello?"

"This is Harry Holy."

"Harry! Pleased to hear you're up early. A good habit. I've been waiting for you to ring. Are you alone?"

"I'm alone."

There was heavy breathing at both ends of the line.

"You're on to me, aren't you, mate?"

"I've known for quite a while, yes."

"You've done a good job, Harry. And now you're ringing because I've got something you want, right?"

"That's correct." Harry wiped away the sweat.

"You understand that I had to take her, Harry?"

"No. No, I don't understand."

"Come on, Harry, you're not stupid. When I heard someone was digging, I knew of course it would be you. I hope for your sake you've been smart enough to keep your mouth shut about this. Have you, Harry?"

"I've kept my mouth shut."

"So there's still a chance you could see your red-haired friend again."

"How did you do it? How did you take her?"

"I knew when she was finishing work, so I waited outside the Albury in the car and drove behind her. When she went into the park I thought someone ought to tell her it wasn't advisable to go there at night. So I jumped out of the car and ran after her. I let her have a sniff of a cloth I had with me, and after that I had to help her into the car."

Harry realized he hadn't found the transmitter in the bag.

"What do you want me to do?"

"You sound nervous, Harry. Relax. I don't intend to ask for much. Your job is to catch murderers, and that's what I'm asking you to do. To continue to do your job. You see, Birgitta told me that the main suspect was a drug dealer, a certain Mr. Evans White. Innocent or not, every year he and others like him kill many more than I've ever done. And that's not such a small number. Ha ha. I don't think I need to go into details. All I want is for you to make sure Evans White is convicted for his crimes. Plus a couple of mine. The conclusive evidence could be traces of blood and skin belonging to Inger Holter in White's flat? Since you know the pathologist he could supply you with some samples of the requisite evidence and you could plant it at the crime scene, couldn't you? Ha ha. I'm joking, Harry. Perhaps I could get some for you? Perhaps I have traces of blood and skin of the various victims, and the odd hair, lying neatly sorted in plastic bags somewhere? Just in case. After all, you never know when you might need it to send people off on the wrong track. Ha ha."

Harry squeezed the clammy receiver. He was trying to think. The man obviously didn't know that the police were aware of Birgitta's kidnapping and had revised their view of the possible murderer. That could only mean Birgitta hadn't told him she'd been on her way to meet White, watched by the police. He had snaffled her right under the very noses of a dozen officers without even realizing.

The voice brought him back from his thoughts.

"An alluring possibility, Harry, isn't it? The murderer helps you to put another enemy of society into the slammer. Well, let's keep in contact. You have . . . forty-eight hours to bring the charges. I'll be waiting to hear the glad tidings on Friday night's TV news. In the meantime, I promise to treat the redhead with all the respect you might expect of a gentleman. If I don't hear anything I'm afraid she won't survive Saturday. But I can promise her one hell of a Friday night."

Harry rang off. The fan was groaning and screeching wildly. He examined his hands. They were trembling.

* * *

"What do you think, sir?" Harry asked.

The motionless broad back that had been in front of the board the whole time stirred.

"I think we should nab the bastard," McCormack said. "Before we call the others back, tell me exactly how you knew it was him."

"To be honest, sir, I didn't know for sure. It was just one of many theories that occurred to me and one in which at first I didn't really have much faith. After the funeral I got a lift with Jim Connolly, an old boxing colleague of Andrew's. With him was his wife who he said had been a contortionist with the circus when he met her. He said he had wooed her every day for a year before he got anywhere. At first I didn't give this a second's thought, then I realized that perhaps he meant it literally—that in other words the two of them had had the opportunity to see each other every day for a whole year. It struck me that the Jim Chivers crew were in a big tent when Andrew and I saw them in Lithgow, and that a fair was there as well. So I asked Yong to ring the Jim Chivers booking agent to check. And I was right. When Jim Chivers goes on tour it's almost always as part of a traveling circus or fair. Yong had the old itineraries faxed over this morning, and it turns out that the fair Jim Chivers had been traveling with in recent years also had a circus troupe until a while ago. Otto Rechtnagel's troupe."

"Right. So the Jim Chivers boxers were at the crime scenes on the relevant dates as well. But did many of them know Andrew?"

"Andrew introduced me to only one of them, and I should have bloody known it wasn't to look into an inconclusive rape case that he dragged me to Lithgow. Andrew saw him as a son. They'd experienced so many similar things and there were such strong ties between them that he may have been the only person on this earth the orphaned Andrew Kensington felt was real family. Even though he would never admit he had strong feelings for his own people, I think Andrew loved Toowoomba more than anyone else precisely because they were from the same people. That was why Andrew couldn't arrest him himself. His innate moral concepts clashed with his loyalty to his people and love for Toowoomba. It's hard to imagine what a brutal conflict this must have been for him. That was why he needed me, an outsider he could steer toward the target."

"Toowoomba?"

"Toowoomba. Andrew had found out he was behind all the murders. Perhaps the desperate, rejected lover, Otto Rechtnagel, told Andrew after Toowoomba left him. Perhaps Andrew made Otto promise he would never go to the police by saying he would solve the case without involving either of them. But I think Otto was close to spilling the beans. With good reason—he had begun to be frightened for his own life as he realized Toowoomba would hardly want an ex-lover wandering around who could give him away. Toowoomba knew Otto had met me and it wouldn't be long before the game was up. So he planned to murder Otto during the show. Since they'd traveled together with an almost identical show before, Toowoomba knew exactly when to strike."

"Why not do it in Otto's flat? After all, he had the keys."

"I asked myself that, too." Harry paused.

McCormack waved his hand. "Harry, what you've said already is so much for an old cop to absorb that any new theories won't make much difference one way or another."

"The rooster factor."

"The rooster factor?"

"Toowoomba isn't only a psychopath, he's also a rooster. And you can't underestimate a rooster's vanity. While his sexually motivated murders follow a pattern akin to compulsive acts, the Clown Murder is something quite different, it's a rationally necessary murder, you see. With that murder he suddenly had a free hand, he was uninhibited by the psychoses that had set the pace in the other murders. A chance to do something really spectacular, to crown his life's work. The Clown Murder will be remembered long after the girls he killed have been forgotten."

"Fine. And Andrew legged it from the hospital to stop the police when he realized we were going to arrest Otto?"

"My guess is he went straight to Otto's flat to talk to him, to impress on him how important it was that he kept his mouth shut about Toowoomba for now. To calm him down by saying Toowoomba would be arrested as Andrew had planned, if he could have some time. If *I* could have some time. But something went wrong. I have no idea what. But I'm convinced it was Toowoomba who in the end saw off Andrew Kensington."

"Why?"

"Intuition. Common sense. Plus one tiny detail."

"What's that?"

"When I visited Andrew in hospital he said Toowoomba was going to drop by the next day."

"And?"

"At St. Etienne Hospital all visitors have to register at reception. I asked Yong to check with the hospital to see if any visitors or phone calls for Andrew had been registered after I'd been there."

"I don't follow you, Harry."

"If something had cropped up, we have to assume that Toowoomba would have called Andrew to say he wasn't coming. As he didn't do that, it would have been impossible for him to know Andrew was no longer in the hospital until he was standing in reception. After signing the visitors' book. Unless . . ."

"Unless he had killed him the night before."

Harry opened his palms. "You don't visit someone you know isn't there, sir."

* * *

It was going to be a long day. Shit, it's been a long day already, Harry thought. They were sitting in the conference room with rolled-up sleeves trying to be geniuses.

"So you rang a mobile phone number," Watkins said. "And you don't think he's at his address?"

Harry shook his head. "He's cautious. He's holding Birgitta somewhere else."

"Perhaps we can find someone at home who might have a lead as to where he's got her?" Lebie suggested.

"No!" Harry snapped. "If he discovers we've been to his flat he knows I've been talking and Birgitta's had it."

"Well, he'll have to go home some time and we could be ready for him," Lebie said.

"What if he's thought of that and can kill Birgitta without physically being present?" Harry countered. "What if she's tied up somewhere and Toowoomba won't tell us where?" He looked around. "What if she's sitting on a ticking bomb that has to be switched off within a certain number of hours?"

"Stop right there!" Watkins slapped the table. "This isn't a cartoon. For Christ's sake, why would the bloke be an explosives expert just because he's killed a few girls? Time's moving on and we can't sit on our arses waiting any longer. I think it would be a good idea to have a squiz at Toowoomba's place. And we'll make sure we set up a trap that will snap shut on him if he approaches his flat, trust me!"

"The guy's not stupid!" Harry said. "We're putting Birgitta's life at risk by trying a stunt like this. Don't you see?"

Watkins shook his head. "Sorry to say this, Holy, but your relationship with the kidnapped girl's affecting your ability to make rational decisions right now. We'll do as I say."

51

A Kookaburra

The afternoon sun shone through the trees in Victoria Street. A little kookaburra bird was standing on the back of the second empty bench testing its voice for the evening concert.

"I suppose you think it strange that people can walk around smiling on a day like today," Joseph said. "I suppose you take it as a personal affront that the sun is playing on the leaves at a time when you'd rather see the world collapse in misery and weep tears. Well, Harry, my friend, what can I say to you? Things aren't like that."

Harry squinted into the sun. "Perhaps she's hungry, perhaps she's in pain. But the worst is knowing how frightened she must be."

"Then she'll be a good wife for you if she passes the test," Joseph said, whistling to the kookaburra.

Harry gazed at him in amazement. Joseph was sober.

"A long time ago an Aboriginal woman had to pass three tests before she could marry," Joseph said. "The first was to control her hunger. She had to hunt for two days without food. Then she was set before a fire with a juicy kangaroo steak or some other delicacy. The test was to see if she could control herself and not be greedy, just eat a little food and leave enough for others."

"We had something similar when I was growing up," Harry said. "They called it table manners. But I don't think it exists anymore."

"The second test was to see if she could tolerate pain. Nails were put through her cheeks and nose, and they made marks on her body."

"So? Today girls pay to have that done."

"Shut up, Harry. At the end, when the fire was dying she had to lie across it with only a few branches between her and the embers. But the third test was the hardest."

"Fear?"

"Right, Harry. After the sun had gone down the members of the tribe gathered round the fire and the elders took turns to tell the young woman terrifying, hair-raising stories about ghosts and Muldarpe, the shape-shifting evil spirit. Pretty rough stuff, some of it. Afterward she was sent off to sleep in a deserted place, or near the burial places of her forefathers. At the dead of night the elders sneaked up on her with their faces daubed with white clay and wearing bark masks—"

"Isn't that a bit like taking sand to the beach?"

"—and making eerie noises. You're a poor listener, Harry." Joseph was offended.

Harry rubbed his face. "I know," he said at length. "Sorry, Joseph. I just came here to think aloud and to see if he'd left any clues that might give me a pointer as to where he might've taken her. But I don't seem to be getting anywhere, and you're the only person I can use as a sounding board. You must think I sound like a cynical, insensitive bastard."

"You sound like someone who thinks he has to fight the whole world," Joseph said. "But if you don't drop your guard now and then, your arms will be too weary to fight."

Harry cracked a smile. "You're absolutely sure you don't have an older brother?"

Joseph laughed. "As I said, it's too late to ask my mother now, but I think she would have told me."

"You two sound just like brothers."

"You've said that a few times now, Harry. Perhaps you should try to get some sleep."

Joe's face lit up when Harry came in through the door of Springfield Lodge.

"Nice afternoon, eh, Mr. Holy? By the way, you're looking good today. And I've got a parcel for you." He held up a package in gray paper with "Harry Holy" written on it in capital letters.

"Who's it from?" Harry asked, taken aback.

"I don't know. A taxi driver delivered it a couple of hours ago."

In his room Harry placed the package on the bed, unwrapped it and opened the box inside. He had already more or less worked out who it was from, but the contents eliminated any lingering doubt: six small plastic tubes with white stickers on. He picked up one and read a date he instantly recognized as the day Inger Holter was murdered, bearing the inscription "pubic hair." It didn't require much imagination to guess that the other tubes would contain blood, hair, clothes fibers and so on. And they did.

Half an hour later he was woken by the phone.

"Have you got the things I sent you, Harry? I thought you'd need them as soon as possible."

"Toowoomba."

"At your service. Ha ha."

"I've got the things. Inger Holter, I assume. I'm curious, Toowoomba. How did you murder her?"

"Easy as wink," Toowoomba said. "Almost *too* easy. I was in a girlfriend's flat when she rang late one evening."

So Otto's a *girl*friend? Harry almost asked.

"Inger had some dog food for the girl who owns the flat, or should I say, owned the flat? I had let myself in, but spent the evening on my own as my girlfriend was out on the town. As usual."

Harry noticed the voice sharpen.

"Weren't you taking a huge risk? Someone might have known she was going to . . . er, your girlfriend's flat."

"I asked her," Toowoomba said.

"Asked her?" Harry replied, skeptical.

"It's incredible how naive some people are. They speak before engaging the brain because they feel safe and therefore don't have to think. She was such a sweet, innocent girl. 'No, no one knows I'm here, why?' she said. Ha ha. I felt like the wolf in *Little Red Riding Hood.* So I told her she'd come just at the right time. Or should I say wrong time? Ha ha. Do you want to hear the rest?"

Harry did want to hear the rest. Preferably everything, right down to the last detail, how Toowoomba had been as a child, when he had first killed, why he didn't have a fixed ritual, why he sometimes only raped, how he felt after a murder, whether he became depressed after the ecstasy the way serial killers do because it hadn't been perfect that time, either, it hadn't been how he had dreamed and planned it would be. He wanted to know how many, when and where, the methods and the tools. And he wanted to understand the emotions, the passion, what the driving force of his madness was.

But he didn't have the energy. Not now. Right now he couldn't care less whether Inger had been raped before or after she had been killed, whether the murder was a punishment because Otto left him alone, whether he had killed her in the flat or done it in the car. Harry didn't want to know whether she had begged, cried or if her eyes had stared at Toowoomba as she was on the threshold, knowing she was going to die. He didn't want to know because he wouldn't be able to stop himself exchanging Inger's face for Birgitta's, because it would make him weak.

"How did you know where I was staying?" Harry asked, for something to say, to keep the conversation going.

"Harry, are you beginning to feel tired? You told me where you were staying last time we went out together, didn't you. Oh, yes, thank you for that, by the way. I forgot to say."

"Listen, Toowoomba—"

"I've been pondering in fact why you rang me to ask for help that night, Harry. Apart from to slap the two anabolically enhanced dinner jackets about a bit. Well, that was fun, but were we really at the nightclub just to pass on your gratitude to the pimp? I may not be much good at reading people's minds, Harry, but I couldn't make that stack up. You're in the middle of a murder investigation and you waste time and effort getting your own back after being roughed up in a club."

"Well . . ."

"Well, Harry?"

"That wasn't the only reason. The girl we found in Centennial Park happened to work at the club, so I had a theory that the person who killed her might have been there that evening, waited at the back exit and followed her home. I wanted to see how you would react if you discovered what we were up to. Besides, you're a pretty conspicuous sort, so I wanted to point you out to Mongabi to check whether he'd seen you that evening."

"No luck?"

"Nope. My guess is you weren't there."

Toowoomba laughed. "I didn't even know she was a stripper," he said. "I saw her walk into the park and thought someone should tell her it's dangerous there at night. And demonstrate what can happen."

"Well, at least that case is solved," Harry said drily.

"Shame no one else but you will have the pleasure," Toowoomba said.

Harry decided to take a risk.

"Since no one else will have the pleasure of anything, perhaps you could also tell me what happened to Andrew at Otto's flat. Because Otto was your *girlfriend*, wasn't he."

The other end of the line went quiet.

"Wouldn't you rather know how Birgitta is?"

"No," Harry said. Not too fast, not too loud. "You said you would treat her like a gentleman. I trust you."

"I hope you're not trying to give me a bad conscience, Harry. In any case, it's a pointless exercise. I'm a psychopath. I know that, you know," Toowoomba said with a low chuckle. "Frightening, isn't it. We psychopaths aren't supposed to know. But I've always known. And Otto did. Otto even knew that now and then I would have to punish them. But Otto couldn't keep his gob shut. He'd already told Andrew and was on the point of cracking up, so I was forced to act. The afternoon Otto was due to appear at St. George's I slipped into his flat, after he'd left, to remove anything that could connect him with me—photos, gifts, letters, that sort of thing. The doorbell rang. I carefully opened the bedroom window and, to my great surprise, saw that it was Andrew. My first instinct was not to open the door. But then I realized my original plan was about to be ruined. You see, I'd been intending to visit Andrew at the hospital the next day and discreetly donate him a teaspoon, a lighter, a disposable syringe, as well as a little bag of much-desired heroin with my own homemade mix added."

"A deadly cocktail."

"You might say so."

"How could you be sure he would take it? He knew you were a murderer, didn't he."

"He didn't know I knew he knew. If you follow me, Harry. He didn't know Otto had told me. Anyway, a junkie with withdrawal symptoms is willing to take risks. Such as trusting someone he thinks regards him as a father. But there was no point speculating about all of that anymore. He'd left the hospital and was standing at the entrance to the block."

"So you decided to let him in?"

"Do you know how fast the human brain can work, Harry? Do you know that those dreams with long, convoluted plots which we think we spent all night concocting, in reality took place in a few seconds of feverish cerebral activity? That was how quickly it came to me, more or less, the plan to make it look as if Andrew had been behind everything. I swear I hadn't given it a thought until then! So I pressed the buzzer and waited for him to come up. I stood behind the door with my magic cloth—"

"Diethyl ether."

"—and afterward tied Andrew to a chair, found his gear and the little dope he had left and gave him the lot so I could be sure he would be quiet until I returned from the theater. On the way back I got hold of some more shit and Andrew and I had a real party. Yes, it really took off and when I left he was hanging from the ceiling."

Again the low chuckle. Harry concentrated on taking deep, calm breaths. He had never been so afraid in his whole life.

"What do you mean by *you had to punish them*?"

"What?"

"You said before you had to punish them."

"Oh, that. Yes, as I'm sure you know, psychopaths are often paranoid, or they suffer from other delusions. My delusion is that my mission in life is to avenge my people."

"By raping white women?"

"*Childless* white women."

"Childless?" Harry repeated, bemused. That was a feature common to the victims that the investigation hadn't picked up, and why would they? There was nothing unusual about such young women not having had children.

"Yes, indeed. Had you really not noticed? Terra Nullius, Harry! When you came here you defined us as nomads without property because we didn't sow seeds in the earth. You took our country from us, raped and killed it in front of our very eyes." Toowoomba didn't need to raise his voice. The words were loud enough. "Well, your childless women are now my terra nullius, Harry. No one has fertilized them, therefore no one owns them. I'm only following the white man's logic and doing as he does."

"But you call it a delusion yourself, Toowoomba! You know how sick it is!"

"Of course it's sick. But sickness is normal, Harry. It's the absence of sickness that's dangerous, for then the organism stops fighting and it soon falls apart. But *delusions*, Harry, don't underestimate them. They're worth having in every culture. Take your own, for example. In Christianity there is open discussion about how difficult it is to have faith, how doubts can nag at even the cleverest, the most devout priest. But isn't the very acknowledgment of doubt the same as admitting that the faith you choose to live by is a delusion? You shouldn't renounce your delusions so easily, Harry. At the other end of the rainbow there may be a reward."

Harry lay back in bed. He tried not to think about Birgitta, about her not having had any children.

"How could you know they were childless?" he heard himself say in a husky voice.

"I asked."

"How . . . ?"

"Some of them said they had children because they believed I would spare them if they said they provided for a bunch of kids. They had thirty seconds to prove it. A mother who doesn't carry a photo of her child is no mother, if you ask me."

Harry swallowed. "Why blonde?"

"This isn't a hard and fast rule. It just minimizes the chance of them having any of my people's blood in their veins."

Harry tried not to think about Birgitta's milky-white skin. Toowoomba gave a low chuckle.

"I can see there's a lot you want to know, Harry, but using mobile phones is expensive and idealists like me aren't rich. You know what you must do and what you mustn't."

Then he was gone. The quickly falling dusk had cast a gray darkness over the room during the conversation. Two circling feelers of a cockroach poked through the crack in the doorway, checking to see if the coast was clear. Harry pulled the sheet over him and huddled up. On the roof outside the window a solitary kookaburra started the evening concert, and King's Cross wound itself up for another long night.

Harry dreamed about Kristin. He may have done that during two seconds of REM sleep, but there was half a lifetime to unravel, so it might have taken longer. She was wearing his green dressing gown; she stroked his hair and told him to accompany her. He asked her where to, but she was standing in the half-open balcony door with the curtains flapping around her and the children in the backyard were making such a racket that he didn't hear her answer. Every now and then he was so dazzled by the sun that she completely disappeared from view.

He got off his bed and went closer to hear what she was saying, but then she laughed and ran onto the balcony, climbed up the railing and floated off like a green balloon. Up she floated to the rooftops, shouting: "Come on, everyone! Come on, everyone!" Later in the dream he ran around asking everyone he knew where the party was, but either they didn't know or they'd already gone. Then he went down to Frogner Lido, but he didn't have enough money for a ticket and had to clamber over the fence. Once on the other side, he discovered he'd cut himself, and blood was leaving a trail behind him on the grass, over the tiles and up the steps to the ten-meter diving board. No one else was there, so he lay on his back and looked up at the sky, listening to the tiny wet splashes as drops of blood fell and hit the edge of the swimming pool far below. High up, toward the sun, he thought he could discern a floating green figure. He put his hands in front of his eyes, like a pair of binoculars, and then he could see her quite clearly. She was so beautiful and almost transparent.

He was woken once by a bang that might have been a gunshot, and lay listening to the rain and the hum of life in King's Cross. After a while he went back to sleep. Then Harry dreamed about Kristin again, or so he imagined, for the rest of the night. Except that, in brief moments, she had red hair and spoke Swedish.

52

A Computer

Nine o'clock.

Lebie rested his forehead against the door and closed his eyes. Two policemen in black bulletproof vests stood beside him watching closely. They had their weapons at the ready. Behind them on the stairs were Watkins, Yong and Harry.

"There we are!" Lebie said and carefully withdrew the picklock.

"Remember, don't touch anything if the flat's empty," Watkins whispered to the officers.

Lebie stood to the side and opened the door for the two officers, who entered the flat textbook style, each holding a gun in both hands.

"Sure there's no alarm here?" Harry whispered.

"We've checked all the security companies in town, and no one has anything registered for this flat," Watkins said.

"Shh, what's that sound?" Yong said.

The others pricked up their ears, but couldn't hear anything unusual.

"There goes the bomb-expert theory," Watkins said drily.

One of the officers came back out. "It's OK," he said. They breathed a sigh of relief and went in. Lebie tried switching on the light in the hall, but it didn't work.

"Odd," he said, trying the light in the small but clean and tidy sitting room, but that didn't work either. "A fuse must have blown."

"Doesn't matter," Watkins said. "It's more than light enough in here to do a search. Harry, you take the kitchen. Lebie, you take the bathroom. Yong?"

Yong was standing in front of the computer on the desk by the sitting-room window.

"I have a feeling . . ." he said. "Lebie, take the torch and check the fuse box in the hall."

Lebie went out, and immediately the light came on and the computer sprang into life.

"Shit," said Lebie, as he returned to the sitting room. "There was a piece of thread tied round the fuse that I had to remove first. I followed it along the wall and it goes into the door."

"That's an electronic lock, isn't it? The fuse was connected to the lock in such a way that the electricity went off as we opened the door. The sound I heard was the fan in the computer switching off," Yong said, pressing the keyboard. "This machine has rapid resume, so we can see which programs were on before it turned itself off."

A picture of the earth appeared on the screen, and a cheery jingle rang out through the speakers.

"Thought so!" Yong said. "You crafty bastard! Look there!" He pointed to an icon on the screen.

"Yong, for God's sake, let's not waste time on this now," said Watkins.

"Sir, may I borrow your mobile phone for a moment?" The little officer snatched Watkins's Nokia without waiting for an answer. "What's the number here?"

Harry read out the number on the phone beside the computer while Yong tapped it in. Then he pressed the call key. As the phone rang a buzzing sound came from the computer, and the icon on the screen became larger and jumped up and down.

"Shh," said Yong.

After a few seconds a beep sounded. He quickly switched off the mobile phone.

Watkins had a deep frown between his eyebrows. "What in the Lord's name are you doing, Yong?"

"Sir, I'm afraid Toowoomba has rigged up an alarm for us after all. And it's gone off."

"Explain yourself!" Watkins's patience had clear limits.

"Do you see the program coming up? That's a standard answering phone service connected to the phone via a modem. Before Toowoomba goes out he reads in his welcome message to the computer through this microphone. When people ring they activate the program, play Toowoomba's message, and after the little beep you heard, you can leave your message on the computer."

"Yong, I know what an answerphone is. What's the point?"

"Sir, did you hear a message before the beep when I rang just now?"

"No . . ."

"That's because the message was given, but it wasn't saved."

Watkins began to see the light.

"What you're saying is that when the power went and the computer turned itself off the answerphone message went, too."

"Exactly, sir." Occasionally Yong's reactions were unusual. Like now. His face was beaming. "And that's his alarm system, sir."

Harry wasn't smiling when he grasped the scope of the disaster. "So all Toowoomba has to do is ring his own number and hear the message is missing to know that someone has broken into his flat."

The room went silent.

"He'll never turn up here without ringing first," Lebie said.

"Shit, shit, shit," said Watkins.

"He could ring at any moment," Harry said. "We have to gain some time. Any suggestions?"

"Well," Yong said. "We could talk to the phone company and get them to block the number and deliver a malfunction message."

"And if he rings the phone company?"

"Cable fault in the area due to . . . er, digging."

"That sounds fishy. He'll just check his neighbor's number," Lebie said.

"We'll have to get the whole area cut off," Harry said. "Can you do that, sir?"

Watkins scratched behind his ear. "There'll be chaos. Why the hell—?"

"It's urgent, sir!"

"Shit! Give me the phone, Yong. McCormack will have to sort this one out. Whatever happens we can't have the phones in a whole district down for too long, Holy. We'll have to start planning our next move. Shit, shit, shit!"

Eleven thirty.

"Nothing," said a desperate Watkins. "Not a bloody thing!"

"Well, we could hardly expect him to leave a note saying where she was, could we," Harry said.

Lebie emerged from the bedroom. He shook his head. Not even Yong, who had gone through the whole block, had anything to report.

They sat down in the sitting room.

"It's actually a bit odd," Harry said. "If we'd searched each other's flats we would have found *something*. An interesting letter, a stained porn mag, a photo of an old flame, a stain on the sheet, something. But this guy's a serial killer, and we've found absolutely nothing to suggest he has a *life*."

"I've never seen such a tidy bachelor pad before," Lebie said.

"It's *too* tidy," Yong said. "It's almost weird."

"There's something we've overlooked," Harry said, studying the ceiling.

"We've been everywhere," Watkins said. "If he's left any clues, they aren't here. All the bloke does is eat, sleep, watch TV, shit and leave messages on his computer."

"You're right," Harry broke in. "This isn't where Toowoomba the murderer lives. The person who lives here is an abnormally tidy guy who isn't worried about any close interest being taken in him. But what about the other one? Could he have another place? Another flat, a holiday cottage?"

"Nothing registered in that name anyway," Yong said. "I checked before we set out."

The mobile phone rang. It was McCormack. He had spoken to the phone company. To the argument that this was a life and death matter they had retorted that it could also be a life and death matter for neighbors ringing for an ambulance. But with a little help from the mayor's office McCormack had managed to have the lines blocked until seven in the evening.

"Nothing to stop us smoking in here now," Lebie said, plucking out a thin cigarillo. "Or dropping ash on the carpet and leaving big, fat footprints in the hall. Anyone got a light?"

Harry cast about for some matches and struck one. He sat staring at the box. And found his interest engaged.

"Do you know what's special about this box?" he said.

The others dutifully shook their heads.

"It says it's waterproof. And it says it's for use in the mountains and at sea. Do any of you walk around with waterproof matchboxes?"

More head-shaking.

"Would I be wrong to say you can only buy these in specialist shops, and they cost a bit more than standard boxes?"

The others shrugged.

"They're not standard anyway. I've never seen any like it," Lebie said.

Watkins scrutinized the box closely. "I think my brother-in-law had boxes like that on board his boat," he said.

"I was given this box by Toowoomba," Harry said. "At the funeral."

There was a silence.

Yong coughed. "There's a picture of a yacht in the hall," he said tentatively.

One o'clock.

"Thanks for your help, Liz," Yong said, ending the call. "We've got it! It's in the marina in Lady Bay where it's registered to one Gert Van Hoos."

"OK," Watkins said. "Yong, you stay here in case Toowoomba turns up. Lebie, Harry and I will head out there now."

The traffic was light and Lebie's new Toyota purred with contentment doing 120 kph up New South Head Road.

"No backup, sir?" Lebie inquired.

"If he's there three men are more than enough," Watkins said. "According to Yong, there's no arms license registered, and I have a feeling he's not the type to brandish weapons."

Harry was unable to restrain himself.

"What feeling is that, sir? The same one that told you it was a good idea to break into the flat? The same one that said she should keep the radio transmitter in her bag?"

"Holy, I—"

"I'm just asking, sir. If we have to use your *feeling* as a guide for anything, that will mean, in light of what's happened so far, he'll be brandishing a gun. Not that—"

Harry realized he'd raised his voice, and shut up. Not now, he told himself. Not yet. In a lower voice he finished the sentence.

"Not that I mind. It just means I can pepper him with lead."

Watkins chose not to answer; instead he glared sulkily out of the window as they drove on in silence. In the mirror Harry saw Lebie's cautious, inscrutable smile.

One thirty.

"Lady Bay Beach," Lebie said, pointing. "Fitting name, as well. You see, this is Sydney's number-one gay beach."

They decided to park outside the fence to the marina, and walked down a grassy mound to the little harbor where the masts huddled together each side of narrow pontoons. At the gate was a sleepy guard wearing a sun-bleached, blue uniform shirt. He perked up when Watkins flashed his police badge and described to them where Gert Van Hoos's boat was moored.

"Anyone on board?" Harry asked.

"Not as far as I know," said the guard. "It's a bit difficult to keep track of everything in the summer, but I don't think there's been anyone in the boat for a couple of days."

"Has anyone been there at all recently?"

"Yes, if my memory serves me right. Mr. Van Hoos was here late Tuesday. He usually parks close by the water. He left again later that night."

"And no one's been on the boat since?" Watkins asked.

"Not on my watch. But, luckily, there are several of us."

"Was he alone?"

"Far as I remember, yes."

"Was he carrying anything to the boat?"

"Probably. I don't remember. Most do."

"Could you give us a description of Mr. Van Hoos?" Harry said.

The guard scratched his head. "Well, no, in fact I can't."

"Why not?" Watkins asked, surprised.

The guard looked sheepish. "To be quite honest, I think all Aborigines look the same."

The sun glittered on the water inside the marina, but further out the breakers rolled in off the sea, big and heavy. Harry could feel the wind was fresher here as they made a cautious approach along the pontoon. He recognized the name of the boat, *Adelaide*, and its registration number painted on the side. *Adelaide* wasn't one of the biggest boats at the marina, but it looked well kept. Yong had explained to them that only boats with engines over a certain size had to be registered, so actually they'd had more than their share of luck. So much more that Harry had an unpleasant feeling their luck had been used up. The notion that Birgitta might be on board the boat made his heart throb.

Watkins motioned for Lebie to enter first. Harry took the safety catch off his gun and pointed it at the lounge hatch as Lebie circumspectly placed his feet on the aft deck. Watkins tripped over the anchor rope as he went on board and landed on the deck with a thump. They stopped and listened, but all they could hear was the wind and the waves lapping and gurgling against the hull. Both the hatch to the lounge and the aft cabin were secured with padlocks. Lebie took out his picklock and got to work. After a few minutes both had been removed.

Lebie opened the lounge hatch and Harry clambered in first. It was dark down below and Harry crouched with his gun in front of him until Watkins descended and drew the curtains aside. It was a plain but tastefully furnished boat. The lounge was made of mahogany but otherwise the interior bore no signs of excess. A sea chart lay rolled up on the table. Above it hung a picture of a young boxer.

"Birgitta!" Harry shouted. "Birgitta!"

Watkins patted his shoulder.

* * *

"She's not here," Lebie confirmed after they had been through the boat from prow to stern.

Watkins stood with his head buried in one of the boxes on the aft deck.

"She might have *been* here," Harry said, scanning the sea. The wind was up and the tips of the waves beyond frothed white.

"We'd better get Forensics over here and see what they can find," Watkins said, straightening. "This can only mean he has somewhere we don't know about."

"Or—" Harry said.

"Rubbish! He's got her hidden somewhere. It's just a question of finding her."

Harry sat down. The wind ruffled and teased his hair. Lebie tried to light a cigarillo, but gave up after a couple of attempts.

"So what do we do now?" Harry asked.

"Get out of his boat quick," Watkins said. "He can see us from the road if he drives this way."

They got up, locked the hatches and Watkins took a high step over the anchor rope so as not to trip again.

Lebie stood still.

"What is it?" Harry asked.

"Well," Lebie said, "I'm no expert on boats, but is this normal?"

"What?"

"Dropping the anchor when you're moored fore and aft?"

They exchanged glances.

"Help me to pull it up," Harry said.

53

The Lizards Are Singing

Three o'clock.

They raced down the road. The clouds raced across the sky. The trees beside the road swayed and waved them on. The grass lay flat at the roadside and the radio crackled. The sun had paled and fleeting shadows rushed across the sea.

Harry was sitting at the back, but saw nothing of the storm blowing up around them. He saw only the slimy green rope they had dragged from the sea in spasmodic jerks. The drops of water had fallen into the sea like glistening crystals, and deep below they had glimpsed a white outline slowly rising toward them.

One summer holiday his father had taken him out in a rowing boat and they had caught a halibut. It had been white and unimaginably large and even then Harry's mouth had gone dry and his hands had begun to tremble. His mother and grandmother had clapped their hands with excitement as they entered the kitchen with their catch and straightaway began to cut up the cold, bleeding fish with big, shiny knives. For the rest of the summer Harry had dreamed about the huge halibut in the boat with its protruding eyes and expression frozen with shock, as though it could not believe it was actually dying. The following Christmas

Harry had been given some jelly-like pieces on his plate, and his father had proudly told everyone how he and Harry had been fishing for halibut in Isfjorden. "We thought we would try something new this Christmas," his mother had said. It had tasted of death and depravity, and Harry had left the table with tears in his eyes, furious with indignation.

And now Harry was sitting in the back of a car as it sped along; he closed his eyes and saw himself staring down into the water where something resembling a sea nettle jellyfish gathered its red tentacles alongside at every heave of the rope, stopped and spread them out into a new swimming stroke. As it approached the surface it spread them into a fan shape trying to conceal the naked white body beneath. The rope was wound around her neck, and the lifeless corpse seemed strangely alien and extraneous to Harry.

But when they turned her onto her back, Harry felt it again. It was the expression from that summer. Dimmed eyes with a surprised, accusatory final question: Is this all there is? Is the purpose really that it should all end like this? Is life, and death, really so banal?

"Is that her?" Watkins had asked, and Harry had answered in the negative.

When he repeated the question Harry spotted her shoulder blades sticking out, showing red skin next to a white strip where her bikini top had been.

"She was sunburned," he answered in astonishment. "She asked me to put sun cream on her back. She said she trusted me. But she was burned."

Watkins stood in front of him and placed his hands on Harry's shoulders. "It's not your fault, Harry. Do you hear me? It would have happened anyway. It's not your fault."

It had become noticeably darker now, and gusts of wind tore in with such force that the eucalyptus trees shook and waved their branches, seemingly intending to detach themselves from the ground and lumber around like John Wyndham's triffids, brought to life by the storm that was on its way.

"The lizards are singing," Harry said suddenly from the backseat. They were the first words that had been spoken since they'd got into the car. Watkins turned and Lebie watched him in the mirror. Harry coughed.

"Andrew said that once. That lizards and humans from the lizard family had the power to create rain and storms by singing. He told me the Great Flood was created by the lizard family singing and cutting themselves with flint knives to drown the platypus." He smiled weakly. "Almost all the platypuses died. But a few survived. Do you know what they did? They taught themselves to breathe underwater."

The first large drops of rain landed with a shiver on the windscreen.

"We haven't got much time," Harry said. "Toowoomba will soon realize we're after him, and then he'll disappear like a rat into the ground. I'm the only link we have with him, and now you're wondering whether I can handle it. Well, what can I say? I think I loved the girl."

Watkins looked uneasy. Lebie nodded slowly.

"But I'm going to breathe underwater," Harry said.

Three thirty.

No one in the conference room took any notice of the fan's lament.

"OK, we know who our man is," Harry said. "And we know he thinks the police *don't* know. He's probably thinking that I'm trying to falsify evidence against Evans White. But I'm afraid this is a very temporary situation. We can't keep households without a phone for much longer, and besides it will soon start to look suspicious if the alleged fault isn't fixed.

"We have officers in position if he should appear at his home. Ditto the boat. But personally I'm convinced he's much too careful to do anything stupid without being one hundred percent sure that the coast is clear. It's probably realistic to assume that at some point this evening he'll know we've been in his flat. That gives us two options. We can sound the alarm bells, go out live on TV and hope we find him before he disappears. The counterargument is that anyone who's rigged up a system like the one he has is certain to have planned ahead. As soon as he sees his picture on the screen we risk him going underground. The second option is, therefore, to use the little time we have before he feels us breathing down his neck, to catch him while he is relatively unsuspecting."

"I vote we go for him," Lebie said, removing a hair from his shoulder.

"*Catch* him?" Watkins said. "Sydney has over four million inhabitants and we don't have the slightest idea where he could be. We don't even bloody know if he *is* in Sydney!"

"No question about that," Harry said. "He's definitely been in Sydney for the last one and a half hours."

"What? Are you saying he's been seen?"

"Yong." Harry gave the floor to the ever-smiling officer.

"The mobile phone!" he began. As though he had been asked to read his essay aloud to the class.

"All mobile-phone conversations are linked via what are known as base stations, which receive and transmit signals. A phone company can see which subscriber's signals the various base stations receive. Every one covers a radius of about ten kilometers. Where there is good coverage, i.e., in built-up areas, your phone is generally covered by two or more stations at once, a bit like with radio transmitters. That means that when you're talking on the phone a phone company can locate your position to within ten kilometers. If the conversation can be picked up by two stations at once, that will reduce the area to the zone where the coverage of the two stations overlaps. If your signals are picked up by three stations, the zone is even smaller, and so on. Thus, mobile phones cannot be traced to a single address like a standard phone, but we do have a pointer.

"At this minute we're in touch with three blokes from the phone company following Toowoomba's signals. We can connect them to an open line here in the conference room. For the moment we're receiving simultaneous signals from only two stations and the overlapping area covers the whole of the city, the harbor and half of Woolloomooloo. The good news is that he's on the move."

"And what we need is a spot of luck," Harry chimed in.

"We hope he moves into one of the small pockets covered by three base stations or more. If so, we can launch all the civilian cars we have at a moment's warning and have a crumb of hope that we might find him."

Watkins didn't look convinced. "So he's spoken to someone now, and he also called an hour and a half ago, and both times the signals were picked up by base stations in Sydney?" he said. "And we're dependent on him continuing to chat on the bloody phone to find him? And what if he doesn't ring?"

"We can ring him, can't we?" Lebie said.

"Wonderful!" Watkins said. His cheeks were very flushed. "Great idea! We can ring him every quarter of an hour pretending to be the speaking clock or some such bollocks! Which will tell him it might not be a smart idea to talk on the phone!"

"He doesn't need to do that," Yong said. "He doesn't need to speak to anyone."

"How . . . ?"

"It's enough for his phone to be switched on," Harry said. "It seems Toowoomba isn't aware of this, but as long as a phone isn't switched off, it automatically sends out a little beep every half an hour, to say it's still alive. This beep is registered by the base stations in the same way as a conversation."

"So . . ."

"So let's keep the line open, brew up some coffee, sit tight and keep our fingers crossed."

54

A Good Ear

A metallic voice came through the telephone loudspeaker.

"His signal's coming through on base stations 3 and 4."

Yong pointed to the map of Sydney spread over the board. Numbered circles had been drawn to show the areas of coverage for the various base stations.

"Pyrmont, Glebe and a chunk of Balmain."

"Bloody hell!" Watkins swore. "Much too big an area. What's the time? Has he tried to ring home?"

"It's six," Lebie said. "He's dialed the number of his flat twice in the last hour."

"He'll soon twig there's something amiss," McCormack said, getting up again.

"He hasn't yet though," Harry said quietly. He'd been sitting still on a chair tilted against the back wall for the last two hours.

"Any news on the weather warning?" Watkins asked.

"Only that it's going to get worse," Lebie said. "Gale-force winds, hurricane force tonight."

The minutes ticked by. Yong went for more coffee.

"Hello?" It was the telephone loudspeaker.

Watkins jumped up. "Yes?"

"The subscriber's just used his phone. We have him in base stations 3, 4 and 7."

"Wait!" Watkins looked at the map. "That's a bit of Pyrmont and Darling Harbour, isn't it?"

"That's right."

"Shit! If he'd been in 9 and 10 as well, we'd have had him!"

"Who did he call?" McCormack said.

"Our central switchboard," said the metallic voice. "He asked what the matter was with his home number."

"Shit, shit, shit!" Watkins was as red as a beetroot. "He's getting away! Let's sound the alarm bells now!"

"Shut up!" came the stinging response. The room fell silent. "Apologies for my choice of words, sir," Harry said. "But I suggest we wait until the next beep before we do anything hasty."

Watkins looked at Harry with his eyes popping out.

"Holy's right," McCormack said. "Sit down, Watkins. In less than an hour the block on the phones will be lifted. That means we have one, maximum two, beeps left before Toowoomba finds out it's only his phone that's still cut off. Pyrmont and Darling Harbour are not large areas in geographical terms, but we're talking about one of Sydney's most populated central districts at night. Sending a load of cars down there will only create the kind of chaos Toowoomba will use to escape. We wait."

At twenty to seven the message came over the loudspeaker:

"A beep has been received at base stations 3, 4 and 7."

Watkins groaned.

"Thank you," Harry said, disconnecting the microphone. "Same area as last time, which suggests he isn't moving anymore. So where can he be?"

They crowded round the map.

"Maybe he's doing some boxing training," Lebie said.

"Good suggestion!" said McCormack. "Are there any gyms in the area? Anyone know where the bloke trains?"

"I'll check, sir," Yong said, and was gone.

"Other suggestions?"

"The area's full of tourist attractions which are open in the evening," Lebie said. "Maybe he's in the Chinese Gardens?"

"He'll be staying indoors in this weather," McCormack said.

Yong returned, shaking his head. "I rang his trainer. He wouldn't say anything, so I had to say I was the police. Toowoomba's gym's in Bondi Junction."

"Nice one!" said Watkins. "How long do you think it'll be before the trainer rings Toowoomba's mobile phone and asks what the hell the police want him for?"

"This is urgent," Harry said. "I'll ring Toowoomba."

"To ask him where he is?" Watkins asked.

"To see what's happening," Harry said, picking up the receiver. "Lebie, check the tape recorder's on and everyone keep quiet!"

Everyone froze. Lebie cast a glance at the old tape recorder and gave Harry a thumbs-up. Harry gulped. His fingers felt numb on the keys. The phone rang three times before Toowoomba answered.

"Hello?"

The voice . . . Harry held his breath and pressed the receiver to his ear. In the background he could hear people.

"Who's that?" Toowoomba said in a low voice.

There was a sound in the background followed by children's exuberant cries. Then he heard Toowoomba's deep, calm laugh.

"Well, if it isn't Harry. Odd that you're calling, because I was just thinking about you. There seems to be something wrong with my home phone, and I was wondering if you had anything to do with it. I hope you don't, Harry."

There was another sound. Harry concentrated but he was unable to identify what it was.

"It makes me nervous when you don't answer, Harry.

Very nervous. I don't know what you want, but perhaps I should switch off this phone. Is that it, Harry? Are you trying to find me?"

The sound . . .

"Shit!" Harry shouted. "He hung up." He flopped onto a chair. "Toowoomba knew it was me. How on earth could he know?"

"Rewind the tape," McCormack said. "And get hold of Marguez."

Yong ran out of the room while they played the tape.

Harry couldn't help himself. The hairs on the back of his neck rose when he heard Toowoomba's voice again over the speakers.

"It's definitely a place with a lot of people," Watkins said. "What's that bang? Listen, children. Is it a fair?"

"Rewind and play it again," McCormack said.

"*Who's that*?" Toowoomba repeated, followed by a loud sound and children's shouts.

"What's . . . ?" Watkins began.

"That's a pretty loud splash," said a voice from the door. They turned. Harry saw a small brown head with black curls, a little moustache and tiny, thick glasses, attached to a large body that looked as if it had been inflated with a bicycle pump and could burst at any moment.

"Jesús Marguez—the best ears in the force," McCormack said. "And he's not even blind."

"Just almost blind," Marguez mumbled, straightening his glasses. "What have you got here?"

Lebie played the tape again. Marguez listened with closed eyes.

"Indoors. Brick walls. And glass. No muffling of any kind, no carpets or curtains. People, young people of both sexes, probably a number of young families."

"How can you know all that from listening to some noise?" Watkins asked suspiciously.

Marguez sighed. It clearly wasn't the first time he had come across skeptics.

"Do you realize what fantastic instruments ears are?" he said. "They can distinguish between a million separate differences in pressure. One million. And one and the same sound can be comprised of tens of different frequencies and elements. That gives you a choice of ten million. An average dictionary contains only about a hundred thousand headwords. A choice of ten million, the rest is training."

"What's the sound in the background we can hear the whole time?" Harry asked.

"The one between 100 and 120 hertz? Hard to say. We can filter away the other sounds in our studio and isolate it, but it takes time."

"And that is what we haven't got," McCormack said.

"But how could he identify Harry even though Harry never spoke?" Lebie asked. "Intuition?"

Marguez removed his glasses and polished them absentmindedly.

"What we so nicely call intuition, my friend, is always supported by our sensory impressions. But when the impression is so small and delicate that we only perceive it as a sensation, a feather under a nose while we're sleeping, and we cannot put a name to the associations, the brain cuts in and we call it intuition. Perhaps it was the way . . . er, Harry was breathing?"

"I held my breath," Harry said.

"Have you rung him from here before? Maybe the acoustics? Background noise? Humans have sensationally good memories as far as noises are concerned, generally better than we ourselves are aware."

"I've rung him from here once before . . ." Harry stared at the old fan. "Of course. That's why I can recognize the background noise. I've been there before. The bubbles . . ."

He turned.

"He's in Sydney Aquarium!"

"Hm," Marguez said, studying the shine of his glasses. "That makes sense. I've been there myself, of course. A splash like that can be made by the tail of a pretty big saltie."

When he looked up again he was alone in the room.

55

A Straight Left and Three Shots

Seven o'clock.

They would perhaps have endangered the lives of civilians on the short stretch from the police station down to Darling Harbour, had it not been for the storm that had cleared the streets of people and cars. Lebie did his best, nevertheless, and it was probably the blue light on the car roof that allowed a solitary pedestrian to jump for his life at the last moment and a couple of oncoming cars to swerve to safety. Watkins was in the backseat swearing non-stop, while McCormack was in the front ringing Sydney Aquarium to prepare them for some police action.

As they turned into the car park the flags in the harbor were flying horizontal, and waves were crashing over the edge of the quay. Several police cars were already there and uniformed officers were closing the exits.

McCormack gave the final orders.

"Yong, you distribute the photos of Toowoomba to our people. Watkins, you stay with me in the control room—they've got cameras there covering the whole aquarium. Lebie and Harry, you start searching. The aquarium closes in a few minutes. Here are the radios, put the plugs in your ears, fix the mikes to your lapels and check you have radio contact at once. We'll guide you from the control room, OK?"

As Harry got out of the car a gust of wind caught him and almost knocked him over. They ran for shelter.

"Fortunately it's not as full as it usually is," McCormack announced. He was already breathing heavily from the short sprint. "Must be the weather. If he's here we'll find him."

They were met by the security manager who showed McCormack and Watkins to the control room. Harry and Lebie checked their radios, were ushered past the ticket windows and set off along the corridors.

Harry checked for the gun in his shoulder holster. The aquarium seemed different now, with all the light and all the people. Besides, it felt like an eternity since he had been here with Birgitta, as though it had been in a different era.

He tried not to think about it.

"We're in position." McCormack's voice sounded secure and reassuring in the earpiece. "We're studying the cameras now. Yong has a couple of officers with him and is checking the toilets and the cafe. We can see you, by the way. Keep going."

The corridors in the aquarium led the public in a circle back to where they had started. Harry and Lebie were walking anticlockwise so that all the faces were coming toward them. Harry's heart was pounding. His mouth was dry and his palms were wet. There was a buzz of foreign languages around them, and to Harry it seemed as if he were swimming through a maelstrom of different nationalities, complexions and apparel. They walked through the underwater tunnel where he and Birgitta had spent the night—where children were standing now with their noses glued to the glass watching the marine underworld go about its undisturbed everyday business.

"This place gives me the creeps," Lebie whispered. He walked with his hand inside his jacket.

"Just promise me you won't fire a shot here," Harry said.

"I don't want half of Sydney Harbour and a dozen sharks in my lap, OK?"

"No worries," Lebie answered.

They emerged on the other side of the aquarium, which was as good as deserted. Harry swore.

"They close the ticket office at seven," Lebie said. "Now the people who are still here have to be let out."

McCormack contacted them. "Afraid it seems as if the bird's flown, boys. You'd better come back to the control room."

"Wait here," Harry said to Lebie.

Outside the ticket-booth window there was a familiar face. He was wearing a uniform, and Harry grabbed him.

"Hi, Ben, do you remember me? I came here with Birgitta."

Ben turned and looked at the animated blond hair. "Yes, I do," he said. "Harry, wasn't it? Yeah, yeah, so you've come back? Most do. How's Birgitta?"

Harry swallowed. "Listen, Ben. I'm a police officer. As you've probably heard by now, we're on the lookout for a very dangerous man. We haven't found him yet, but I have a feeling he's still here. No one knows this place better than you do. Is there anywhere he could have hidden?"

Ben's face was swathed in deep, thoughtful folds.

"Well," he said. "Do you know where Matilda is, our saltie?"

"Yes."

"Between the crafty little sod we call Fiddler Ray and the big sea turtle, well, we've moved her now, and we're going to make a pool so that we can have a few freshies—"

"I know where she is. This is urgent, Ben."

"Right. If you're fit and not too jittery, you can jump over the plexiglas in the corner."

"Into where the crocodile is?"

"It spends most of its time half asleep in the pool. From the corner it's five or six steps to the door we use when we wash and feed Matilda. But you'll have to be nippy because a saltie's incredibly fast. It'll be on you, all two tons of it, before you know what's hit you. Once we were going to—"

"Thanks, Ben." Harry broke into a run and people scattered to the side. He folded his lapel and spoke into the mike: "McCormack, Holy here. I'm going to check behind the crocodile pen."

He caught Lebie by the arm and dragged him along. "Last chance," he said. Lebie's eyes widened with alarm as Harry stopped by the crocodile and took a run-up. "Follow me," Harry said, jumping onto the Plexiglas wall and swinging himself over.

As his feet hit the ground on the other side, the water in the pool began to ferment. White froth rose and as Harry headed for the door he saw a green Formula One car accelerating out of the water, low-slung, with small lizard feet on the sides whirling round like rotary whisks. He kicked off and slipped in the loose sand. From far behind him he heard the roars and from the corner of his eye he saw the raised bonnet of the racer. He was up again, sprinted the few meters to the door and grabbed the handle. For a fraction of a second Harry's mind dwelt on the possibility that the door might be locked. The next moment he was inside. A scene from *Jurassic Park* appeared at the back of his mind and made him bolt the door behind him. Just in case.

He unholstered his gun. The damp room stank of a nauseous mixture of detergent and rotten fish.

"Harry!" It was McCormack on the radio. "First of all, there is a simpler route into where you are now than straight through that beast's food bowl. Secondly, stay right there, nice and calm, until Lebie's walked round."

"Can't hear . . . bad re . . . ion, sir," Harry said, scratching a nail across the mike. "I'm . . . go . . . n alone."

He opened the door at the other end of the room and emerged into a tower with a spiral staircase in the middle. Harry guessed that the stairs led down to the underwater tunnels, and decided to go up. On the next landing there was another door. He peered up the stairs, but there didn't appear to be any more doors.

He twisted the handle and pushed the door open carefully with his left hand while keeping the gun trained ahead of him. It was as black as night inside, and the stench of rotten fish was overwhelming.

Harry found a light switch on the wall inside the door, which he operated with his left hand, but it didn't work. He let go of the door and took two probing steps forward. There was a crunch beneath his feet. Harry guessed what it was and retreated soundlessly to the door. Someone had smashed the bulb in the ceiling. He held his breath and listened. Was there someone else in the room? A ventilator rumbled.

Harry slipped back onto the landing.

"McCormack," he whispered into the mike, "I think I've found him. Listen, do me a favor and call his mobile phone."

"Harry Holy, where are you?"

"Now, sir. Please, sir."

"Harry, don't make this a personal vendetta. It's—"

"It's hot today, sir. Will you help me or not?"

Harry heard McCormack's heavy breathing.

"OK, I'll call now."

Harry nudged the door open with his foot and stood legs akimbo in the doorway, his gun held in front of him with both hands, waiting for the phone to ring. Time felt like a droplet that would never fall. Perhaps two seconds passed. Not a sound.

He's not here, Harry thought.

Then three things happened at once.

The first was that McCormack started talking. "He's switched off . . ."

The second was that Harry realized he was silhouetted against the doorway like a wild creature in flight.

The third was that Harry's world exploded in a shower of stars and red blotches on his retina.

Harry remembered fragments of Andrew's boxing lessons from their drive to Nimbin. Such as that a hook performed by a professional boxer is normally more than enough to knock an untrained man unconscious. By moving his hip he gets the whole of his upper torso behind the hook and gives the punch so much power that the brain short-circuits instantly. An uppercut placed precisely on the point of the chin lifts you from the floor and sends you straight into dreamland. For certain. Also a perfect straight right from a right-handed boxer leaves you poor odds for being able to stand upright afterward. And most important of all: if you don't see the punch coming, the body won't react and swerve away. Just a minor movement of the head can considerably soften the impact of a punch. It's very rare for a boxer to see the decisive blow that knocks him out.

The only explanation for Harry not being unconscious must therefore have been that the man in the dark had been standing to Harry's left. Because Harry was standing in the doorway he couldn't hit him in the temple from the side, which according to Andrew in all probability would have been sufficient. He couldn't throw an effective hook or an uppercut as Harry was holding his arms with the gun in front of him. Nor a straight right, because that would have meant standing in front of the gun. The only option remaining was a straight left, a punch Andrew had dismissed as a "woman's punch, most suited to irritate or at best bruise an opponent in a street fight." Andrew may have been correct about that, but this straight left had sent Harry flying backward down the spiral staircase where his back had met the edge of the railing and he had almost flipped over.

When he opened his eyes, though, he was still standing upright. A door was open at the other end of the room, through which he was fairly sure Toowoomba had made his escape. But he could also hear a clanking sound he was fairly sure was his gun rolling down the metal stairs. He decided to go for the gun. With a suicidal dive down the staircase Harry grazed his forearms and knees, but caught the gun just as it was about to bounce off the edge and plunge twenty meters to the bottom of the shaft. He struggled to his knees, coughed and confirmed he had lost his second tooth since coming to this bloody country.

He stood up and almost immediately passed out.

"Harry!" someone shouted in his ear.

He also heard a door being flung open somewhere below him and felt running feet shaking the stairs. Harry aimed himself at the door in front of him, saw the door at the other end of the room, half hit it and staggered out into the dusk with a sense that he had dislocated his shoulder.

"Toowoomba!" he screamed into the wind. He looked around. Before him lay the town, and behind him Pyrmont Bridge. He was standing on the roof of the aquarium and had to hold on tight to the top of a fire escape in the gusting wind. The water in the harbor had been whipped into white foam and he could taste the salt in the air. Below him he saw a dark figure on his way down the fire escape. The figure stopped for a second and looked around. To its left was a police car with a flashing light. In front of it, behind a fence, the two tanks of water that protruded from Sydney Aquarium.

"Toowoomba!" Harry yelled and tried to raise the gun. His shoulder refused point-blank, and Harry screamed with pain and fury. The figure jumped down from the ladder, ran to the fence and began to climb over. Harry realized at that moment what he was intending to do—to get into the building housing the tank, go out through the back and swim the short distance to the quay on the other side.

From there it would take him only seconds to disappear into the crowds. Harry stumbled down the fire escape. He charged at the fence as if intending to tear it down, swung himself over with one arm and landed on the cement with a thud.

"Harry, report in!"

He pulled the plug out of his ear and lurched toward the building. The door was open. Harry ran in and fell to his knees. Beneath the arched roof ahead of him, bathed in lights hanging from a steel cable over the tank, was an enclosed piece of Sydney Harbour. A narrow pontoon crossed through the middle of the tank, and a fair way down it, there was Toowoomba. He was wearing a black roll-neck sweater and black trousers and running in as relaxed and elegant a manner as a narrow, unstable pontoon would allow.

"Toowoomba!" Harry shouted for the third time. "I'm going to shoot!"

Harry leaned forward, not because he couldn't stand upright, but because he couldn't raise his arm. He got the dark figure in his sights and pulled the trigger.

The first shot made a tiny splash in front of Toowoomba, who seemed to be running with consummate ease. Harry aimed a bit to the right. There was a splash behind Toowoomba. The distance was almost a hundred meters now. An absurd thought occurred to Harry: it was like shooting practice inside the hall in Økern—the lights in the ceiling, the echo between the walls, the pulse in the trigger finger and the deep meditative concentration.

Like training on the shooting range in Økern, Harry thought, and fired for the third time.

Toowoomba plunged headlong.

Harry said later in his statement that he assumed the shot had hit Toowoomba in the left thigh, and that therefore it was unlikely to kill him. Everyone knew, however, that this was no more than a wild guess, firing as he had from a hundred meters away. Harry could have said anything he liked without anyone being able to prove the contrary. Since there was no body left on which to do an autopsy.

Toowoomba lay screaming half submerged in the water as Harry advanced up the pontoon. Harry felt dizzy and nauseous, and everything was beginning to blur—the water, the lights in the roof and the pontoon tilting from side to side. As Harry ran he remembered Andrew's words about love being a greater mystery than death. And he remembered the old story.

Blood rushed in his ears, in surges, and Harry was the young warrior Walla, and Toowoomba was the snake Bubbur, who had taken the life of his beloved Moora. And now Bubbur had to be killed. By love.

In McCormack's statement later he was unable to say what Harry Holy had shouted into his mike after they'd heard the shots.

"We just heard him running and shouting something, probably in Norwegian."

Even Harry was unable to say what he'd shouted.

In a life-and-death race, Harry sprinted up the pontoon. Toowoomba's body was jerking. Jerks that made the whole pontoon writhe. At first Harry thought something had bumped into it, but then he realized he was being cheated of his quarry.

It was the Great White.

It raised its white skull from the water and opened its jaws. Everything seemed to happen in slow motion. Harry was sure it was going to take Toowoomba, but it couldn't get a proper grip and only succeeded in dragging the screaming body further into the water before having to dive again.

No arms, Harry thought, recalling a birthday with his grandmother in Åndalsnes a long, long time ago when they were doing apple bobbing, trying to grab apples with their mouths from a tub of water, and his mother had laughed so much she'd had to lie down on the sofa afterward.

Thirty meters to go. He thought he would make it, but then the shark was back. It was so close Harry saw it roll its cold eyes, as if in ecstasy, as it triumphantly showed its double row of teeth. This time it managed to catch hold of one foot and tossed its head from side to side. Water shot up in a jet of spray, Toowoomba was flung through the air like a limbless doll and his screaming was cut short. Harry arrived.

"You bloody monster, he's mine!" he wailed through tears, pointing his gun and emptying the magazine into the pool in one burst. The water was suffused with a reddish color, similar to a red squash drink, and down below Harry saw the light of the underwater tunnel where adults and children were thronging round to see the finale, a genuine drama in all its true horror, a feast that would compete with "The Clown Murder" for tabloid event of the year.

56

The Tattoo

Gene Binoche looked and sounded exactly like what he was—a guy who had lived a rock 'n' roll lifestyle to the full and didn't intend to stop until he was at his journey's end. And he was well on the way.

"I guess they need a good tattooist down there too," Gene said, dipping the needle. "Satan appreciates a bit of variety when he's torturing, don't you think, mate?"

But the customer was plastered and his head was drooping, so he probably couldn't comprehend Gene's philosophical observations or feel the needle puncturing his shoulder.

At first Gene had refused to deal with this bloke who'd entered his little boutique and slurred his request in an odd sing-song accent.

Gene had answered that they didn't tattoo people in his condition and asked him to return the following day when he'd sobered up. But the bloke had slapped 500 dollars on the table for what he reckoned was a 150-dollar job, and to tell the truth business had been a bit slack in recent months, so he took out his Ladyshave and Mennen stick deodorant and started the job. But he refused when the bloke offered him a swig from the bottle. Gene Binoche had been tattooing customers for twenty years, was proud of his work and in his opinion serious professionals didn't drink on the job. Not whiskey at any rate.

When he'd finished he taped a bit of toilet paper over the rose tattoo. "Keep out of the sun and, for the first week, wash with water only. The good news is the pain will subside this evening and you can take this off tomorrow. The bad news is you'll be back for more tattoos," he said and grinned. "They always come back."

"This is the only one I want," the bloke said and staggered out of the door.

57

Four Thousand Feet and an End

The door opened and the roar of the wind was deafening. Harry crouched down on his knees by the opening.

"Are you ready?" he heard a voice shout in his ear. "Pull the rip cord at four thousand feet and don't forget to count. If you haven't felt the chute within three seconds something's wrong."

Harry nodded.

"I'm going!" the voice yelled.

He saw the wind take hold of the black outfit worn by the little man climbing out onto the stay under the wing. The hair protruding from under his helmet flapped. Harry glanced at the altimeter on his chest. It showed a little over ten thousand feet.

"Thanks again!" he shouted to the pilot. The pilot turned. "No worries, mate! This is a lot better than taking snaps of marijuana fields!"

Harry stuck out his right foot. It felt like when he was small and they were driving up Gudbrandsdalen Valley on their way to another summer holiday in Åndalsnes, and he opened the side window and stuck out his hand to "fly." He remembered the wind catching his hand when he turned the palm into it.

The wind outside the plane was extraordinary, and Harry had to force his foot forward onto the stay. He counted internally as Joseph had told him—"right foot, left hand, right hand, left foot." He was standing beside Joseph. Small patches of cloud floated toward them, speeded up, surrounded them and were gone in the same second. Beneath them lay a patchwork quilt of different nuances of green, yellow and brown.

"Hotel check!" Joseph screamed into his ear.

"Checking in!" Harry shouted and glanced at the pilot in the cockpit, who gave him the thumbs up. "Checking out!" He glanced at Joseph, who was wearing a helmet, goggles and a big smile.

Harry leaned away from the stay and raised his right foot.

"Horizon! Up! Down! Go!"

Then he was in the air, feeling like he was being blown backward as the plane continued its undisturbed flight ahead. From the corner of his eye he saw the plane turn before realizing that he was the one turning. He looked toward the horizon where the earth arced and the sky gradually became bluer until it merged into the azure Pacific Ocean that Captain Cook had sailed to get here.

Joseph grabbed him and Harry adopted a better free-fall posture. He checked the altimeter. Nine thousand feet. My God, they had oceans of time! He twisted his upper torso and held his arms out to make a half-turn. Jeez, he was Superman!

Ahead, to the west, were the Blue Mountains, which were blue because the very special eucalyptus trees gave off a blue vapor that could be seen from far away. Joseph had told him that. He had also said that behind them was what his forefathers, the semi-nomadic Indigenous people, called home. The endless, arid plains—the outback—constituted the greatest part of this immense continent, a merciless furnace where it seemed improbable that anything could survive, yet Joseph's people had done so for thousands of years until the whites came.

Harry looked down. It seemed so calm and deserted below, it had to be a peaceful and kind planet. The altimeter showed seven thousand feet. Joseph let go of him as they'd agreed. A serious breach of training rules, but they'd already broken any rules there were by coming out here alone and jumping. Harry watched Joseph put his arms to his sides to gain horizontal speed and swoop down to his left at an amazing rate.

Then Harry was alone. As we always are. It just feels so much better when you're in free fall six thousand feet above the ground.

Kristin had made her choice in a hotel room one gray Monday morning. Perhaps she had woken up, exhausted by the new day before it had even started, looked out of the window and decided enough was enough. What mental processes she had gone through Harry didn't know. The human soul was a deep, dark forest and all decisions are made alone.

Five thousand feet.

Perhaps she had made the right choice. The empty bottle of pills suggested that at least she'd had no doubts. And one day it would have to end anyway; one day it would be time. The need to leave this world with a certain style bore testimony, of course, to a vanity—a weakness—only a few people had.

Four thousand, five hundred feet.

Others just had a weakness for living. Simple and uncomplicated. Well, not only simple and uncomplicated perhaps, but all that lay far below him right now. Four thousand feet below, to be absolutely precise. He grabbed the orange handle to the right of his stomach, pulled the rip cord with a firm wrench and began to count: "A thousand and one, a thousand and . . ."

ALSO BY JO NESBØ

HEADHUNTERS

Roger Brown is a corporate headhunter, but one career simply can't support his luxurious lifestyle and his wife's fledgling art gallery. At an art opening one night, he meets Clas Greve, who is not only the perfect candidate for a major CEO job, but also, perhaps, the answer to his financial woes: Greve just so happens to mention that he owns a priceless Peter Paul Rubens painting that's been lost since World War II—and Roger Brown just so happens to dabble in art theft. But when he breaks into Greve's apartment, he finds more than just the painting.

Crime Fiction

The Inspector Harry Hole Series

THE SNOWMAN

One night, a boy named Jonas wakes up and discovers that his mother has disappeared. Only one trace of her remains: a pink scarf, his Christmas gift to her, now worn by the snowman that inexplicably appeared in their yard earlier that day. The case deepens when a pattern emerges: over the past decade, eleven women have vanished—all on the day of the first snow. But this is a killer who makes his own rules . . . and he'll break his pattern just to keep the game interesting, as he draws Harry ever closer into his twisted web.

Crime Fiction

THE LEOPARD

Inspector Harry Hole has retreated to Hong Kong, escaping the trauma of his last case in squalid opium dens, when two young women are found dead in Oslo, both drowned in their own blood. Media coverage quickly reaches a fever pitch. After he returns to Oslo, the killer strikes again, Harry's instincts take over, and nothing can keep him from the investigation, though there is little to go on. Worse, he will soon come to understand that he is dealing with a psychopath who will put him to the test, both professionally and personally, as never before.

Crime Fiction

PHANTOM

When Harry Hole moved to Hong Kong, he thought he was escaping the traumas of his life in Oslo and his career as a detective for good. But now, the unthinkable has happened—Oleg, the boy he helped raise, has been arrested for killing a man. Harry can't believe that Oleg is a murderer, so he returns to hunt down the real killer. Although he's off the police force, he still has a case to solve that will send him into the depths of the city's drug culture, where a shockingly deadly new street drug is gaining popularity. This most personal of investigations will force Harry to confront his past and the wrenching truth about Oleg and himself.

Crime Fiction